Dedication

To my three daughters, Nicole, Emily and Jaclyn

Acknowledgments

I want to acknowledge the wonderful people of Pangnirtung, or as called by the locals, Panniqtuuq. The people of this Nunavut village taught me respect and admiration for the Inuit culture. I am grateful to the *Panniqtuuq Panik* girls' volleyball team, the artists of that remarkable village, the 2006 Administration students from Silattuqsarvik (Nunavut College), and my language teacher, Rosie Kilabuk, whom I hope will forgive me if I have misspelled any Inuktitut words. I especially wish to thank my Nunavut friend, Phoebe Sowdluapik, who has the fortitude, beauty and intelligence of Ashoona, the protagonist in this novel.

Thank you to Kaija Farstad and Tianna Behr who read the manuscript and offered valuable comments, to fellow paddler David Smith for his assistance, to my husband Paul, who helped proof the book, and to my patient and skilled editor.

I want to thank Canada Council for their support of Canadian literature and aboriginal culture.

Preface

In 2006, when I was an instructor at Nunavut College in Pangnirtung, an Inuit elder with tolerance and an amazing sense of humor told us her story of being forced into an arranged marriage to an older hunter. "I hated his short neck, his squat body and the smell of him," she told us. And so, Ashoona's story was given a voice.

This work of fiction draws upon the many remarkable accounts by explorers, anthropologists, fur traders, historians, doctors and researchers, including Knud Rasmussen's anthropological study, Jennifer Niven's excellent research on the Stefansson expedition, Pat Sandiford Grygier's account of the Inuit tuberculosis epidemic, Daphne Bramham's research on polygamy in British Columbia and *Uqalurait*, an oral history of Nunavut, Canada. The characters in this novel are purely fictional, with the exception of the survivors of the doomed Stefansson expedition, some of whom existed, but speak in fictional dialogue, others who are fictional. I have taken advantage of literary license in this work, changing names and adjusting dates.

Baffin Island scholars and residents, especially the people of Pangnirtung, will notice that I revised the dates of several events and developments on Baffin Island. The government did not take tuberculosis patients to Charles Camsell Hospital until after World War II, and the federal government only began building in the communities in the mid-1950s, not the mid-1940s.

In several places in this book, the people of the North are referred to in dialogue as "Eskimo" rather than Inuit. Inuit means "the people" in the Inuktitut language. Up until the late 1970s, the Canadian government referred to the indigenous people of the Canadian Arctic as Eskimos. However, that term is from the Algonquian language and is considered pejorative among Canadians and especially among the Inuit.

I wanted this fictional story to show the significant changes on Baffin Island from the days of travel by dog team to the settled life in the communities, and I chose to show these changes over eight years of a young woman's life. Ashoona's journey takes us through the Inuit transition from the hunting and fishing lifestyle to a culture heavily influenced by Western society.

> *In the sumptuousness of our temperate zone, we live quite ignorant of the terrific struggle that goes on among a little human unit that inhabits the icy shores of our upper continental edge. Beyond the treeline, beyond the cropline, far into the area of eternal snow, are buried a score of Nomadic Eskimo tribes. These tribes eke out an existence by hunting and fishing. They have no...real interests save preservation thereof. Their struggles are sacrifices, while tragic, make a great story of the human race.*
>
> –Knud Rasmussen, *Across the Arctic America*, New York: G.P. Putman and Sons, 1927

Glossary of Inuit Terms and Other Words

There may be misspellings of Inuit words in this fictional novel. The Inuktitut language was first written in syllabics and later translated using the Roman alphabet, and as a result, variant spellings are used in each of the three Nunavut regions as well as in the many research documents used in writing this book. We have made our best effort to correctly spell the Inuktitut words and phrases consistently. Any errors are our own and unintentional.

amauti —a woman's parka designed to carry a baby on the back of the wearer with a wide hood that in cold weather covers both mother and baby

anaq—shit

Angakkut—Shaman; religious leader

arnaq—wife

Atagoyak Ilisiviak—Atagoyak School

Ati, panik, qamutikmi—Come on the sled, girl

ayunqnaq—it can't be helped

Eeee—"yes" or exclamation

igunaq—fermented, putrid walrus

kaju—blood soup

kamik / *kamiit* (plural)—sealskin boots

katabatik winds—a wind that carries high-density air from a higher elevation down a slope under the force of gravity

lead—a stretch of open water within the sea ice, caused by movements of ice due to wind or currents

muktuk—whale meat

nanuq—polar bear

natsik—seal

Nuliarsuit—man possessed by the spirit of wives who sow chaos

panik—little girl

paniga—possessive for *panik*

Panniqtuuq/Pangnirtung– settlement where Ashoona was born and raised

qaggiit—big snow house used for large gatherings, including celebrations and games

Qallunaaq / Qallunaat (plural)—white person / people

qamutik / qamutiit (plural)—sled pulled by dogs; sleigh, sledge; sometimes spelled "komatik"

qujannamiik—thank you

qulliq / qulliit (plural)—oil lamp, made out of stone and shaped like a long narrow bowl

Quviasugisi Quviasuvvimi—Merry Christmas

snow knife—a long knife used by Inuit for cutting and shaping blocks of snow in building snow houses

Ullaakkut—good morning

ulu—a curved knife, an all purpose tool called the woman's knife

Unnasakoot—good afternoon

Sources for Inuktitut Words and Phrases

The author used the following sources for spelling and definitions of Inuktitut words:

Bennett, John and Susan Rowley (eds). *Uqalurait, An Oral History of Nunavut*. Montreal: McGill-Queen's University Press. 2004.

Intensive Inuktitut Wordlist for Senior Executives. Iqaluit, Nunavut: Pirurvik Centre for Inuit Language, Culture and Wellbeing. 2006.

Mallon, Kublu, Piugattuk and Kublu-Hill. *Drills in Inuktitut*. Arviat, Nunavut: Nunavut Arctic College. 1994.

Mallon, Mick. *Inuktitut the Hard Way: There is no Easy Way*. Arviat, Nunavut: Nunavut Arctic College. 1997.

Sawdluapik, Phoebe, Inuktitut speaker from Pangnirtung, Nunavut.

Ashoona's Arctic Homeland

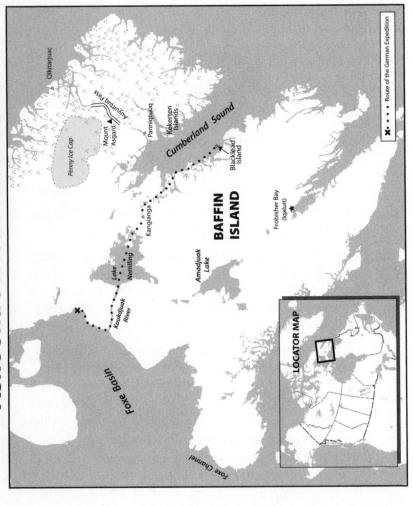

Chapter One

Captured!

How was she to escape her captor over this landscape of ice and through the bitter January winds that swept over the barren lands of Canada's Arctic? Ashoona was miles from her home in Panniqtuuq, having spent twenty long hours tied up on the *qamutik* as the dog team pulled her along sea ice, over the jumble of ice blocks formed by the tidal flow and then into this windy valley. They needed food, and her captor, Qillaq, expert hunter that he was, left her in the snow house while he went out onto the sea ice to hunt seal. She considered escaping on foot, but he had taken the dog team and would soon overtake her even if she was able to survive walking in the depths of the arctic winter. Ashoona's head spun with possible escape plans until she felt drowsy. She was asleep on the caribou skins when the barking of the dog team woke her.

Oh my God! He's back!

Ashoona was curled up in the corner of the sleeping platform. She had a sharp-edged *ulu* clutched in her hand and hidden under the sleeping robes. Her heart was pounding, and she could taste the terror in her throat.

11

She sat up, the *ulu* hidden behind her back. She watched in fear as the big man pushed through the entrance to the snow house. He was in his mid-fifties, short, broad and powerful. His skin had a grizzly cast; his face, scarred by fights, was frosted with ice. He glared lustfully at Ashoona, sending a sick feeling through the young girl.

Qillaq pulled a large seal through the entrance after him. "We have food."

The animal had been cut up the middle and the intestines pulled out to feed the dogs. Qillaq removed his parka, squatted beside the seal, cut a piece of the raw meat and stuffed it into his mouth. Ashoona's stomach lurched as she listened to him noisily chew the seal meat and watched the blood drip from the corners of Qillaq's mouth.

I hate the sound of his chewing. I hate the smell of him. I'd rather have a hot poker stuck in my eye than sleep with that old man.

"You cook this now," he ordered, after gulping down several chunks of raw meat. "After food, I take my young wife to bed."

He eyed Ashoona and grinned lasciviously and began pulling off his clothing. First, he removed the outer caribou skin and then the inner layer, with the fur next to his body, revealing a muscled torso and a big stomach that pressed against sealskin trousers. He took off his trousers and scratched his groin before pulling on a dry pair; his eyes remained riveted on Ashoona's body.

"Tonight. I will have you tonight."

"Not yet, Qillaq. Twelve is too young. Remember your promise to Auntie. Not until I have my first bleeding." *I can't fight him off,* she thought. *I have to try to reason with him.*

"Did you think I would keep that stupid promise after all I've gone through to get you? You're mine now. I paid for you, and we will have strong sons together." He studied Ashoona, grinning at the thought of taking her. He had the look of a hungry dog anticipating a long-awaited meal.

"Qillaq, you already have three wives. They won't want me in their house. Your children will hate me. What will your wives think of you when they find out I didn't come willingly, that you had to trick me and tie me up on the *qamutik* so I couldn't escape? A man like you can find willing wives. Why steal a girl who is not ready for marriage? It is wrong. You should take me back to Panniqtuuq."

"I made a bargain with your aunt. I traded for you, and I will have you. You can't run away; you would die out there without a dog team and food. When we go to Igloolik, my wives and children will get used to you. By the time we reach the village, you'll be with child." Once more his beady eyes moved up and down her slim frame, lusting for this young girl who had never been with a man.

"Fight me," Qillaq said, rubbing his hands together. "That'll make the conquest all the more exciting. I'll rip your clothes off and fuck you all night. Soon you will ask for it like my other wives, and soon you'll have my child in your belly."

"I hate you, and I will always hate you! I hate John for tricking me. I hate Aunt Amaruk for selling me to you, for who knows what prize. You may force yourself on me, but I'll never be your wife. I'll get away from you, even if I die escaping. When the police find out that I have been kidnapped, they will rescue me. James will rescue me," Ashoona sobbed into her hands.

"James?" scoffed Qillaq. "That boy with only fuzz on his chin, the one who has eyes for all the girls? You think he cares enough to come after someone like me? He isn't even a policeman yet, and when he gets his badge, he will not interfere with Inuit marriage customs." Qillaq laughed a guttural sound and then glared at Ashoona. "Now, get my meal ready. I've been out on the ice for hours, waiting at the seal's breathing hole. I need to warm my blood with hot seal meat."

Maybe he will eat, get tired and fall asleep, Ashoona thought as she hung the cooking pot above the oil lamp. She moved as far away from Qillaq as she could, skillfully slicing off pieces of meat and throwing them into the pot. *Could I open up Qillaq's throat as easily as I sliced into this seal? Hopefully it won't come to that.*

Soon the food was simmering. Qillaq was exhausted from a day of running alongside the *qamutik*, building the snow house and long cold hours out on the ice. When the food was ready and the nourishing seal meat warmed Qillaq, he laid his head down, his large girth filling the sleeping platform. His eyes grew heavy, and in seconds, he was snoring.

Ashoona finally had time to think and to plan an escape. Her Aunt Amaruk had urged her to accept Qillaq as her husband; despite his bad temper, he was a skillful hunter, and she would never go hungry. That was just yesterday, but it seemed like a lifetime for Ashoona. Remembering brought back all the anger she felt for her aunt, the one person who was suppose to care for Ashoona and instead sold her to this hateful old man.

She knows I'm too young! What kind of life will I have? I'd rather die of starvation than sleep with this hideous, rude, putrid-smelling hunter. If only Mother had lived, she would have protected me; if only my father had kept his promise!

While the pot boiled above the lamp, Ashoona quietly put on her parka and pulled sealskin *kamiit* onto her feet. She took all the hot meat from the pot and placed it in a skin bag. Ashoona didn't really have a plan, but she knew she had to get away quickly, while Qillaq slept.

As silently as possible, Ashoona gathered up as many supplies as she could carry and crept out of the igloo into the bitterly cold, starlit winter evening. She returned to the snow house, dragged the fat seal outside and stashed it in the *qamutik*. She knew that taking meat killed by someone else was thievery, but stealing food was a small crime compared to the one she was about to commit.

Should I dare take Qillaq's gun, ammunition and his dog team? That was a crime that must be paid for in blood.

It was a calm evening for a change. Maybe the fierce arctic wind would hold up on Baffin Island's glaciers and give Ashoona time to reach the safety of a friendly community.

The dogs were sleeping contentedly next to the sled. She hooked them up and led the team away from the camp. One of the younger dogs yelped. Ashoona's heart skipped a beat. "Ssshhhh!"

She stood still, listening for Qillaq, but all was quiet in the snow house. The dog yelped again. Ashoona made a run for it, snapping the whip over the lead dog. They were off across the hard-packed snow, the dogs' yelping filling the frigid night air. The sound awakened Qillaq, who charged out of the igloo, naked from the waist up.

"I'll catch you! You'll never escape me, you bitch!" She looked back at Qillaq, who was running after her, shaking his fist and screaming obscenities. He chased after the sled, his fury shielding him from the cold bite of the arctic night.

She urged the team on, flicking the whip and yelling to urge them forward. The dogs were well fed and rested, so they bounded over the snow, opening up the distance between them and her pursuer. She glanced back again. Qillaq had returned to the igloo, but she knew he would never let her go easily. He would track her down. It might take months or even years, but she knew enough about vengeance among the Inuit to realize the gravity of what she had done. Stealing everything a hunter depended on was a crime that never went unpunished no matter how many years passed.

Ashoona was able to ride on the sled as the dogs raced over the windblown snowpack. Soon she reached the jumbled ice at the flow edge. The lead dog skillfully maneuvered through the jagged ice heaved up by the high tides around the rocks. The sled bumped and crashed between the towering pillars of ice. Ashoona held on, not wanting to hinder the team.

Finally they reached the smooth surface of the sea ice on the fjord. Her eyes grew heavy, and as the dogs continued through the night, Ashoona lay on the sled, sometimes dozing off.

Suddenly, the sled hit a ridge of snow on the sea ice, bumping Ashoona into wakefulness.

I can't afford to fall asleep. She looked nervously back up the fjord. No one was in sight. She had left Qillaq behind, at least for the time being. *This would never have happened if my father hadn't left us, if he had just kept his promise.*

As the dogs raced across the fjord, the arctic wind stirred. She remembered how her father complained about the fierce gales. He was never far from her mind.

"Does that blasted wind ever stop?" Ashoona's father grumbled. "They told me it would be windy on Baffin Island, but they didn't warn me that the roof would blow off the trading post, or that my entire house might be lifted from its foundation if I didn't chain it to iron pegs pounded into the pre-Cambrian rock of the Canadian Shield."

"It is not always so," Ashoona's mother answered in her soft Inuit accent. "Remember the day we were married? There was not a breath of wind, and it was so warm we bathed in the pool along the creek." Minnie was a beautiful, dark-eyed woman.

"Yes, for one day, it was warm and calm. But what about the day our little Ashoona was born? That day we were out on the land with only a tent for shelter, and she decided to greet her father a month early. I sat on the flaps of the tent while helping you with the birth. The wind whipped around our tent all through the next day, but our little Ashoona just nursed and slept through all the wailing of the winds as if she knew it was not time to fuss. The *Qallunaat* ladies down south could not imagine having a baby out on the land with no hospital and no doctors. My lovely Inuit wife had a baby in an arctic outpost camp in the middle of a hurricane and never once complained. Only a good Inuit woman could do that."

Ashoona recalled being just six years old and loved by her parents and by the Inuit community. She was special, a bright-eyed girl who learned the ways of the Inuit from her mother and learned to hunt and to speak and write English from her father.

They lived in the Hudson's Bay Post house at Panniqtuuq where Ashoona's father was the chief factor at the whaling station. As an employee of the most powerful company in Canada's north, Dugan Campbell had to maintain British customs, but he also learned and followed the Inuit way of life. They lived in a snow house on the sea ice while out hunting seals and drove their dog team into the hills to hunt caribou in the fall.

Ashoona's mother dressed them in parkas made from caribou skins and decorated with beautiful colorful patterns. She made excellent sealskin *kamiit* that never let their feet get wet, and their snow house always had the best of pots and dishes. They even owned a Primus stove that cooked their food in minutes and a kerosene lamp that kept their home cheery whether it was a winter snow hut, their summer tent, a sod hut at their fishing camp or their wooden house next to the Hudson's Bay Post. Her mother was skilled at trimming the wick and keeping the flame in the oil lamp burning bright without any smoke. Thinking about those wonderful days brought another flood of tears to Ashoona's eyes, then anger. .

Papa, why did you leave? Why didn't you come back like you promised? You're just like all the other damn Qallunaat *who fathered children in the Arctic and left them alone and uncared for. I hate you! I hate you!*

The sleigh sped over the smooth ice, while Ashoona ran alongside sobbing so hard that her eyesight was blurred.

I have to stop this, she told herself. *It's dark, and I must watch where we're going. I could miss a ridge of ice and tip the* qamutik.

***

During the winter months, the sun never appeared over the horizon, but by noon, a faint glow showed on the mountaintops, and the sea ice was lit by the reflection of half-light on the snow. She halted the team, fed the dogs and ate a chunk of cooked meat. She hadn't brought any water, so she ate a handful of snow. It did little to quench her thirst.

Soon Ashoona was once more on the move, racing past the little settlement of Panniqtuuq.

"I'll not risk seeing the people who sold me to a rapist!" she yelled as the sled raced south. She thought about the treachery of her aunt and cousin. Ashoona was an only child. This was unusual, given the large Inuit families, where most children had at least a half dozen brothers or sisters. After Ashoona's mother died, Aunt Amaruk fetched the sad eight-year-old from the Hudson's Bay factor's house. Amaruk had cared for her initially, but all that changed. She became a snarly woman, thin with a pinched face that always wore a scowl. Amaruk's bad moods landed on Ashoona and poor Adamie, Ashoona's uncle, but never on their haughty daughter, Natsiq. When Ashoona approached marriageable age, Natsiq delivered the fateful news with ill-concealed glee.

"So, I guess you don't know about the marriage arranged for you. Qillaq is on his way here to take you to Igloolik as his fourth wife. I'm sure you are delighted."

"I'm not marrying that old man! You're lying! Aunt Amaruk would never do that to me." But even as she spoke the words, a little voice told Ashoona that her sharp-tongued aunt was indeed capable of such treachery.

"I suggested the union, and it's all settled. Ask Mama."

"Aunt Amaruk!" Ashoona yelled. "Please tell me it's not true. I can't marry that ugly old man!"

"It's the best for you and for us. We are a poor family and can't keep you. I spoke to Qillaq months ago when he came here for supplies. He's a strong man and a fine hunter. You will always be well fed, have warm clothes and many, many children."

"I'm not ready, Aunt Amaruk," Ashoona pleaded. "I'm only twelve, and I haven't even started to bleed. I'm not old enough to marry. Please don't do this to me!" Ashoona felt the anger and fear rise in her chest.

"You'll be old enough soon. Thirteen next spring. Am I right? That is the age we marry. Old enough to be a mother and strong and young enough to run behind the sled for hours. Besides, I asked that he wait till you start your bleeding before he takes you to his bed. He will honor that."

"But he's older than Uncle Adamie and much older than my father."

"What father?" Natsiq said with a sneer. "You mean the Hudson's Bay factor who dropped in, fucked your mother and left? Don't you understand? You're a burden to us, and Qillaq is rich. It is a match made in heaven as the Christians say."

"How would you know anything about Christianity? Or you, Aunt Amaruk? My mother believed in Christ and always acted in a Christian way. I feel as though I've been given to heathens who care little for the happiness of a blood relative. Mama trusted you to look after me, Aunt Amaruk. It was just before my eighth birthday, but I remember the day she told you she was dying, the day she begged you to take me in. How could you hate me so much that you would give me to that hideous man?

"It's still little Davidee, isn't it?" Ashoona continued. "You never believed me." Ashoona was now in tears. "I didn't kill him. I didn't." Then turning to Natsiq, she screamed, "You shot him, not me! I just tried to save him! You lied about it!"

Reliving the deception sent Ashoona into a rage, sucking her energy and the strength she needed to endure the long journey across the ice. Once more she told herself to stop dwelling on the past.

I need to focus if I am to stay ahead of Qillaq.

———

But she couldn't keep the black memories of that tragic day from controlling her thoughts. Ashoona had been with a group of five families that traveled by dog team across the ice of Cumberland Sound in late June to camp at the Clearwater fishing site. Throughout July and August they fished for char and in the fall, they hunted caribou, food that would supplement the winter seal harvest when the families returned to Panniqtuuq. Ashoona remembered that sunny day at the camp near the ocean, when the sea ice was melting and tents would soon replace the snow houses.

Seven-year-old Natsiq and Ashoona, eight, were playing near the camp along with Natsiq's little brother, Davidee, the two-year-old who was cherished by his parents. He was the son they had always wanted, the son who would hunt for the family when Adamie was old, who would be a fast runner and the most patient hunter at the seals' breathing hole. But all their dreams turned to nightmares in one moment on that beautiful spring day.

Natsiq's father could never say no to his daughter. Adamie cringed at Natsiq's temper, which could be brutal whenever either parent denied her. When Natsiq asked to play with his gun, Adamie gave it to her even though he knew it was wrong to allow a child to play with a gun. Unlike Ashoona's father, Adamie had not taught Natsiq how to handle a gun. Instead, he allowed his daughter to play unsupervised, never thinking that the gun might be loaded. When Ashoona learned to shoot a gun at the age of six, her father was always right next to her, holding the gun, instructing her and reinforcing warnings about how dangerous guns could be if not handled properly.

On that fateful day, at the Clearwater camp, Natsiq aimed at the dogs, pretending she was hunting caribou. Ashoona watched as her seven-year-old cousin aimed the gun at Davidee. She saw Natsiq move her finger to the trigger. It wasn't loaded, Ashoona remembered Adamie saying. But, what if it was? Ashoona tried to grab the gun. But as she reached for it, Natsiq pulled the trigger. Davidee fell, and in a heartbeat, Natsiq shoved the gun at Ashoona yelling, "Ashoona shot my brother!"

From that moment, Ashoona's relationship with Davidee's family was poisoned.

———

I have to stop thinking about Davidee's death and Natsiq's treachery, Ashoona told herself. *Keep your mind on the trail; watch for open leads in the ice.*

Ashoona could not stay awake for a second night. Her eyes grew heavy and her body sluggish as she drove the team out on to Cumberland Sound. She had to remain alert. Here the ice was seldom solid; it was in constant motion, moved by the strong tidal stream, with floes smashing against each other. Slabs jammed up on one another, making the journey in the dim light precarious.

She brought the dog team to a halt behind a towering slab of ice, pushed up by the tidal stream. She was nervous about resting but conceded, knowing the dogs needed to sleep as much as she did. She worried about Qillaq. In his anger he wouldn't stop to sleep. Spurred by fury, he would run through the night until he found her. If he caught her, he would beat her and take her back or he might kill her. Nightmares of Qillaq disturbed her sleep, and within a few hours she was up, harnessing the team and moving on.

Once more out on the expanse of sea ice, Ashoona looked back nervously. In the distance, she could see a faint black speck.

Is that him? She strained her eyes but couldn't tell if it was a man moving across the ice or a seal, poking up for air. Her heart pounded as she flicked the whip in the air, cracking it loudly above the lead dog's head to tell the team they had to run fast.

Ashoona had to make a decision. Should she try to make the whaling station at Kekerten or risk the long dangerous trip across Cumberland Sound to the settlement of Blacklead? She had already passed Panniqtuuq, the village where she was raised, where her aunt bargained with Qillaq, trading Ashoona for some unknown prize.

When the family first took in Ashoona, Aunt Amaruk cared for her. Ashoona slept beside her aunt, cozy in the caribou skins; her hair was always braided, her caribou parka and *kamiit* were warm and always mended. She missed her parents, but being welcomed into her new family made it easier to accept the loss.

Once again Ashoona thought back to the day Davidee was killed. Ashoona was a shy child and did not contradict Natsiq's lie. Ashoona hid under the caribou skins in the igloo while the adults tried to save little Davidee.

Please don't let him die, Ashoona prayed.

During the hours following the shooting, one of the hunters, a heavy-set man, sat on Ashoona's legs, not knowing the little girl was there. Ashoona cried out in pain.

"It's the little murderer!" the hunter yelled for everyone to hear. "People wish *you* were bleeding to death instead of Davidee." With these words, the man cuffed Ashoona's ear. She put her hand over her mouth to muffle her cries, wishing she was invisible, wishing her mother had not died, wishing her father had not run off to Montreal.

Later that same day, little Davidee took his last breath. Ashoona loved her little cousin and wept quietly. She remained hidden in the caribou skins for hours, listening to the sorrowful moaning of the family. As the news spread, the entire camp began moaning and shrieking in despair. That day they laid the tiny body to rest on a hill above the camp, his face positioned toward the rising sun. They piled rocks on the grave, covering all but his head. Amaruk leaned over the grave and lightly placed a falcon's feather on her son's cold lips.

"Spirit of the bird," she chanted, "help this child fly to the hills and over the mountains." She worried that when winter returned, the families would leave and there would be no one nearby to help Davidee pass into the spirit world.

That evening, Aunt Amaruk took the child's beautifully sewn clothes, heaped them in a pile and burned them as was their custom. While the skins smoked and finally burned, the women's wails increased in volume, some crying for the loss of the child and others for the loss of the jackets, caribou pants, sealskin mitts and *kamiit*.

Angered by the tragic loss, the five families that lived in the camp targeted Ashoona as a murderer. No one defended her. Everyone shunned her. Life with Aunt Amaruk became unbearable. No one gave Ashoona food or made her clothing. Her clothes became tattered. Her hair was never combed, and her head was crawling with lice. At night the little eight-year-old slept on the tent floor with only a scrap of caribou hide to protect her from the cold.

Chapter Two

Shunned

J uly to October passed in misery for young Ashoona. The
Clearwater fish camp was a favored spot for families during
the summer, a wonderful time of year for the children. They
could play outside dressed in light clothing, and at night sleep in
skin tents with only a light cover. But the summer and fall after
Davidee's death was different for Ashoona. No one spoke to her.
No one would even give her food; she was so hungry that she had
to snatch a few scraps of caribou meat from the food tossed to
the dogs, which was a dangerous undertaking because dogs in
the Arctic are not pets. A hungry pack of dogs could take down
a small child for their meal. Ashoona had to beat them away to
steal a chunk of fat or piece of intestine. Aunt Amaruk did not
seem to care that Ashoona was wasting away.

The cold winds of November swept down on the camp,
which was a sign for Agalukjuq, the chief hunter, to order the
move back to Panniqtuuq for the winter where they would hunt
seals. The people of the camp hitched up their dog teams, and

Ashoona, along with her aunt, uncle and Natsiq, left that sad place and the small grave on the desolate hilltop.

They crossed Cumberland Sound stopping twice to make temporary snow houses. Agalukjuq chose the overnight camp spots where the snow was packed into firm drifts, sites where the men could easily cut blocks for igloos. The men worked with their long snow knives while the women and children filled the chinks with snow. In less than an hour the igloos were up. The families ate, slept and rose early the next day to continue their journey back to Panniqtuuq. During the day, Ashoona walked behind the dog team, while Natsiq sat on the sleigh with her mother. Night comes early in November, and as the light faded, Ashoona dropped behind. She didn't care. She felt so isolated that she even thought it might be best to let go, to lie down in the snow and die.

The last *qamutik* in the group carried Aula, an old crippled woman who looked back and saw the little figure disappearing far behind the group.

"Wait! Stop the dogs!" Aula shouted. "Ashoona will die out there."

"You want us to risk being left behind so we can help the little murderer?" scoffed Kakik, Aula's seventeen-year-old grandson. He was a small, wiry man who, after the death of his parents, reluctantly assumed the task of provider for his two brothers and elderly grandmother. The responsibility of hunting and fishing for a family made him petulant and sour. Anger was always close to the surface; he was edgy unless he had a cigarette in his scowling mouth. By contrast, even though Aula suffered chronic pain, she couldn't help feeling sorry for the small child that no one seemed to care about.

"It is not Christian to treat anyone this badly," the old woman retorted. "Now stop, and wait for her."

As they waited, Aula spoke to Kakik and the others traveling with the dog team. "I remember when the old were left behind to die. My mother, who I still miss to this day, was left behind in an igloo because she could no longer walk and was a burden to her family.

"My older sister and my aunt took my own baby girl from me. They did not want me to have that baby. And what did they do? They took my child and left her naked outside in the snow. I listened to my little baby cry until she was mercifully silent.

"I had named the child Ashoona. Now another Ashoona is crying out for my help, and I will not abandon her."

The old woman was silent for a moment, and despite the passage of a lifetime since her baby's death, telling the story brought tears streaming down her wrinkled face.

"We are different now," she continued. "We are Christians. We do not abandon our old people to die in the cold. We do not kill babies because we fear there is not enough food or we need a boy more than a girl. You call little Ashoona a murderer. What if you are wrong? One day, when Ashoona looked like a starved bird, I gave her some soup and combed the lice from her hair. Do you know what she said? She did not pull the trigger. She tried to take the gun from Natsiq. Of course, no one believes her. I'm not sure that I do, but at least it gives me some pause when all of you want to persecute the little one every day of her life."

By the time Aula finished her admonition, the exhausted girl had reached the sled.

"*Ati, panik, qamutikmi, panik*...Come on the sled, daughter."

"*Qujannamiik*...thank you, Aula," Ashoona said. A small, shy smile crossed her face, the first since Davidee's death. Ashoona sat on the sled with the elder, and Kakik whipped the team into a fast pace to get to their overnight camping spot.

From that day on, Aula took Ashoona into her care. When the families returned to Panniqtuuq, Aula accepted that she could no longer travel out on the land with her grandsons. She suffered from joint pains and could not withstand the long, cold and bumpy journey on the *qamutik*. So she lived year-round in a small wooden shack, the type called a matchstick house because it was cobbled together using pieces of wood from packing crates that came on ships.

Kakik and his two teenage brothers were mostly away seal hunting on the sea ice, across the fjord at the caribou grounds, or in summer and fall, at Clearwater. Meat was plentiful in the house, but Aula needed help with the sewing, cooking and cleaning. Ashoona fit into the household like a cat in a house full of troublesome mice. She was not really loved by everyone, but at least she was useful.

———

The next three years were bearable for Ashoona. Aula became like a mother to her even though Aula was old enough to be Ashoona's great-grandmother. When Ashoona turned twelve, Aula told her that soon she would become a woman and would need to go back to live with her aunt once the young men returned from the hunt.

"My grandsons are beginning to look at you as a woman, not a girl. You cannot continue sleeping under the same caribou skins as they do."

"Aunt Amaruk does not want me. I will be miserable there. But I understand. Aula, I have to tell you something that makes me feel ashamed. One cold, cold night, Kakik held me tightly and then started to put his hands all over me. I had to tell him to go away and sleep next to his brother."

"Then you know why you have to go, *panik*," Aula said sadly.

"Yes, dear Aula. I know, but I'm afraid."

"At least stay with Aunt Amaruk until you are a woman. By then that young man James may be able to take you for his wife. He looks at you and I see that you like him. You would like to be his woman, right?"

"Isn't he going back to Blacklead with his father?"

"They'll return to the police post, but that does not mean he cannot promise to marry and come back for you when you become a woman. He will have a house as soon as he finishes his studies and will be a policeman like his father. They say he will be the first Inuk policeman. You can bring your children up to be good Inuks but have all the wealth of the *Qallunaat*."

Ashoona blushed at the thought of lying with a man and having his children. But it was not unpleasant to think about James.

"They will never let me be his wife. His mother will shun me, and besides, Aunt Amaruk told me Natsiq is promised to James."

"That may change," the old woman smiled at Ashoona. "There are ways to win a man's heart, and then who knows if Natsiq will succeed in getting her own way again."

Thinking about her love for James cemented Ashoona's determination to escape Qillaq. Running alongside the dog team, Ashoona conjured up a picture of James. He was such a good-looking young man with black hair and dark eyes, features that were the best of his beautiful Inuit mother and his tall, handsome English father.

If Qillaq found her and raped her, the dream the young girl had kept alive would be tarnished, the dream of being married in a church to the man she loved. Ashoona had to escape Qillaq even if she died trying.

The team and sled bumped over the ice of Cumberland Sound. Ashoona was so weary that she feared she would fall asleep, that the dogs would halt and Qillaq would catch her. It was noon of her third day on the run. She had no seal meat left for the dogs and only a few morsels to sustain her energy.

During the lightest part of the day, Ashoona halted the dogs to let them rest. She strained to look back at the expanse of ice. In the distance, she saw a small speck at the entrance to the fjord.

It must be him. He's picked up a dog team at Panniqtuuq! Ashoona's heart jumped.

She hurriedly packed up the *qamutik* and urged the dogs forward.

"I need to find a place to hide. If I try to make it across Cumberland Sound, he'll see me and catch me!" she whispered to herself.

To the east, Ashoona could see the scattered islands that made up the Kekerten Chain, dozens of islands, some little more than rocky outcroppings rising out of the sea ice. Kekerten Whaling Station was located on the last island in the chain, but she needed shelter immediately, and the whaling station was too far away.

"I need to make it to shelter behind the cliffs, and I need a wind, a big wind to cover my tracks. Dear God, please help me!"

She whipped at the team, hoping the tired, hungry dogs could muster the strength to run the ten miles to the first island. Although the sun's rays had not reached the frozen lands of Baffin Island, at mid-day there was a faint light, enough to allow

Qillaq to see Ashoona's team moving across the sea ice of Cumberland Sound.

I need Qillaq to think I'm heading to Blacklead.

She traveled across the ice for the next hour, then as the curtain of the arctic night descended, she turned the team sharply east, heading for what she hoped would be a safe refuge on one of the islands. Not only were the dogs noticeably tired, but Ashoona also had trouble focusing. Several times she drifted off to sleep on the *qamutik* and jolted awake when she realized the dogs had stopped. After that scare, Ashoona ran along with the dogs.

"I can't afford to sleep. Qillaq cannot catch me," she chanted to herself over and over in order to keep up the relentless pace. The island drew closer. Ahead she could see the outline of the steep rock cliffs of the shoreline, cliffs that hid sheltered bays. She needed a hiding place so she could rest without being discovered.

Only a few more miles!

Just when she thought safety was at hand, one of the dogs staggered, fell and was dragged for several feet before Ashoona could bring the team to a halt. She yelled at the dog to mush. The old sled dog struggled to get to his feet but collapsed.

"Damn! Why now!" she cried.

Ashoona unhooked the exhausted dog. He was so thin that she could easily lift him into the *qamutik*.

"I should leave you behind, but who knows whether I'll need your skinny body for food for the team. Sorry, old fellow. You did your best."

She worked quickly, re-harnessing the team so that it could pull with one dog less. Ashoona was so tense that her hands would not work properly. *Qillaq must be closing in on me.* She peered into the blackness, her nerves on edge.

What if he saw my tracks? A light wind blew but not enough to cover her trail. *I must stay awake. Don't think about Aunt Amaruk's treachery. If I can survive this journey and escape Qillaq, just possibly, if dreams come true, James will marry me.*

———————

She remembered the last time she saw James. It was in August when the young police trainee spent three weeks in Panniqtuuq. Ashoona had blossomed into a lovely girl. She'd styled her hair in intricate braids and wore a caribou skin *amauti* that Aula helped her make. It was decorated beautifully and fitted snugly to emphasize her slim figure and full bosom. Ashoona had the dark eyes of her Inuit mother and the classic nose and oval-shaped face of her Scottish grandmother. When she walked, it was with a grace that exceeded anything the villagers had seen.

"Is this the one they call the little murderer?" someone whispered. Some less kindly of the group said that under her beauty and gentle personality lurked an evil nature capable of killing babies.

Natsiq noticed the changes in Ashoona and became fiercely jealous. Natsiq was a year younger, and although pretty, had not developed the grace and beauty of a woman. Still an awkward pre-teen, she did not receive admiring glances from the young men. More worrying to Natsiq was the fact that James had not come to visit her and did nothing to seek her out when he was in the village.

"Don't worry about Ashoona. She'll be going away soon," her mother said when she noticed Natsiq sulking. "And you need not concern yourself about James. His mother and I made a promise that he will be your husband, and she is not one to break her word."

"Then you better arrange Ashoona's marriage immediately because I saw James looking at her, and every day she walks beside the house where he stays. She is such a little bitch; she'll do anything to win him and get away from us and this town. I hate her!"

"Be patient. James and his father are leaving next week. Ashoona is too young to go with him. He may look, but he can't take her until she is a woman. His father won't let him, and his mother would sink a knife into Ashoona if James brought her home as his wife. I have plans. Don't be so upset; it makes your face look pinched."

Ashoona also knew that James would be leaving soon. When she went for walks along the ocean, he sought her out. Each day he would smile at her and say hello, then go on his way. Ashoona was shy and could only whisper a greeting.

The day before James was to leave, Ashoona was walking in the hills above the town searching for the patches of blackberries. She carried a basket made from a seal stomach. The basket was stitched with delicate embroidery around the top; it was a work of art, similar to her mother's designs that had won the heart of Ashoona's father. Ashoona wore the summer dress she had made from skins, also beautifully decorated, and a pair of light *kamiit* on her feet.

For once there was no wind and no bugs. The sky was clear blue. The cliffs rose above the village starkly etched against the sky. Ashoona felt happy, not just because of the splendor of the day, but because she felt her life might change, that happiness was possible after years of misery.

Ashoona found the berry patch and knelt to pull the fruit from the tiny plants clustered close to the ground. She was so intent on her task that she did not hear him approach.

"Let me see how much you've picked."

Ashoona was startled. She felt her face flush, and she was unable to speak. She held the basket up to show him.

"Like everything else you do, you're wonderful at picking berries. I need a bite," he said, flashing the most radiant smile.

Ashoona offered the berries to James. He took the basket, lightly brushing his fingers against her hand. The heat of the sun and his touch made Ashoona feel faint. In the past four years she'd had so little pleasure, and apart from Aula's care, so little love, that the prospect of winning the affection of this handsome young man overwhelmed her.

"You can talk to me, or maybe you only speak Inuktitut?"

"I can speak English, but I prefer that we speak in our language."

"Good, I am glad you have a tongue," James continued in the language of their mothers. "Are you promised to anyone? Has some old hunter spied your beauty and bargained to take you as his wife?"

Ashoona laughed at this jibe. "I will marry the man I love. I know about the arranged marriages that happened in the early days. Christians don't believe in promising young girls to old men."

"Many parents are still arranging marriages, so I must make my bid early just in case you get hitched to someone's great-grandfather."

"And what about you? I heard you are promised to Natsiq."

"That is only what your aunt believes. My father would never agree. It's my mother who made some stupid promise to your aunt, believe it or not, on the day Natsiq was born."

"So you are promised." Ashoona was no longer smiling. Once more, bad luck stalked her.

"You don't know my Aunt Amaruk, and you have not tangled with Natsiq. Auntie hates me because she believes I was responsible for her son's death, and Natsiq hates me because the only person she cares about is herself."

"My father told me about the little boy being shot. He wasn't sure that you were the one who pulled the trigger. He investigated Davidee's death."

"I didn't kill him. I loved him like a brother. Natsiq was playing with a gun, and to be fair to her, I think she accidentally pulled the trigger."

"How is it that you were blamed?"

"I tried to take the gun from her when I saw her pointing it at Davidee. But I was a second too late. The gun went off, and we both saw little Davidee fall. Natsiq put the gun in my hands, and everyone saw me holding the gun and the little boy bleeding to death. I didn't even try to defend myself. I was doomed then, and if you marry Natsiq, I will be doomed again. I feel powerless in this hard world. For a few days I believed that you might care for me, that I could be yours some day. Now I think we have everything against us."

"You are pessimistic for such a young woman. You're the prettiest girl I've ever seen, and I'm pleased that you care for me." He placed his hand gently on her cheek. The touch made Ashoona shiver. "Meet me tonight when your family is asleep? I want to hold you close just once before I have to leave."

"I can't lie with you," Ashoona said in the most serious voice. "My mother said I have to be wed in a church before I take someone to my bed."

"I didn't mean that we would be like man and wife. We will only kiss and touch, not more, at least not yet. Do you see the towering pillar of rock? Meet me there late tonight, my sweet darling girl."

"I'll meet you, but remember, we will just talk."

"I only want to get to know you better so I can picture your lovely face during the next year. I guess you know I'm going to Regina to be trained as a Mounted Policeman. I'll be eighteen when I return. And how old are you?"

"I'm twelve and cannot can't marry until two more winters have passed. Then I will be fourteen and old enough to marry. Aula said she would help me make the most beautiful clothes in our land, and that for my wedding, I will be dressed like a princess."

"You will be my princess," James said, taking her hand. "Until tonight then, my sweet." He pulled her close, kissing her lightly on the lips. "There will be more kisses tonight, my love. I can't wait."

"I love you, James. You've made me happier than I have been all my life. I can't believe this is happening to me. It's almost too wonderful to be true. Then till midnight when we will meet." Ashoona danced down the hill carrying her basket of berries. Her heart sang with happiness. She felt as light as a bird and filled with hope and love.

Later that night, Ashoona pretended to fall asleep next to Aula, who was snoring loudly. Ashoona felt her aunt's and cousin's resentment whenever she stayed at her Aunt Amaruk's house, so she slept at Aula's home whenever her grandsons were away on hunting trips. The old woman enjoyed Ashoona's companionship.

Ashoona waited until the sun disappeared behind the steep mountaintop. It was mid-August, and the midnight sun was replaced by a few hours of darkness. Ashoona slipped out the door and checked to see if anyone was out and about before she moved into the open. The village was asleep, and she was safe to make her way behind the rows of small wooden shacks and skin huts and up the mountain path, anxious to reach the rendezvous spot. Her heart pounded in anticipation of seeing James once again, and this time, away from prying eyes.

She reached the towering rock where they were to meet. She waited, thinking about his touch and recalling his handsome face, the wonder of every part of him. He would come soon. She was sure.

Hours passed, and Ashoona began to worry. *I can't believe he would make a promise and then not meet me.*

Ashoona was distraught. It was as if a fleeting promise of happiness was snatched away.

I should never expect anything in life, and then I'll never be disappointed.

The sun was shining over top the mountain peaks when she trudged back to the village. Aula was up making tea when Ashoona came in.

"Where have you been?"

"I don't know if I should tell you." Ashoona looked so sad that Aula could feel the young woman's pain.

"Tell me, because if you keep that much sadness inside you, it will eat away your heart."

"He said I was his love and then did not keep his promise," Ashoona said, tears pouring down her face.

"By *he*, I assume you mean young James? Well, maybe he couldn't keep his promise because he is gone. He left with his father in the boat to investigate an accident at the end of the fjord. When they return, James will go to Regina for his training, and his father will go to a new posting on Baffin Island."

"But shouldn't he have left me a message at least? How could he just leave like that when he knew I was counting on him?" Ashoona felt a little better but still did not believe that James would ever be hers.

"Have faith, *panik*."

Chapter Three

Abandonment

The island never seemed to get any closer as Ashoona continued to drive the dog team across the sea ice. It was the third day since her escape from Qillaq through the bitterly cold winds of January. A faint mid-day light turned her world into shades of white and grey. The pewter sky overhead blended into the grey-white wasteland of ice at her feet. It was mesmerizing, and Ashoona had to shake her head to keep her focus on the trail, to look ahead and try to pick out the open leads in the ice that could swallow them in a single moment of distraction. When she grew tired of running beside the *qamutik*, she stood on the back runners, but it was even more difficult to concentrate.

The monotony of ice tired her, and her thoughts drifted back to all the betrayals. Her mind filled with turmoil; anger toward her aunt, toward the man who would have raped her had she not escaped, toward her father who abandoned her. She tried to replace the anger with sweet memories of her childhood because the broiling anger sucked her limited energy.

Good thoughts. I need to remember my mother who loved me till the day she died.

She thought back to the days when she had both parents, lots of food and beautiful things, when her mother taught her to sew and her father took her out with the dog team to hunt caribou, seal and walrus. The home where she spent her first eight years was dear to her heart.

I still can't understand how you could leave us? You told mother and me that you loved us so much that you would die for us. You called me your little bird. So how could you just leave and then let Mother die without you by her side?

Her father had been so devoted to his family. When Ashoona was six years old, he told her about the day he met Ashoona's mother.

"You know, little bird, your mother came into the store one day, saw that I didn't have warm boots for my feet and asked if she could make some clothing for me in exchange for food for her family. I told her that would be fine, and I expected to wait months. But the very next morning your mother came to the post with a pair of caribou pants. The next day she brought a sealskin parka, then the sealskin mitts and finally the *kamiit*. It was the *kamiit* that were so special. They were sewn with tight stitches that kept my feet completely dry, and around the top of the boot she made an exquisite design in many colors."

Dugan Campbell would pick up the *kamiit* and show them to Ashoona. "Even after seven years, they are still beautiful and special enough to be in a museum. I was so impressed that I asked your mother to make more clothes that I could take south and sell. She could whip up a parka in one night. Every day she came to the post, and within a month, my day was not worth living if I didn't see her lovely face.

"So we were married in the church—your mother, the beauty of Baffin, and me, a hairy red-headed Scot." He smiled at his wife, hugged his little daughter and said, "You, my little bird, will not only be a wonderful seamstress like your mother, but I will also teach you to be a good hunter."

He kept his word, and little Ashoona went out on the land with her father. At four years old she pulled the trigger of a Winchester and killed her first caribou. Her father had steadied the gun so the kickback would not hurt his little girl. At seven, Ashoona was skilled enough to hunt for rabbits, but always under the watchful eye of her father. It was on one of their last hunts together that Ashoona first learned that something was troubling him, when she first suspected that events far from their peaceful community would destroy her idyllic life.

"Why do they kill seven hundred whales in a day? They can't even cut them up before they rot on the beach or are swept out with the tide. And now we hear that no one wants the whales anymore, that corsets are not being made out of baleen, and whale oil is not needed. Not needed," he said in a sad voice. "Just like me. I won't be needed either."

Ashoona's father was told he must return to Montreal and that changes were underway for him. "Only a short trip," he told his family. "I'll be back on the next boat."

That was the worst day of my life, Ashoona thought. *Well, maybe not the worst day because that was the day my mother died or it was the day my mean-spirited, spiteful aunt traded me to Qillaq, the day I knew I would never be with James again. And were they to be married soon? Natsiq and James? Natsiq wanted James. Since the day my mother died, Natsiq has spent her life making me and everyone else miserable.*

Okay, thinking about Natsiq's treachery isn't going to save me from Qillaq; pull yourself together, girl, and watch the trail. If I stew over the past, I won't see open leads, and my dog team and I will plunge into icy ocean and die.

She yelled at the team, and once more they were under way, but the pace was slow. She needed to be quick, but she also needed to keep the speed reasonable for the weary, hungry dogs. She could not afford to lose another dog.

It was late afternoon, and the one sure thing about Baffin Island is that the winds usually come up in the afternoon. As predicted, the sky grew white as swirling snow and gusts of wind blew from the north, winds at her back, winds that helped her tired team move a little faster.

I'll make it to safety. She felt more confident as the island drew closer. She guided her team over the hummocky ice along the base of the rocky cliffs into the shelter of a small inlet. She found a flat area between high blocks of tidal ice; relief flooded her body like a deep drink of hot tea. Exhausted, she dropped to the snowy surface as the katabatic winds descended from the high glaciers, picking up speed as they dropped to Cumberland Sound to rage against the walls of her rocky shelter.

Ashoona could not rest long. She had to unhitch the team, tying the traces to the rocks surrounding her campsite. She lifted the old dog out of the sled, so he could sleep with the other dogs and gain some warmth from their bodies.

She desperately needed food and water. But first she needed to sleep.

Everything will be better once I sleep, she thought as she climbed wearily into the *qamutik,* covering herself with caribou robes.

"What's that?" Ashoona woke with a start. *Oh no! Qillaq caught up and was shaking the* qamutik!

Her heart pounded as she poked her head out of the caribou robes. But it wasn't Qillaq; it was the wind, and not just a little wind, but one of the fierce hurricane-force winds that sweep across Baffin Island, winds that can pick up boats and *qamutiit* and toss them across the ice.

"I asked for wind, and I got more than I wanted," she laughed at herself. Although her camp was protected from the worst of the winds, occasional gusts descended into her little space. It licked at the caribou skins, rocked the sled and whipped at the harnesses and anything else left loose. Ashoona reluctantly crawled out of her warm nest to check the team and her belongings. It was not wise to let a storm descend on your camp without making sure everything important to your survival was tied down fast or tucked away.

Back in Panniqtuuq, she once saw a matchstick house lifted from the rocky ground and blown away into the fjord during a storm. No one was in the house at the time, but the family lost all their belongings and could have lost their lives. After that, many families anchored their little wooden houses with cables drilled into the rocks. Everything precious—boats, *qamutiit*, sheds—was tied up or weighed down with rocks. Children were never allowed outside when the winds blew, otherwise they could be lifted from their feet, blown into the air and dropped like sacks. Mothers kept their children close during these hurricane-like storms.

The dogs were awake and howling when she checked on them, patting each one to quiet them. The old dog lay motionless.

"Wake up, old man." But the dog didn't stir. She reached over to shake him, but felt only cold under his fur and a body already showing signs of rigor mortis.

"Poor fellow," she said with a tear. "I'm being silly! Inuit don't cry over their dogs!"

Ashoona remembered being reproached by her uncle for treating the dogs like pets. "They are not pets," Adamie scolded. "They're wild animals and will eat you if you are too small or too thin. Remember that, and don't spoil them."

But Ashoona's father was a *Qallunaaq,* and Ashoona was different—part Inuit, part Scottish, the two cultures always a little at war with one another.

Ashoona couldn't get back to sleep. *We need food, but first we need water.* Ashoona had filled a pouch with snow and warmed it under her armpit, giving her a few sips of water that made her only want more.

She rummaged in the sledge for the *qulik* and found a little piece of seal fat. She lit the lamp after wasting two matches and filled a pot with snow. Soon she had water to drink.

One sip for me and then some for my dogs.

She gulped the water and immediately felt revived. She gave a few sips to each dog, careful not to spill the water or let one dog take more than his share.

"More water is coming, and if my hunt is successful, we will have food."

The next task was the hardest for Ashoona. The old dog had to be used for food, and Ashoona could not stop her tears as she first removed the dog's hide. She skillfully worked her sharp *ulu* to slice off chunks of meat that she threw to the dog team. It was food; they didn't care that it was another dog. She gave the team small portions of meat, putting several hunks in a skin cover to freeze for future use.

"If I were a real Inuit, I would eat some of you old dog, but I just can't. I'm too much of a *Qallunaaq.*"

Ashoona still had a few pieces of seal meat. As soon as she swallowed the meat, she could feel heat return to her body. "Mmm, at least I know that seal meat is the best food. What would we do without seals to nourish us, give us our clothes, heat the food in our cooking pots and warm our houses? Let's see what else?"

Food, water and a sense that freedom might be at hand put Ashoona in a playful mood. She amused herself with a game.

"I know...I can make a waterproof container from the seal's stomach, strong ropes from the intestine, waterproof *kamiit* to keep my feet dry and baskets for berries." As she thought about the berries and that beautiful fall day on the hill behind the village, her heart broke again over the loss of James.

I have to stop loving you, James. I must be strong to stay alive. Forgive me if I forget you.

"Tomorrow, I will hunt for seal, and my dogs and I will be well fed, warm and safe. I will never have to put up with that smelly, cruel man, forcing himself on me, making me have his babies. Yuk! Yuk!"

With the small amount of nourishing seal meat in her stomach, Ashoona snuggled into the *qamutik*. The wind rattled the *qamutik*, and the incessant roar kept Ashoona awake. The trauma of her past was difficult to put out of her mind, and as she listened to the raging wind, she could not help but fume over the mistreatment by her relatives.

Once Natsiq realized her cousin had caught James' eye, she was delighted that Qillaq would take Ashoona to Igloolik. Ashoona would be Natsiq's rival for all the handsome boys in the village or other young men that might come to Panniqtuuq in search of a wife.

Despite Ashoona's protests, Aunt Amaruk would not renege on her promise to Qillaq. She was unwavering.

"There is no point in wailing, Ashoona," Aunt Amaruk said. "Qillaq will be here when he is able to travel on the ice from Igloolik, and you will go with him. There will be no arguments about this. And your uncle supports me, so don't go crying to him."

"Adamie is afraid to stick up for me. You just push him around, and you always get what you want. I saw you hit him once," accused Ashoona.

Amaruk's face contorted in anger. She bristled at Ashoona's accusation because she knew that her niece spoke the truth. "Shut up, you ungrateful girl. We gave you a home after your mother died and your father abandoned you, found you a good husband, and now you fight me every step?"

"I won't go with him, Aunt Amaruk. You can't make me go!"

"We'll see about that," Aunt Amaruk said in a tone that meant the discussion was over.

~~~~~~~~~~

Once the ice on Panniqtuuq Fjord was solid, Ashoona often scanned the sea, fearful for the day when Qillaq would arrive. She had seen him at the Hudson's Bay Store when she was six years old. He was a disgusting-looking man who frightened her and sent her hiding behind the packing boxes. And now her aunt expected her to go with him, lie in bed with him, have him touch her body and steal her innocence? Ashoona shuddered. She considered stealing a dog team and a gun in Panniqtuuq and escaping to another village, but that was a crime so grievous she would be an outcast among the villagers for the rest of her life.

No, I cannot take a neighbor's dogs or gun, and I know I can't survive alone without them. I will plead with Qillaq to leave me in Panniqtuuq. He will surely hear my request and give me up.

Ashoona planned the words she would use to convince Qillaq to leave her be.

As the deep cold of winter set in, Aunt Amaruk sewed beautiful clothes for her niece—caribou pants decorated with colorful patterns, a heavy sealskin parka, perfectly sewn *kamiit* that would withstand the cold and keep her feet dry when the spring melt came. She also made an *amauti* for the day when Ashoona would carry a baby on her back. These were the first clothes Ashoona's aunt had made for her since before little Davidee's death.

"Aunt Amaruk, I won't go with him, and I won't wear these clothes. I would rather burn them in front of you than put them on for a husband I will despise. You can't make me go with Qillaq, no matter what you say."

Amaruk threw her sewing on the table and approached Ashoona, her fists clenched. "It's a bargain that cannot be broken. You will shut up and go with him." Amaruk's fury was so intense that Ashoona backed off, concerned that if her aunt hit her, she would strike back and then be accused of assault.

Late fall passed with no sign of Qillaq. Then the fierce winds of December pelted the village, keeping the hunters, including Aula's grandsons, in Panniqtuuq. Ashoona reluctantly returned to her aunt's home, hoping that the hurricane-force storms would make Qillaq stay in Igloolik. If he did not get here by break-up, she might have a chance to escape. She could plead with one of the families to take her with them to their summer fishing camp. If that failed, she might be able to sneak onto the supply ship, or if the new minister arrived in time, she could beg for his protection.

Christmas brought no joy to Ashoona. Villagers gathered in St. Luke's Anglican Church for the service, led this year by Moses Agalukjuq, an Inuit layperson. He had grown up attending the mission in Blacklead, where the missionaries first translated the Bible into the Inuktitut language using syllabics. Moses chanted the familiar Anglican prayers that he learned as a child. He was proud to lead his villagers in prayer, but he was reluctant to interfere with the villagers and the old customs and taboos. He followed the flock, he did not lead them, except when chanting the prayers and selecting the hymns.

Ashoona knew that Moses would refuse to protect her. She sat in the pew, staring at the Inuktitut hymnal, mouthing the words of the Christmas songs, while Aunt Amaruk sang out in a high-pitched screechy voice. The distraught girl wondered how her aunt could sing the words of peace and love yet force her own niece into a life worse than prison.

Aula sat beside Ashoona, aware of the treacherous bargain that Amaruk had struck with Qillaq. Aula was saddened at the depth of the girl's despair. She was Ashoona's only defender. What upset the old woman was that Amaruk acted as if Ashoona was a possession that could be traded off like a dog or a gun.

That same day, while the villagers walked from the church to the mission house for food and gifts, Aula approached Amaruk.

"You can't give Ashoona to that man. Haven't you heard about him? He is *Nuliarsuit*…a man possessed by the spirit of wives who sow chaos. Have you not heard the stories of the time when he was young and not yet skilled as a hunter, the time when he did not have the patience to wait at the seal breathing holes, the time when his small family was without food for weeks? Did you know that he ate two of his own children? Killed them and ate them! Would you risk the lives of Ashoona and her children?"

Aula, generally a quiet woman with a soft voice, felt her face flush and her hands clench at the thought of Ashoona being traded off to one of the most evil men ever born an Inuit.

"It is a lie, stories spread by women who are idle and have nothing better to do but gossip. Go away, Aula. You have nothing to say about Ashoona. She does not belong to your family."

Amaruk had more power in the village than the old woman, and so Aula's pleas went unheeded. No one was willing to stand up to Amaruk, and one of the women in the craft circle observed that since Ashoona had killed Amaruk's only son, the unfortunate marriage was justified.

The Christmas celebrations ended, and the deep, bitter cold of January settled over the town. With each passing day, Ashoona felt more trapped and helpless. She tried to get someone, anyone, to help her. She visited every family in the village, pleading for a place to hide or begging a hunting family to take her to another village. But no one would help her.

Amaruk's nephew, John, overheard Ashoona's pleas and thought his aunt would find the news useful. "Auntie, you should keep watch on Ashoona. She's looking for an escape."

"Do you want to help me, John?"

"Eeeee," John replied, using the Inuit expression for agreement.

The next day, Qillaq arrived in the community. He had made the long journey from Igloolik driving a team of dogs along the west coast of Baffin Inland, over the pass and then across the sea ice arriving in Panniqtuuq in the dead of winter. As Qillaq drove his dog team off the tidal ice and up to the Hudson's Bay Store, the other dogs in the community barked wildly, alerting the villagers. People pulled on their parkas and went to greet the hunter, hoping to get news of friends or relatives in Igloolik and the other villages he passed en route.

Aunt Amaruk joined them, anxious to let Qillaq know that Ashoona would be his, provided he kept his side of the bargain. Qillaq asked that Amaruk take him to see Ashoona immediately, but the villagers coaxed him to come to the mission house for tea and bannock and to share news.

Ashoona heard the commotion, and with her heart in her throat, peeked out from her aunt's doorway. Her stomach clenched in fear. She pulled on her *amauti* and was about to run out the door when Aunt Amaruk burst in.

"Stay in the house," she ordered, blocking the door. "Qillaq will come for you soon. Get your things ready. He will take you over the pass to his mother's village at Qikiqtarjuaq where you stay till next winter because it is too late now to reach Igloolik before break-up. It will be cold crossing the mountains, so take your new *amauti*, your thick sealskin pants and caribou furs. If you die on the *qamutik*, you are no use to me. Now pack your things quickly and sit and wait."

But Ashoona, frantic to find an escape, found the strength to push her aunt aside.

"Let me go! I won't be his wife. I won't!" She ran from the house in a panic, her breath turning to ice crystals in the sub-fifty degree air. Aunt Amaruk could not run to catch her, but yelled after Ashoona as the girl disappeared behind the houses.

I have to hide before he sees me.

Ashoona ran to the church to pray, hoping to find a cupboard to squeeze into, someplace she would not be found. But before she could find a place to secret herself, the door opened, and light seeped into the dim church interior. She spun around, certain that it was Qillaq and that she was trapped with no one to help her. Instead, it was John. She didn't like him much because he often taunted her, calling her a killer and a bastard. At the mission school, Ashoona remembered John digging boogers out of his nose, inspecting his find and then wiping them under the desk. She cringed at the revolting image.

"I know you want to see James again and that you will do anything to avoid marrying Qillaq," said John. "James has sent me to get you; he has a dog team a few miles down the fjord. He will take you to Blacklead Island, and from there you will go with him to Regina."

That James would take her to stay with him at the police academy in Regina seemed preposterous, but she put aside reason and accepted the amazing turn of events, not because it seemed plausible, but because she desperately wanted to believe.

"John, I will always remember this wonderful thing you have done for me."

"Run and get your belongings, especially your new clothes, and meet me here. I'll have a dog team ready to take you to James. But hurry."

"John, thank you again," Ashoona said. "Is he really there? I can't believe I am so lucky. It's what I have dreamed. But we must be careful. Qillaq cannot discover my escape."

"Don't worry. He's still eating seal, char and everything else the community can spare. And don't worry about your aunt; she is with him at the mission, guzzling tea. Qillaq may even sleep overnight before looking for his bride."

Ashoona had never run so fast; she dashed in the door of her aunt's small wooden house, grabbed a sealskin bag with her wedding clothes, her heavy parka and pants and a few keepsakes and was back at the church in minutes.

"Let's go. I can't stand the thought of Qillaq taking me!"

Ashoona rode in the *qamutik* while John drove the team onto the ice. It was a fast trip because the team was fresh and the dogs were anxious to run. In ten minutes, they rounded the peninsula. Ashoona's heart pounded in her chest. John told her that James would be in sight as soon as they headed into the next bay. Despite the dim light of the arctic winter, she finally spotted the dog team and the loaded *qamutik*, but where was James? Ashoona felt a twinge of concern.

Ashoona scanned the rocky shoreline trying to see him. But it wasn't James who stepped out from behind the rock cliff. It was Qillaq.

"You wicked boy! How could you?" Ashoona jumped from the moving sled and broke into a run, but she wasn't fast enough. Qillaq whipped his lead dog and stepped onto the sled runners. Within minutes, Qillaq caught up with Ashoona and pulled the team to a halt a few feet ahead of her. She turned to run back the other way, but John had anticipated her, cutting off any escape. Qillaq grabbed Ashoona by the hair, dragged her over the ice, bound her hands and feet and tethered her securely to the *qamutik*.

———

It was three days since Qillaq kidnapped her, days that seemed endless: the long day of anguish tied to the *qamutik* and bounced along the ice up Auyuittuq Valley; her daring escape and then two days on the run away from Qillaq and into this sheltered cove. She lay in her *qamutik*, trying to sleep through the noise of the raging storm. She was free of hateful Qillaq, but for how long? Thinking back on her aunt's treachery again brought on a renewed flood of angry tears.

"How could they trick me? It's so unfair! So cruel!" Ashoona cried herself to sleep as the winds buffeted the island and her dogs dug deeper into the drifts to find some shelter from the fierce, bitterly cold wind.

Chapter Four

The Shaman's Camp

Ashoona awoke with a start. Her first thought was that, earlier in the day, during the short period of mid-day light, Qillaq might have followed the tracks of her *qamutik* to her hiding place. She peeked around the cliff, careful to keep her head low, and scanned Cumberland Sound, a desert of ice stretching to the horizon. The night was calm, the sky aglow with stars, the planet Venus on the horizon a brilliant diamond. The constellations etched their familiar designs against the backdrop of the black sky with a myriad of faint clusters completing the tapestry. Ashoona marveled at the beauty of the land without sun.

She melted ice for water to drink and gave the team the rest of the meat of the old dog. Ashoona ate sparingly from the remaining seal meat. She was in no rush to begin the hunt. She went back to sleep and slept late into the morning and spent the early part of the day mending harnesses, thankful she had grabbed Qillaq's sealskin bag that held his supplies of knives and needles. She waited for the short period of half-light that she needed if she was to hunt successfully. As noon approached, a rosy hue lit the mountaintops of Baffin Island. She poked her head around the protective cliffs and looked out onto the flat ice of Cumberland Sound. She saw a dark speck moving away from her island.

"That must be him! And he's heading for Blacklead," she said smiling, "We dumped him! You outran the mean old bugger!" Ashoona was so happy that she jumped among the dogs, hugging and petting each one. "Now, I'm going to do something for you."

Ashoona knew she could not venture out on the side of the island where Qillaq might see her, but she also had to search for seals while it was light. During her exhausting two-day run across the ice, Ashoona dismissed any thought of halting her escape to hunt seals. A hunter often spent hours, sometimes entire days, waiting patiently for a seal to poke its nose above the ice. Remaining out in the open was a risk Ashoona was not willing to take. She would choose starvation rather than let Qillaq catch her again.

Her camp was in a sheltered cove, protected from view by steep cliffs on the ocean side. If she tried to walk around the island either to her left or right, Qillaq might see her as soon as she ventured out of the cove. She decided to climb up a ravine that rose up from the cove and then cross the top of the island to the far side. She took the gun and a few supplies from the *qamutik* before checking the tethers securing her dog team to the rocks. She held the gun in one hand and began climbing the cliff, careful to remain hidden. When she reached the top, Ashoona turned briefly toward the ocean and was relieved to see Qillaq and his dog team continuing across Cumberland Sound, just a small black speck in the distance.

"The most wonderful sight in this world is seeing you disappear, you mean bastard!" she yelled, shaking her fist.

"Enough! He's gone, and if I can help it, I will never see his ugly face again." In a few minutes, she made her way over the top of the island to the far side.

"This isn't what I expected," Ashoona said as she peered down over the sheer drop. Halfway down she could see a narrow ledge that would possibly give her some purchase. Just then, a seal came up onto the ice below and lay near its breathing hole.

"I gotta get there fast," she said. "We need you, little *natsik*. But how do I get off this blasted cliff without breaking my neck?" She looped her rope around a rock at the top, but she couldn't tie it off because she would need it later to drag the seal back to camp.

Quietly and cautiously, Ashoona rappelled down the cliff. A few more feet, and she would reach the narrow ledge.

Is the rope long enough for me to safely get my feet onto the ledge? With only a foot of rope left, she slid down to the ledge.

"Made it," Ashoona sighed with relief. At the sound of her voice, the seal moved, preparing to dive under the ice. "No you don't!" Ashoona moved with the speed and skill she had learned from her father. She turned her back to the cliff and aimed. It was a perfect shot.

But her stance was precarious; the kickback from the gun threw her off balance, and she slipped off the ledge.

"Oh, my God! Nooo!" Down she went, falling several feet onto the jagged ice below. She landed hard on her left wrist. At first she was in shock, but within seconds, she was overcome with pain. Her wrist was broken.

"Owww!" she cried. "It's not fair! It hurts! I can't stand it! Mama, I need you," she cried, overcome by the most excruciating pain. She lay curled up on the ice waiting for the worst of the agony to subside.

Ashoona could hardly bear to look at the break, but she saw that her hand was twisted and a bone protruded out of the skin on her wrist.

"Oh, my God!" she cried, realizing the seriousness of her situation.

The short interval of the winter sun's half-light had ended by the time Ashoona was able to stand up. She gasped at the pain. She cut off a piece of the rope to use as a sling for her injured arm. She grasped her fractured wrist and moved it slowly, testing her tolerance for pain. Her stomach churned, and she thought she might vomit. Ashoona paused, taking deep breaths as she adjusted her arm against her chest and awkwardly secured it with the rope.

She struggled over to the seal, wondering how she was going to get it back to her camp. She took one end of the rope, poked a hole in the seal's hide with her *ulu* and threaded the rope through. Gritting her teeth, she began pulling the seal with her good arm while trying to ignore the pulsing pain from her broken wrist.

She had to try to pull the seal over the ice and hope to reach shelter before the pain became too intense and she fainted. Fainting meant death out in the open. The arctic night had deepened by the time she reached the far end of the island. She had pulled the seal for at least three miles, every step a struggle, but she realized that she could not possibly pull the hundred-pound seal to her camp. From her estimate of the island's size, she still had about a mile to go. It was too much for her to think about.

"*Nanuq*, don't you dare take my seal," she admonished, looking around for polar bears that might have caught the dead seal's scent. Ashoona sliced off a large chunk of seal meat for herself and the dogs, covered her kill with snow, stood her gun upright in a snowdrift as a marker and continued on to her camp.

Just a mile! I can make it. She plodded toward camp, each step slower and slower. An hour later, Ashoona struggled into the camp and collapsed on the *qamutik*. Despite her weariness, she could not sleep. The pain returned with vengeance. Ashoona decided that she had to go for help.

"I can't go to Panniqtuuq. Aunt Amaruk will force me to go back to Qillaq. Besides, it's too far. I need someone who can fix my wrist as soon as possible."

"I guess I'll have to go to the *Angakkut's* camp. Padluk has to be the worst person I've ever met next to Qillaq, but he can set broken bones. It's not far, just the next island."

When Ashoona was a shy five-year-old, Padluk had come to the Hudson's Bay Post in Panniqtuuq. She remembered seeing the strange-looking man with cruel eyes, and she asked her mother who he was and why he looked so odd. Ashoona's mother explained that the *Angakkut* was the spiritual leader and healer in the old days before the missionaries arrived. Only a few of these shamans still held their power. Some helped their people, others enforced the old customs. They meted out brutal punishment to anyone ignoring taboos and blamed innocent people when the hunt failed. As a young child, Ashoona dreaded being in the same room as Padluk, but for the time being, he was her only source of medical help.

Once she had made up her mind to go to the *Angakkut's* camp, she did not delay. It was hard to hitch the team up with only one hand, but she managed, and soon they were heading over the ice, first to pick up the frozen seal she had left behind, and then onward five miles to the village. The trip tested Ashoona. Her face white with the intense pain and holding her arm close, she tried to run alongside the team, but every step she took jarred her arm. If she rode on the sled, the team slowed down, or worse, the lead dog took the team off course.

Dogs barked as she approached the camp, and as was tradition, the people of the village came out of their huts and raised their arms to indicate that they were friendly. Ashoona raised her good arm in greeting and drove into the camp as forty or more adults and children gathered to inspect the new arrival.

"I'm hurt." Ashoona spoke to crowd. "Please…where is Padluk? My wrist is broken. I hope he can set it?"

A man separated himself from the crowd. He had long, dirty hair and piercing eyes. He chose to wear dirty, ragged skins, even though he could have the best clothing made by the most skilled seamstresses.

"So, here we have the Hudson Bay man's bastard. What is your name? I never remember names of children born of the *Qallunaat*."

"Ashoona. And you should know me because I remember you well even though I was only a little child helping my father in the store."

"Well, Ashoona, what will you give us if I help you?"

Ashoona did not expect this question and thought for a few minutes. "I did not think that the shamans asked for payment to heal people. Why are you asking me to give something? I have nothing of value."

"There is always something to give," Padluk answered, a cadaverous smile on his thin, wrinkled face. "You will be my helper for twelve moons. I need someone young to fetch water, to cook my food and keep the snow house warm. Agree to that, and I will tend to your injury."

"One year! That's too long. I will help you until I reach my thirteenth year, four months from now."

"You should not bargain with me, *Qallunaaq* child. You are not welcome in this camp, and if you do not get help, you could die. You have nothing but your labor to bargain with while I hold your life in my hands."

"Yes, I have more to bargain with. My father is rich. He will come back and bring many wonderful things. Whatever he brings, I will share with this camp. I give the people here my word. But I will not be your slave for a whole year."

A murmur rippled throughout the camp. Many of the old ones remembered Ashoona's parents. They recalled her father's generosity and believed the young girl would bring them many wonderful things from the big cities to the south.

"Let her stay. We should help her," said one of the adults.

"Yes," said Lasalosie, one of the elders. "We should help her. That is what Inuit do. They help someone in trouble."

The shaman understood the camp would not let him send the girl away. He had to keep control of the people. He could not assert his authority when the community did not agree with him. He nodded angrily, signaling defeat.

"We will help her. She will stay for three months and be my helper, and when and if her useless father returns, we will demand our share of the wealth. Maybe this *Qallunaaq* will return and maybe he won't."

Ashoona smiled at the people in the camp. "*Qujannamiik*...Thank you."

The shaman watched with a calculating look as Ashoona struggled out of the *qamutik*, cringing in pain with every movement. A young woman with a baby on her back came over to help Ashoona.

Ashoona smiled at the woman. "What is your name?"

"Aula," the woman replied.

"Another Aula that is helping me. *Qujannamiik*, little mother. Not so long ago, an old woman named Aula saved me when everyone wanted me dead. Now I have found another Aula, and I love you immediately."

Ashoona was so grateful for the woman's offer of help that she burst into tears. Since the day her father left on the ship to Montreal and the desperately sad day her mother died, she had experienced little kindness.

Aula supported Ashoona, steadying her as they walked to the shaman's snow house. She guided Ashoona to one of the sleeping platforms. The dwelling was untidy and had a damp chill, quite unlike igloos Ashoona was accustomed to. In her mother's igloo, several blubber lamps were always kept burning, filling the home with warmth and light. In Padluk's snow house, on the other hand, rotting bones littered the floor, and the caribou robes on the sleeping platform were worn and smelly.

"He does not like older women to help him, and there are no single young women in the camp to clean, sew and cook for him," Aula explained.

"But is he capable of fixing my arm?" Ashoona asked.

"He knows more than anyone else on the island and maybe even more than anyone, except maybe the doctor at Blacklead or the nurses at Igloolik and Panniqtuuq."

Just then a noise at the entrance announced the shaman as he pushed through the narrow passage into the igloo.

"Aula, get out! I don't want you here." The shaman turned to Ashoona. "I'll have to cut your parka off to fix the arm. I assume you are a seamstress and can sew it again once you are healed?"

"Do whatever is needed so I can be healed as soon as possible."

Unlike most Inuit houses, Padluk had no neat shelf for storing *ulus* and knives. The shaman searched for a knife, tossing caribou robes, sealskins and other implements willy nilly, making an even bigger mess than was there originally.

"Damn this messy house. I can never find a knife, my *kamiit* or sometimes even my gun. Once you are well, you will put this place straight. Right?"

"If you can't find your knife, just pull my parka off. I need my arm in a splint as soon as possible. My fingers are turning blue!"

"You…a *Qallunaaq*…will take that kind of pain? I'll do it, but you will scream when your arm is pulled from the sleeve."

"Get on with it," Ashoona repeated, gritting her teeth to prepare for the broken wrist bone grinding against the sleeve of her parka.

Not the gentlest healer, Padluk first tugged on the parka sleeve, freeing her good arm, lifted the parka over Ashoona's head and with a quick pull, removed the sleeve from her fractured arm.

Ashoona couldn't help moaning as the sleeve tugged on her broken wrist.

"That is a bad break, right through the skin," the shaman said, feeling around the broken bone that protruded from Ashoona's wrist. Her arm was swollen and blue from her fingers to her elbow. Padluk worked quickly, first placing a straight piece of caribou bone against the break. As he moved the fractured bone into place, Ashoona gasped with pain and almost fainted from the throbbing in her arm. But Padluk aligned the break properly, and Ashoona knew that in time she would heal. Next, he tied a dampened rabbit skin around the supporting caribou bone, securing the skin like a cast.

"That should do. My sister Meena has been cooking for me, so I'll have Aula bring you a bowl of her soup. If you can make it through this night of pain, tomorrow the healing will be well underway. You are young. You will heal."

Ashoona sighed with relief that the tugging and pressure on her injured arm was finished. The pain was still intense, but at least it was tolerable.

Soon, Aula came with a bowl of hot caribou soup.

"Take a few sips, *panik*...my little daughter," Aula said gently. "I wish he would let me stay with you, but he despises me." Ashoona could see the thin, pinched face of a baby in Aula's *amauti*. Holding onto the edge of the *amauti* was a toddler whose little face was so drawn that she looked like an old woman.

"Your children look unwell. Are they sick?"

"Sick from lack of food. We have had only scraps to eat and my milk is drying up. The *Angakkut* refuses to share food with us."

"You should take some of the food I am given. You must feed your little ones."

"Padluk would sentence me to death if I stole a mouthful from your bowl. Just go to sleep and get well. Maybe then you and I can escape together."

"But why are you bringing me food, rather than Padluk's sister?"

"Meena is too important to fetch food for anyone, and Padluk gave me the task to increase my suffering and that of my starving babes. His devoted followers watch me constantly, and if I as much as dip my finger in the soup to let my child have one drop, Padluk would kill me. Now drink your soup, and do not ask any more questions. I am not supposed to speak to you."

When Aula left, Ashoona dropped off to sleep like a person falling from a high cliff. Although she was still in a great deal of pain, exhaustion carried her into a fitful sleep until morning.

"Ahhhhhhh!" Ashoona moaned when she accidentally rolled over onto her injured arm. The shaman was already up, trying to light the lamp.

"So, you slept through the night. I'd give you some water to drink, if I could just get this damn lamp lit. It never wants to light even with these *Qallunaaq* matches. There...finally it's going."

Ashoona waited anxiously, wondering if Aula or one of the other women would come to help her. Her throat was parched, and she felt dehydrated. First, she needed to pee, but she did not want to ask the shaman for help. Meanwhile, he pulled down his caribou pants and peed, unconcerned that Ashoona was just feet away.

"You can use the pot. I don't care. As soon as you are better, you will carry it outside to dump. That is why I helped you, so you can help me. See, we both will benefit. Your arm will be healed, and I will have someone to light the lamp, clean the house, empty the pot. It will work for both of us. Right?"

Ashoona nodded, but she wasn't as happy as Padluk about the arrangements for the next three months. However, for Ashoona, a deal was a deal, and no matter how hellish her duties were, she would keep her side of the bargain, providing the bargain did not include sexual favors.

"Would you ask Aula to help me get up so I can pee?"

"Aula! That witch married an outsider. He is unwelcome here; his children are unwelcome here. Since they came here we have had fewer seals and no caribou. She is wicked and has brought bad luck to our camp."

"All right, I'll do it myself, but I would like you to go outside while I use the pot."

"What? Go out of my own house? I don't think so. That is ridiculous *Qallunaat* thinking. Who cares whether I see your backside? Get up. Pee. Then take a cup of tea. You need to drink several cups if you are to heal."

Ashoona struggled from the sleeping platform, carefully placing her feet on the floor. Her head spun as she tried to stand.

Okay. Slow down. She rose cautiously from the bed, holding on to the edge to steady herself. Her arm throbbed with the movement. Ashoona fumbled with her pants, pulling one side, then the other and finally squatting over the pot.

She staggered to the lamp where a pot of tea steamed over the flame. She scooped out a cup for herself and gingerly made her way back to the bed. The liquid was so refreshing, and she immediately felt revived and then sleepy again. As soon as she lay down, Ashoona fell into a deep sleep. For the next three days, the young girl slept, woke to drink tea or broth and then slept again.

When Ashoona woke on the fourth morning, the first thing she saw was a bowl of stewed caribou covered with gravy. It was only in her imagination, of course. She had not eaten a proper meal for days, and now she could eat a small seal all by herself.

"Do you ever eat in this house?" she asked the shaman, who was dozing on the sleeping platform across the igloo from her bed.

"I would eat if the hunters would bring meat. They've been out hunting every day for two weeks without a single kill. We have little food left, only a few chunks of your seal, a few bones from a caribou and fat from a walrus.

"If the hunters are unsuccessful today," Padluk continued, "the entire camp will soon starve. Already, the children are ill from lack of food, and the mothers are barely able to nurse their babies. Aula brought a curse on the camp, and now her useless husband has left, hoping that we'll send a few scraps to her bastard children."

"How can you say that? It's not Aula's fault that the caribou herd has moved or that the seals do not come to their breathing holes. How can you blame Aula? She has nothing to do with it!"

"She brought bad luck here. Before she came here with that hateful man, the hunters brought many seals home each day. The people had so much food that we were able to give the good dark meat to the dogs. Now we have nothing but scraps. I will look after my own people before I will help that wicked woman and her children. You'll see. As soon as Aula and her two children die, our luck will return."

"Surely you don't intend to starve Aula and her children? That is wrong. The Inuit always share."

"Who are you to talk about Inuit ways? You are not one of us either. But I allowed you to come into our camp, so I have an obligation to give you a share of the little food that is left."

"I'm famished, but I don't want to eat a bowl of stew when I know Aula and her two little children have nothing. Let me take them something."

"It is forbidden," Padluk stormed. "No one in this camp is allowed to help the witch. You hear me?"

"I hear you, but you are wrong. Someday you will have to account for your actions. Do you think the outside world is going to allow you to starve a member of the camp and do nothing about it? Policemen and government people know what goes on. You cannot act this way anymore."

"I can do whatever I want. Do you think those useless *Qallunaat* will ever come here?"

"Yes. If they knew the village had no food, they would come, and they would find out that you are starving Aula and her two children. Send them a little broth today, please. The two wee ones are dying. I beg you to help! I beg you to save them just to save yourself if for no other reason."

"Never. Let her and her bastards die. If the police come here, no one in the camp would tell them anything. The people on this island do not dare to disobey me. It has happened before. A young woman disobeyed me. She was stripped naked and placed in a snow hut with the door and windows filled in. She could not escape, and within a week she was dead. After that, no one opposed my word."

Ashoona heard the evil in Padluk's voice. *What he is doing is not just wrong, it is murder. He's starving a family because of his stupid superstitions. If he thinks I will let a mother and two innocent babies die, he'd better think again.*

Each day the hunters left with dog teams or on foot to head out onto the ice in search of seals, and each evening, they returned with nothing. It was as if all life had escaped from Cumberland Sound. No matter how far the hunters traveled, sometimes out for days, they saw no sign of caribou or seal.

Then more tragedy. Many of the dogs became ill with distemper. Soon only a few dog teams remained, and only a few hunters were able to travel any distance in search of seals and caribou. The dogs that perished became a sparse meal for the surviving dogs and the starving villagers.

But one other dog team may have been spared. Amo, Lasalosie's son, had not returned. Most believed he was dead; others hoped that he had made a dash across Cumberland Sound to get help for the starving community.

"I hope Amo went for help," Ashoona told Padluk, as she worked cleaning the snow house. "Unless you want everyone to die of starvation, someone must get to Blacklead where there are stores of food. The Mounted Police never let people die out on the land if they know people are starving."

"That would suit the *Qallunaat*, wouldn't it?" Padluk replied, his high-pitched thin voice rising in anger. "They could prove that we cannot live out on the land; they would bring their priests, make us live in their warm smothering houses and send our children to *Qallunaat* schools. No one from the village is allowed to go to Blacklead. If Lasalosie's son has gone there, I will kill the old man and his disobedient son."

Lasalosie was an old man; his wife was younger but was blind from birth. Ashoona was sure the elder could be counted on for help if matters in the camp worsened. She said nothing more to Padluk; she would wait until the shaman was asleep. She could not let babies die when all they needed was a tiny bit of food.

Chapter Five

Rescued

T he long, dark days of the arctic winter were nearing an end. A week earlier, the sun only shone for a few minutes before disappearing in an array of color behind the ice-crowned peaks of Cumberland Sound. But at noon today, the sun held its position in the sky for an hour, and shone over the frozen sea, coloring the cliffs of the *Angakkut's* island camp in shades of rose. The sun had sunk below the horizon when the doctor from Blacklead came upon Padluk's camp. Henry Russell did not know what he would find but had heard from Amo, one of the hunters from the village, that people at the *Angakkut's* camp were starving.

As Henry and his guide, Kilabuk, approached the community, Henry could see the shapes of the snow houses but no movement in the encampment. All was quiet, even the dogs did not welcome the newcomers.

Henry and Kilabuk crawled through the opening of an igloo. The passageway opened up into a roomier space. It took them a moment to adjust to the dimness of the damp, odorous dwelling.

Henry could see two forms on the sleeping platform and another huddled in the corner.

"Are they dead?"

"The lamp is still burning," Kilabuk said. "Someone must be alive."

Kilabuk was a muscular man in his early thirties. He had dark skin, and like most Inuit, he had no facial hair. He wore traditional Inuit winter clothing of caribou skins and sealskin boots.

Henry, who was also dressed in Inuit clothing, had a three-day beard and dark brown hair that hadn't seen a pair of scissors for many weeks. He was several years younger than Kilabuk and considerably taller. Despite his lack of grooming, he was pleasant to look at with his gray eyes and long lashes, a feature women noticed but which was lost on Henry.

The two men searched the snow house for any sign of life. Henry spotted movement from the form in the corner and went over to find Ashoona, who was crouched on the floor, caribou skins drawn up around her. Her face was gaunt, the bones in her cheeks stood out.

"We've come with food. We heard you are starving."

Ashoona said nothing. She had accepted the inevitability of death and could not comprehend that survival was at hand.

Henry poured a warm drink from his thermos and held it to the girl's mouth. "Take just a little. It's caribou broth. It will revive you."

She sipped slowly at first then grabbed the cup and gulped down the warm liquid. She immediately felt restored.

"Can you speak now?" Henry asked in a gentle voice. "Who are you, and what happened here?"

"I'm Ashoona. We've had no food for weeks." Ashoona whispered between sips of broth. "The hunters haven't killed any animals for more than a month, no seals, no caribou. We boiled our boots and sleeping robes to survive."

"Old Lasalosie helped me," she said, pointing to the sleeping ledge, "and Padluk punished him. Lasalosie is so very sick." Her voice broke, and tears fell down her emaciated cheeks.

Henry went over to the old man, who was moaning in pain. When Henry drew back the caribou robe, he could see that the man's leg was swollen and blue, clear signs of blood poisoning. Next to the old man was Annie, his blind wife. She stirred but was too weak to speak.

"You speak their language as well as English? Can you interpret for me?"

Ashoona nodded.

"How did this happen?" Henry asked the old man. Lasalosie muttered something about hunting the caribou, but his words made no sense. He seemed to be talking about some long-ago hunt.

Henry turned to Ashoona. "Do you know how he was injured?"

"No," she whispered. She feared the abusive shaman and was reluctant to reveal the worst of what had taken place. Henry realized that the young woman was not going to be forthcoming and turned his attention to Lasalosie.

Henry examined the leg again. He didn't want to tell Ashoona that he couldn't possibly save the old man without a surgeon and a hospital.

"I have some medicine. Come with me to the *qamutik*, and I'll give you a little for him. Then I need you to help me with the others. Kilabuk is already busy constructing a large igloo where we will cook food for the villagers. But for now, are you strong enough to go around to everyone and give each person

68

a bowl of broth? Once the igloo is built, I will ask that you tell those who can walk to come to the new igloo where they can eat and warm up."

"What about Lasalosie? You think he will die, don't you?"

"The gangrene has spread to just below his knee. He will only live if we amputate. I can't do that without help, and we must save the ones who are not beyond hope. Do you understand?"

"Yes. You're right. Everyone needs food and water immediately, and I'll help you look after them. But I beg you to save Lasalosie. Annie cannot live without him. She is blind and depends on him. Please help them. They have been so kind to me after I was no longer allowed to visit my only friend in the camp."

"I can't promise anything right now. Let's get to work. While I help Kilabuk build the igloo, I want you to visit all the snow houses as quickly as you can."

Ashoona was off before he finished speaking.

Kilabuk worked feverishly cutting the blocks for the igloo. By the time Henry joined him, the experienced builder had completed the first round of the spherical dwelling.

"Good God, Kilabuk, you're fast!" Henry smiled as he lifted the cut blocks to form the second layer.

"I'm not fast, and besides, you did not ask for a *qaggiit*... the big snow house where the whole village can gather, the kind that takes many hands and much skill to place the final blocks in the high ceiling. But that type of igloo is for games and dancing and no one will be dancing this day, will they, Boss?" Kilabuk gave a little chuckle. "This big enough, Boss?"

"Wonderful. It's a work of art, and please call me Henry. I don't feel like your boss because as we build this igloo, you're my boss. Now what do you want me to do?"

"If it is okay with you, Boss...I mean Henry...could I ask that girl to light the *qulliit*? We need to heat the interior to make the walls icy and keep the inside warm. And the floor has to be solid ice so I can spread out the caribou skins."

"You mean Ashoona?"

"Yes, the pretty one who just needs more seal meat to fill her out."

When Ashoona returned, Kilabuk dug out several oil lamps and the Primus stove from his *qamutik*.

"We are just clumsy men and need your help, Ashoona." He spoke to her in Inuktitut, although his English was almost equal to hers. "We need a good flame in each *qulliq*. I can see that you are the kind of girl who knows how to light a clean, hot flame."

Ashoona smiled at the compliment and went to work. Soon she had several lamps burning and a pot of food boiling on the Primus stove.

Ashoona left the igloo and returned to find the villagers. "Some people can't walk," Ashoona told Henry as she led a group of ten into the large igloo.

The men, women and children were stone-faced; they could not grasp the idea that their lives were being saved. Their clothes were tattered, their bodies so thin; their faces showed that death had stalked them. Kilabuk filled cups with broth and a few small pieces of meat.

"Eat slowly. You don't want to be sick," Kilabuk warned.

No one among the desperate group spoke. Some gulped down the food; others sipped their meal slowly. An old woman took a few sips and vomited, heaving over and over again.

"I have something that may help her," Henry offered. He dug in his medical supplies and took out a bouillon cube that he placed in a cup of warm water. "Ashoona, give her this."

The girl held the cup to the old woman's lips. This time she sipped the liquid and kept it down.

When the group finished their broth, Kilabuk gave each family some oil for their lamps and a pot of food to take to the ones who could not walk.

"More food will arrive soon. Amo will return with as many seals as his sledge can hold. He came to Blacklead to ask for our help and is hunting. Eat now, but not too much, and eat slowly."

Henry enlisted Ashoona's help as he made the rounds of all the dwellings. His first stop was to check on Lasalosie. The painkiller Henry had given him offered some respite from the torture of the past days and allowed the old man a few hours of sleep. But now he was awake, thrashing about and moaning. Henry gently lifted his head so he could drink a few sips of warm tea laced with more painkillers.

"The gangrene will spread unless you amputate his leg. He won't live, will he?" Ashoona asked. "Most of the people are looked after. Why can't you operate on him? That is what we should do."

"You're an insistent young woman. But you're right; the poison has spread. I can only help him with the pain. I'm not ready to ignore the others to work on what I believe is a hopeless case. Now tell me, did you visit all the houses? Do you know who still needs care?"

Ashoona led Henry to the neighboring snow houses, giving him the names of the people and showing him those who were in most urgent need of medical attention. Some were debilitated to the point that their survival was uncertain, but he reasoned that if he demonstrated confidence in his abilities to heal them, the very sick would have hope, and hope was a big part of the cure.

As they walked through the destitute camp, Ashoona seemed even more distressed.

"I can't help that Lasalosie is ill."

"I know. It's not him."

"So what's troubling you? Before we came, you were all facing death. Are you not relieved? Already your health is improving. A few hours ago, you could not even get up from your sleeping robes."

"I am so grateful to you that I don't want to make you angry with me."

"Why would I be angry with someone who has helped me when the others, even the camp's leader, are of no help."

"There is something I should have told you, but the *Angakkut* ordered us not to speak of it."

"The *Angakkut*? You mean the minister?"

"No. The people's *Angakkut*. His name is Padluk."

"But I thought shamans were no longer among your people. How can he give commands and order you to be silent?"

"He has a great deal of power over the people, especially in times of famine. When people are starving, it's up to the *Angakkut* to find a reason for the hardship, and usually that reason is a family or a person in the camp."

"So Padluk blames someone here for the death of the dogs and the starvation? And who would this be?"

"Aula. She lives in a tent away from the main village. I'm being watched, and I was afraid to take you there, but now I don't care." Ashoona whispered as if Padluk could hear her and make her a target of the camp's vigilante justice.

"Where is she? I thought we had visited everyone."

"Not all. Her tent is hidden by that big rock." Ashoona pointed off in the distance, far past the edge of the camp.

Henry set off, with Ashoona in tow. He felt this would be an easy matter to clear up—just another family who needed oil for the lamps and a pot of stew to restore their health.

They approached a sealskin tent, tucked in between the rocks. It was a sorry-looking dwelling made of animal skins patched together unevenly, leaving gaps for the snow to blow in.

He pulled aside the flap and stepped in. Ashoona didn't follow him.

A sickly smell permeated the room. A faint light filtered in through the thin tent walls. A woman sat in the middle of the room, staring off into nothingness and ignoring Henry. The bowl of soup Ashoona had brought earlier lay untouched beside the woman. Henry wondered why there was only one cup when three people were in the tent. He could see the heads of two small children in robes on either side of the woman.

Henry poured more warm soup into a cup and tried to make the woman take it. She said nothing but gently pushed Henry's hand away.

"Please eat something. I came to the Arctic to help people who are in need. It would be so sad for me if you refused food and died, rather than allow me to care for you. Why not eat?"

Ashoona had entered the tent and was listening. "Have you checked the children?"

Henry touched the sleeping robe of one of the children. The child did not move, and the robes were cold to his touch.

"This child is dead. Both are dead? Oh, my God!"

"They died a few days ago." Turning to Aula, Ashoona rested her hand on the woman's shoulder. "This good doctor has come to save us. He has brought food; you must eat something."

"I do not wish to eat," she replied, as she stared past Ashoona at the wall, expressionless.

"How did they die?" Henry asked, choking on his words. "Were there not scraps enough to feed these little ones to keep them alive?"

Aula's lips began to move, but she could not find her voice. Then suddenly she began in a voice too loud for the small space, her words punctuated with tormented sobs. "My husband had no relatives here. He comes from Kivatou. The *Angakkut* blamed my husband, telling the villagers that the stranger in the camp caused the seals and caribou to disappear and made the dogs ill. He said it was an evil spirit brought here with my husband. Padluk wouldn't allow any of the people to help us, even though my husband is a good hunter and always shared the best pieces from his kill with the others. To save me and the children, my husband left, traveling on foot.

"Still, villagers shunned us. The *Angakkut* even took the food we had and gave it to the dogs. He said that no one could help us, and if we died, the sickness would leave and the hunters would once more find food." She sobbed. "My beautiful babies died two days ago; they suffered for weeks. I had no breast milk, and we were left to starve."

"Even after her husband left, Padluk said we could not help her," Ashoona continued for Aula. "But I snuck in a little food and oil from Lasalosie and Annie. That was until the *Angakkut* caught me and left me naked in a snow hut with the door covered over as punishment."

Henry sighed and turned to Aula. "You are not to blame for the dogs' sickness or for the unsuccessful hunt. The dogs died because there were too many foxes; the foxes became sick, and the same sickness was passed on to the dog teams. I've seen this happen before. The people here are starving because they have too few dogs for the hunt and the weather has been poor. Winds and too much snow in the mountains made it impossible for the caribou to migrate to the nearby hunting grounds. Don't give up; you're still a young woman, and you can have more children."

"You can live with Lasalosie and Annie," Ashoona said. "Lasalosie is very sick, and I can't be there through the night to help him. I have to go back to the *Angakkut's* house. It would help me if you could stay with the old couple."

Aula was listening now, their kind words bringing her back from the brink of death where she could join her beloved babies.

"Drink this now," Henry said. He gave her the bowl of caribou broth, and she lifted her face to sip the reviving liquid. Before they left, Ashoona lit the lamp and left a supply of oil for heat and a bowl of stew.

"Others are sick, so I must go now," Henry said gently to Aula. "The Christians in the camp will bury your children tomorrow, and the little ones will rest in peace. When you feel stronger, take your things to Lasalosie's house. Get well soon; Ashoona and I need your help." The thought that Aula may be needed gave the distraught mother the will to live.

Henry and Ashoona carefully picked up the bodies of the two children, Mary, three, and Kilabuk, only a year old. Aula had given her daughter the name of the child's deceased maternal grandfather, as was their custom. Now little Kilabuk's name would be passed down to a newborn so that the child's soul would live on.

They carried the tiny bodies through the camp for all to see. As they passed the snow houses, they met several camp residents walking back to their homes with bowls full of stew, people who'd had food while these babes were left to die. Henry did not have to say a word. He could see the shame etched on their faces.

Henry and Ashoona left the two small bundles beside the trail and covered them with caribou skins and rocks. Next they visited Padluk's home.

"I've come to see how you are and to bring you food and oil." Henry wanted to bring up the matter of the children's deaths, but he felt this was not the time. Meena, the *Angakkut's* sister, was ill. Although she had eaten the broth and a little meat, she was unable to keep the food down and had spent hours vomiting.

"Try this broth." Henry mixed one of his beef bouillon cubes in hot water and gave it to the ill woman. She sipped the broth and smiled weakly.

"It's good," she pronounced.

Henry asked Padluk to come over to the main igloo to get oil and food. While they walked, Henry thought over what he could say to this obviously powerful leader. Government officials had warned him not to get involved with the Inuit beyond seeing to their physical welfare in times of need. Questioning the Inuit's religious practices was definitely beyond the scope of his job. But Henry feared Ashoona would be punished for revealing the deaths of Aula's two innocent babies and the expulsion of Aula's husband.

"I heard that you would not let the people share food with Aula's family and that you blamed the death of the dogs and famine on the man who came from another community."

"It is no concern of yours what I do among my people. You're only here for a little while and should not interfere with our taboos and spirits."

"I also have taboos I must follow. I must see to the well-being of my fellow man. Because of your actions, two children are dead. The father, who was shunned by this community, is also likely lost to us. I'm speaking up for Aula to ensure her safety. You must tell the people that it is not her husband's fault or hers that the camp has suffered. Tell them the truth—that the foxes spread the disease to the dogs and that the heavy snowfall had nothing to do with that unfortunate family. If you continue to deny food to Aula, or if she is harmed in any way, the police will hear of it and take you away."

This seemed to strike home. Padluk's aggressive manner changed abruptly, and he slunk away carrying the oil and food back to his house.

"Ashoona, will you come back to Blacklead with me? I could use someone like you to interpret for me. I worry about you staying here for even another day."

"I still have my dog team and can leave anytime if I'm threatened."

"You mean your dog team survived?"

"Yes. Cruel as he is, Padluk allowed me to feed them intestines and skins to keep the dogs alive but denied even a bone for Aula and her babies."

"I still feel it's too dangerous for you here. That man is crazy with power."

"I gave my word to Padluk. He healed my arm, and I promised to work for him for three months. Besides, I am hiding from a man named Qillaq. My aunt sold me to him, and I escaped from him. I need to wait here to make sure he will not find me. But in five weeks, I will leave for Blacklead, once I have fulfilled my promise to Padluk."

"When you come, I'll give you a job helping me with the sick at my clinic."

"Speaking of the sick, you said we might need Aula's help. Are you going to operate on Lasalosie?"

"If you and Aula assist me, I will try to save him, but I make no promises."

"You're a good man, Henry." She hugged him tightly, tears in her eyes. His kindness and caring overwhelmed her. "I will help. We will use the big igloo, right?"

They returned to the big snow house where many people in the community had gathered and were chatting with Kilabuk. He was related to several families and was catching up on their news. The visiting continued for several hours until one by one, the families returned to their snow houses to sleep with food in their bellies for the first time in many weeks. They were exhausted physically and emotionally, but sleep, meat, and tea with sugar would bring them back to good health.

Kilabuk and Henry planned to sleep in the big igloo and insisted that Aula stay with them because her tattered tent would not provide adequate shelter.

Ashoona retired to the old couple's house to watch over Lasalosie and assist Annie. She gave Lasalosie a double dose of painkiller and made a cup of tea for Annie.

"The doctor has agreed to amputate Lasalosie's infected leg," Ashoona explained to Annie, "but he needs to know that you agree. He will not live if the leg is not amputated; everything below his knee is black with gangrene."

"Of course, I agree. I can smell the poison, and I know he will die without help from the fine doctor. When will he do this amputation?"

"First thing tomorrow," replied Ashoona. "We'll set up a table in the big igloo. Aula, Kilabuk and I will help Henry."

The next day, Ashoona was up early, brewing tea and checking on Lasalosie. Henry and Kilabuk placed the old man on a litter and carried him to the big igloo where Kilabuk had built a makeshift operating table. Aula was busy over the Primus stove boiling Henry's surgical instruments.

Henry began the amputation, instructing his helpers as he went. "I've given Lasalosie ether to put him to sleep. He will feel nothing until he wakes after the operation. Ashoona, watch carefully and interpret for Aula.

"He's asleep, so we'll begin. First we cut the skin below the knee, through the fascia and the subcutaneous tissue, leaving a flap of skin that we'll close below the amputation. I'll amputate the leg below the knee so there is sufficient blood supply to the wound. The big muscles must be tapered and later pulled down over the severed bone."

Ashoona concentrated on the operation. She knew she would not be queasy watching Henry cut into the flesh. The Inuit were accustomed to butchering seals and caribou, and Lasalosie was a friend who had been wounded protecting her. She wasn't going to let him down.

"Is everyone okay? If you feel dizzy, sit down. I can't have you collapsing on the operating table."

Ashoona looked at Aula, who was standing by waiting to be given tasks. Her color looked good. "We're okay," Ashoona assured him.

"The next step is the hardest because you'll hear the saw cut through the bone." Ashoona kept telling herself that the procedure would save the old man. She could see the putrid flesh on his foot and ankle. If not treated, the infection would creep up his leg and poison him.

The handsaw bit into the bone.

"We're through the bone," Henry said. "It's a clean cut. Now I need to pull the muscles and skin over the severed bone and stitch the wound. Ask Aula to bring the needles but to hold them with the forceps. She must not touch anything with her hands."

Ashoona felt relieved as Henry closed the wound with small, neat stitches. *I'm sure Aula and I would be skilled at closing wounds. There is little difference between sewing seams of caribou skins for a jacket and sewing up a leg wound.*

Aula and Ashoona took turns watching over Lasalosie until he regained consciousness. Then his wife Annie stayed by his side, and Aula remained to help. Ashoona felt the tug of duty and returned to the shaman's house to clean and cook. She was afraid of Padluk and kept her distance. She would finish out her obligation, just a few weeks now, and she would leave with Aula.

When Henry and Kilabuk prepared to leave, Ashoona hugged both men. The older women wept and hugged the men who had saved them from starvation, and the men solemnly shook hands. Only the *Angakkut*, his sister Meena, and their two closest allies stood off to the side, frowning and looking disgruntled.

Kilabuk touched Aula on the shoulder and drew her aside. She could see that he was disturbed about something; he looked worried. "I'm sorry, but I have terrible news for you. When I was on patrol with the policeman, we found your husband. It looks like he just lay down near the trail and died."

"I knew I would never see him again. No one can walk that far in winter without a gun, a dog team and food. He left to save our family, but Padluk let my babies die. I want to die, too. I only keep going because I worry about Ashoona. She brought me food, and they tried to kill her, but the old man rescued her."

"Is that how Lasalosie was injured?"

"Padluk and his followers stripped off her clothes, put her in a snow house and blocked off the entrance. Lasalosie smashed the walls and rescued her but not before Padluk slashed his leg with a snow knife."

"I don't understand why you and Ashoona are staying. You are both in danger. If there is anymore treachery from Padluk, you must promise me that you will escape." Kilabuk placed a comforting hand on Aula's shoulder. "Take care, and may your pain be healed."

Ashoona was sorry to see them leave, but felt relief that Henry and Kilabuk would be in Blacklead to meet them when her commitment to the *Angakkut* was finished.

A few weeks. I can survive for that long. Besides, I need to care for Lasalosie to see that he recovers.

For an old man, Lasalosie was strong. Already he was drinking soup and wanting to get up from the sleeping platform.

"When the sun returns, you can help him walk outside," Kilabuk said, as he handed Ashoona a crutch he had made from a caribou bone.

"Ashoona, you should go with Henry," Aula said hugging Ashoona. "I will look after Lasalosie. You have already helped us by saving Lasalosie and being my only friend. You can help out at the clinic, and I will come as soon as our patient is better. Your arm is healed. You are ready to travel and to work,"

"No, Aula. I have to stay. I've made a promise, and I will keep it."

———————

When she decided to finish out her time with Padluk, Ashoona never imagined that things could possibly get worse, but once the rescuers left, the mood of the camp changed dramatically. Once again, the *Angakkut* asserted his authority. Once again, the hunters followed the *Angakkut's* directions out to hunt seals on the ice or into the hills to search for the caribou herd. The hunts were successful, and so the people believed that the shaman was responsible for the return of the caribou and the abundance of seals, and that the death of the two children was the reason for the success of the hunt.

Their stomachs were full, the dogs were well fed and the women had seal blubber to burn in their lamps. Despite the well-being of the camp, a schism occurred between the *Angakkut's* followers and the Christians. Aula was one of the strongest Christians. She had been baptized and married in the church, which was unusual in the 1930s. It was far more common for couples to live together or for girls to accept an arranged marriage. In those cases, the unions were seldom sanctified by the church or registered with the government.

"When I marry," Ashoona told Aula, "I will wear a white dress, and go to church, like my grandparents in Scotland."

The two young women were sitting outside sewing and enjoying the returning sun. It was mid-March, and a promise of spring floated in the air. The temperature was mild, only a few degrees below freezing, with no wind and a warming sun that angled its rays over the camp.

Soon the igloos would melt, and the people of the camp would move into skin tents. When the men returned from the hunt, they would build adjoining tool sheds with wood salvaged from the crates left at the Kekerten Whaling Station. Everyone looked forward to moving out of the smelly, wet snow houses into their summer tents.

Even Lasalosie and Annie came outside for the first time since his operation. He sat on an upturned *qamutik* with his crutch nearby and his wife by his side.

"I saw a picture of my Scottish grandmother," said Ashoona. "She was the most beautiful woman I've ever seen. I dream about wearing a dress just like hers. My mother and father were married in the church, but mother wore a dress of caribou skins that were tanned and bleached until they were white. The dress was as soft as silk and intricately embroidered along the hem and cuffs."

"And who is it that you want to walk down the aisle with you?" Aula asked.

"His name is James. He's going to be a policeman, and he is so handsome. He called me his loved one," Ashoona said, blushing.

"So, where is this wonderful man?"

"James is studying to be a policeman in Regina. I wanted to ask Henry if he'd heard any word about him, but I was afraid."

"Silly girl!" Aula said, laughing. "Why didn't you send a letter to the RCMP post? They could send it on to Regina. Don't you think James needs to know you still love him, and you need to know that he is waiting for you"?

"There are days when I no longer believe James is waiting for me because he was promised to another woman. You know what it's like when parents get together to arrange a marriage for their children. Even though he loves me, his mother might convince him to marry Natsiq. The two mothers arranged the marriage when Natsiq and James were babies. I doubt that I could ever be lucky enough to have James for my husband. Ever since my father left Panniqtuuq, my life has been unlucky."

"Well, you are unlucky to work for the *Angakkut*. Watch out for him, or he will take you to his bed," Aula warned. "And speaking of the devil, there he is calling the camp together. I wonder what nastiness he has in mind today."

Chapter Six

I am God

Aula and Ashoona left their sewing to join the circle around the *Angakkut* who stood with several of his closest followers: Meena, his bossy sister; Jaco, a middle-aged man who was so ugly no woman wanted him; and Charlie, a strong, healthy man in his fifties, who had in the past, guided for the Mounted Police. A few of the weaker camp members also gathered around Padluk to show their admiration and support for the powerful shaman.

"I am God, and Charlie is Jesus," the *Angakkut* shouted. "Do you believe?"

"Eeeee," Charlie crooned. "I believe you are God, and I am Jesus." He turned to the people. "We are your saviors."

"Follow us," the *Angakkut's* voice rose in volume and emotion. "I am the true God. Do you believe?"

The crowd hesitated, glancing at each other in fear. It was dangerous to oppose the *Angakkut*.

"Oooo," the people crooned, showing their support for the *Angakkut*.

"What he is up to?" Aula whispered. "First, he tries to tell everyone that God and Jesus do not exist, and now he tries to convince us that *he* is God. I have a very bad feeling about this."

"Well, I'm not going to agree with that crazy man." Ashoona folded her arms over her chest in indignation.

"Be careful," Aula warned. "He still has much power over the camp."

The *Angakkut* continued to chant, "I am God. Follow me. Charlie is Jesus, sent to save your souls."

"Oooo!" the people chanted.

"Who refuses my word?" Padluk continued, his voice at a fever pitch.

"I don't believe you!" Ashoona cried out.

All eyes turned on her.

"You heard me," Ashoona repeated. "I'll say it again. You are *not* God, and Charlie is *not* Jesus!"

The *Angakkut* rushed at Ashoona, his arm raised in anger. "You *Qallunaaq* brat! And *you*! Bitch who brought us months of starvation! How dare you? Say that you believe that I am God. Say it!"

"Yes," Aula said quietly, "I believe you are God, and so does Ashoona. Don't you, Ashoona?" And then in a whisper to her young friend, "Please Ashoona, just tell him what he wants to hear."

"God is God, and Jesus is Jesus!" Ashoona yelled. "You are *not* God, and Charlie is *not* Jesus!"

Padluk brought his upraised hand down and struck Ashoona across the face with his fist. Ashoona's cheek stung, but Padluk was not a big man, so a blow from him did little damage. Then one of the *Angakkut's* followers handed Padluk a board.

"Tell me I am God," he screamed, slamming the board down on her head and knocking her over. Once she was on the ground, others sprang to life. Several caught hold of her, grabbed

Ashoona by the hair and dragged her to the igloo where Lasalosie and Annie were sitting. Aula stepped in front of the attackers to try to save Ashoona from the blows. Padluk dropped the board and took a harpoon that Charlie gave him. The shaman raised the weapon and thrust it at Aula, piercing her eye. She shrieked in pain and collapsed to the ground, her blood staining the snow. With Aula out of the way, the attack on Ashoona intensified.

"Hit her! Hammer her!" Padluk demanded. In frenzy, the *Angakkut's* followers struck at her, with blow upon blow.

Then Meena grabbed a 30-30 rifle and raised the butt above Ashoona's head, holding it in the air while Meena readied herself to bring it down on Ashoona's head for a deathblow.

Lasalosie moved with astonishing swiftness for a crippled man. One minute he was on the *qamutik*, and the next he was in the mêlée. Lasalosie struck the gun barrel with his crutch, deflecting the blow that would surely have killed Ashoona.

Lasalosie turned to Padluk. "You are *not* God, and Charlie is *not* Jesus! Stop this insanity!"

"What did you say?" Padluk demanded, directing his fury at Lasalosie.

"You are not God, Padluk, and you, Charlie, are Charlie Ouyerak, not Jesus."

Charlie lunged at Lasalosie, trying to knock him to the ground. Lasalosie balanced on his good leg and swung at Charlie with his crutch, connecting with the crazy man's chin. Charlie staggered and fell, giving Lasalosie time to get away from the fight and join his wife.

"Ashoona! Aula! Run! Go to Blacklead!" Ashoona and Aula helped each other up and staggered away from the bloody scene. Lasalosie spoke to his friends and relatives. "I need your help. Won't anyone come to our aid, you who believe in the one true God?"

The crowd grew silent; all eyes turned to Lasalosie. Some whispered to each other; one woman began to speak, but her husband silenced her. In the end, fear muzzled them.

Padluk stalked up to Lasalosie, and raising the board, smashed it into Lasalosie's face. Blood poured from the crippled man's nose. He staggered and fell to the snow, but his wife helped him up. A moan issued from the crowd. This blow to an old man they loved was unacceptable.

Padluk turned to the group, but he could not see who had uttered the offensive sounds. Unsure of total support, Padluk let the old couple retreat to their igloo, both knowing they had only a short reprieve and that a death sentence hung over them. They would have to leave the camp or Padluk would surely kill them.

Fear invaded all corners of the camp. The people felt the danger and were cautious about every word and every action. While they made a pretext of supporting the *Angakkut*, many were repulsed by the attacks, especially by the treatment of their beloved elders. Lasalosie and Annie were parent, aunt, uncle, grandparent or great-grandparent to many people in the camp.

Meanwhile, Ashoona and her wounded friend hid in Aula's makeshift tent beyond the camp. Ashoona's wounds were not life threatening, so she was able to patch Aula's face, pushing the hanging eyeball back into the socket and binding a piece of caribou skin over the ghastly wound. Ashoona tried to comfort her friend. She carefully laid Aula down on the caribou skins and wrapped the injured woman in furs.

"Let me die," Aula begged. "I am in so much pain, and I won't be able to escape with you. Get supplies, hook up your team and flee to Blacklead."

"I must try to save Lasalosie and Annie. Their son is away hunting. They have no one to protect them."

"You can't save them, and if you try, Padluk will surely kill you. You must leave immediately. If you try to take me, both of us will die."

"Can I leave you for a few minutes while I see what I can do to help Lasalosie and Annie?" Ashoona asked.

"Be careful, my friend," Aula cautioned. "You need more than courage to live through this craziness, but live, you must. I gave an eye for you, girl, so now don't make my sacrifice useless."

"I promise I won't let them get me."

Lasalosie and Annie could not sleep; they knew Padluk would come after them. Others lay on their sleeping platforms, disturbed by the events of the day, sharing their true feelings with their partners, sons and daughters. Lasalosie's son, Amo, had returned late that evening from hunting and listened in disbelief as his wife Ruby recounted the violence Padluk had inflicted on the camp.

"Do you believe that Padluk is God and that Charlie is Jesus?" Amo asked his plump wife as they held each other under the caribou skins.

"No. I don't believe such foolish words," Ruby answered. "But I was not going to risk the lives of you and my children just to say what I think. I wanted to defend your parents, but I knew it would be suicide. Lasalosie and Annie are safe. Padluk won't go that far. We must keep quiet and get away from here."

"You believe they are safe, but if Padluk is so incensed with revenge, he may even take the lives of two respected elders. I'll check on my parents tomorrow; I'm sure they must be asleep by now. I need my sleep if we are going to escape in the morning with my parents. We must warn our older children to say nothing of our plans. The shaman can look into someone's eyes and see the truth. We must be careful."

While Amo and his wife commiserated over the evil events of the day, the *Angakkut* still had business to carry out. Padluk picked up a harpoon, walked through the village and tapped on Charlie's igloo.

"Come with me. We must do God's work. We must rid this camp of Satan." Padluk and Charlie crept up to the old couple's igloo. A muffled sound came from within.

"Come out, Satan. Face your punishment!" Padluk yelled.

Padluk looked through the transparent window made of stretched seal intestine. He could see shadowy forms.

"Come out, or I will come in, and you and your wife will be executed." Again the only sounds coming from the hut were the soft voices of Lasalosie and Annie reciting the Lord's Prayer in their native language as taught to them by the missionaries.

Lasalosie and Annie's calm acceptance infuriated Padluk. The shaman and his follower squeezed through the entrance into the snow house.

Lasalosie had his back to them as he knelt on his one good knee in prayer. Annie sat on the sleeping platform chanting the prayer along with her husband.

Padluk thrust the harpoon at Lasalosie, piercing the old man's shoulder. Lasalosie winced but remained kneeling. Annie cried out and moved to try to protect her husband, groping in her own personal darkness to find him.

"It's all right, Annie. Pray with me."

Lasalosie and Annie continued praying.

Padluk's rage overwhelmed him. "Say you believe, and you shall live!" he screamed. The couple continued their prayer, and despite the blood pouring from his shoulder, Lasalosie did not yield.

Padluk passed the harpoon to Charlie, who was a strong hunter. With a powerful thrust Charlie sent the weapon deep into Lasalosie's chest.

The old man fell and gasped, "Pray for me," and then died.

In her blindness, Annie became disoriented. The man that had shared fifty years of her life lay dead beside her.

"I want to go to my savior!" she screamed, tears pouring down her gaunt face from sightless eyes. "You are not God, Padluk, and you are not Jesus, Charlie! So put that harpoon through me so I can leave all this suffering and go to heaven with Lasalosie."

Padluk grabbed the old woman with his thin, strong fingers and strangled her until she lay motionless on the floor. It took only minutes for Padluk and Charlie to snuff out two lives that had contributed to the welfare of the camp for two generations.

Padluk and Charlie left the house of death.

Charlie grinned at Padluk. "We did good work, didn't we? You are God, and I am Jesus. Everyone will worship us."

"Yes, I am God. We can sleep now. Tomorrow we will find the girl and the witch. We will make them pay for their sins. Soon, we will punish the wicked, and the camp will be cleansed."

"Yes," Charlie added. "Tomorrow they will pay, and tomorrow will be another day of good work."

Ashoona arrived in time to see Padluk and Charlie emerge from Lasalosie's igloo.

"Oh, no!" Ashoona gasped, her heart pounding. She ducked behind the snow house, fearing the worst. Once the two madmen were out of sight, Ashoona dashed to the entrance of Lasalosie and Annie's home. At first, she couldn't see anything because the lamp was low. Feeling along the floor with her hands, she came upon something warm and sticky.

"Oh, my God! No!" Ashoona raised her hand in horror. The floor was covered in blood. She was too late; her chest filled with sorrow. Her eyes had finally adjusted to the faint light, and she could see the bodies of Lasalosie and Annie, her two beloved old friends, side by side, as they had lived their entire adult life. She could do nothing for them now. Her own life and that of Aula's were clearly in danger. She kissed the two old people, took the cross from around her neck and placed it over them.

"Bless you, and may you find peace in heaven, away from this place of hell."

She could not hold back her tears as she crept behind the houses and back to the tent to Aula.

"They're both dead, Lasalosie killed with a harpoon and Annie strangled. They did nothing wrong in this life, yet they were executed by someone who calls himself a leader. We are next, Aula. We have to go."

"Go without me," Aula commanded. "I am no good to you. I'm in terrible pain."

"I will not leave without you, Aula, so you must come, or we both face death. Now is the time to go while Padluk and Charlie sleep. I'll help you. Come now. You must!"

"Okay, girl, I'll come, but if I am a burden, you must promise to leave me in a snow cave. I won't be responsible for you falling into Padluk's web of evil."

"Stay here while I get the dogs and some supplies. I will come back to get you when I am loaded and ready to travel."

Quietly and quickly, she made her way to Lasalosie and Annie's snow house.

They will no longer need their pots, cooking oil, that harpoon, their caribou robes. All they need now is my cross to protect them from the hate and stupidity that holds the camp in its clutches.

If Ashoona thought the insanity was at an end, she was terribly wrong. As she gathered up supplies, she heard a soul-piercing voice.

"I have seen a vision. I have seen stars shoot across the sky. I have seen signs. Jesus is coming again."

Ashoona could not place the voice. It wasn't Padluk; it was a woman's voice, shrill and commanding.

"Come out, and be with God! Meet your savior."

Ashoona realized it was Meena, Padluk's crazy sister. "She is the one who tried to kill me," Ashoona whispered. "What is she up to now?"

Meena's voice grew in intensity. "Come out! Jesus commands you to come!"

Ashoona peeked through the opening and watched as families staggered out of the igloos, rubbing the sleep from their eyes.

"Jesus is coming, and we must meet him!" Meena yelled, moving from house to house, demanding that everyone wake up and join her.

Soon most of the people were outside; Padluk and Charlie, having dispensed with the old couple earlier, were exhausted and fast asleep.

Old men, women and children staggered from their snow huts, some grumbling, others too terrified to utter a sound, but finding Meena's insistence impossible to ignore. Meena looked at each face in the crowd to see who was not among them. She knew Ashoona and Aula were missing, but she considered them to be Padluk's affair. Meena would deal with the rest of the camp.

She continued chanting, weaving her head back and forth as she shrieked, "We must go out on the sea ice and meet Jesus. Leave all your belongings; Jesus wants us to come to him naked."

Meena herded the people onto the ice, dancing around them and chanting in her high-pitched, eerie voice. Who could ignore her? Marie, one of the young mothers, lagged behind, holding her two little ones back. Meena, shrieked at her, hit her and slapped the children until the three joined the larger group.

Meena forced her victims farther and farther out onto the ice. Amo and Ruby remained in their snow house with their three children, fearful of what Meena was up to. Now Amo was truly concerned for his parents' safety because if they joined Meena in the bitter cold night, they would perish. Amo slipped out of the snow house, making sure that Meena did not see him.

Amo entered his parent's snow house. "My God! What has he done!" Amo cried in anguish at their senseless death.

Ashoona watched as the group disappeared onto the sea ice. She had no idea what was about to happen, thinking only that this gave her and Aula an excellent opportunity to escape their own death sentence. As Ashoona hooked up her dog team, she still heard Meena's chanting but could no longer see her hapless captives. Ashoona took the dog team to the tent, and Aula staggered up, dressed and ready for the trip.

"What is all that shrieking from the camp?" Aula asked as Ashoona led her injured friend to the *qamutik*.

"It's Meena. She's demented, trying to convince the people that Jesus has sent her a message. At least they won't notice us leaving." Ashoona had little time to think about Meena's real intentions. After all, Ashoona and Aula were condemned; the people Meena had forced out on the ice were believers, so maybe they would not be harmed.

But as Ashoona and Aula sped away into the night, they didn't know that the people of the camp were far from safe.

"Strip off your clothes!" the crazy woman screamed. "We must meet Jesus naked as the day we were born into this sinful world!"

Parents were aghast. Some were able to escape, but four mothers and one man, the weaker members of the camp, could not break away. When they tried to protect their children, Meena, beat them with a whip, screaming until the wretched victims complied with her demands.

"Be naked as you meet your savior!" Meena yelled, tearing the clothing off the young mothers and one elderly man. Once the adults were naked, Meena pulled off the children's parkas, their pants and their boots. She cracked her whip, making them dance barefoot and naked in the bitter wind.

Ashoona and Aula were oblivious to this scene of torture. They could hear Meena screaming and children crying as they sped toward Blacklead, and they wondered but never guessed at the horrible events taking place across the ice.

Suddenly it was quiet. Too quiet. The northern lights streaked across the sky, and the wind died down to a whisper.

With Aula nestled in the sleigh, Ashoona directed her team around the houses and protective rocks taking a secret route, in the hope that Meena, Padluk and Charlie would not see them.

As Ashoona moved the team out onto the sea ice, she was startled. A dog team was coming up quickly behind her.

"Aula, they're after us!" Ashoona screamed, as she whipped at the dogs to speed them across the flat sea ice. *If only we can outrun our enemies!* Ashoona tried to concentrate on driving the team and did not dare look back at their pursuers.

"Ashoona! Wait! I won't hurt you!" someone called from the pursuing team.

Ashoona was certain this was a lie, and she urged the dogs on.

Ashoona kept the team moving, unable to comprehend the tragedy occurring out on the sea ice, but also not wanting to be caught.

"Wait, Ashoona! It's Amo and Ruby. Look what Meena did. She killed them, and Padluk killed my parents. They will kill us too. We are escaping like you!" he yelled.

Ashoona halted the team and looked back to see Amo and his family approaching. Ashoona turned to the scene played out in stark relief under the snapping and crackling of the northern lights. She could not believe her eyes. Across the flat sea ice, they could see Meena holding her arms up to the heavens, dark shapes at her feet.

In moments, Amo's team reached them.

"Oh, dear God!" he cried. "Those poor people!"

"We even saw babies out on the ice naked and dead," Ruby cried tearfully. "They all died from exposure, Ashoona. They were naked! Meena made them dance naked, yelling at them until the little ones dropped to the ice and died. Shocked and tearful, the adults all stared transfixed at the lifeless forms and the eerie sight of Meena, a black silhouette against the crackling lights of the night sky.

"Amo," Ruby continued, "we have to tell the police at Blacklead. Maybe we can save the rest of the camp from this madness."

Chapter Seven

Blacklead Island

It was an easy trip across Cumberland Sound. No wind, a moon overhead and smooth ice. It was as if the earth displayed its beauty in stark contrast to the evil of its humans. The horror of Padluk's camp slowly dissipated for Ashoona, and her thoughts turned to James. She wondered if he had returned to Blacklead, if she might see him soon. Her heart raced at the thought of him.

Once they were well away from Padluk's camp, Amo brought his team to a halt.

"We need a rest, and the children need to eat," Ruby explained as Ashoona stopped her team next to them.

"And I need to change Aula's dressing," she replied, as she helped her friend out of the sled. While Ashoona tended to Aula's injuries, Ruby brought out bannock and dried char. Her children's faces were bright with smiles as she gave them their meal. The trip was like a holiday for them.

"We will be at the mission soon, my little ones," Ruby said. "I was born there, and your parents were wed in the church.

Soon you will meet the wonderful Reverend Worthington who taught me how to write in our language."

"I thought Blacklead was a whaling station," Ashoona remarked.

"Most of the whaling was done on Kekerten Island, just across the sound. The mission at Blacklead opened many, many years ago about the same time that the whalers arrived in the Baffin Island region, and thank goodness. The whalers brought about the downfall of many of our people, taking our girls, corrupting our men with liquor and turning us into slaves, just like the *Qallunaat* always do." Ruby's voice rose in pitch as she recounted these injustices. "The Anglican mission protected us from the abuse."

"There you go again, Ruby," Amo interjected. "Ashoona is going to get the entire history of the wrongs inflicted on our people. You forget she is part *Qallunaaq*."

"I'm sorry, my friend. I did not mean to offend you," Ruby said. "You are not like them. Anyway, I'll stop complaining about the *Qallunaat* now that I've seen such wickedness brought on by the Inuit like Padluk and his crazy followers. At least at Blacklead, a doctor can care for Aula. We can report Padluk's crimes to the police, and all of us can go to church and hear our own language in prayer. All will be well."

"If you have finished your rant, maybe we can move on," Amo said, grinning. "And how is our patient fairing?"

"I'm feeling much less pain," Aula answered, "and I'm quite ready to travel."

The children were tucked into the *qamutik*, and they slept until the first faint light of morning lit the landscape. As the group moved across Cumberland Sound, the weather was mild, with only a light breeze.

On the second morning, Ashoona spotted the rocky outline of Blacklead, or Omanakdjuak, "Big Heart." The mountain rising above the settlement was in the shape of a heart, with two rounded peaks linked by a shoulder. As soon as the dogs picked up the scent of the settlement, they increased their pace, anxious to reach camp so they could eat and rest. In minutes, the two *qamutiit* were bouncing through the rough tidal ice and along a rugged trail between the massive chunks of ice heaved up by the tides.

"Ashoona, take Aula to the clinic. That's where you will find Henry and the nursing station," Ruby advised, always taking control. "Amo and I will report in at the police station. Meet us there later."

Dogs barked, and people came outside to see the new arrivals.

"We've come to see the captain. There's trouble at Padluk's camp," Amo called out as his team reached the first of the cabins on Blacklead Island.

Ashoona dropped Aula off at the clinic and joined Amo and his family at the police station. The captain listened to Amo's story.

"And you said Charlie was involved?" the officer asked in disbelief. The captain of the RCMP post was a middle-aged man, dressed impeccably in his uniform. He was just feeling his way into his new job, having recently been transferred from Regina to take the position James' father had held.

"Yes, Charlie claimed he was Jesus and followed Padluk's every word. It was as if he was possessed," Ruby explained.

"I was told that Charlie was one of the best guides and that I could trust him with my life. Now I have to bring him to justice?"

Ashoona did not add to the discussion. Her thoughts were focused on James, but she was too shy to ask this *Qallunaaq* officer about the young man.

"I'm going back to the clinic," Ashoona said. "I want to find out how Aula is doing and to see Henry. I'll stay there for the night." She was concerned about Aula, but her main reason was to find out if James had returned to the community.

Back at the clinic, Henry greeted Ashoona with a warm embrace, "Your friend will recover, although she will be blind in that eye. It is the loss of her children that will take more healing than I can offer. And you, Ashoona…I wish you had listened to me when I saw you at Padluk's camp. Why did you stay with that vicious man?"

"I know, Henry. Sometimes I wish I could ignore my obligations. But that's how my parents taught me, and that's the way I am. If I say I will do something, no matter how impossible or pointless, I will finish the job."

"Well then, work for me at the clinic. I need that kind of dedication. I also need someone who is fluent in both languages. You could look after Aula and help her move past the loss of her family."

"Will you pay me a wage, or would I just work for my food like so many of our people? My Inuit grandmother worked at the hospital in Panniqtuuq for years, sweeping the floors and cleaning up after the *Qallunaaq* nurses. Her only wage was *Qallunaaq* food, which she found unappetizing, and a bed in a hot room, where she couldn't get a decent night's sleep."

"Wait a minute, Ashoona. That isn't the way I run my clinic. And I didn't know you had such strong opinions. Maybe you can advise me on how Canada should treat the Inuit."

"I don't know about national affairs. I'm just a simple Inuit girl who didn't finish school."

"Well, my simple Inuit girl, are you going to work at the clinic or are you going to continue to be chased across Baffin Island by Qillaq until he finally catches you and rapes you or worse."

"First, I need to know something. And please don't tell anyone that I asked."

"You want to know if James is still here. Am I right?"

Ashoona blushed. "How did you know?"

"You asked about him when I saw you at Padluk's camp. I could see in your eyes that it was not a casual question. I know this young man means a great deal to you. I don't want you to be hurt, but you should forget him. He is not for you."

"What do you know? He is perfect, and he loves me, or at least he loved me more than anyone has ever loved me, except my parents."

"In any case, he's not here. James is still in Regina completing his training. His father is white, an experienced policeman, so, despite his son's poor grades, the boy was accepted at the police academy. I hope you don't mind, but I'm going to give you some advice, Ashoona. James stayed in Blacklead for several months, and he treated the young women badly. Don't wait for him because he will hurt you even more than anyone in Padluk's camp hurt you."

"Why are saying this? What do you know about James? He is a good person, and we are meant for each other. Both of us are part Inuit and part *Qallunaaq*; both of us want to make something of our lives."

"You are a smart girl. You can get an education and be more than an obedient wife to someone who won't appreciate you. But if you are determined to keep the flame burning for James, then stay here and help me with my patients. James will be back on the last supply boat in the fall. Maybe it will work out for the two of you."

The prospect of seeing James again was enough to convince Ashoona to remain in Blacklead and take the job at the clinic. She poured herself into the work, not only cleaning and cooking, but also helping Henry treat the sick. Henry also hired Aula, who did a lot of the cleaning and cooking.

The two women shared a room at the hospital, waking early and working until late. Ashoona was the one who answered the calls in middle of the night, tending to hunters with injuries and mothers with sick babies.

Chapter Eight

Inuktitut Lessons

In May the sun grew brighter, shining down on Blacklead village well into the night. Soon there would be twenty-four hours of sun—a season of lighthearted activity among the Inuit. The villagers waited for the ice to go out so the men could fish for Arctic char and go out on the sea to harpoon seals.

While Ashoona became increasingly involved with her work at the clinic, Aula had a new interest. Since arriving in Blacklead, she spent any spare time she had with Kilabuk, the guide and hunter who had come to help rescue them when Padluk's camp was starving.

Life does go on despite dreadful loss and heartache, Ashoona thought as she watched them walk outside the village one sunny afternoon.

Time passed quickly as long as there was lots of work at the clinic. Ashoona celebrated her thirteenth birthday with the staff at the clinic. There were two nurses' aides, Olive and Evelyn, middle-aged sisters who had sailed from England to work among the Natives in the Canadian Arctic.

"We're going to save the heathen Eskimos," they told their church friends at the farewell tea hosted at Saint Andrews Anglican Church in London.

When Ashoona first arrived, they ordered her around using sign language, assuming she did not have a complete grasp of English. Aula fared worse because the two English women treated her like a servant. The women were pleasant enough but of the opinion of most Brits that Aboriginal people were not intelligent and that without help from the "civilized nations," the Natives of the land would not survive.

Three months after Ashoona and Aula arrived at Black-lead, Aula was a changed woman. She had found a new love with Kilabuk, and the two were married at St. James Church by one of the Inuit laymen. Once Aula moved in with her husband, Ashoona had a room to herself, but spent little time sleeping, since she was always ready to assist Henry with the midnight emergencies. Olive and Evelyn were tired by evening and were grateful for Ashoona's youthful energy.

Ashoona ate her meals with Inuit staff in the kitchen while the two aides and Henry ate in a small, fancy dining room where Aula served their meals.

"Henry, why is there a separate eating area for the Inuit?" Ashoona asked one day as they made the rounds of the clinic. "I thought we were all to be treated equally? I've heard that in Frobisher Bay, Inuit people are managers in a few of the government offices and local stores and that my people are now being educated as nurses and teachers. Yet here we are separated, as if we are heathens and the English-speaking people our rulers."

"Language is the main problem," Henry answered. "Except for you, the Inuit staff members do not understand English, and Olive and Evelyn do not speak Inuktitut. It would be difficult for the two English women in a room where everyone was chattering in another language. I understand a little, but I doubt that I could keep up with a conversation."

"I could teach the three of you the language. It would make it so much easier to be a healer to my people if you and the nurses spoke Inuktitut."

"You are an interesting young woman, Ashoona. What are you going to do with your life? Become a politician and a leader among the Inuit or maybe even among the *Qallunaat*?"

"You know what I want, Henry? I want to marry James and have children. I want to work hard and make enough money for a strong dog team, guns, fancy dishes and a sewing machine. I also want to own my own house instead of a government-issued shack."

"You consider yourself an Inuit, yet you want all the things the white people have and more."

"I don't want to become a *Qallunaaq*, but I want the comforts you have and the life the Inuit have, hunting for food and making my own clothes."

"So you haven't given up on James. I thought you said he was to marry Natsiq."

"I dream about being his wife and love him with all my heart, but I have to wait patiently until he finishes his training. But you're right. Bad luck may continue to haunt me, and he might end up marrying my cousin."

"That might be a sentence, if it's true what I've heard of her bad temper."

⁓

The next day at suppertime, Henry and the two aides were eating a meal of caribou stew served by Aula when Henry delivered the news. "I have decided that Aula and Ashoona will give us lessons in Inuktitut three evenings a week."

The two sisters stared at him in disbelief. Olive, the older of the two, was the first to object. "I don't understand why we should learn Inuktitut. The language will die in a few more years, so what use is it to us? Besides, we're returning to England this fall, and we will have no use for a language that is only spoken by a few thousand Inuit."

"It will allow you to communicate better with our unilingual patients and improve our patient care," Henry tried to explain. "Even a few sentences in their language make a significant difference to someone in distress. And if I were you, I wouldn't tell the Inuit people that their language is threatened. There is a strong sense of culture wrapped up in the language."

Olive frowned, obviously dubious of Henry's rationale.

Evelyn also raised her own objections. "Look at the Indians in the Yukon, and you will see how their languages are being lost," she argued. "Only the old people speak, and soon the language will be gone along with them. I have a friend working in Whitehorse. She tells me that there are a handful of Tagish speakers still living and that all the young Indians speak English."

"I regret what is happening in the Yukon," Henry replied. "Mission schools are wiping out the Native culture and language, but that has not happened among the Inuit. Here, I believe the language will survive, and we should support that. Language class will begin tomorrow." The tone of his voice told the two English women there was little point in arguing. He was in charge of the clinic, and in the end, it was his decision.

Classes began the following week. Aula had beautiful handwriting and used a blackboard to write the Inuktitut words in both the syllabic and Roman alphabets. Aula pronounced the words and Ashoona gave the English translation. After a few lessons, Olive and Evelyn were resigned to the program and became

enthusiastic students, concentrating on the phrases and practic-
ing the pronunciation during the day.

When the two sisters met Aula or Ashoona in the hallway, they greeted them in Inuktitut. "*Ullaakkut,*" they would say,
along with an expression of accomplishment.

The language classes also brought Henry and Ashoona
closer. The two walked together each afternoon, taking the path
up the mountain. It was late June, and the sun never left the sky
but beamed down on the village twenty-four hours a day. All but
a few patches of ice and snow had melted from the rocky hill, and
small ponds formed in the depressions between the rocks. The
wind blew softly for a change, and the summer sun shone brilliantly high above the mountain peaks.

"So, Ashoona, you have a couple of months before you
see the man who will take you for his wife. Am I saying that correctly in Inuktitut?"

Ashoona almost doubled over with laughter.

"What is so funny?"

"You said that I would be his *anaq,* which means 'shit,'
instead of *arnaq,* 'wife,'" Ashoona explained still chuckling.
"The two words are similar. It's an easy mistake to make."

"So, how do you say 'it is a beautiful day'?"

And it was. The hike to the summit was exhilarating,
and from the peak, they could see the rows of little matchstick
houses facing the blue waters of Cumberland Sound.

"Look, there is Taluttarusirk. It means "a hidden place,"
Ashoona said, pointing to the concealed harbor at the north end
of the village. "Try to pronounce that word; it's a tongue twister.
I noticed that the *Qallunaat* have trouble with our place names
and have been busy for two centuries giving our places English
names. Iqaluit is now called Frobisher Bay. Iqaluit means "the
place of many fish." The names we use describe the places. It
makes more sense than calling a bay or mountain by a person's

name. Frobisher means nothing to our people, just another explorer who passed through one year."

Henry tried to pronounce Taluttarusirk several times until Ashoona broke the word into syllables and pronounced it phonetically. Finally Henry was able to master the pronunciation, much to Ashoona's delight.

"Over there is where James will land when the supply boat arrives," Ashoona mused. "I'll be there to greet him. I will make a *Qallunaaq* dress in blue, I think, with a ribbon around my waist. I have a nice small waist, don't you agree?"

"You are beautiful," Henry answered, looking at Ashoona appreciatively. "If you were a few years older, I might be the one seeking your hand in marriage. James is lucky."

"It's almost a year since James promised to be mine. He will be back soon, and in another year we will marry."

"You'll only be fourteen. That is still too young, Ashoona. Girls in my culture wait until they are eighteen or nineteen, and most marry in their early twenties. Why do the Inuit marry so young?"

"Inuit women are considered mature when they are thirteen. By that age, girls are competent seamstresses and cooks, and they are strong enough to care for babies and run behind a *qamutik*."

"That will change in the north. At fourteen, you are still considered a child, and you should be in school. Marriage is hard, especially in the Arctic. Girls from Frobisher Bay are going out to Ottawa to complete high school. You might change your mind and take a different path."

"Maybe. But now we should take the path back to the clinic and return to our jobs."

Ashoona marked off each day on the calendar. Finally, it was August, and she could not take her eyes off the sea. She walked to the trading post each morning because it was located on a site with the clearest view of approaching ships. Near the end of August, she spotted the *Nascopie* steaming up the sound.

"It's coming!" Ashoona yelled. As the ship approached, all the people of the settlement came to the harbor. But the boat could not dock because the tide was out, so instead, the ship anchored a half-mile from the harbor to wait for high tide.

"When are they going to launch the small boats?" Ashoona asked Ishulutuq, an elder, who had watched many ships land over his lifetime.

"Be patient, *panik*. When the tide rises, they will send smaller boats out from the big ship. It will be later tonight. You're waiting for James, the Mountie's son. Am I right?"

"Yes. He will be my husband." She was still so uncertain, but declaring her hopes to this old man was her way of trying to make her dream come true.

Ashoona waited by the shore, watching for the first sign of the incoming tide. But waiting for high tide is akin to staring at a pot set on the fire to boil. The more you stare at the pot, the longer it seems to take. So she chose a rock on the shoreline.

When the seawater covers that rock, I will know the tide is coming in. She stared at the rock. It remained above the waterline. *Maybe I'm looking at the wrong rock because I've been here an hour, and the tide should be coming in.*

As the August sun moved across the sky, she sat on the shore, until she realized the water was almost lapping at her feet.

He'll be coming on shore any minute, she said to herself, heart pounding at the thought of seeing her handsome young man after all the trauma and heartache she had suffered.

Ashoona kept watching for the small boats to be launched. Finally, a boat powered out from the ship heading for the dock. Ashoona raced up the dock searching to see if James was aboard.

"Damn tourists! Why are they coming here? They just want to stare at us and take pictures. James, please come!"

The southerners struggled out of the small craft and onto the dock.

"Miss, do you speak any English?" one of the tourists said slowly and in a loud voice, enunciating each word clearly.

Ashoona nodded.

"Could you tell us how to find the mission?"

In the group was a slim, beautiful woman with pale white skin and long red hair. "And the clinic. Do you know where that is? I've come to work there."

Ashoona realized the young woman was the nurse sent to replace Olive and Evelyn. The two sisters were leaving the next day on this same boat.

Ashoona gave them careful directions, and when they turned the wrong way, she ran after them and pointed out the mission and the clinic.

She wanted to ask if they had met James onboard the boat but was too embarrassed. Ashoona wondered about the *Qallunaaq* woman. Only recently had Ashoona earned respect from the two English women, and now she would have to prove herself again to this new nurse.

By the time Ashoona walked back to the beach, the boat had returned. Once again, she ran down the dock to see who was in the boat, but it was the captain and his officers.

She recognized Captain Armstrong, a short man in his fifties with a barrel-like chest pressing against the brass buttons of his uniform. He had a well-trimmed graying mutton chop beard framing a round, pleasant face.

"Hello there. It's Ashoona, right?" he greeted her warmly with a hug. "I haven't seen you since your father was at the Hudson's Bay Post in Panniqtuuq. Can't believe I actually recognized you. But those beautiful, dark eyes haven't changed much since you were a babe."

"Hello, Captain Armstrong," Ashoona replied, blushing at his compliment.

"Captain, was James on the boat? We were expecting him back today."

"Aye," he said with a wink and smiled. "So the handsome James has caught your eye, has he? All the girls are after that boy. He should be so lucky to land a proper girl like you."

"He's on the boat isn't he, and he'll be coming on shore soon?"

"Yes. He'll be in the first group of Inuit passengers coming on shore. First, the tourists, then the captain and crew, then the locals. It won't be long. In fact, I think I see the boat loading up now."

"Really!" Ashoona stared out to sea where the supply ship was anchored. "I think I see him! Did you speak to him, Captain? Did he tell you I was his sweetheart in Panniqtuuq?" Now Ashoona was throwing caution to the wind.

"Well, not that I recall, girl. I'm sure he thought about you every minute so just wait here, and he'll be on shore in minutes. Now, I must get myself up to the mission because supper is waiting, and at my age, I long for a good meal as much as I once longed for young love. Look after yourself, little Asha." The captain picked up his bag and strode up the gravel bank toward the town, puffing as the incline increased.

Chapter Nine

The Mountie

Ashoona waited for hours sitting on the shore at Talut-tarusirk, the harbor on Blacklead Island. She felt a chill as the August afternoon wind stirred, buffeting her light cotton dress and loosening a strand of black hair from her intricate braids. Finally, the boat carrying her loved one pulled away from the ship. Ashoona walked out on the dock, her eyes fixed on the boat.

"James!" Ashoona called out as the dinghy came closer.

"And who might you be?"

"It's me," Ashoona replied, her voice a nervous whisper.

"Okay, but who are you?"

Ashoona's throat felt so tight she could barely answer. *Surely he remembers me.* "It's Ashoona. You remember me, don't you?"

By this time the boat had docked, and Ashoona was smiling shyly at the handsome young man. He wore the standard RCMP uniform—navy blue trousers with the yellow stripe down the side, brown leather boots and the brown Sam Steele

Stetson. He wore a blue jacket, not the red serge, which was reserved for special occasions.

"Of course, I remember you, Ashoona. I was just teasing you." James jumped out of the boat in one leap, swinging his bag onto the dock. "What a surprise. I thought you were in Panniq-tuuq. Come here, my sweet girl. I've missed you."

He threw his arms around Ashoona and would have kissed her in front of the other Inuit passengers if Ashoona hadn't pushed him away.

"Not here, James. I don't want everyone talking about us. Let's go to the clinic. I want the people I work with to know you are back and that you still care for me."

"Later, okay. I'm invited for dinner at the mission. I'm starving, and they have the best food. How about we meet behind the church after dinner?"

"Of course," Ashoona answered trying to hide her disappointment, "you must be hungry for a proper dinner after so many weeks at sea. Besides, I have work to do at the clinic. I'll see you in a few hours."

As they parted, James leaned toward Ashoona. "How about that kiss? No one's looking now."

Ashoona had dreamt of this moment, and her heart pounded as he pressed his lips against hers and held her tight against him.

"More tonight, right? Now back to your sickies."

Ashoona's faced burned as she ran back to the clinic, coming in just as Henry and Olive had finished their rounds.

"So where is Prince Charming?" Olive asked. "I thought you were bringing him to the clinic. I haven't seen the young man for a year, and I'd like to say hello."

"I saw him, but he went to the mission for dinner. He looks so incredibly handsome in his uniform. I'll ask him to walk with me to the dock so we can both bid you goodbye when you leave tomorrow."

At dinner, Ashoona could not get any food down her throat. Her face burned with a fever. She felt as if she must be breaking out in hives, her skin was so hot.

Is this what love feels like? Feeling sick and tense? She cleared the dishes, but her hands were damp with anxiety. A cup slipped from her hand and shattered on the floor.

"Oh, dear!" cried Olive. "Remember the old saying: 'A broken glass at morning; a broken heart at night.' Well, it's evening, so you'll be all right. But I can't help feeling you are not yourself."

"I'm fine, just a little preoccupied."

"Why don't you run off and see that fellow of yours. It would be a mistake to let you handle another dish anyway. I didn't bring this beautiful china all the way from London just to see it smashed to pieces on our very last day."

Ashoona ran to her room and splashed cold water on her face, combed her long, dark hair and once more braided it into the style traditional for Inuit girls. Her face still looked flushed, but the rosy hue of her cheeks and lips only added to the contrast between her black hair and dark eyes. She examined herself, thinking that she did look beautiful, and now she felt more mature than the shy girl James had kissed so many months ago in Panniqtuuq.

He will want me for his wife. I just know it!

James was still at dinner, so she took her time walking to the church. The mid-day heat had given way to a gentle breeze that cooled her feverish face. Ashoona sat on a rock behind the church; she took deep breaths to calm herself.

The wait seemed unbearably long. *Why isn't James anxious to see me? If it were me, I couldn't possibly have stayed for dessert. I've yearned to see him every minute since I first fell in*

love with him and every second since his boat anchored offshore.
I'm too anxious; I must relax. Letting him know how much I care
may push him away.

Ashoona was exhausted by the tension of the day's
events. An hour passed, and eventually, Ashoona lay down
against a rock and dozed off.

"Ah, sweet Ashoona," James laughed. "You have so little
interest in me that you sleep instead of keeping watch."

"James!" Ashoona jumped up, blushing and stammer-
ing. "I'm so sorry I fell asleep. It's been a long day for me and,
well, I expected you much earlier. It's almost eight o'clock! Why
did you take so long at dinner?"

"So, my little beauty is already checking up on me. I'm so
sorry I kept you waiting. We talked about the future of the Inuit,
and it was difficult to break away. I'm here now. Come, my sweet.
Let me taste those wonderful lips again." He drew Ashoona
close, pressing his body against hers. "And that kiss; it was only
a little taste. I need all of you, my sweet one."

She wanted his kiss, but he was holding her tightly, pressing against her. She could feel him growing hard against her.
Surely he did not expect her to lie with him, to give herself to
him. She felt the first tinge of anxiety.

"Come with me, sweet girl. Let's find a place away from
prying eyes."

"I love you more than I can say, James, but I don't think
we should go somewhere secret. I don't want the villagers to gossip. Let's get together tomorrow and talk about our future."

"What is there to talk about? I love you, and I want you."

"I want you too, James, but only after we are married.
I promised my mother that I would be married in a church."
Ashoona remembered her mother's soft voice, speaking in her
Native language, telling her to remain a Christian, to marry in
a church, to always do what was right. She could smell the

soap her mother used and the rich aroma of the tanned caribou skins her mother worked on.

Had Mama foreseen that life would present me with a test I might not have the strength to manage?

"You understand that I must be innocent when I marry, don't you, James?"

"Yes, darling, and I want you for the rest of my life, Ashoona. Just come with me. We can sneak into the Hudson's Bay warehouse. No one will see us. I need to be alone with you. Come, please."

James pulled Ashoona along the trail. She resisted at first, worrying that what she was doing would end badly.

"I can only stay a few minutes. I'm expected at the clinic." Ashoona's voice was barely a whisper. Her face burned and her stomach was in knots.

They slipped through the heavy doors of the warehouse. The pungent scent of pelts, fish and ropes assaulted Ashoona's senses, and she felt suddenly dizzy from the odors and the intensity of her emotions.

James pulled her down onto a pile of furs. "Ah, so comfortable. I could stay here all night with you."

"But, James, you know I can't stay. I should go back to the clinic. I'm expected to be in by nine each evening."

"Relax. You've waited a year for me. Why are you struggling against me?"

He pressed his mouth against hers and pinned her to the soft mattress of furs. Ashoona sank into the wonder of his kiss. When he moved his hands up under her dress, she stiffened and tried to break away, to ask him to stop. But he covered her mouth with a hard kiss, and she couldn't cry out. When he ran his hand up the inside of her leg, Ashoona struggled against him, feelings of love and affection replaced by panic. He pulled her panties down in one rough move and thrust himself into her. Ashoona pushed against his chest, trying to free herself. Now that he no longer held her mouth with his kiss, she screamed in protest.

"No, James! Don't!"

Despite her cries, James held her down and continued to thrust into her. Then, with a groan, he was finished. Ashoona could feel the wetness flood between her legs.

"Oh, my God. You're beautiful, my sweet. Wasn't that wonderful?"

"No, James. I did not want to be with you like that until we were married. We have to go to the church as soon as possible."

"Whatever you wish, my love. I've been posted to Panniqtuuq, and I'll be back in a couple of months. We'll talk about it then. You should get back to the clinic now. I don't want a search party out looking for you."

"You do love me, don't you, James?"

"I love all women," James said, chuckling. "But, Ashoona, you are the most beautiful, so I love you the most."

"But James. You will marry me, won't you? You must. I've given myself to you, and now we have to marry."

"Let's talk tomorrow, my sweet," James pulled his clothes together and offered his hand to Ashoona to help her up. She was silent as they walked out of the shadows. James bid her goodnight when they reached the mission, and Ashoona continued along the path to the clinic, her thoughts in turmoil.

Ashoona met Henry at the clinic door.

"It didn't go well, did it?" Henry said. "Meeting with James stole your rosy color. You look as if you've seen a ghost. He has upset you."

"How do you know what happened? James is my sweetheart, and he will be true to me. We'll talk tomorrow and settle on a date. It'll work out, I'm sure." But in her heart, she wasn't sure at all.

"I hope James will be honorable. Your happiness is important to me. Take care, little one," Henry said, placing a comforting hand on her shoulder.

Ashoona slept fitfully, waking often, sobbing and then falling back into a troubled sleep.

Oh, James, why would you do that to me? Oh, please marry me, or I don't know what I'll do.

She woke several times during the night hoping morning would come soon. If he would set a date, then all would be well.

Ashoona was the first one up in the morning, doing rounds of the clinic. She did not expect James until nine; she tried to stay calm. She decided to go to the mission and ask him to walk with her. She tried to keep her emotions in check.

Ashoona made her way through the village, trying to mask her anxiety, managing a weak smile when she passed anyone. No one noticed her nervousness as she approached the mission.

Mrs. Worthington, the minister's wife, opened the door and smiled at Ashoona.

Ashoona was so tense, she forgot the manners her mother taught her, and without even greeting the minister's wife, she said, "Is James here?"

"He left for the police station, Ashoona. They are busy this morning preparing for the boat trip to Panniqtuuq. Hurry if you want to see him because they'll be leaving shortly and won't be back for several months."

Ashoona ran to the station, bursting through the door. "James! Are you still here?" Her heart pounded as she waited for an answer.

"Ashoona! You look so upset," James said, walking calmly toward her. "Are you all right? Is something amiss at the clinic?"

"Everyone is fine." Ashoona's face burned. "I just thought you would come to talk to me today, that we would set a date for our wedding."

"Why do we have to marry?" He had a thin smile on his face as if he found her pleading tiresome.

"But last night…?" Ashoona stammered. "You took me last night, and I thought that meant we would be wed. You must agree to marry me, James…please. If you don't, I don't know what will become of me." Her voice was frantic, almost hysterical.

"You're very young and not wise in the ways of the world, darling girl. Of course, I love you, and I want to be with you, but getting married is impossible."

"It's Natsiq, isn't it? You're still being pushed into marriage with her."

"My mother thinks I'll marry Natsiq. My father won't allow me to marry anyone for five years because that is the rule for new police officers. If I marry, I'll be kicked off the force, and I certainly can't marry a girl of thirteen. What would they think of me!"

Ashoona gave a desperate cry and ran away, tears pouring down her cheeks. She sobbed so violently that she could barely see the path. She staggered to the ocean edge, sat on a rock outcropping beside the water and sobbed till her chest hurt.

There is no hope now. My life is over. I want to walk into the ocean and let the waves take me out to sea. I don't want to live without James.

Ashoona remained on the shoreline until the chill winds blew off the ocean, making her shiver. She had cried herself out and sat stone-like, staring out to sea. At last, she struggled to her feet and made her way back to the clinic, hoping to reach the seclusion of her room without anyone seeing her.

She crept down the hallway, opened her bedroom door and was surprised to see a redheaded woman sitting on the cot opposite hers.

"Hello, Ashoona. I'm Joanna. It looks like we'll be sharing this room." It was the nurse Ashoona had met at the dock. Joanna was brazenly beautiful, her long hair in gentle curls that reached her shoulders. She wore tight pants and a brightly colored shirt that hugged her breasts.

Her new roommate had been busy colonizing the entire room. Dresses filled the closet, and jewelry, lotions and perfume covered the top of the shared dresser.

"Oh… Happy to meet you, Joanna," Ashoona whispered hoarsely. "Sorry, I'm not feeling well. I'll be fine tomorrow, but right now, I have to sleep."

"I'm a nurse. Tell me what's wrong; maybe I can help."

"I just need to sleep. Then I'll be all right."

Joanna continued to hover over Ashoona, placing a hand on her forehead to check for fever.

Could she please just go, and leave me alone?

"I must meet the doctor now and see what needs to be done. You must be one of the chambermaids?"

Ashoona didn't bother to tell her that she had been helping Henry with cuts, broken bones and even operations and that he appreciated her work.

Now, to make matters worse, I may not even be Henry's helper anymore. I'll become the chambermaid!

Joanna closed the door with a bang, not considering that every loud noise reverberated through Ashoona's fragile state like a bomb blast. Ashoona could hear the sound of Joanna's steps as she sashayed down the hallway to Henry's office.

Ashoona dozed off in a feverish sleep and awoke to a light knock on her door.

"It's Henry. May I come in?"

"I'm very sick Henry. Maybe we could talk tomorrow."

"Please, I just need to talk to you for a minute. I can imagine what happened Ashoona, and I'm worried about you." He opened the door slowly and gazed at the young woman's tortured face.

"It's so hard when you love someone who is unworthy of you, someone who takes advantage. I know you won't believe me, but someday, maybe in a few months or a year, you will no longer feel this pain."

"I don't want to live, Henry. I love him so much, and he doesn't intend to marry me. It's more than I can bear."

"The cure is in work, Ashoona. We need to give you more tasks and help you get an education. You're still so young. Much too young to be married but just the right age to study and find a vocation. You could be a teacher, a nurse, a doctor. Your whole life is ahead of you."

"You don't need me anymore. You have a real nurse now, not just a couple of old women with first aid training or an uneducated local. Joanna has proper training. Why bother with me? She thinks I'm the chambermaid. Is that what I'll be, now that Joanna is here?"

"Definitely not. Your position at the clinic won't change. In fact, it will be more important because you'll have a new pupil in your language class. Now, why not get up and have a little supper and then do the rounds with me. Joanna needs to settle in, and I no longer have Evelyn and Olive to help me. You are important to this clinic. Don't forget that."

Ashoona pulled herself out of bed. Henry held her arm to steady her until she could regain her balance. She felt weak from all the emotion of the day.

Henry rested his hand on Ashoona's shoulder, hoping to comfort her as they made the rounds. Her heart still ached, but when they visited a young mother nursing her newborn and then an old man suffering from pneumonia, Ashoona's attention became focused on her patients and for a short time, she didn't think about James and his betrayal.

When Ashoona returned to her room that night, she was relieved that Joanna was sound asleep in her bed across the room. Ashoona turned her face to the wall, her tears dampening the pillow.

How will I survive the winter, knowing James is lost to me forever?

Chapter Ten

The Chambermaid

Before her heartbreaking encounter with James, Ashoona had been hopeful. She had useful work at the clinic and her dreams had come to life. However, as winter approached, Blacklead Island became a depressing place for the young girl. Her heart ached over James' deception, and she found little enjoyment in her work at the clinic. Joanna objected if Ashoona carried out even the simplest medical task.

The trouble all started with the first snowfall. The village children picked a steep slope behind the houses and were competing to see who could start the downhill slide at the highest point on the mountainside. They had found a metal sheet that made an excellent, but fast and dangerous, sled. Eight-year-old Jacobie climbed higher for each run and descended faster and faster. He finally climbed up to the very top of the hill, but this time he slid out of control and at a ferocious speed, careening into the thick wooden wall of the old Hudson's Bay warehouse. He didn't cry. He just lay quietly on the snowy surface, clutching his broken arm.

His friends carefully placed him on the metal sheet and pulled him to the door of the clinic. Ashoona took control of the situation, shooing away the children and getting Aula to help her lift the little boy onto the examining room table.

Rather than wait for Henry, Ashoona began to cut away his clothes, all the time soothing the small boy with gentle endearments.

"Now, my little one, you will be all right. I won't hurt you. I'm just cutting your jacket carefully so that your mother can sew it back up when we're through. Now that I can see your arm, I can tell you had a very wild ride down that hill."

Jacobie, who didn't cry at all during Ashoona's examination, gave her a proud smile.

"First, I want you to swallow this pill with a little gulp of water." She held his head up and gave him a sedative. "Just breathe deeply, and the medicine will help lessen the pain so that I can examine your arm and see what we need to do to make you all better."

Ashoona gently touched his swollen arm and felt a break. She thought it might be a fracture to the radius, one of the small bones between the wrist and the elbow. She was trying to decide if they needed to x-ray his arm when Joanna burst into the room.

"You don't have the training to examine patients. And I see you've given him drugs. You mustn't overstep, or the clinic will get into trouble." Joanna's voice was harsh, her face stern and angry.

Ashoona was not accustomed to conflict with the *Qallunaat*. Her throat went dry and her chest tight with anxiety. Henry had assured her that she was competent and could treat this type of injury.

"Henry said…" she muttered.

"You're not going to tell me that he has permitted this? Is that what you're saying? Well, I don't believe it, and if it's true, I will report him to the authorities."

"No, please don't make trouble for him. He's a wonderful doctor. He's helped me so much, and I don't want to cause him problems. Look, if you don't tell anyone, I will stop treating these injuries. I just want to stay here at the clinic. I hope to study to be a nurse."

Joanna looked at Ashoona in disbelief as if to say that for an Inuit girl to even think about a career in nursing was ridiculous. *Was there even one Inuit with a high school education?* Joanna wondered. *Likely not,* she concluded.

"It's wonderful that you are ambitious," Joanna said coolly, not wanting to totally deflate Ashoona's hopes for her future, "but do you have any idea how difficult it will be to leave the north to study? Working as an aide might be a more realistic goal, don't you think?"

"Henry wants me to go south to get an education. He has promised to help me."

"Oh, does he?" Joanna replied. "Well, since he and I have become good friends, he has changed his mind about a lot of things. But in any case, please do not give drugs to the patients. That is a job for a nurse or a doctor. Promise me you will stop, and I won't report Henry."

With that pronouncement, Joanna took Ashoona's arm and steered the Inuit girl out of the room. When Joanna touched the little boy's arm, he let out a holler that echoed throughout the clinic corridors. Just then the door opened, and a young Inuit woman came in followed by Ashoona who was trying to prevent her from entering.

"That's my son. What are you doing to him?" The mother spoke Inuktitut and was obviously upset to hear her son's cries.

Jacobie's mischievous nature often landed him with bruises and scrapes, but she had never even heard a whimper from him.

"Get her out of here," Joanna said harshly.

"This is Elisipi, Jacobie's mother. She needs to know what is happening. I'll interpret for her." Ashoona began to explain to the young mother that Jacobie had a broken arm and that they would set the bone and he would be completely healed in a couple of months.

The mother seemed to calm down after listening to Ashoona. She leaned over to kiss her son and then asked him why he was crying. Jacobie whispered anxiously to his mother, clutching her *amauti* with his uninjured hand.

"What's going on? What are they saying?" Joanna asked.

"Jacobie says that he wants me to fix his arm, and his mother asks that I look after her little boy."

"That's not going to happen, Ashoona. I want you to leave now and take the mother with you."

Ashoona knew it would be easier for Jacobie if his mother could stay and if Ashoona could set the break, but it was pointless to try to argue with Joanna. The new nurse was not cruel, just a person who expects to be in charge, especially with the Inuit.

Reluctantly, Ashoona coaxed Elisipi to leave, offering her a cup of tea and store-bought cookies. As they left, they could hear Jacobie crying.

"Is she some kind of witch?" Elisipi asked.

"She's a real nurse, and I'm not," Ashoona said. "But, someday, I will get an education, and then I won't be pushed aside. I will be as good a nurse as Joanna."

And I'll certainly be a better mother, Ashoona thought. She did not mention that Joanna had embarked on the extraordinary journey to the North, leaving her own two children with her ex-husband's parents.

Ashoona didn't understand why it was wrong for her to examine the child. *Haven't I been in the operating room and assisted in far more severe injuries? How far will Joanna go to exclude me from any meaningful work at the clinic.*

Jacobie recovered despite his treatment by the new nurse. Soon he was out running around town, showing off his cast to his friends. Even Joanna's attitude softened and she would smile at Jacobie and ask him how he was doing. Jacobie did not understand her and would look blankly at the English-speaking nurse.

Life for Ashoona became increasingly tense. Joanna constantly craved attention from Henry. During dinner, she would pose her body so that he would be aware of her low-cut blouse and full breasts. It seemed that she had to catch the eye of every good-looking or rich man she encountered. Because she was beautiful, Joanna was used to having men desire her.

Over the next month, Ashoona observed Joanna's extreme mood swings. One minute Joanna gushed and spoke sweetly to Ashoona and the next, she called her names—stupid Eskimo, ignorant half-breed—insults that hurt Ashoona and made her suspicious of Joanna's real feelings toward the Inuit people.

"Henry, you did such a wonderful operation on Ida today," Joanna purred, touching Henry lightly on his shoulder to command his full attention. "Henry and I worked for six hours in almost primitive conditions, compared to the Toronto hospital I worked at. It's a great experience to work in the wilderness with such a clever doctor." Joanna leaned toward Henry, this time skating her fingertips over his hand.

"Thank you for your compliments," Henry said, "but what I do here is not at all extraordinary. What is quite exceptional is the life the Inuit live out on the land. Can you imagine surviving in temperatures down to 60 degrees below, with only a snow house for shelter? The hunter and his wife must keep the family clothed, sheltered and fed."

"It is extraordinary. I'd like to see the remote hunting camps. Maybe I could go with you." Joanna smiled sweetly at Henry.

"Yes, of course you should come. I've been taking Ashoona because she speaks the language. Now that I can speak a few words in Inuktitut, I think I could manage without my young helper." Henry smiled at Ashoona and then noticed a dark look cross her face.

"You could come as well, Ashoona," Henry added, not wanting to hurt her feelings. She had been at his side on trips over many months.

"We'll be fine on our own, Henry," Joanna chirped. "Ashoona needs to stay at the clinic in case there are any emergencies. "Isn't that right, Ashoona?"

"I think I'll be off to bed," Ashoona answered despondently. *Now that it suits Joanna, I'm apparently capable enough to remain alone at the clinic to handle childbirth and accidents when before she wouldn't even let me set a small fracture.*

Ashoona lay on her cot wishing that she didn't have to share the small room with Joanna.

She's trying to snare Henry and wants me out of the way. I should warn Henry about her in the same way he warned me about James.

But no warning could stop the progress of the web Joanna was weaving. Every moment she was in Henry's presence, she made certain he saw her figure at its most attractive. When they worked on a patient together, she moved close to him so he could smell her perfume. She touched him often, and soon he was thinking about her every minute.

In late October, Henry asked Joanna to go for a walk, hoping to escape the halls and wards of the overheated clinic.

"But Henry," Joanna pleaded, "it's freezing out there, and my parka isn't warm enough. Let's take our break inside where it's cozy."

So instead of a refreshing walk, they shared tea in the dining room. Henry held Joanna's hand.

"Joanna, I noticed on your job application that you're divorced. Do you mind telling me about your marriage?

"John was a brute, and I couldn't stand to be with him. Our two children are with his mother and much happier now that their parents aren't bickering day and night. Once I make enough money working in the north, I will get my children back. John may fight for custody, but the mother always wins. And if I remarry, I will have a more stable situation and be capable of supporting them."

"You have children?" Henry paused, feeling a moment of concern, wondering how a mother could leave her children. "And how old are they?" he continued, an uneasy feeling rising in his chest.

Joanna didn't want to talk about her previous life so she tried to distract him, "Let's go to your room. I want to be with you, and we can't go to my room because Ashoona is there and she's quite jealous of me?"

"Ashoona doesn't have a jealous bone in her body. She is just attached to me because I helped her escape from a bad situation."

"Enough about Ashoona," Joanna replied. She rose and took Henry's hand, leading him to his room. Joanna undressed gracefully, revealing her breasts then, slowly removing her tiny silk panties. Henry watched mesmerized and excited.

When she was completely naked, she posed for Henry. "What do you think?"

"You're perfect. More beautiful than any woman I've ever seen." Any doubts Henry had earlier were erased when he saw her body. He led her to the bed and took her in his arms.

When Joanna did not return to her cot that night, Ashoona knew that she and Henry had become lovers.

Anyone but Joanna! She'll betray him as surely as James betrayed me.

Ashoona stayed clear of Henry and Joanna. She was aware of their growing attraction for each other but unwilling to watch the relationship progress.

"Ashoona, I know you're unhappy about my relationship with Joanna, but I've fallen in love with her. I had a sad experience in my first relationship. I never expected to love again or to find such happiness, especially here in the Arctic."

"Just be careful, Henry. Remember your warnings to me about James. I care for you as a good friend, and I don't want her to hurt you. I truly believe that is what she'll do. For her, everything has to be about Joanna, and she'll always want to be admired. She told me shortly after she arrived that she had to have a new man every six months because she became bored with the same partner. Even when she was married, she had love affairs. I thought it strange that she would tell me, but you need to know who she is. She's not ashamed of her exploits; she even brags about them. Once you are firmly in her clutches, she will start looking for other conquests."

"So, Joanna was right. You *are* jealous. I don't want to hear another negative word about her." Henry gritted his teeth. It was the first time he had ever spoken to Ashoona in anything but a kindly manner. Now he was furious with her, and she was deeply wounded.

"I'm not jealous," Ashoona said, tears welling up in her eyes. "It hurts me so much to have you think poorly of me."

Henry immediately regretted his harsh words.

"Look, there is no shame in caring about a man and disliking the other woman. You'll get over me just like you recovered from losing James. But please understand, Ashoona, that I won't tolerate mean-minded and false stories about Joanna. She's everything I have ever dreamed of, so please say no more."

"Henry you are so wrong. I'm not jealous; I am concerned for you. All I want in my relationship with you is to be your friend, keep up my studies and someday, make you proud of me."

"Then let's agree that my personal life is off limits."

From that day on, the mood in the clinic was tense. Henry spent his days and nights with Joanna, and when he worked with Ashoona he was polite but detached. Ashoona distanced herself from Henry and Joanna, and as the winter approached she became increasingly dissatisfied with her life on the island.

But her life and that of the villagers was to change drastically when a supply ship sank offshore. The shipwreck brought strangers to the village and an opportunity for Ashoona to escape what had become an unbearable situation.

Chapter Eleven

The German Explorer

"The hunters spotted the supply ship out in the sound," Henry remarked on a windy fall morning. "We expect the Reverend back from Scotland along with about a ton of gear and food." Henry held onto Joanna's arm to support her as the strong winds buffeted them during one of their daily walks. "There. I see the ship. Look at about two o'clock. Think of the hand on the clock; straight ahead is twelve and two o'clock, a little to your right."

"I see it. My order of face cream and perfume should be on board," Joanna murmured to Henry. "Then you will find me even more irresistible."

"You don't need perfume to smell sweet to me," Henry chuckled, encircling her small waist proprietarily. "I just hope my supply of coffee makes it to shore. Look at the waves and that ice pack moving toward the ship. It'll be difficult bringing the ship in through that storm."

Henry and Joanna were nearing Taluttarusirk, the harbor surrounded by rock cliffs and hidden from view. As they reached the shoreline, Kilabuk and two other Inuit hunters landed a motorboat on the dock.

Kilabuk jumped onto the dock, tied up and yelled excitedly at Henry. "The British ship is trapped in the ice pack! The captain, crew and passengers managed to get into the lifeboats. We're going to take all the boats out to where the ship is foundering and try to save the supplies."

"I'll go with Kilabuk. Find Ashoona, Joanna," Henry called back as he ran to join the boats, "and make sure you're both ready at the clinic in case anyone is injured."

"I'll keep the home fires burning while you face danger," she laughed. "Take care of yourself out there."

Henry jumped into the boat with Kilabuk, who pointed the craft out to sea. Soon a flotilla of motorboats headed out through the ice-strewn sea. Several miles east, they could see the ship being buffeted by the winds and the heaving ice pack.

The Inuit on the six motorboats were experienced at finding a path through rough waters laden with large chunks of ice. But the wind was gusting and whipping up even higher waves that threatened to swamp the boats of even the most skilled Inuit boatmen.

"We won't be able make it to the ship until the wind dies down!" Kilabuk yelled over the storm. The other boatmen signaled that they should turn back. But before they had time to bank the boats and head for shore, the supply ship capsized.

"She's going under!" Henry yelled into the gusting winds. "God help anyone left on board."

"Look!" Kilabuk yelled, pointing to a light on a rocky peninsula. "I see the survivors on the point." Kilabuk and the other boatmen turned toward the shore.

A gravel beach allowed the boatman to land, and as they brought their boats on shore, they spotted the shipwreck survivors waving at them from the top of a cliff. It was a sorry-looking group, including the captain, three sailors, a foreign-looking man and someone they all recognized, the Anglican minister.

The Inuit men shook hands with Reverend Worthington, delighted to have him back home safely. The minister was a sturdily built man in his mid-thirties with a ready smile for everyone and a willingness to make the best of any situation.

"Thank you for coming. We all made it off safely," said the Reverend with obvious relief. "This is Ludwig Reiner," indicating a stern-faced man in his late twenties. He was dressed in a dark woolen suit with shoulder pads that did little to broaden his narrow frame. "He is a scientist planning a research expedition," the Reverend added. Ludwig shook hands with everyone, nodding coolly.

"Yes, I'm here to learn about the vildlife and vays of the Eskimo people," he explained in a heavy German accent. "Ve vill go to Kangianga to hunt the caribou, live in the snow houses, then to Lake Nettilling and vest to Foxe Basin. But sadly, my project is now in jeopardy," Ludwig added. "I've lost most of my supplies—my film, record books and most of the food for the trip."

"It will be a difficult winter for everyone," the Reverend said. "Most of the supplies for the clinic, the mission and the trading posts at Blacklead and Kekerten Whaling Station sank to the bottom of the sea. What remains is what you see here. We each saved what was most important to us, but we had only these four lifeboats, plus Ludwig's rowboat. It was tough to see the tobacco, and especially the coffee, go down, but at least we have our lives. I thank God for that."

Kilabuk brought out his kit containing a pot, cups, tea and sugar. He lit a fire using the dwarf willows and heather that grew in crevices along the cliff top and boiled up hot drinks for the survivors and rescuers.

"Let's rest here until the wind dies down," he suggested. They used the piles of supplies and one of the lifeboats as shelter from the wind, and the rescuers and weary sailors settled in around the fire.

"It has been a dreadful sailing," Captain Osgood Littleheart explained. "When I took command of this ship, I couldn't have imagined the difficulties we would encounter. We have faced strong winds since passing the south point of Greenland. At our stop in Frobisher Bay, we were delayed again, waiting for the supplies to be unloaded. Then I had to sail into these waters with winter approaching. Now I've lost my ship and all the supplies for Blacklead and Kekerten."

Littleheart was young for a captain and had obtained his commission with the intervention of his rich and powerful father. Captain Littleheart was in his mid-twenties, a tall, blond-haired athletic man with handsome features. His good looks were further enhanced by his neatly pressed and well-tailored officer's uniform.

The captain continued his description of the sea journey. He seemed to want the locals to understand that the shipwreck was unavoidable and not at all related to his lack of experience sailing in arctic waters.

"We made it into Cumberland Sound, when the shifting ice pack blew into our path and we couldn't take the ship forward or back. When the ice jammed up against the ship, she listed far to the port side and started taking on water, which was a few feet deep in the hold of the ship when I ordered everyone into the lifeboats."

"The vater destroyed my books and seeped into my supply of biscuits," Ludwig complained. "Until I have a chance to unpack my supplies, I vill not know how much vas lost." The German looked despondent.

As Captain Littleheart and Ludwig recounted the problems they experienced on the journey from England, the Reverend translated for the Inuit.

"Looks like we'll have to hold up at Blacklead for the winter," the captain said. "I doubt that we'll see another ship make it into the sound until the ice goes out next spring."

A chorus of grumbles erupted from the sailors who knew from experience the deprivation they would face wintering in a community without adequate supplies.

"Look, men," the captain continued, "it will be difficult for all of us. My family will be worried about me. I'm an only son, and my father, Lord Littleheart, is unwell. Not knowing whether I am dead or alive could send him to an early death."

"We have family, too," one of the sailors grumbled, "who will also be worried. Maybe your poor seamanship caused this misfortune."

"Keith knows what he's talkin' about," Donald, the younger of the two sailors added. "You should have listened to McInnis. He knows these here waters; he would have landed us safely."

"It was an act of God that brought the winds and ice," Reverend Worthington said as he stepped forward. He had spent his life bringing peace to conflict. "Let's not blame the captain for the shipwreck. Be of good faith. We'll make sure everyone has a bunk or a piece of floor to bed down on, and I'm sure our German compatriot will share his supplies with the community."

"Vat you say?" Ludwig was livid. "I can't give even a box of bouillon cubes from these supplies. I've lost half my food for my expedition. I vill need all things."

"You can't be serious about continuing on your expedition without tents and cooking gas, not to mention so little food!" the Reverend argued, as surprised as everyone. "Surely you will send word with the next ship to order a re-supply."

"No. Dat cannot be. The next ship comes only after eight months, and then I vill vait a year for re-supply. I must continue vit my expedition. It is my God-given duty. I'm an instrument of science bound to my project."

"That's bullshit!" Second Officer McInnis barked. "You're in the Arctic; people look after one another here. No one hoards supplies, and they don't put their small, selfish interests ahead of the community."

McInnis was a burly man from Scotland who had sailed the Arctic for twenty years. He had spent the trip advising the neophyte captain but found that the arrogant Englishman had little respect for the seasoned sailor. Here was another European arriving in the Arctic afflicted with a belief in his superiority and entitlement.

"Vat do you know about the scientific world?" Ludwig yelled. "Vat are you? A Brit with no education who's made his way up to second officer. Am I to listen to you?"

McInnis scowled at the German, trying hard to contain his anger. The Scot was thinking about the days ahead when they would all be housed in close quarters waiting months for the next ship.

Keep your temper in check, he told himself.

"Let's remain calm and be thankful that no lives were lost," the Reverend said calmly, trying to keep tempers from flaring. "We can discuss this when we are back in the village, dried out and have some hot food in our stomachs."

"It's true that there won't be enough food for the Europeans unless we all take to a diet of seal and caribou," Henry said, "and then only if the hunters are successful. If the caribou herd moves far away or if the dogs can't sniff out the seals' breathing holes, we will all be in serious trouble this winter. Ludwig, you may want to give some thought to postponing your journey. I heard about a trip that would take you by dog team to Lake Nettilling. Is that still the plan?"

"Have I come all the vay from the best university in the vorld to listen to a gaggle of men vitout a high school education?" the German asked none too politely. "You're the factor at the store, right?"

"No, I'm the doctor, and I run the clinic, along with one nurse, my young Inuit helper, a housekeeper and a janitor. It may seem unimportant to you, but my work at the clinic and healthy food for the patients are critical to the community."

"Not my food. Never!" With this Ludwig left the warmth of the fire and stalked up the steep hill. From the top, he looked back with anguish as the ship's hull slowly sank into the icy waters of Cumberland Sound, along with his precious supplies and equipment.

The gales blew until midnight then died down somewhat. The crew, passengers and their rescuers slept for a few hours until Kilabuk woke them.

"Winds are calm now. We should load the boats and set out for the village."

The Europeans shivered as they crossed the bay, heading into Blacklead. The village was asleep, with only the lights from the mission and clinic casting a dim glow out onto the icy waters.

"Follow me," Reverend Worthington said cheerily. He jumped nimbly out of the lifeboat, looking more like an athlete than a man of the cloth. He had earned the respect of the community because of his interest in hunting and his willingness to sleep in an igloo and accompany the hunters out onto the ice to hunt seal. "I'll take you, Ludwig and McInnis. Henry, can you find a bed for the captain and the two sailors?"

McInnis worried that it would be difficult to share quarters with the arrogant German, but because he had known the

Reverend for many years, he had enough respect for the minister's judgment to accept the arrangements.

"Let's see if the staff will brew a little tea to warm us," Henry said, leading the smartly attired captain and the two roughly clothed sailors to the clinic.

Ashoona met them at the door. She looked tired but smiled at the newcomers and asked if they were well.

"They just need a cuppa and a biscuit. Where's Joanna? Maybe she could find a place for the men to sleep."

"She turned in because we didn't think you would be back tonight. After I make the tea, I'll see where we can put our guests."

Keith, the older of the two sailors drank his tea sullenly, so exhausted from the ordeal he lacked the energy to make small talk. Donald, who was still a teen, could not help but notice Ashoona's beauty, but was too shy to speak to her. The captain was energized now that he was safely on shore and warmly housed. He gazed admiringly at the pretty teenager.

"How long have you worked at the clinic? Are you the chambermaid who will tuck us in at night?"

Ashoona's face burned at the suggestion that the only job an Inuit could do was to pick up a chamber pot and make beds.

"I was the doctor's assistant until recently when a registered nurse arrived," she replied softly. "I'll show you to your room now?"

"There's a nurse, too!" the captain said as he sipped the last of his tea. "And is she young and pretty as well? Maybe she'll look after me." His smile, not warm but contrived to show off his straight, white teeth, reminded Ashoona of James.

I'm sure she will, Ashoona wanted to say. Instead, she smiled at Keith and Donald. "Come. You must be tired. I'm sorry we only have one room available. The three of you will have to share. It has two sets of bunk beds."

Donald took the upper bunk, not even waiting to see if Captain Littleheart wished to take the less convenient spot.

———————

The first month passed with occasional conflicts over food and growing antipathy between the captain and his sailors. While Keith found the days unbearably long and yearned to be back at sea, young Donald spent his time out hunting or helping Kilabuk build *qamutiit* and kayaks. Both sailors found the evenings long unless Ashoona and Aula could be coaxed to play cribbage with them. However, it was dinnertime that grated on Donald and Keith. During every evening meal, Captain Littleheart entertained Joanna with lively stories of the British rich and privileged class. Keith and Donald ate their meals silently and left as soon as their plates were empty.

"It's bad enough eating that disgusting seal stew," Donald complained to anyone who would listen, "but to have it served up with an all too generous helping of Osgood's ego turns my stomach. I don't mind spending time with the Inuit, but the thought of months cooped up with that arrogant bastard is already wearing on my patience. I've only sailed for three years but sure as hell, this is my last trip to sea."

"It's always the same. They promote men who know shit about sailing, and we have to suffer," Keith replied. "But the sea is my life, and I need a wage to look after the wife and six youngins. I just wish to hell that man would button his mouth for two minutes so I can eat in peace."

As winter approached and the ice froze solidly, the hunters were able to go out and shoot enough seal to feed the entire community, but the supply of biscuits, coffee and jam had to be severely rationed at both the mission and the clinic.

Ludwig lived at the mission with McInnis, sharing what little food was available there, and Henry gave Ashoona the task of portioning out the dwindling supplies at the clinic. He never considered asking Joanna to take on that task, partly because she was not as meticulous as the young Inuit and partly because Joanna chose to spend her time with the captain.

It's just a phase, Henry told himself. *She loves me. I'm certain of it.* However, as the nights grew longer and winter set in, he was less and less certain of Joanna's continued affection.

Fortunately, the cruelest days of winter had not arrived, and the hunters continued to be successful throughout November and December.

With the ice now a safe, solid surface, Angus McKenzie from the whaling settlement on Kekerten Island crossed Cumberland Sound with a dog team. He was the factor at the Hudson's Bay Store on the island where a group of Inuit hunted whales, seals and walrus.

When the whale hunt was on, the Inuit worked for an American whaling company rendering whale blubber into oil in huge vats and cutting out the baleen, the long strips of teeth-like structures that hang from the whale's mouth, a product that was indispensable to the manufacture of corsets.

The Inuit also traded sealskins at the Hudson's Bay Post in return for guns, ammunition, biscuits and goods. The Inuit who traded with McKenzie often felt they did not receive true value for their pelts, but when the hunt failed, the Inuit depended on the factor's supplies to keep them from starvation. With the loss of the supplies for the store, there would soon be no tobacco, flour, sugar, coffee, biscuits and jam, items that made life marginally bearable throughout the bitter winter months.

Angus was grim-faced as he pulled his dog team up the hill toward the mission.

"*Ullaakkut*...good morning," one of the elders greeted the visitor in Inuktitut. Angus could not even muster the minimum courtesy of a reply. Instead his thoughts were on the arguments he would make to obtain a share of the remaining supplies rescued from the sunken ship.

Angus strode purposefully to the mission, where he hoped the Reverend would persuade the German scientist to be reasonable and give up his foolhardy expedition. He was in a foul mood when he knocked on the Reverend's door.

"I got all the news about the supply ship from one of my hunters. You must make the German share his supplies fairly," he demanded in a grating voice the moment the Reverend opened the door.

"Angus. Please be calm. Take off your jacket and boots, and let me get you a cup of tea before we begin this discussion."

"This is no time for tea parties and niceties! If that German does not relinquish control of those supplies, all of us will suffer. I'm not going to spend a winter without coffee and tobacco because of some puffed-up scientist."

"He intends to continue his expedition. I tried to talk to him, but he's adamant."

Angus was beside himself with rage. "That is a crock of...!" he yelled. He stopped himself when he remembered where he was and to whom he was speaking. But it was difficult to contain his fury. His face flushed red with anger.

Angus was a big man with a stomach that hung out over his belt, the kind of man who often settled arguments with his fists. As the representative of the Hudson's Bay Company in a remote arctic settlement, he was accustomed to unrestrained power.

Reverend Worthington did not submit to Angus' bluster. Instead, he replied in a quiet, steady voice, trying to appeal to the factor's better nature.

"This will be a hard winter for all of us, and of course, we must talk to Ludwig about sharing his supplies. Try to remain calm until we've had a chance to discuss the situation with everyone involved. I'll arrange a meeting with Ludwig, Doctor Russell and the captain.

"There should be no need to negotiate," Angus grumbled. "In the Arctic, food is shared not hoarded. I can't see the need for a meeting, but for now, I'll go along with you."

Before the meeting, Henry approached Kilabuk regarding the issue of sharing the food.

"I don't need to get involved; you *Qallunaat* work it out," Kilabuk said. "But I appreciate that you asked me. I would like to be asked about many things but not food that comes from the south. If there is no flour and sugar, we will hunt and fish to survive; if the hunt fails, we will manage. *Ayunqnaq*...it can't be helped."

Later that day, the Reverend greeted everyone at the meeting affably and offered coffee. His strategy to diffuse conflict was to begin with a joke, often off-colored.

"I heard a story when I was in London, a true story." The minister chuckled as he began. "Following the death of a young British soldier killed in the Great War, the army sent his belongings to his only surviving relatives, two elderly aunts. When the minister came to offer his condolences, the aunts showed him the photographs and letters and then pointed to an object prominently displayed on top of the organ. 'We don't know what it is,' one of the aunts said, 'but the instructions on the package said that we should open the package, take out the small rubbery sleeve and place it carefully on the organ. It is so interesting that we show it to all our friends who come to visit.'"

The joke brought guffaws from the captain and Henry. Angus and the dour German remained stone-faced. Neither had even listened to the story because they were preoccupied with constructing arguments they would use to acquire ownership of the supplies.

Ludwig had prepared a list of the supplies he felt were essential to the expedition, a list that exceeded those rescued from the ship. He crumpled his papers spasmodically, unable to remain calm even though he knew he should appear composed if he was to succeed in retaining the required supplies.

"If everyone is ready, let us begin the meeting." Ludwig stood up and led off in his thick German accent, each phrase sounding harsh and clipped, "I vant you to know how hard and long I have vorked to prepare for this expedition. I have a degree from the University of Dresden. Many important Germans have contributed to this project. If I have to give up any of my supplies, my expedition vill fail. I risked my life to get boxes and boxes into the boats, with little help from the crew. I saved enough of the supplies, such as soup, cocoa, coffee, biscuits and ammunition, to allow my expedition to continue. I refuse outright to give up a single biscuit." He sat down abruptly and crossed his arms over his chest.

"I don't think it's wise to take such an uncompromising position so early in our discussions," the Reverend said in a calm, sonorous voice. "We need to hear from everyone, and each person must listen to the others. Shall we start with you, Captain Littleheart, and then Angus."

"I can't expect to get myself and my crew on a ship until next July—eight more months! We already depend on the hunters for food, and frankly, seal meat for breakfast, lunch and dinner is not to my taste. If the hunt fails even for a month, we all face starvation."

"What the captain says is true," Angus added in his thick Scottish brogue. "It's only civilized and fair that the German's supplies be turned over to the community."

"Vat do you know of civilization?" Ludwig barked. "You and the Americans on Kekerten slaughter vales by the hundreds, giving the poor Eskimos only liquor for their work."

"The vats of whale oil we send to Europe keep your damn drafty castles heated," Angus bellowed, "and the baleen is used to make corsets for your fat German fraus."

"My country has scientists who develop goods to make the vale products a thing of the past, and colonialists like you will be back in Britain standing in a bread line."

"We don't need a war to break out in the Arctic," Worthington cautioned. "Leave the conflicts in Europe, and let's work out a solution right here and now. Angus, what is your situation at Kekerten?"

"It's totally ridiculous that this man comes to the Arctic and thinks he can hoard the only food available. No one in the north would believe me if I told them about the stupidity of his expedition."

Ludwig stood up, so angry at these words that the Reverend feared a fistfight would break out.

"Please refrain from name calling. Angus, we need you to tell us what your needs are at your post in Kekerten—how many hunters, how much food you have and how many Europeans are at the trading station. Are the American whalers still at Kekerten?"

"Everyone knows that the entire year's supplies for Kekerten went down with the ship. We've been eating seal meat for months already. The Americans left, but ten Eskimos are still on the island along with two Europeans, one assistant trader and me. If the German doesn't give up his supplies voluntarily, we'll take them by force."

"You von't touch my supplies!" cried Ludwig, enraged by Angus' remarks. "Who are you to oppose me and my project? Vat are you? A carpenter who thinks he is important because he rules a little island in the middle of the Arctic? Did you even complete grade school?"

"Enough! Enough!" Worthington interrupted. "No one will use force, and we don't need to insult one another. Come gentlemen, we can work out a compromise. And Ludwig, you must realize that if you keep all your food to yourself, you may condemn some of your fellow educated Europeans to starvation along with the Inuit."

"I don't vant anyone to die from lack of food. I see the hunters out each day bringing back seals, and soon they vill go after the caribou. No one vill starve. There is more than enough meat in the village, and I assume the same is true at Kekerten. You just vant to have food like biscuits and jam to make your dreary life more pleasant."

"That's total bullshit!" Angus yelled. "You know nothing of life in the Arctic. Do you realize that last year the hunt failed for more than a month, and I fed the Eskimos from my supplies? For an educated man, you're as dumb as a sack of hammers. I've had enough of this. The only way this will be resolved is by force."

With that, Angus left, slamming the door behind him.

"Henry," Reverend looked over at the clinic's doctor. "My apologies for not asking you to speak. And…let me tell you how much I appreciate your calm in the face of so much conflict. Please tell us your needs for the clinic."

"We don't mind surviving on seal meat, although I believe Joanna objects to the taste. The patients are all Inuit, so a diet of seal and caribou suits them. My concern is the possible failure of the hunt. I know from the experience of my first year in the Arctic that the hunters sometimes fail to kill a seal for weeks. We hold no reserve of frozen meat, so when there is no kill, there is no food. That could happen this winter, so we would need at least a portion of your supplies, Ludwig."

Reverend Worthington nodded in agreement as Henry spoke and then added, "Ludwig, you must realize the position we're in. No one wishes to take your goods by force, but I tell you clearly that if you don't give up some of your supplies willingly, that is exactly what will happen. We know you're a good man and that you don't want to place your fellow men at risk of starvation over the many months until a supply boat comes. What say you, man? Can you not give up this expedition and return another time? No one will blame you for the ship sinking."

"It is impossible! I have vorked hard for so many years to organize this expedition. I vill not be able to raise the funds for another trip." Ludwig paused. "But I vill give up a portion of the ammunition, soup, biscuits, flour and sugar. You must promise to leave me sufficient food and equipment to allow my expedition to continue."

"I appreciate your willingness to compromise. Without some give on both sides, we may have had an unbearable incident. When I was in London, I heard talk of war with Germany, and for all we know, Britain may have already declared war. I don't want our little enclave in the Arctic to add to the conflicts. We can't have German authorities accusing England of thievery. Without your willingness to compromise, violence would have erupted. It is the very thing I have spent my life avoiding. So let's meet tomorrow to decide the division of the food. Captain, you have said little. What do you think of a compromise?"

"My dear Reverend, you are so accomplished at bringing diverse interests to a common understanding, I think you should negotiate the end to all wars." The captain smiled and shook hands with Henry, the Reverend and the still-sullen Ludwig.

"Let's go to the clinic together," the captain said amiably, "and see if the charming Joanna is still about. We can ask her to brew us a cup of tea. On second thought, Ashoona brews a much better cup of tea, and the beautiful Joanna knows how to keep a man company. We seldom find such delightful female company in the far Arctic. Right, Henry?"

"Um...Oh...?" Henry replied awkwardly. "Why yes, the young women will be happy to do that. Better still, I'll bring out my treasured supply of rum. Perhaps if you have a dram with us, Ludwig, you will forget the loss of your supplies." Henry, who seldom imbibed, needed a drink to heal the ache in his heart, the growing sense of doubt about Joanna's feelings for him.

Ludwig was neither a drinker nor much of a social creature. When they arrived at the clinic, he declined the offer of a drink and remained silent while Joanna and Captain Littleheart engaged in a lively conversion about the captain's travels. The captain pressed Ludwig to accept a small drink to seal the agreement over the supplies.

"Let's toast to the good Reverend's negotiating skills."

Ludwig barely lifted his glass off the table in a half-hearted toast.

"Ashoona, please come with me on rounds before dinner," Henry said, trying to hide his concern over his lover's attentions to the jaunty captain. "Joanna, Ashoona needs help serving dinner because it's Aula's day off."

"I'll be along soon," Joanna said, not looking at Henry.

After Henry left for his rounds, Joanna continued her conversation with Littleheart, keenly aware of how her voluptuous beauty affected the man who had been at sea for months.

"Tell me more about life in London. Did everyone suffer from the Depression like we did in Canada?"

"My parents are well off, so the Depression did not affect us. As prices fell and with it the increased cost of every item from sugar to houses, it became possible for my family to buy properties in America. Depression has hit that country hard. Work is difficult to find for many people, and houses are reduced to half price. It's sad to see, but our family fortune has become more valuable as a result. You should come with me to London and see how we live. You would love it there, Joanna."

"I've always wanted to see the world. I have two children, but I'm sure they could stay a little longer with my mother-in-law. They're happy with her, and I'm happy without my miserable ex-husband. Perhaps I can get a job as a nurse in London."

"I can help you find a position in one of the hospitals, if you wish. However, you don't have to work. Providing war hasn't broken out between Germany and Britain, we could travel on the continent, go skiing and visit the French Riviera for the sun. All I need is companionship and time to train with my rowing team. In 1936, we were lucky enough to compete in the Berlin Olympics. It was amazing; the German people are so prosperous under Hitler. We need someone like him to lift Britain out of the Depression."

Joanna basked in the attention from the rich, handsome captain and seemed oblivious to the pain she was causing Henry.

The discussions between Joanna and the captain upset Ashoona because she knew how hurt Henry was by her actions. It was as if his life ended when Joanna abandoned him. Her capriciousness tormented him, and his suffering seemed even worse than the pain Ashoona had felt at James' betrayal. At least now Ashoona was firmly convinced that James was not the man she wanted to share her life with.

Ashoona was busy serving the patients their meals when Henry joined her to check on a boy injured during a hunt.

"*Ullaakkut*...good morning. My Inuktitut is inadequate, so please interpret for me, Ashoona. Ask him if he's in pain."

Paloosie replied to Ashoona, and she interpreted for Henry. "He says he will be out hunting caribou when his family leaves in the spring." She explained to Henry that Paloosie was Kilabuk and Aula's adopted son.

Henry was unaware that his guide and the woman from the shaman's camp had opened up their home to this boy who had lost his family. It pleased him that the young mother who suffered the tragic loss of her babies had found a new life, a husband to love and a boy who needed a mother. He felt good about his job. If only Joanna would remain faithful, his life would be perfect.

Jealousy consumed Henry as he thought about Joanna, who declined to make the clinic rounds with him, choosing instead to spend time with the captain. All the warm feelings he'd had momentarily for his job instantly vanished.

Henry and Ashoona moved on through the ward, with Ashoona pushing the food cart and chatting with the patients as if they were part of her family. There were five patients in their care, including one elder in his eighties.

"*Ullaakkut*, Pilipusi." Ashoona smiled at the old man and greeted him in Inuktitut. "Today, I have hot seal broth for you, and I want you to try just a little." She held his head and spooned the soup into his mouth.

"That tastes good," he said. He swung his feet around to sit on the edge of the bed. "I can feed myself if I sit up."

"How on earth did get him to sit up?" Henry asked, amazed that this dying man could find the strength.

"I have my ways, Henry. Someday I'll be a good nurse with all the right papers, like Joanna. By the way, where is she?"

The question seemed to embarrass Henry. He hesitated a second before replying, "Having tea with Ludwig, Captain Littleheart and the sailors." He tried to conceal his jealousy.

"You mean the dashing Captain Littleheart? He has his eye on her, Henry. Watch out for him."

"And you had better keep to your job, Ashoona," Henry answered sharply, before walking off.

His remarks hurt Ashoona, and she immediately regretted her words.

Why don't I just shut up rather than hurt the one person who has given me a chance in this world.

Her face burned, and tears pooled in her eyes at the thought of having Henry think poorly of her. *Now I will just have Aula as a friend, and even she is too busy with her new husband and son to spend much time with me.*

Ashoona watched Joanna flirt with the handsome Captain Littleheart and felt vindicated but also terribly sad for the pain Joanna was inflicting. Henry began to follow Joanna around the village, and he questioned Ashoona. "Does Joanna sleep with that man?"

"I don't know, Henry. She sleeps in our room at night, but what she does during the evenings is her business."

"I apologize for being angry with you when you warned me about her. Now we are even. I cautioned you regarding James, when everyone knew he had his eye on a new girl every month. But Joanna appeared so loyal; I thought we would marry and be together forever, that she would send for her children and be a happy mother." Henry's voice cracked as he spoke of the dream that had been sunk as surely as the ship now at the bottom of the ocean.

"We're both sad cases," Ashoona said. "I'm not that happy at the clinic because Joanna has taken away the work I enjoyed the most, helping my people get better. I love learning new things."

"You need to complete your schooling, Ashoona. Without good school grades, you can't get into college."

"I can write in Inuktitut using the syllabics that the good Reverend Peck taught my mother, and I can write fluently in English as my father and the mission school teachers taught me. But math and science are still a mystery to me."

"You should ask Ludwig to help you. He is a doctor of science and has studied all his life."

"I lost my respect for him when I learned that he would not willingly share his supplies with the community. How can I learn from someone who is so selfish?"

"Ludwig is coming around. Reverend Worthington found a way to get him to compromise. I don't think Ludwig will give up on his expedition; however, he will give a good part of his provisions. Hopefully the hunters will be able to keep Blacklead and Kekerten supplied until the ice goes out and ships bring supplies next summer."

Ashoona took Henry's advice and spoke to Ludwig about lessons.

"I vill make you a bargain. I teach you mathematics and basic science, and you vill tell me about your people's customs and traditions," the German suggested.

"That would suit me," Ashoona replied. She wondered what kind of man would leave his country to travel among strangers and devote his life to studying animals.

However, as the lessons progressed, Ashoona became intrigued by the theory of evolution and the study of the various animal kingdoms. She watched for the tracks of the arctic fox and the rabbits and wrote reports on her observations.

"You're an excellent student, Ashoona. I always thought the Eskimos are so much smarter than the Europeans who come to your land. I've noticed that the older women cut up the seal and have names for each part of the body. You must tell me the meaning of the Inuktitut words they use."

The lessons continued over the next few months as the daylight disappeared. Life at the clinic and the mission was not pleasant for the sailors marooned on the desolate island, now without pay as their wages stopped the day the boat sank. Even more difficult was the monotonous choice of food—seal stew, seal soup or fried seal.

Time passed much more agreeably for Captain Little-heart since he spent most of his time with the vivacious Joanna. On the other hand, Henry was tortured by Joanna's sudden and unexpected change of heart.

A week before Christmas, Henry asked Ashoona to place a package on Joanna's bed.

"It's a bottle of hand lotion that I was able to purchase from Angus' supplies at Kekerten. I know she'll like it. I've also asked her to forgive me for not caring enough. If only she would speak to me again, I could stand losing her. But she won't even say hello in the morning. She treats me with disdain as if I was the one who betrayed her."

"Women do not like to be pursued when they have clearly broken off a relationship. Maybe it would be better if you didn't follow her or send her gifts or letters. I know you've been writing her notes. She doesn't even open them. She throws them into the coal fire."

"No! I don't believe you." Henry's voice cracked. "I can't bear this. I can't watch them together. I'll have to leave if they stay here openly flirting in front of me."

"I don't think that will be an issue because Joanna is leaving with the captain. They plan to live together in London. He's some big-time athlete, a rower, I think. I guess the idea of marrying an Olympian and an aristocrat has captivated Joanna."

Henry felt as if Ashoona had taken a knife to his heart. He clasped his head in his hands and sobbed, "Can't she see the pain she causes me?"

"Oh Henry, I'm so sorry I told you. I thought you knew?"

"It's too much for me. I wish I was dead. I can't imagine life without Joanna. Is it really true that she is going away with Osgood? Is she really lost to me?"

"Yes, my dear friend. I'm so very sorry for the pain you feel. I have to tell you that even though I'm still angry over James' betrayal, now that several months have passed, I don't feel as tortured. Besides, I realize that he was lying to me. He just wanted to take advantage of me. I know it's hard, but the pain will pass, and you'll find another."

"There will never be another woman like Joanna. Never!" Again his voice cracked, and Ashoona feared he would begin to cry. She had never before witnessed a man in such misery.

Time did pass, although not that pleasantly for the marooned sailors, Ludwig or the Inuit. As Christmas approached, the community began to prepare for the Christian celebration. Many of the hundred or so Inuit in the Cumberland Sound area had been baptized in the Anglican Church and looked forward to the Christmas services and the parties that followed.

Twenty Inuit and the Europeans gathered in the church for the Christmas Eve service, the men shaking hands and the women hugging each other.

"*Quviasugisi Quviasuvvimi*...Merry Christmas," they said, greeting each other, before retiring to their snow huts or simple matchstick houses. They walked to their homes along the snowy wind-swept pathways, with the stars dancing above in the black sky and the northern lights streaking across the heavens. A feeling of peace and love settled over the Inuit people of the little village.

Unfortunately, the celebrations brought a renewed sense of loss to Henry, who had looked forward to celebrating his first Christmas with the woman of his heart. Ashoona joined her friends in the festivities, exchanging gifts and special treats the Reverend and the clinic staff had saved for this important day.

On Christmas Day, the winds were calm, and the faint light that filtered over the land at noon illuminated the trails as the entire community, Christians and non-Christians alike, made their way to the church, first for service and then for a celebration of gift giving.

Ashoona kept Henry company, hoping to lift him out of his despondency. But the doctor found little joy in the celebrations. He participated solemnly, pleading with God to send him peace. He had given up praying that Joanna would care for him again.

Ashoona asked only for a future of happiness; she knew that James would never come back to her, and she realized that her life would go on, even though the pain of his betrayal would always be with her.

The factor from Kekerten also joined them in the Christmas celebrations. Once again he traveled the long distance across Cumberland Sound to enjoy the company of other Europeans. But he had more on his mind.

He took Reverend Worthington aside and once more pressed his case for access to the supplies that Ludwig had salvaged from the sunken vessel.

"He's just a selfish German," Angus blurted out. "We beat them in the war, and now they come to our Canadian North and try to take over. Germany is once again arming itself, expanding across Europe. I've heard that Britain declared war on Germany months ago. Why do I have to let my people go without because of this enemy to the British Commonwealth?"

"No more arguments about the food, Angus! We've made an arrangement with Ludwig, and I don't want to press it further. He is giving up a great deal."

"He should give it *all* up. He's a fool to set off on a lengthy expedition without sufficient supplies. It can only end in tragedy."

"I worry more about Ludwig on this journey than I worry about the Inuit who have agreed to accompany him. I've told Amo and Kilabuk that they must return if they feel their lives are in danger."

"I hear that Ashoona may join the expedition," Angus continued. "Do you think it's wise to let a beautiful young girl go with the German? She'll come back with a bastard."

"No, I think you're wrong. Ludwig is a good Christian. He has assisted me with the services in the church. He wouldn't betray us in that way."

"Well, maybe it's best that Ashoona leaves the village. I've heard from the factor in Igloolik that Qillaq has abandoned his family to search for her. Eventually, he'll figure out that she is here in Blacklead. That man won't stop until he finds Ashoona and either kills her or rapes her or both. She took his dog team and his gun. That's a violation of Inuit law that must paid for in blood."

"It's also a crime against the church and humanity that a little girl, not even in her teens, is bargained off to a man older than her father. If he comes here, I will do everything in my power to protect her."

"There's not much you can do if he gets here while she is in the village unless you hire hunters to watch her day and night. Come to think of it, she'll be better off on the expedition. Amo and Kilabuk would never let her be kidnapped again. Yes, let the young woman go, but warn her about being compromised by the German."

"Enough, Angus. It's Christmas, and although we have few supplies, it is a time to love one another and celebrate the birth of Christ. It's one of the happiest days of the year in this remote Christian enclave at the edge of the Arctic."

Reverend Worthington brought out a bag of gifts for the community, presents supplied by the good people of the Church of England; it was the one bag the good Reverend rescued from the shipwreck. He called out names, and the members of the community came forward to accept gifts. It wasn't much, needles for the women and sharp knives for the men.

For the children there were European dolls and for the boys trucks or trains. The presents for the adults were useful, but Ashoona noticed the Inuit children played briefly with the fancy dressed dolls or the trains before returning to the small dolls and *qamutiit* made by their parents.

Christmas passed, and by late January, the faint light at noon began to grow brighter. In early February, Ashoona whooped with joy as the sun finally showed over the mountain for the first time in months, lighting the community. The villagers walked along the pathways at noon enjoying the warm rays of the returning sun. Spring was coming! The long winter was ending.

With the return of the sun, Ludwig increased his efforts to prepare for his expedition. It was a stressful time because he was aware that there were insufficient supplies for the long journey he had planned.

The evening of the return of the sun, Ludwig gathered Ashoona for her math studies. "I hope ve leave in March. I vould ask that you come on the expedition," Ludwig said in his awkwardly phrased English.

"What do you want me to do on the expedition?" Ashoona asked.

"You are a quick learner. You know science better than my first-year university students. You vill help me catalog the specimens I collect and speak to the Inuit for me."

"Dr. Reiner, I must say something to you. Often foreigners take advantage of young Inuit women. I want to make it clear that I will only sleep with the man that I will marry."

"That is an insult to me, Ashoona. I vould never proposition you. I am truly a scientist, and I vill be focused entirely on my task. I hope you vill agree to come and help make the expedition a success."

"I believe that you are unlike most of the white men who came north and left Inuit women with children. I believe you care only about your project. I would be pleased to join the expedition."

"For my part, I'm delighted that you no longer despise me. I know you blamed me for not sharing my supplies. I hope you understand how important this expedition is to me, how hard I have vorked all my life to succeed at the university and then to find sponsors for this journey to your land. It has not been easy for me, and I understand, life has not been easy for you. A man is searching for you, correct? Another reason for you to come along is the news Angus brought. Qillaq is searching for you, and the earlier ve leave, the better."

"Yes, Reverend Worthington warned me about Qillaq. But you must tell Amo and Kilabuk that they may have to stand up to Qillaq if he is able to track me down. "

"I hope he does not show up. I can have no distractions on this trip. I must concentrate on my objectives. However, I know Kilabuk thinks of you as his daughter. He vill protect you. So it is settled; we vill leave as soon as the hunters are ready and the veather permits."

The preparations for the trip filled all of Ludwig's time. Ashoona and the Inuit accompanying him spent long hours preparing. The plan was to take three *qamutiit* along on the trip. The party would leave while the ice was still firm and reach Lake Nettilling at breakup.

Ludwig, a fanatically organized person, spent hours going over lists of supplies and making travel plans. He often missed meals because he was meticulously packing supplies and equipment. He grew thinner, and he seemed tense and preoccupied.

Chapter Twelve

The Journey Begins

The warmer days of March were ideal for traveling in the Arctic. The sea ice wouldn't break up until late June or early July, but the spring sun shining across the white landscape would give the travelers longer sunlit days.

The Inuit men were busy tying the supplies to three *qamutiit* that were to be pulled by teams of twelve dogs. *Qamutiit* were built of whalebone with runners made from wood salvaged from shipwrecks, abandoned packing crates, driftwood or leftover building supplies. The sledges were heavy and sturdy enough to carry the rowboat, which was required since part of the journey would be on water.

Kilabuk, along with Aula, their baby and Paloosie, would drive the dog team that carried Ludwig and the rowboat. Ludwig would be the only adult riding on a sledge; he was unaccustomed to strenuous exercise and would not be able to keep pace with the dog teams. Amo and Ruby would drive the second team loaded with supplies and their three children, and Ashoona would drive the third team of dogs.

The entire community gathered at the ocean's edge to say their goodbyes and hug their loved ones. The expedition would travel along the western edge of Cumberland Sound and then to Kangianga and to Lake Nettilling. They would cross the lake and continue up the western shore of Baffin Island by boat and dog team. The party would be away for at least a year. Friends brought small gifts for the expedition members—dried caribou and char, a knitted hat, an extra pair of sealskin boots. Every item was made with skill and love.

Ludwig paced back and forth trying not to show his anxiety over the delay. He was paying for each day of the journey with tobacco, ammunition, biscuits and the Sunday treat of cocoa. He could not afford to waste time on farewells.

Henry joined the group and took Ashoona's hand.

"Take care, my young charge. Come home safely," he whispered. He put his arms around Ashoona and held her tight, almost as if he was sinking into the sea and needed her to rescue him. Ashoona had never thought of Henry as anything but a friend, but his warm embrace would remain with her throughout the many hardships she endured during the months of the expedition.

Reverend Worthington realized that Ludwig was highly agitated at the delays. "Come," he said gently. "Let us pray."

The chatter died, and the people bowed their heads.

"Please, oh God, protect this small band of hunters and their families and look after the scientist who has come to our shores to further his knowledge of our remote lands. Look after our young sister, Ashoona, who needs your guidance and protection. Amen."

After more farewells and embraces, Ashoona realized that Ludwig was almost beside himself with impatience. She took the harness and yelled at her team to move out. Her dogs were anxious to be on the trail and took off at such a fast pace that Ashoona had to jump onto the runners lest she be left behind. Amo and Kilabuk followed with their more heavily loaded *qamutiit*.

The weather was favorable, and the expedition with its fresh dogs made good time. When Kilabuk brought the party to a halt for the midday meal, Ashoona peered out across Cumberland Sound trying to make out the chain of islands that included Padluk's camp. However, the Kekerten Chain was too far in the distance, and Ashoona could only see gray-blue shapes of the mountain peaks that framed the eastern edge of the sea.

"I still get the shivers," she said to Aula, "when I think about how Padluk starved you, and how Meena forced the women and children out on the ice and made them dance till they perished. I can't believe that Padluk and his sister are Inuit. How could Inuit people be so evil?"

"My mother told me a story," Aula replied. "Padluk and his sister were young children, and their family lived at Blacklead Island when it was a whaling camp. Most of the whalers had no respect for the Inuit. They brought alcohol into the community and abused the women.

"Padluk's parents became the village drunks," Aula continued, "leaving the children, seven in all, to fend for themselves. The five younger children died of disease or starvation, and Padluk and Meena were blamed because they lived. The parents beat the two children and left them, only eight and nine, to the vagaries of the whalers. The abuse those two suffered would turn most of us into deranged people. I have no love for Padluk and Meena, but when I heard their story, I could see what brought them to such evil deeds."

"Qillaq is like that, too, a vicious inhuman spirit inside him. I must ask you all to be on the alert for that man. If he finds me and captures me again, he will kill me."

"Little sister, fear not," Kilabuk promised. "We will be your guardians."

"Enough talk and rest," Ludwig ordered. "Ve must make more miles vile the veather is good."

The expedition headed north, through the scattered islands that hugged the shoreline of Cumberland Sound. The first three days passed in bright sunshine, calm in the morning with increasing winds in the afternoon. With insufficient snow to build igloos, the group set up camp using the sledges and the boat as windbreaks for their tents and cooking area.

Ludwig was occupied every evening writing in his journal and photographing the surrounding landscape. On the fourth day, they spotted seals sunning themselves on the ice, but the hunters had no cover as they approached their prey, so the seals slipped back down their holes in the ice before Kilabuk and Amo could get within range.

"You must kill at least one seal," Ludwig advised. "There is not enough food for the dogs and for us without at least one seal a day."

"Then we'll stay at the breathing holes until we are successful," Kilabuk replied. The hunters were extraordinarily patient. Amo and Kilabuk took up positions behind a hummock of windswept snow and waited for hours. Ashoona also positioned herself near a breathing hole, but after four hours in the bitterly cold wind, she returned to the camp.

"I must have too much *Qallunaaq* in me," Ashoona explained, as she dropped down tiredly beside Aula and Ruby and accepted a cup of tea and a biscuit.

"Ashoona, please tell them that they must preserve the biscuits," said Ludwig, emerging from his tent, journal and pen in hand.

"Tell them yourself," Ashoona answered with a smile. "Remember I taught you how to say that in Inuktitut."

"The language is so difficult I cannot repeat the words even though I've written them in German. When I read vat I have written, the Inuit do not understand; they laugh at my pronunciation. The problem with your language is that the sounds cannot be found in either English or German."

"You can learn. Our dear friend, Duval, who came from your country, speaks the language fluently as does Reverend Worthington. Before him, Reverend Peck not only spoke Inuktitut but also wrote in our language. He was the Anglican minister who set up the mission on Blacklead and translated the bible into our language using syllabics."

"Dat is precisely vat I mean. You don't even use the Roman alphabet!" Ludwig pouted in exasperation. "You and Kilabuk vill interpret for me. I do not need to speak the language."

"Aula is learning English, which I have to tell you is not easy either," Ashoona admonished him lightheartedly. "Aula, can you translate what Ludwig said to me?"

Aula interpreted for Ruby and then looked to Ashoona to see if she had it correct.

"No one needs to translate for me," Ruby said defensively. "I already understand more English than our German academic understands Inuktitut."

"Vat she say?" Ludwig asked, feeling like a little boy among these self-assured Inuit women.

"Ruby just says that it is a nice day to sit and have tea," Ashoona answered.

"I think I'll get some salt water to boil up the seal bones to make a good seal soup," Aula announced. "That will be enough for our supper as long as we can have biscuits as well."

The sound of a gunshot pierced through the winds now howling through their campsite. Kilabuk had killed a seal. He quickly harpooned the animal and brought it up on the ice.

A moment later, a second shot rang out; Amo had snagged his prey.

"A good supper for us all," Ashoona said to her companions, clapping her hands together. "No soup. No biscuits. Hot seal stew for us and food for the dogs."

"They killed the seal?" Ludwig asked. "*Das ist sehr gut. My people are gut.*"

"Ludwig," Ashoona interrupted, "you may have hired us, but we are *not* your people."

"Ya," Ludwig said, embarrassed as a first-year college student caught with the wrong answer. "You are correct. I am wrong. I learn from you children of nature. You vill see."

"I believe you, Ludwig," Ashoona said kindly. "You're a much better man than I first thought."

Although there was a fourteen-year difference in their ages, Ashoona was not a submissive employee and often openly challenged the expedition leader. Ludwig had to rely on the people he traveled with. They knew how to survive in the Arctic.

When the hunters were out on the ice searching for seals with their binoculars, Ashoona remained in camp and assisted Ludwig with his notes and drawings. She helped him describe the life of the Inuit out on the land—how to build snow houses and anchor tents against the wind. He asked her about Inuit marriage customs and relationships. Ashoona wrote notes for Ludwig in English, but when she could not find the correct English word, she would write in Inuktitut using syllabics.

"How do you expect me to make any sense of these notes ven I return to Germany," Ludwig asked with a grimace. "There is not even a single Inuktitut dictionary in our entire country, and no one knows this alphabet except your people. It is inferior."

"You're wrong." Ashoona felt her temper rising. "As we continue on this journey across the lake and into the western sea and then endure a winter on the trail, you will learn not only how to speak, and I hope, write our language, you will also learn respect for the skills of our people. For a while, I thought you had changed, but I see you still cling to your old prejudices that we Inuit have suffered from the time the first explorers came north looking for a way to sail their ships to India. Learn to be an Inuit; speak our language and learn our ways, and you will survive in the Arctic."

"I have to learn English to be an academic; now I must learn this strange language and even stranger alphabet? Is that vat you say?"

"Do as you wish, Dr. Reiner," Ashoona replied, more than a little annoyed by his attitude. "We are all in your employ. We agreed to come with you on this dangerous journey. You will see as we travel that our knowledge will be far more important than all the science you have stuffed in your head."

"Vat vill I see?"

"This expedition is poorly equipped, and if we cannot find seals and caribou, we will all die. Our lives do not depend on the scant supplies of soup, biscuits and cocoa that you brought. This expedition depends on the success of the hunters and the skill of the women to keep the blubber lamps burning through the night, make boots that stay dry and parkas that protect you from the wind and keep you from freezing to death."

Ludwig had little to say in response. He thought about the many boxes of food, sturdy tents, stoves and kerosene now at the bottom of Cumberland Sound.

Could I really perish out here? Was the expedition so poorly planned and equipped that starvation was possible?

Ludwig experienced a wave of fear, for at that moment he realized he could die out on this land, cold and far from his loved ones at home in Germany. It took considerable mental fortitude for him to shake off Ashoona's dire warnings about the future, but soon Ludwig had reverted to his earlier view of himself as the superior among the "Children of Nature."

"Ve Europeans who explore or vork in the Arctic believe we fulfill the white man's burden. We will educate you and change the indigenous people so you can live like us, comfortably and in safe villages." Although Ludwig truly cared for the Inuit, especially the people in his expedition, he could not abandon his prejudices.

"What's really the case on this expedition, as with most trips with your people," Ashoona replied coolly, "is that my people know that the Europeans are the Inuit's burden. We have to teach you how to light the blubber lamp, start a boat motor in cold weather, keep you from freezing your face and your feet and keep you fed while out on the land."

"My young assistant has strong opinions." Ludwig sank into a gloomy silence as he listened to her words, and for a few minutes, the truth of what she said seemed to sink in. He had a bleak premonition of what could transpire during a year out on the land.

And so Ludwig discovered that Ashoona was right, that he was dependent on his Inuit companions for survival. They traveled the first leg of the expedition over ice and snow. The sun had returned, but temperatures at night dropped to minus thirty, and fierce winds often blasted their camp. Every task had to be carried out with utmost precision. At the end of each day of travel, when the snow was good, Amo and Kilabuk constructed the snow houses, carefully selecting the packed snow with the correct density, cutting the blocks and building the structure to its rounded ceiling. They built a passageway into the igloo, to retain the small amount of heat generated by the blubber lamps and the occupants' bodies.

Although space was limited, Aula and Kilabuk, Paloosie, Ashoona and little Minnie shared the igloo comfortably. During meals, they sat on the sleeping platforms at the back of the snow house.

Ashoona often rocked the baby as Aula cooked over the lamps at the front. At night, Ashoona and the family slept, nestled like spoons, lying on two layers of caribou skins and covered by two more layers. Ashoona slept next to Aula and Kilabuk next to his son. The baby lay snug and warm between her parents. Ashoona's only problem was Kilabuk's unbearably loud snoring.

"I am thankful that Ludwig is sharing a tent with Amo and Ruby," Ashoona told Aula and Kilabuk. "I do not find his company pleasing, despite all his education. I will work with him during the day learning all I can, but at night I enjoy returning to our happy igloo. I hope Ruby can put up with Ludwig's fussiness. She's even more strong-minded than I am."

"Ruby can handle just about anything," Kilabuk replied. "But she is not someone I'd want to share my igloo with. Great housekeeper and seamstress, but too sharp-tongued for me."

The three teams pulled heavy loads. Kilabuk's team carried the rowboat lashed to the *qamutik* along with the boxes of supplies. Ashoona's sledge was loaded with frozen meat, when they had meat to carry. Most often, Ludwig would ride on Kilabuk's sledge. Paloosie ran effortlessly for hours, and despite Aula's urging, refused to climb on the *qamutik* to rest.

Amo's sledge carried tents, stoves, cooking utensils, Ruby and their three children: Elisapi, age six; Moses, age five; and Jonasie, two. It was common for a hunter's wife and children to come on long hunting expeditions. The roles of the women and men were well defined, and only seldom, as in Ashoona's case, did the females take on the job of driving the team and hunting. The women made the clothing and tents and kept them mended, tended the blubber lamp and cooked the food. Sewing skill was the most critical of all. In the arctic climate, travelers out on the land perished simply because of a small tear in a tent or a broken seam in a boot.

The Inuit thought most Europeans were beyond learning how to survive an arctic winter. In Ludwig's case, they were right. However, Ludwig knew enough from his studies that he should not attempt the journey without Inuit guides. John Franklin, who searched for the Northwest Passage in 1845, perished along with his crew because he was equipped with only European goods and did not have Inuit people to guide and care for him and his crew. Ludwig was following in the path of Franz Boas, an anthropologist who depended on the Inuit, but unlike Boas, the German scientist did not adapt well to Inuit life.

As the group of Inuit and their European employer moved west up the saltwater fjords toward Lake Nettilling, nature did not cooperate. Strong winds buffeted them each afternoon. Then, instead of firm ice and snowpack, warm weather melted the snow, revealing slushy snow patches and a windswept rocky landscape that impeded the dog teams.

"Ve have to sleep during the day and travel at night ven the snow is firm and the ice freezes," Ludwig said.

"That's asking too much," Ashoona told him. "Aula has a baby who wakes every few hours, and she needs rest so she can nurse. Minnie has just started to sleep through the night. Now Aula's family will be kept awake all day and all night. No one will sleep as we travel over these bumpy ice hummocks."

"It has to be dat vay," Ludwig insisted. "Tell them it is my decision and explain that we have to make progress or ve vill not be able to cross on the ice through the fjords to reach Lake Nettilling by dog team."

"*You* explain to Kilabuk," Ashoona said. "He speaks English, and the others understand most of what you say. I can't tell them to risk the health of their families."

"You are a stubborn woman, Ashoona," Ludwig answered grumpily, before walking away to find the men.

Ludwig was persuasive, and at midnight, he woke everyone and asked Ruby to make tea and prepare breakfast. Within the hour, the tired expedition members had loaded the *qamutiit*, harnessed the dogs, and were on their way. The wind had died down, and the northern lights lit up a cloudless sky. Despite the difficulty of getting their children dressed and fed, both Aula and Ruby enjoyed the beauty of the arctic night.

"That is Orion above us to the west," Ludwig pointed out, thinking that only he knew the constellations. "Over there is the planet Venus, I think, and Mars should be in the sky, but I don't know vich one."

"It is there," Kilabuk said, pointing out the red planet to his son. Then the experienced Inuit guide described all the well-known constellations to young Paloosie using, for the most part, the English names.

Ludwig was surprised. "How did you learn the English names for the stars?"

"I have traveled many times with the missionaries, the Mounted Police and also with scientists. The Inuit often use the stars to navigate because in midwinter, there is no sun, and the wind often blows the snow over the inukshuks we have placed to show us the pass through the mountains."

The children fell asleep again as the sledges bumped over the path, hitting icy hummocks, then over sections of rock swept bare of snow by the fierce winds that funneled down the valley. At last, they reached a small frozen lake. The dogs sped across the smooth surface, and the party made good progress until the strong rays of the sun lit the ice and snow. It was one of those spectacular arctic mornings when the light turns the mountains pink, and the stars disappear in a clear blue sky.

"It's time to stop," Ruby called to Ashoona. "Tell the boss man that we need to feed the children, and Aula must nurse Minnie."

Ashoona could hear the five-month-old raising her voice to a fever pitch. She knew that sound. Minnie would stir before uttering a little cry. If her mother did not feed her within two minutes, the baby's voice rose to a pitch that could pierce their eardrums.

"Time to stop!" Ashoona yelled.

Ludwig sat on Kilabuk's sledge, where he had been peacefully gazing out at the landscape. He was reluctant to halt their forward progress.

"Na, not now," Ludwig replied. "Ve must make another hour because soon the sun vill melt the snow and ve von't be able to travel. I must have the cooperation of my people."

"Once again," Ashoona answered, "we are *not* your people. We work for you, but we must see to the health of the children. If you insist on going on, leave me with the mothers and their children. We will feed them, and Aula will nurse little Minnie, and then I'll catch up. My sledge is lighter and travels more easily over the melting snow."

Ludwig reluctantly agreed. "I am concerned about being separated. How vill ve be fed and looked after without you women?"

"I will make the tea and food," Kilabuk offered. "I've done it before when I traveled with the missionaries."

The women removed a few of Ruby and Aula's belongings from the other *qamutiit* before bidding goodbye to the men. Young Paloosie accompanied the men.

Soon the mothers were seated on Ashoona's sledge caring for their babes, and peace was restored. In a just few minutes, Ashoona had water boiling and food prepared.

"It's good for us to have time with just the women," Aula said. "We can do everything they can do," she laughed. "Who needs them?"

"I need my man once a week at least," Ruby replied, giggling. "And you, Ashoona, when will you go to bed with a man and have babies?"

James' betrayal was still too raw for her to share her feelings. "I want to go to school. If I have a job and can make good money, no one will ever mistreat me again. I don't trust men anymore, and I don't want to depend on anyone but myself."

"If you reject men, maybe you should consider a young boy," Aula chuckled. "We could arrange a marriage just like in the old days, and you could wait for Paloosie to grow up. "

"That's a good idea," Ruby chimed in. "Have you noticed how he has google eyes for you?"

Even Ashoona laughed; she had noticed how the boy, less than a year younger than Ashoona, became tongue-tied whenever she was close by.

"This is so much fun just having the women and children alone. No tea or food to prepare for the men," Ruby said. "I love Amo, but since we married, I seem to have another baby before the last one is entirely off the breast, and with three little ones, I never get enough sleep. Soon there will be one more, and I am not even through nursing this one." Ruby had her two-year-old at her breast. Jonasie finished nursing and toddled off to play with his siblings.

"You're with child?" Aula said. "Are you happy to have another babe?"

"What is there to say? Unless Ludwig lets us turn back soon, my child will be born on the trail with a boss I don't trust. Of course, I will love my child. I'm just not happy about traveling with a baby in my womb and worrying that the big boss won't let us return home in time for the birth. I know you help mothers deliver babies, Ashoona. Will you help me with this one when the time comes?"

"Hopefully you will be in Blacklead for the birth. But if not, of course, I will help you. I'll also make certain the trip doesn't become one of pure survival."

Spring brought relief from the threats arctic life imposed. The sun grew brighter each day, and the children scampered up the rocky slopes and played in the streams that trickled down. Ashoona loved spring, the renewal of new growth. Willows grew up in the gullies, and early spring flowers sent up their shoots. In a few months, berries would be plentiful on the bushes, and as soon as they found the caribou herd, there would be an abundance of food.

"Our time together has been fun, but we must pack and catch up with the men," Aula warned. "The sun has warmed the snow to slush. It will be a slog."

Filled with the joy of spring, the women and children moved along the fjord toward Lake Nettilling where they would cross the lake by boat. They only had the rowboat, which would not hold everyone in the party. Ashoona guessed Amo and his family would return to Blacklead Island once Amo and Kilabuk harvested sufficient caribou to supply the expedition. Then Ruby could give birth at the clinic in the safety of the village.

Meanwhile, the men and young Paloosie had reached a stretch of exposed rock.

"Auch, I knew ve could not make it to the lake with the dog sleds," Ludwig scowled. "Ve must get to the lake no matter how hard it is."

"It's okay, Boss," Kilabuk said calmly. "We will get there. We can carry the supplies on our backs and drag the *qamutiit*. It will take several trips, but we'll make it."

Ludwig was steaming with anger over the delay. It was even more difficult for him because Ruby wasn't there to make him a cup of tea and set up his bed.

"Boss. You want me to make tea?" The ever-congenial Kilabuk had noticed the frustration in Ludwig's actions and voice.

"Why, yes." Ludwig answered in a more pleasant tone than he had used all through the difficult day. "Dat is most kind of you."

"I'm happy to do whatever you need," Kilabuk said.

"Why is Amo putting up tents instead of hunting?" Ludwig inquired. "Ve need caribou to feed the dogs and all my people."

"He searched for the caribou but found no trace. There are summers when the animals do not come to the Nettilling watershed, but most years they come in the hundreds, especially at the main grounds at Kangianga. We take what comes. We manage." There was a sense of peace and acceptance in everything this man of the Arctic said or did.

"I'll go and get us a bird or two for our meal," Paloosie told his father. Paloosie had the uncanny ability to hit a bird in flight by throwing small stones with the force and accuracy of a major league ballplayer. Paloosie hit two birds and was collecting his kills when he saw a sledge approaching from the west, traveling fast. He could see the man whipping the dogs so severely that the lead dog yelped. He saw that the whip drew blood. One of the lead dog's flanks was whipped so badly the dog's entrails were exposed.

Paloosie did not recognize the man, but ran back to the camp at top speed.

"A man is approaching with a dog team!" he said excitedly. His father was getting the cooking pots out, and Amo was erecting another tent.

"I see him, and I think I know who that is," Kilabuk said calmly. "Be careful now, Paloosie. That man is trouble."

"He beats his dogs, so he won't be good company to share our birds with."

"They are just dogs," Paloosie's father said. "Girls worry about the sled dogs, not hunters."

An unkempt, burly man brought his team to a halt close to the camp.

"Where is she?" he barked. "I'm told you have the witch with you. She belongs to me. When I catch that bitch, she will suffer." His eyes were bleary as if he had not slept for days.

"She's not here," Paloosie blurted out, "and we won't let you take her. We've heard all about you."

"I will kill all of you to get the truth," Qillaq growled. "I know she left with the expedition. You're the German, right? You had Ashoona with you. So maybe the women returned to Blacklead."

"The women are headed to Lake Nettilling," Paloosie lied.

"You lying little scum!" Qillaq yelled. "I came from Lake Nettilling, and no one has crossed there recently. You tell me she went that way, which means she is heading for Blacklead." He pointed east along the path that the women would be taking. There seemed no way to head Qillaq off.

"You're lucky I don't have time to kill all four of you," Qillaq said as he whipped his dogs and forced them to pull his sledge across the rocks and slushy snow. He had a light sledge and a strong dog team, so he was able to make progress despite the impossible trail conditions.

Paloosie watched him leave and looked helplessly at his father, praying Kilabuk would go to defend Ashoona. Ludwig realized that Kilabuk intended to pursue Qillaq.

"You cannot leave your employer to run off and protect Ashoona; you must fulfill your agreement and not turn back. If you go, you vill lose all the tobacco, food and supplies you are promised."

"I won't let that horrible man steal her again. He will kill her or worse." Paloosie was beside himself as he appealed to his father.

"You can do little against Qillaq," Ludwig warned. "He has guns, and he is ready to murder whoever gets in his way."

"I'm going back!" And with that, Paloosie ran after Qillaq. Kilabuk, realizing Paloosie was no match for the insanely vicious Qillaq, dropped the cooking pots, grabbed his rifle and ran after Paloosie.

"You vill lose your vages!" Ludwig yelled after Kilabuk. But Kilabuk remembered his promise to protect Ashoona. More important, the life of his adopted son was far more precious than any amount of tobacco or any guns.

Paloosie could not catch up to Qillaq, but he kept the dog team in sight as he ran like a deer over the slushy snow and uneven ground. He never tired, driven by his affection for Ashoona and concern for her safety. He covered the ten miles in a little over an hour. Kilabuk, also a fit runner, could not keep up with his son, but he never lost sight of him either.

Ashoona saw Qillaq coming, halted the team and looked for a gun, but she realized all the weapons were with the men. Her heart pounded with fear as the vicious man closed the gap. All she could do was arm herself with an *ulu* and a long knife used for making snow houses.

"You witch!" Qillaq screamed at Ashoona. "You will pay for stealing from me and running away. After I fuck you till you faint, I will strangle your beautiful neck."

Paloosie caught up to Qillaq just as the angry hunter reached the women's *qamutik*.

"Don't you touch her!" Paloosie yelled, aiming a rock at the hunter. The missile flew straight and swift as an arrow, a direct hit on the murderous man's head. Qillaq hollered and staggered. Paloosie launched another rock, this time knocking the big man to the ground. Qillaq rolled over on the rocky surface and took cover behind a large boulder. His head was bleeding heavily, but the big man was not easily felled.

Qillaq raised his rifle and aimed at Paloosie. Before he got the shot off, Kilabuk was within shooting range.

"Paloosie! Hit the ground!" Paloosie obeyed just as the first shot whizzed by the boy's head.

Qillaq reloaded and fired a second shot, this time hitting Paloosie in the thigh. The next shot came from Kilabuk, a hunter who never missed. He did not aim to kill. The bullet hit Qillaq's arm, knocking the gun out of his hand. A second bullet hit the same spot, shattering the hunter's right arm.

"I will kill all of you...your son, your wife, your baby!" Qillaq screamed in pain and rage. "You are a dead man, Kilabuk, and the young witch will wish she had never resisted me. Her life will end in torture."

But Qillaq could not do much. He was in excruciating pain as he picked himself up, holding his bloodied arm against his chest.

"Stay away from me," Ashoona said, and she kicked the gun away from Qillaq.

"Aim this at Qillaq," Ashoona said as she picked up the gun and handed it to Ruby. She grabbed the first aid kit she had brought from the clinic and ran over to Paloosie.

Aula and Kilabuk knelt beside the injured boy, but it was Ashoona who took control. Her months as Henry's assistant had given her enough first aid training to deal with most traumatic injuries. She cut the clothing away from the wound and applied a tourniquet to stop the bleeding. The bullet had passed through the upper part of Paloosie's leg severing an artery. Paloosie remained quiet as Ashoona stitched the wound and bandaged his leg. Ashoona's sure and quick actions halted the worst of the bleeding and saved Paloosie's life.

Qillaq had had enough. He had no gun, and his arm was useless; he would need a skilled doctor to repair the shattered bones. He wrapped his arm in a piece of caribou skin and tied it tight to his chest. He could no longer whip the dogs, and besides, his lead dog lay bleeding from the merciless whippings and would not get up. Qillaq kicked at the dog with no result, so he unhooked the lead. The injured dog ran away, whimpering and leaving a bloody trail. With only one good arm, it took Qillaq some time to hook up a new lead dog and harness his team. Qillaq and his dogs moved slowly over the bare, rocky ground heading east.

Ashoona watched him disappear, wondering whether he would head for Blacklead Island or try to get to the mission hospital at Panniqtuuq. She was certain he was not gone from her life or her nightmares.

"He's gone, Ashoona," Kilabuk said. "I'll make sure the police know about his attempted murder of Paloosie. We now have laws in this land that will catch up with a man like that."

"He could be in prison for twenty years, and when he gets out, he will still come for me. I wish you had killed him."

"I will kill him for you," Paloosie said. He had recovered somewhat from the initial pain and trauma of his wound and was resting on caribou skins. "Ludwig is going to give me my own gun when we finish this expedition, and then I will find Qillaq and make sure my bullet goes through his mean, ugly brain."

"You don't need a death on your conscience," Aula said. "We are Christians now, my son. I want you to grow up and be a fine hunter and guide like your father."

"Paloosie won't get his gun from Ludwig if we don't get moving," Kilabuk warned. "He threatened to cut our wages when I ran back to help. I'm glad I came, but now we have to move quickly and join up with Ludwig and Amo. I couldn't risk losing my son." He hugged Paloosie in a rare show of affection.

The trek to join the forward part of the expedition was difficult. The sun still shone down on the land, making the snow slushy and extending the bare spots. The sledge was heavily loaded with the injured Paloosie and the children. The adults pushed and pulled the sledge through the melting snow, which in places was a foot deep, wet and heavy. Occasionally, they hit a patch of bare ground and had to lift the entire sledge over the rocky outcroppings.

Paloosie remained calm as they bumped along, jarring the bandages loose and sending shocks of pain up his leg. The boy had survived so much adversity since the death of his birth parents that he refused to utter even the smallest complaint. The three Inuit children understood that Paloosie was in trouble, so they stayed close by his side. Ruby's daughter, Elisapi, placed her hand on Paloosie's forehead and asked him if he was okay. He smiled at the small girl's thoughtfulness.

The adults were perspiring from the task of moving the laden sledge, and to make matters worse, the wind had picked up and was buffeting them and the sledge. After an hour, Aula called a brief halt.

"I just need to catch my breath," she explained. "This day has drained me. My adopted son is so dear to me, and I thought I was going to lose him when I saw Qillaq aim directly at his heart." Aula, not accustomed to tears, started crying and put her head on Kilabuk's shoulder. "I'm so grateful that you came to save him. I will never forget this."

"You might when you find out how much Ludwig cuts from our wages. First to go will be the cooking pots he promised and then the kerosene lamp, all things that I know you desire. The last thing I will give up is my tobacco," he laughed.

"Have your smoke," Aula said. "I have my son and will give up any number of pots for him. But now we must get moving again."

It was cold and dark by the time they reached the forward camp. Amo had put up Ludwig's tent, made him tea and cooked seal while the German busied himself writing in his diary.

"I see you are here at last," Ludwig said impatiently. "Ve have lost hours that ve could have been on the trail. The temperature has dropped, and the snow is hard now. Ve can travel and make camp in the morning."

The women looked at one another in disbelief.

"Is he serious, Ashoona?" Aula asked. "Are we to continue tonight and not let Paloosie rest and mend? Please say something to him."

But it was Kilabuk who interceded on behalf of the group. "Ludwig, I know you are basically a good man, and you wouldn't want my young son to die. He is badly wounded and needs a night of rest before we can continue on. I beg you as the Christian I know you are, to let us stay here for the night."

Ludwig was silent for a minute, thinking about his responsibilities to his employees and his conflicting drive to succeed. "Yes, you are right; ve must give him time to heal. I'm sorry. Sometimes my vork gets in the way of my being a good boss and a strong Christian."

The next day the sun rose over the eastern hills lighting the mountains in a dazzling display of pink. The spring day brought a lighthearted spirit to the camp. The children ran around with lighter clothing and played with boats in the rivulets formed from the melting snow, and the women bathed in the small pools warmed in the depressions formed on the rock surface. It was a cherished time of year.

Ruby, however, was not in the best of spirits. "Before his injury, Paloosie would climb the cliffs to gather auk eggs," she complained. "I have no eggs to boil for our meal. Amo, why don't you get up those cliffs?"

"I'm going out with Kilabuk to hunt caribou," he answered. "You'll just have to make do with the leftover seal and some tea."

"I can climb up there," Ashoona offered. "And don't worry, I'll be especially cautious. When I fell and broke my wrist and landed in Padluk's clutches, that was an experience worse than breaking a bone."

"You must not risk the climb. It's too dangerous," Aula said gently, "and we need you to tend to Paloosie's wounds. But for myself, I will miss your company if you end up smashed at the bottom of the cliffs. And, remember, coming down is much more dangerous than climbing."

"I'll take a rope. Ludwig, may I borrow one of your ropes?"

"You may use vatever you need if I can have eggs for lunch rather than that tiresome seal meat."

The sun shone brilliantly as Ashoona scaled the cliffs that rose up steeply along the narrow gorge. She moved higher and higher, then looked toward the west.

I can see the route we will take to the lake.

In the distance she could see the ice glistening on Lake Nettilling. It was early June, but the lake was still frozen. Breakup would come in a few weeks, and by that time, the expedition would be at the shores of the lake and ready to set sail in the rowboat.

A few more feet up the steep cliffs and Ashoona reached the first nest. The angry female bird flew at Ashoona's head. She reached into the nest and found three precious eggs, but she needed more. Ashoona placed the eggs in her sealskin pouch and moved farther up the steep cliffs. As she climbed higher, ice coated the rocks, and Ashoona felt her foot slip as she reached for the next ledge. Her heart jumped as she held on tightly and peered down over a hundred feet at the jagged rocks below.

"Eeeee...be careful!" she whispered to herself as she looped the rope around a rocky ledge. If she slipped, the rope would stop her fall. Ashoona continued up the cliff, gathering eggs from several nests. The small black-and-white birds squawked and dive-bombed around her head. Ashoona stayed calm, thinking how delicious the eggs would be after weeks of a monotonous diet of raw seal, seal stew and seal soup.

Lately, Ruby had resorted to boiling sealskin to make soup, and she fed the dogs the remains of the boiled skin, but that was not enough food if the dogs were to continue pulling the *qamutiit* over a trail of rocks and deep slush that was becoming more difficult with each passing day.

They had to find and kill caribou soon or the expedition would be in jeopardy. Ludwig was most worried about the failure of his expedition. Everything he had worked for depended on completing the journey and returning to Germany to publish his findings. At times, an even more troubling image woke him at night. He imagined himself and his little band of Inuit starving to death miles from the comforts of the remote village of Blacklead and far, far away from his friends and family. It was a picture that disturbed his sleep and caused him to stir restlessly throughout the short night.

Ludwig was also distressed over the food supply. He knew that the Inuit he employed would insist on turning back if they had no meat. He also knew that if he insisted on continuing the expedition and his Inuit guides died, word would make its way back to London and then to his homeland. He would be ostracized if he knowingly put the indigenous people at risk, and any opportunities for future funding would evaporate. Ludwig cared about the people he hired, but he cared even more about his career as a scientist.

As Ludwig mulled over the predicament of his poorly supplied expedition, Ashoona came bounding toward the camp with a huge smile on her face. In her sealskin bag, she had more eggs than they could possibly eat. That night, the expedition members feasted on eggs until their stomachs were full and the thought of one more egg made them ill.

Ruby kept a dozen boiled eggs for the next day because she knew Ludwig would order them to continue on the trail despite the impossible conditions. If she were in charge, she would make camp right where they were and wait until the men had been successful at the hunt. She would also wait until the small lakes were free of ice so that they could put the boat in the water and paddle most of the way to Foxe Basin.

Men! Or at least these Qallunaaq *men, don't seem to have the brains of a bear cub! The lives of our children are at stake on this journey, and I long to be rid of the German and his dangerous expedition.*

Ruby approached Kilabuk and Ashoona. "Amo and I want to return to Blacklead. We may have just enough time to travel along the Cumberland Sound coastline before the sea ice goes out, and I know there's not enough food for all of us. You must ask the boss to let us go home. I want to be in Blacklead before winter sets in so my baby can greet us when his father has food in his stomach, and when we can make sure our little one has a warm house."

Surprisingly, Ludwig agreed. "Ya. They should go back. Ve have not enough space in the boat. It is better if they start home. I vanted to have two hunters when ve reach Kangianga. But, once Paloosie's leg heals, ve vill have two hunters, and Ashoona tells me she killed her first caribou ven she was only four years old. Very strange, as our little German boys do not shoot guns at that age." He paused and offered a rare smile. "So ve have enough hunters to supply us until ve reach Foxe Basin and can hunt seals."

"If you grant us another request, I give my word we will work hard for you, Boss," Kilabuk continued. "Paloosie needs another day to heal, so we want to stay here and let him rest."

Again, Ludwig agreed without protest. *Maybe the driven scientist was beginning to be more human,* Kilabuk thought.

And so it was. Ludwig allowed a two-day halt to give Paloosie a chance to heal.

"I hope we can reach Blacklead Island along the ice," Amo said. "The trail will be rough, and we'll have to push and pull the *qamutik* over the bare spots. Worse, if the ice goes out early on the sound, I'll have to spend a summer and fall in a remote camp listening to Ruby complain."

Ludwig laughed. The relationship between the scientist and his bossy housekeeper had been trying at times.

"Whether or not we make it back to Blacklead, my family will be well fed," Ruby added. "We will find many seals on the sound. And hopefully, you will return to Blacklead by Christmas so that you can attend our baby's baptism."

"It will not be so soon," Ludwig said firmly. "Ve must travel in the winter and then return by sled and boat next spring."

"Oh, dear," Ruby said. "May God keep you safe on your journey." She whispered to Ashoona, "Do not let him put all of you at risk. Be strong." Ruby was not the type of woman accustomed to crying, yet tears welled up in her eyes as she hugged Ashoona and Aula.

Ludwig was visibly irritated as the friends said lengthy farewells and sent messages back to family and friends in Blacklead. Finally, Amo called to his team, and he and his family set off heading east, anxious to reach the comforts of their village.

Chapter Thirteen

Kangianga

After Amo and his family left, the expedition got underway again. Ice remained on the river and small lakes, but the trail was a difficult combination of slushy snow and rugged rock. It became impossible for the dogs to pull the sledge and close to impossible for the hardy Inuit to pack supplies and drag a boat and two sledges along the trail.

Over the next month, the weary group trudged on. Kilabuk shot one caribou, which lasted them a week. And once again they had no meat and were boiling skins for the tiny bit of nourishment in the soup. Ludwig carefully rationed the remaining bouillon cubes, flour and sugar, always calculating the supplies remaining and the number of months he intended to continue with the expedition.

Why doesn't he admit this project is doomed? Kilabuk thought. Kilabuk understood a great deal and was intelligent and thoughtful, but he would not oppose his employer. Because of his disposition, the tough, intelligent Inuit had one of the best reputations in the Arctic as a guide and hunter. No European wanted employees who refused to obey orders.

———

The month of June should have brought days of sunshine. Instead the winds became fierce, and the little group had to set the tents up behind a barricade of sledges and the rowboat as protection against the battering gales. The expedition could not continue while the winds raged.

Little Minnie was now crawling, and Aula was careful not to let the little one out of the tent. She could be picked up in the wind and blown away like a leaf in a breeze. As well, the dogs could be vicious and a threat to the small child. But the dogs huddled down among the rocks, hungry and cautious as the storm raged on.

Minnie was a happy, smiling child. Kilabuk nicknamed her the "Princess of Cuteness," and Aula, who worried about dirt on the tent floor that her baby might pick up, called her the "Little Dust Mop." She had first perfected backward crawling, and when she learned to crawl forward, she moved across the tent floor with lightning speed.

The baby became the center of attention and a source of entertainment in the crowded tent, where Paloosie, Ashoona and of course, the devoted parents, spent the evening entertained by Minnie's every move and expression.

Ludwig seemed to ignore the storm and spent his days in his tent, scribbling in his journal. He had laid out on the tent floor the skeletons of birds, seals, foxes and rabbits, and Ashoona had the task of writing down the Inuit names for the parts of the animals. As she became more skilled, she also wrote down the Latin names, proving her unlimited capacity to learn.

"At least the winds will help break up the ice," Kilabuk remarked.

"*Das ist sehr gut.* I am impatient to make our journey to Foxe Basin to research the sea life on the coast and meet the Eskimos from the vest before ve return to Blacklead."

I wish we could be home by Christmas, Ashoona mused. *How wonderful it would be to return and see Henry, to go to the church services, enjoy the feasts and the games.*

Then she thought of the journey ahead with the dwindling supplies and the real possibility of starvation. Even a skilled hunter like Kilabuk could not prevent the expedition from starving. He would never keep his family in a place that had no game; he always moved to a camp where he knew he could find food before all the seal meat was eaten. But it wasn't his choice; he was bound to the German and would do what he could to keep his boss and his family alive.

"If we can get to Foxe Basin," Aula said, "Kilabuk will bring us more seals than we can eat. My husband has traveled this route and told of seals offering themselves up for dinner."

"I would like to see that sight," Ashoona laughed. "I've been so hungry, my dreams are filled with visions of bread baked in the hospital oven and the delicious raisin pies you made."

"Best not to speak of food," Aula advised.

The June sun grew brighter, melting the remaining low-lying patches of ice in the valley.

Ashoona remembered the wonderful summer days in Panniqtuuq when she was five or six. Her mother and father would take her in kayaks across the fjord in search of berries or to hunt caribou in the Qulliq, the narrow valley shaped like a blubber lamp. They would build a fire with dwarf willows and drink tea and eat biscuits. Life was perfect.

But on this expedition, the summer was far from perfect. As the June sun warmed the earth, melted the lake ice and sent streams pouring down the rocks, Ashoona looked at the torn tents, hungry dogs and their shrinking supplies and wondered if she would get back home and if she would ever find love and happiness again.

Kilabuk and Paloosie had been out hunting three days without success. The boy's leg was healing quickly, and although he couldn't run as yet, he was able to keep up with his father. While the men were away from the camp, Ashoona and Aula were trapped with the impatient Ludwig.

"Vere have they gone to find caribou?" Ludwig grumbled. "They told me Kangianga is the best place for the animals and that ve vould have more meat than we need. Now ve are eating the precious biscuits that are needed to complete the journey, and I have to eat your disgusting soup made from boiled skins, with hair swimming on the surface! Vould anyone in my town in Germany believe I vould eat something like dat?"

"The Inuit eat worse to stay alive," Ashoona said.

Aula laughed and recounted all the dreadful things that starvation forced them to eat.

"How about the ptarmigan and the caribou poop that some expeditions have been forced to eat? Not bad when flavored with a little seal oil," she said with a chuckle.

Ludwig's face turned green. "You ate shit?"

"No, I have not ever gone that far, although if I had fed my beautiful children bird droppings, they might still be alive. I never want to suffer that pain again."

Suddenly the fun drained out of the conversation as Aula recalled how her beloved children had starved to death at the hand of the *Angakkut*.

"Don't ever blame yourself, Aula. You could do nothing to save your children. But I promise you that Minnie will not suffer. Ludwig will make sure of that, won't you?" Ashoona said sternly as if she had become the teacher and Ludwig the student.

Ludwig had no time to answer because the sound of the men approaching interrupted them.

"They're back!" Ludwig exclaimed, scrambling out of the tent with more energy than he had shown in weeks. "It's Kilabuk and Paloosie, and they are carrying loads of meat. We are saved!"

The feast of caribou was wonderful. Aula sliced the liver and heart for Ludwig in recognition of his leadership and then cut a few raw pieces of the rump for her husband and son. Ashoona preferred cooked meat, so she helped Aula cut small pieces to boil over the lamp. Soon they were sitting around the igloo enjoying the first filling meal they'd had for days. Life was good again. All but the driven German wished they could remain at Kangianga to enjoy the warm summer days and the abundance of food.

Over the next two days, the hunters killed four more caribou; the herd was so abundant, they could have killed twenty. Aula and Ashoona packed the caribou meat onto the sledges with an uneasy feeling. They were leaving the rich caribou hunting grounds of Kangianga and heading toward Lake Nettilling. Unless the hunters were successful en route, the remaining caribou meat might have to sustain them until they reached the seal-rich seas of Foxe Basin.

"And now we need to think about how we are going to cross that bloody lake and get to the ocean. Next week we will be traveling the trail of the dead, as my husband's family called it. At Kangianga we've had the gifts of the caribou, bird eggs, rabbits and fox. Over the centuries, when Inuit took this road, many starved."

"Don't worry so much. If the food runs out, I will make sure we turn back," Ashoona said, hugging her friend. "Your son saved my life. I will not let Ludwig risk your family."

As they pushed on through the melting snow and ice, the sledge bumped over the rocks and then sank into the slush to the top of the runners. The march was exhausting for the little party of travelers especially because there was little to look forward to. By the time they reached the ocean, the warmth of summer would be over.

"Do you realize that we will be facing winter on the Baffin Coast?" Aula said as they stopped for lunch and a well-deserved rest. "The ice will not be frozen, and seals will be hard to hunt."

"You are being too fearful," Ludwig chastised. "It's best to have a positive outlook. I too am tired because I do not have Kilabuk's or even your young son's physical fitness. I do not complain even though I vant to rest; I vant to go home to my family and see the blond-haired children playing in the street, eat the vonderful food of my homeland. So, all of you...stop this complaining!"

"I sorry," Aula quickly responded in her broken English. "You right, Boss. Ashoona, you tell Boss what I say."

"Ludwig, Aula fears for her children and hopes this journey will end well. She worries about you. She says you do not eat enough, especially when we have no oil to cook with and have only the raw meat. She says you do not sleep well and that you do not have a healthy *anaq*."

"Vat?"

"You do not take a good shit," Ashoona offered.

"Yes," Aula went on in halting English. "You have not health, Ludwig."

"I have never been an athlete. I'm thin but not tall. I vould never be able to eat the two to three pounds of seal or caribou that you people devour. I need hot food and biscuits."

"That is why you have been sneaking into the supplies and taking extra biscuits," Ashoona said goodnaturedly. "It's not that we mind, but you don't have to pretend that we do not see you. We know that you are letting yourself starve because the Inuit food does not suit you, so take as many biscuits as you need."

"Vere are those men?" Ludwig said, checking his watch. "Ve must be on the road an hour ago. Late again. Late always!"

He was visibly angry even as the two men finally approached from the west. But from the expression on Kilabuk's face, it was obvious something was amiss.

"Vat now?" Ludwig demanded.

"You will not believe who and what we have found," Kilabuk said excitedly. "We must hook up our teams immediately. On the trail up ahead is an old woman who needs our help, especially your care, Ashoona. Without immediate help, she will cross the boundary into the spirit world."

Within minutes, the two sledges were underway, and Ashoona spotted a dilapidated tent.

"She told me her name is Pinnaq," Kilabuk informed them as they reached the tent. "She came from Igloolik with her family. She survived, but the rest are dead, her two children and her husband. She has been here alone for months."

They approached the tattered tent. Ashoona peered in and saw a woman in rags, her mouth a dark hole, missing several teeth. She was so thin her bones protruded from her cheeks and her hands.

"I am damned," the woman cried. "I cannot live with people. Let me die."

"Why?" Ashoona asked, examining the emaciated woman. "We are here to save you. Why won't you grab onto the life that moments ago was almost lost to you?"

"Even you, my rescuers, will be disgusted at what I have done!"

"That is not true. What could you possibly have done to turn us against you?" Kilabuk stared at the unhappy woman. "Surely you are not a murderer."

"Worse than thievery or murder," she sobbed. "A sin that is unforgivable. I have eaten my children. I have eaten my husband. Please, leave me to die."

"Did you kill them?" Ashoona asked. If she had, Ashoona thought she would leave her to die.

"No! No! I would not kill those that I love. They died of starvation, first the children then my husband. He was old, and we had no food for weeks. I buried them in the snow, my little ones first and then when my husband passed, I buried him. I was so weak I could barely pull him out of the tent, and only with great effort did I cover my dearest love with snow. I starved for one moon and then I knew that I, too, would die as the longest and coldest days of winter were upon me. I had to decide if I should live. First, I ate my husband, then the children. It makes my heart sick, and I will go to hell, for I am a Christian."

"What you have done is not a sin," Aula said gently. "You must not die. Your family has given themselves to you, and it is your responsibility to live and make their sacrifice worthwhile. Ashoona, help me get her up, and Kilabuk, put up a shelter for her. I will make hot caribou broth for you, and I want you to drink it and live. Will you?"

"Yes, you are right. I must live. Thank you."

"Vat is this?" Ludwig demanded. "Ve do not stop to camp here. Ve must make more miles." His voice grew loud with fury.

"Yes, Boss," Kilabuk said. "We must stop for a time to bring her back to life. She will die if we move her before she has had some food. If you will allow it, once we see she is recovering, we are prepared to continue through the night."

"Ve travel at night. *Das ist sehr gut.* The snow and ice will freeze, and ve vill make more miles." Ludwig seemed relieved at the compromise until he realized that the woman would be coming with them.

"You don't expect me to take her, do you?"

"And what else would we do?" Kilabuk asked coolly.

"Yes, I see. She must come." Ludwig was obviously displeased with the extra burden on their supplies, but once again he realized how it would look to those in his homeland if he left the woman to die and word got back to his sponsors.

Kilabuk erected a shelter from skins, and they lifted the frail woman into the tent and laid her down on clean caribou skins.

"Here," Ashoona said. "Drink a little water, and soon we will have some caribou soup for you."

When Pinnaq sipped the hot broth, energy seemed to pour through her veins. She smiled shyly at her nurses, lay down and was soon asleep. While the woman recovered, Ashoona and Aula spent the time sewing caribou skins into winter clothing, while the men repaired the sledges in preparation for the rough trail ahead. Ludwig, as usual, worked in his tent scribbling his notes and occasionally asking Ashoona to help him with the Inuktitut names. That evening, the women had time to boil a caribou stew on the oil lamp until the meat was so tender it broke apart.

"This will be good for Pinnaq," Aula exclaimed. "I remember when I was starving and could not digest much more than soft mush. I also remember when I had to watch my little ones die of starvation. I could not do what Pinnaq did, but I hold no hard feelings for the poor woman."

They gave Pinnaq the nourishing stew along with a good helping of broth.

"Drink the broth slowly, and then chew the meat well," Aula advised. "Your stomach is not used to food, and it will take a few days before you can eat a proper meal."

As soon as they finished their meal and had cleared away the cooking dishes, Ludwig ordered the group to carry on. The temperature was dropping and would soon freeze the snow and make their journey easier. As the sun sank behind the mountains, the half-light made it difficult to pick out a safe route over water, ice, rock and snow.

Pinnaq did not complain and was an entertaining addition to the group. In her forties, she was old for a mother of eight- and nine-year-old children. Her husband, at sixty, had been considerably older.

"I have many children and grandchildren," Pinnaq told them. I was first married when I was only twelve summers old, and my first husband was older than my grandfather. How I hated being bedded by that old fart!"

"What happened to your first husband?" Aula asked.

"He was so old that he died while my youngest was still at the breast. The day we buried my husband was my salvation."

Ashoona liked Pinnaq's expressive storytelling and told her new companion the tale of how Qillaq had almost succeeded in taking her.

"You mean that old bastard from Igloolik was after you? I know about him. Always wanting a young girl with no experience in bed, getting the young thing to bear an igloo full of babies, then out he would go looking for another wife and abandoning his responsibilities. He is not a true Inuit. He's crazy, and you are lucky to have escaped him. Very lucky."

They told Pinnaq about the encounter on the trail and how Qillaq was likely at the clinic in Blacklead getting his arm stitched up.

"He must have passed your tent on the way from Lake Nettilling."

"I think I heard a dog's yelping and a man screaming and whipping his dogs. He did not slow down, and he did not look at my tent, although I must admit that most people would not think anyone could be alive in that ripped and windblown bit of canvas. But you found me, dear Kilabuk. You are a man that all Inuit should follow, a good man who always cares."

"He's mine, Pinnaq," Aula said with a laugh. "So don't think if you fatten yourself up you can snatch him from me."

"I am too old for him, and after your kindness, Aula, I would never as much as glance at someone that belongs to you."

"No one belongs to anyone," Ashoona added. "Someday I want to find a man to love and to have children with. I want us to stay together because we love one another."

"Eeeee!" Pinnaq exclaimed. "She is still so young; she doesn't know what marriage will bring. Like the times you want to push him into the crack in the ocean because he doesn't clean his teeth and he snores all night.

"But then despite all, you come to care deeply for each other," Pinnaq continued. "When I knew my husband was dying, not my first husband but this one, I was beside myself with grief. When he took his last breath, I cried until I had no more tears to weep. But now, my dear husband nourishes my wretched body. We were a true love match. He was older by twenty years, but we chose each other. He looked after me, and before he died, he told me that I must use his body to save the children and myself. But the little ones died a few days before he succumbed, and I could not tell him that they had already passed to the spirit world."

With the lively Pinnaq joining the entourage, the evenings were more pleasant. Pinnaq came from the west coast of Baffin and knew of many connections between families of the Cumberland Sound area and those from Igloolik. Although the journey was difficult, the Inuit remained energetic, and as long as the supplies of food lasted, the evenings were cheerful with much lively storytelling.

By the time they reached Lake Nettilling, the sun had melted an ice-free passage up the center of the lake, and the group loaded the boat for the long paddle. Before launching the boat, they built a cache of caribou meat, covering it with a pile of rocks and gravel, then marking the site with three inukshuks, positioned in line with the peak of the mountain range that rose up on the north shore of the lake. The dogs were unleashed and left to run along the shore ice, and the two *qamutiit* were tethered to the stern of the rowboat. As they pushed the heavily laden boat into the water, the dogs howled at being separated from the group. Kilabuk's lead dog swam out, following the boat until Kilabuk pushed the dog to the edge of the open water using his paddle. The dog was unable to scramble onto the ice and would have perished if Kilabuk hadn't boosted him up onto the ice shelf.

"We need every dog on the two teams if we are to return home with the sleds," Kilabuk explained when he noticed Ludwig's impatient scowl.

Ashoona, Kilabuk, Aula and Paloosie paddled, while Pinnaq looked after the baby, and Ludwig sat like a monarch on top of his fading kingdom. They had paddled for two hours when the winds came up and waves rocked the top-heavy boat.

"Keep paddling!" Ashoona yelled at Paloosie when she saw him raise his paddle as a wave hit them broadside. "The worst thing to do is to take your paddle out of the water when a big wave approaches."

Paloosie was embarrassed to be found at fault by Ashoona. She noticed his dark look. "Don't feel badly when I correct you, Paloosie. You are skilled in the kayak, but a rowboat is different. You will be a great boatman; it just takes experience. I started paddling with my father in big waves like this when I was six."

The waves grew higher as the winds screamed across the pass and onto the wide surface of the lake, kicking the waves into three-foot peaks. When the heavily laden boat rode up a wave, the paddlers slapped the top of the wave with their paddles to prevent the boat from diving and taking on water at the bow. As the craft plunged into the trough of the wave, they back-paddled to keep the boat from knifing into the steep dip of the wave.

"This is crazy," Aula said in Inuktitut. "Tell the boss we must go ashore. If the boat tips, everyone will drown."

"Just a little longer," Kilabuk said. "We need to make some distance, or Ludwig will again talk of cutting our wages. Be careful, and be strong; we can make it to that island."

Kilabuk and Ashoona, the most experienced paddlers, managed to drive the boat onto a gravel beach, where they took refuge from the summer storm. Ludwig was stiff from the cold as he stumbled on to the shore. They camped for the night, weathering out the storm in their tents while the dogs howled into the night on the far shore of the lake.

It took three more days to cross the lake. Mornings were calm, and the water surface was like glass, but as the day wore on, the winds came up, and Kilabuk and Ashoona had to paddle with all their strength to keep the boat from capsizing. At last they reached the slow, flat Koukdjuak River that drained out of the lake and meandered slowly west to Foxe Basin.

After the harrowing trip across the lake, the drift down the river was completely relaxing. As they approached the ocean, the terrain flattened out and the river split into channels making it difficult to paddle the boat as it scraped over gravel bars and rocks. Often they had to step into the icy waters to push the boat through the shallows.

Each time the river split around an island, Ashoona and Kilabuk had to decide which channel to take, always looking for the route with the deeper, faster water. The current picked up as they veered left into a narrow branch of the Koukdjuak. Suddenly, the boat swirled around the corner in the river and picked up speed in a newly cut channel that neither Aula nor Kilabuk had seen on previous trips.

The river sped around another corner, and before they had time to react, they were in the midst of rapids. Ashoona yelled commands at the other paddlers.

"Right! Strong right!"

The boat narrowly missed a collision with a mid-river boulder, but not without the sharp rock gouging the left side of the rowboat. Pinnaq clutched the baby tightly, ready to save little Minnie should they capsize. Aula's heart raced, worried about her baby being thrown into the icy waters. Despite her fears for her little one, she knew she had to paddle with every ounce of strength if they were to survive the rapids and land safely.

Water gushed into the boat, unbalancing the overloaded craft. They successfully negotiated the rapids and slipped into quiet, deep water. But the danger had not passed. The boat was taking on water and listing precariously. Kilabuk and Aula, on the right side, dug their paddles into the water in a strong, high brace, and Ashoona and Paloosie on the left, did a hard low brace. Their quick action prevented the boat from capsizing. Ludwig clung to his perch, his face white with fear. Pinnaq remained calm and stoic. After escaping death by starvation, she knew they would survive, and the baby would be safe.

"It's shallow. I can touch the bottom," Ashoona called. Relief flooded through Aula; her baby would be safe. The river flattened into a wide expanse of slow-moving knee-deep water. Ashoona could see the gravelly river bottom.

"Let's get out of the boat," Aula said. "We can push it to shore and make sure it doesn't tip over. Stay there, Pinnaq, and hold onto my little darling."

Ludwig remained glued to the supply boxes piled up in the boat.

"Eeeee! It's cold!" Aula exclaimed, as she stepped into the chilly water.

"Feels good to me," Ashoona said with a smile. "Better than being plunged up to my ears in the rapids and swimming for our lives."

"I like the icy water," Paloosie added. "It makes me feel alive."

They pulled and pushed the boat through the shallow water and dragged it up onto the gravel shore. The dogs howled at the river's edge, until everyone was safely on shore.

Two boards had torn off from the side of boat, rendering it useless because the missing pieces had been carried out to sea.

"The boat served us well," Kilabuk remarked "but we won't have a use for it since we will be on ice for the journey home."

With all their concentration on the challenge of the rapids, they had not noticed where they were. To their delight, the ocean was before them. They had made it to Foxe Basin.

They put up tents on a relatively level area that sloped gently for fifteen miles toward the Soper Range. On the south side of the river was the Great Plain of Koukdjuak that stretched along the eastern side of Foxe Basin.

The tidal region was a jumble of rocks, impassible at low tide and covered at high tide. They needed to hunt seal for lamp oil and food, but the seals were far out in the ocean, well beyond rifle range. The caribou meat was gone, and except for ptarmigan, all the birds had flown south. Aula found it impossible to feed six adults and a baby on the few bones and skins that remained.

With the exception of Ludwig and Pinnaq, everyone spent the day searching for food. Paloosie was adept at hitting ptarmigan with his excellent throwing arm, and Kilabuk brought in a few rabbits, but that was still not enough food to keep their group supplied. One rabbit did not satisfy the hunger of people who had been out on the land all day, and a goose was just an appetizer.

Fortunately, they had arrived at the ocean shore in late August, in time to dig for clams, which was a job for the entire camp. But the destitute expedition members couldn't stop thinking about the sea ice. They needed the ocean to freeze solidly so the hunters could go out on the sea ice for seal. If only the ice would form earlier this year. They hoped it would freeze up in September, not October, as was usual. The seals would save them from certain starvation; the brutal cold of the arctic winter was not far away.

"All we have left now is this thin soup," Aula complained. "Soup made from old skins. After starving at Padluk's camp, I didn't think it would come to this when traveling with a *Qallunaaq*. I thought all *Qallunaat* were rich."

"He just wants to be famous when he returns home," Pinnaq grumbled. "He makes sure we do not perish out here because that would destroy his reputation, but does he care if we have to eat bird shit to survive? No!"

Pinnaq went on at length, but then added a sad note and an accusation. "It was a scoundrel who took my little ones and husband! We had a cache on the trail. It was marked carefully with an inukshuk. So many paces away, marked using the sun, making sure the edge of the inukshuk points to our cache. My man buried it deep in the permafrost and covered it with gravel. It was enough food for five families, enough to carry us across the passage of the dead where the birds do not fly and the caribou do not graze.

"We wouldn't have minded if travelers took some of the blubber, some of the dried meat and fish. But a greedy thief took every morsel and left us to starve. We also left *igunaq* in another cache. That putrid walrus, too, was gone. Now that you tell me

Qillaq passed by, I think he must have used this trail earlier this year on his way to Igloolik and was the one to steal from us."

"You're right about Qillaq," Ashoona agreed, "but don't be too hard on Ludwig. He does care for us and has learned to be more human on this trip. Qillaq is a different story. There is only evil in that man. When he lost track of me on Cumberland Sound, I thought he would stay in Blacklead, but Henry told me he stopped there briefly before leaving for Igloolik. That is his home, so he likely came this way. Too bad the *igunaq* didn't poison him," Ashoona chuckled, "but you are probably an expert at preparing that disgusting food so it is always safe. Two elders in my village died from eating *igunaq*."

"I was careful in cutting the walrus, wrapping it in a circle and waiting long enough till it becomes like that stinky cheese the *Qallunaat* eat. Mmm. It is my favorite dish."

"Eeeee! My grandmother gave me a piece when I was little, and I chucked it all up," Ashoona said. "It smells so bad; I don't know how you can eat it. But maybe now that we are facing starvation, I would try a bite and keep it down so that I can have the energy to walk and something to warm my blood."

In September, an early taste of winter descended on the encampment bringing with it the first snowfall. The windy, cold days were interspersed with a few beautiful autumn days. Aula, Ashoona and Pinnaq were out on the lower slopes picking berries. They found a generous harvest of blackberries, the hard, little fruit that gives so much nourishment despite a miniscule size.

Once the berries were gone, the expedition again depended on the occasional ptarmigan or rabbit that the men shot and on the supplies in Ludwig's boxes, now seriously diminished.

"That is the last of the cocoa," Aula announced to the women. "No more Sunday treats till we get home to Blacklead; that is, if we ever get home."

"I survived without food for a month after eating my family's remains. Now, I cannot die, and you cannot die. My survival was a sign, Aula, so don't worry."

"Why shouldn't I worry? We have only a few bouillon cubes and a small box of biscuits, providing the boss has not snitched them. There is no sugar, no flour, no oil for cooking. I need to eat if I am to nurse my baby. Paloosie is young, and he needs food to grow. This expedition is doomed."

"Dat is enough, women." Ludwig was working in the tent and understood by her tone that Aula was complaining. "Stop that talk. You vill not die. The ice vill freeze, and ve vill shoot the seal and eat. If you continue with this talk, I vill fire you."

"Really?" Ashoona replied. "And how do you fire someone when we are months away from our village? Aula is rightly concerned for the safety of her family. We have no food left, and you knew from the beginning that we were not adequately supplied. We must think about turning back before deaths weigh heavily on your conscience, Mr. Boss."

"Never! I must travel up the coastline and meet the people from the vest. Dat is still my plan, and once the ice freezes, there will be no problem."

"I have a proposal," Kilabuk offered. "I will build kayaks like in the old days, and then we can hunt the seals. It will be dangerous because we do not have the right materials. If Paloosie and I can get out on the water, I can shoot seal."

"Ya, do dat and immediately. Why didn't you think of this first?"

"It is not easy to make a safe boat when all I have is a few caribou skins and odd pieces of wood from the rowboat. The best skin for a kayak is walrus, but there are no walrus here. If

I use the wood from the rowboat, I need to know that we will return to Blacklead this winter and not need the boat to cross Lake Nettilling."

"If my people vould not delay all the time and take me north to meet the Igloolik hunters, then ve vill return before the ice breaks up next spring."

"Mr. Boss, I will try. We will make two kayaks, and I will show Paloosie how to bring the seal back to shore."

Kilabuk and Paloosie pulled apart the rowboat to make frames for the kayaks, then stretched caribou and sealskin over the hulls. Kilabuk was a master-builder in whatever project he undertook. He hurried the job, but he still had to be careful because their lives depended on the seaworthiness of the kayaks. It was even more important to build the crafts securely because they had no food, only the smallest scraps. They *had* to shoot a seal.

Kilabuk and his son said their farewells to Aula before they embarked.

"This is dangerous," Aula cautioned. "We always use the walrus skin for kayaks. When we dry and stretch the skin in the sun it makes a kayak as strong as steel. Is there no other way to find food? Maybe ask the boss if we can turn back because we have a cache on the shores of Lake Nettilling. Except for the rapids, it wouldn't be that tough to paddle upstream on the slow-moving Koukdjuak. We could make it as long as the boss has enough biscuits and soup in his box. I can't lose you and Paloosie."

"We won't drown. Paloosie kayaks well. He can handle the waves better than any man I know. Maybe not better than our Ashoona, but very good for someone as young as Paloosie. So don't worry. Soon I will have a fat seal for the pot and blubber for your lamp."

As Kilabuk reassured his wife, he knew that it would be a miracle if they were able to kill a seal and bring it safely back to shore. Kilabuk worried that if the kayaks tipped over, they might not be able to get the wretched little boats to roll up in the waves. And he was certain the powerful winds that blew down on Foxe Basin would kick up fierce waves.

They each stowed a rifle in the cockpit of their kayak and paddled out into the deeper water, heading north up the channel. It was impossible to shoot from the makeshift kayaks unless the ocean was calm, and in the Arctic, calm seas were rare.

"We'll paddle to that peninsula where we can watch for the seals. Once we spot a pod, I want you to launch your kayak. As soon as they come within range, I will shoot, and then you must paddle as fast as you can out to the seal and spear it before it sinks. I'll try to hit the seal in a way that prevents it from sinking and keeps it from losing all its blood into the ocean."

"Why didn't we hunt next to the camp? Is that because the water there is too shallow? Where do seals like to swim?"

Kilabuk patiently explained the way of the seals: the tasty young ringed seal that Aula wanted for cooking and the bearded seal that would keep the dogs from starving to death. But even if all they could bring home was an old, bearded seal, it would be enough to save the expedition from starvation. Even if the seal bled out in the ocean and there was nothing to make the life saving *kaju*, or blood soup, the blubber and rich dark meat would save them.

They reached the rocky outcropping, and Kilabuk and Paloosie climbed up to their observation post. It was an ideal place to hunt from because the ocean was deep there, and even at low tide, there would still be a few feet of water. Now, they had to wait and watch.

But Kilabuk and Paloosie found no sign of life in Foxe Basin. It was as if the animals had departed and all that was left in this dreary region was the small encampment of Inuit and the obstinate scientist with his far-fetched goals. They waited throughout the day, and as night fell, they curled up in a crevice, covered themselves with a caribou skin and slept uneasily through the wind and cold.

"Wake up, Paloosie," Kilabuk whispered. "The seals are here. Launch your kayak, but be careful. The ocean sleeps quietly now, but I feel a breeze so it may get choppy soon." Kilabuk moved slowly and quietly. He lay down on the flat cliff top to give himself the steadiest firing position and aimed at the young seal, a ringed seal. His shot was accurate, but the seal rolled at that same moment, so instead of a head shot, the bullet pierced the seal's chest.

Paloosie was in his kayak and paddled out from the shore as soon as he heard the shot. The ocean remained calm, and for a few seconds, Paloosie could see the seal. Then it disappeared under the water along with the entire pod. Paloosie paddled furiously over to where the body had sunk below the surface. It was gone, sinking to the bottom of the ocean, and the rest of the pod had escaped.

"My shot was poor," Kilabuk said as Paloosie reached shore.

"No, it wasn't. The seal rolled just as you fired, and the bullet likely hit a lung." Kilabuk and his son were disheartened at the loss of their kill, at the continued suffering this would cause the expedition and at the dismal thought of spending another day out on the rocky cliff with no food and little shelter.

They hunkered down out of the wind, but with an eye on the ocean. The waves were kicking up, and spotting the seals among the white caps was difficult. Kilabuk had his binoculars and Paloosie his sharp, young eyes. Both peered intently out to sea. Often Paloosie thought he saw a seal, only to be tricked by boiling white caps and his strong desire for the hunt to succeed.

Finally, after the sun had set and the evening winds screamed about them, Kilabuk spotted a small pod. But he had the wind to contend with as well as the poor light. He motioned to Paloosie to be prepared to fetch the seal.

"My shot must hit directly on your head, so little *natsik*, don't move, swim straight to me."

Kilabuk fired and saw through the scope that his aim was perfect. The seal would stay afloat until Paloosie reached it. Kilabuk felt relief for a moment until he realized that his son was paddling into the biggest waves the youngster had ever attempted. The kayak rode up the waves and then dipped out of sight. Kilabuk held his breath until once again Paloosie appeared above the turmoil of wind and water. Then came the difficult task of harpooning the floating seal without tipping the kayak. Even Kilabuk would have had trouble maintaining balance without both hands on the kayak paddle. Kilabuk's heart beat wildly as he stared out to the ocean looking through the binoculars.

"He throws the harpoon! Good aim. Good boy! Now, careful...Oh no!" Kilabuk exclaimed, as he watched intently.

The fragile kayak flipped, and all Kilabuk could see was the bottom of the makeshift boat. Kilabuk raced to his kayak and headed out to where Paloosie's kayak bobbed up and down. He could see no sign of his young son.

Then, as if in a dream, Kilabuk saw the kayak roll up, with Paloosie still inside and with a smile on his face as wide as an *ulu's* blade. Kilabuk felt such joy that tears came to his eyes. The father took the harpoon from Paloosie and latched the tether onto the seal. Now, Paloosie could paddle with both arms and stay upright in the growing storm. The successful hunters knifed through the waves and into the boiling surf near the shore.

The two had to land safely as the waves churned up along the steep rocks. The closer they paddled to the shoreline, the more turbulent the waves became. The seal dragged on the small kayak, causing Kilabuk's little craft to tip dangerously with each surge. Ahead they saw a small bay between two towering rock outcroppings. They turned their boats toward the sandy shore and drove through the waves and up onto the sand. They were safe. They had food for their family but could go no farther in the storm. They pulled the seal on shore, and Kilabuk gutted it with a few skillful slices. They ate a chunk of the raw seal and felt energized immediately from the nutritious red meat.

When the winds died down during the night, father and son paddled through the calm waters of the channel and soon reached the sleeping camp. It was the end of their starvation, at least for now.

One seal does not last long with six people, and the hunters had little luck in the next month. As ice began forming on the basin, any attempt to kayak in the ocean would be suicidal. Once more the Inuit in the encampment kept their eyes on the ocean waiting for the ice to form so they could hunt safely. Ashoona and Aula begged Ludwig to turn back, but he was adamant that the expedition continue. He would not allow his project to be compromised.

"Ve have to make our way north, and it is my hope that ve vill meet the people from this part of the Arctic," Ludwig told them. Pinnaq was the only one who wanted to travel north along the coast. Her homeland was a month away by dog team, and her people often came to make winter camp in this area. Although she yearned to see her friends and relatives, she also felt concerned that they might turn her away, that they would not accept that she had eaten human flesh.

Will they allow me back into the community? Pinnaq was pulled to her home but also afraid.

Chapter Fourteen

Death at Foxe Basin

Soon all the seal meat was gone, and once again, the expedition was brought to its knees. A thin layer of ice formed out on Foxe Basin, but it would be some time before the ice would be solid enough for the hunters. Kilabuk and his son Paloosie went out on the land every day hoping to find animals. They had seen polar bear tracks, and with the fresh snow, they were able to track the animal across the tundra. It was a big bear, and Kilabuk worried that his Winchester would not be powerful enough to kill it instantly. He wasn't fond of polar bear meat either, especially from an old bear, as this one appeared to be.

Ashoona accompanied Kilabuk and Paloosie on the hunt. She had grown tired of life in the tent, where the lack of food was making everyone irritable. Ludwig had become despondent and often grew angry at Ashoona's slightest mistake in recording information on the animals.

"It is not that I do not appreciate your intelligence. I am just so very homesick, and sometimes I fear that I may never return to my homeland. Everyone has been *gut* to me. I know *dass*, and I regret the days when I was short-tempered because Aula tried to get me to drink that disgusting *kaju*. All I vanted was to have a cup of tea with sugar, and instead she gave me blood soup. My parents, varm and vell fed in their home in Germany, vill be shocked ven I tell them about the life you endure. How can you live day after day in such extreme vant and not become depressed?"

He looked so thin that the women began to fuss over him, giving him the extra broth because he seemed unable to chew even the cooked meat.

"Boss," Aula said, "you get thin like old fox in midwinter. Your mother say, who is this? You get into box of biscuits and sugar. That will give strength."

"There is nothing left. Now I depend on you *gut* people to keep us alive. Soon ve vill go along the coast and meet the northern arctic people. They vill have food to share with us and the hunters vill see many seal on the ice."

He tried to sound hopeful, but it was clear Ludwig doubted that the group would find enough food or be able to travel north to find hunting groups from Igloolik. Again his inner voice told him that he would die out here hungry and cold, far away from his beloved homeland.

Ashoona enjoyed her excursions with Paloosie and Kilabuk on the days when the sun gave its brilliant light for the brief midday period and the wind didn't blow. It was late fall, and snow covered the tundra. They were tracking the polar bear up the lower slope east of the camp. They could see the tracks were fresh, and they closed in on the bear.

"I see him!" Paloosie had the sharpest eyes of the three and pointed to the bear moving along the hillside above them.

"Let's split up. Ashoona, you go with Paloosie. Run to the far side of the bear, and fire a shot to scare him toward me. I will hide behind the rock and shoot when he's close enough that I can be sure of a kill."

Paloosie was off running along the rock-strewn slopes with the grace and speed of a deer. Ashoona had a difficult time keeping up. They had to be quiet and stay downwind because if the bear sensed them, it would head farther away. They needed the bear to head toward Kilabuk.

The young boy got there first. He was about hundred feet away from the bear when he fired his gun into the air. The bear was startled and ran full speed in the direction of Kilabuk. Ashoona and Paloosie followed, but the bear's speed was well beyond anything a human could manage.

Once the bear was in firing range, Ashoona and Paloosie took cover so that Kilabuk could have a clear shot. Kilabuk moved out from behind the rock and fired. His shot hit the bear, but instead of going down, the huge animal lunged at Kilabuk.

"My God, no!" Paloosie yelled, thinking the bear would maul his father.

The fearless hunter stood his ground, took out his skinning knife and held it firm. As the bear reared up to come in for the kill, Kilabuk plunged the long blade deep into the bear's heart. The massive animal dropped at Kilabuk's feet.

"Kilabuk, no one will ever believe me when I tell them you killed a polar bear with a skinning knife," Ashoona said, relieved.

"Then don't tell the story." The humble Kilabuk was not the type of man to seek praise or attention.

Kilabuk, Ashoona and Paloosie skinned and gutted the bear with the skill of accomplished butchers. They removed its heart and liver for Ludwig, not sure he would be able to eat the rich meat. Next they placed as much meat as one person could carry into a large makeshift sack made from the bear's skin. Kilabuk took the heaviest load, and Ashoona and Paloosie each took a hindquarter. They piled rocks on the remaining meat and built an inukshuk over the cache. They planned to return the next day for another load.

The expedition members had no great feast on the hunters' return because no one in camp cared for the acrid taste of tough polar bear meat. However, the kill provided a good supply of fat to burn in the lamp and necessary sustenance to stave off starvation.

Ludwig refused to eat the raw meat and waited until Aula cooked a stew. Even then, when he tried to chew the tough, sinewy flesh, all he could get down was a little broth.

"Auch. I don't mind the cooked seal," Ludwig said, "but this old bear meat is not for me. I vould rather starve than try another bite."

"Drink more broth, Boss," Kilabuk urged. "You have to get your strength back." By this time, Ludwig was confined to his cot, too weak to walk and barely able to sit up for meals.

"Ve still go north to study this part of the Arctic," he mumbled. "I just need to sleep for a day, and I need the seal meat. Then I vill be strong enough to go on. Is the ocean frozen over?"

As he grew weaker, Ludwig continued to ask about the ice and the luck of the hunt. But when the ice was solid enough and the hunters returned with four young ringed seals, Ludwig was too ill to eat. He would sip a little broth and fall back to sleep. He knew his time was running out, and he became overwhelmed by depression and regrets. Then, as he grew weaker, he came to accept his fate. He became childlike with the people whom he'd once commanded with such arrogance.

"You have been so very *gut* to me," he mumbled. "I have brought you here where ve almost starved, and yet, you have always looked after me. You are kind people."

Despite the many conflicts with the driven scientist, the women now fussed over the dying German and were truly sorry for his plight. Aula carefully tucked caribou skins around his cold feet and tried her best to keep him from shivering. He could no longer eat and could barely sip even a little broth. Without food, the arctic cold crept through his body to his very core.

"My papers." They were the first lucid words he had uttered in days. "You must see that all my vork goes back to the university. There are letters to my dear mother. I know I vill never see her again.

"Mine *mutter*..." he whispered, and then he was gone.

"Oh, my God! Our dear boss," Ashoona cried, and Aula, who'd often criticized the German, wept for hours as if she had lost her brother. Even the sharp-tongued Pinnaq became teary-eyed, and Kilabuk, who never said a negative word about his boss, was silent for days. He wondered if he could have done anything differently to save the man he was charged to guide and care for.

But it was not for lack of effort and dedication by Kilabuk that Ludwig had succumbed. The scientist was a man raised in the protective environment of a wealthy Dresden family. As a teen, he spurned athleticism and turned to books. He was too slight, too effete for the demanding rigors of the Arctic.

Following Ludwig's burial, the ice formed solidly on the sea, and the hunters were successful. Kilabuk built a large igloo to house them all. It was not as big or as high as the *qaggiit*, used for dancing and celebrations, but had a large room, a storage area for meat and a lower entrance tunnel that kept the drafts from the living quarters. Kilabuk and Paloosie cut the snow blocks for the sleeping platforms, and Aula and Ashoona gathered flat rocks and dwarf willows to place over the snow platform. The layers of rock, willows and then caribou skins kept the snow platforms from melting from the warmth of their bodies. While the young women worked, Pinnaq looked after Minnie, helping the thirteen-month-old build a small inukshuk.

In preparation for the return journey to Blacklead, Kila-buk and Paloosie continued to hunt for seals. They killed a dozen extra seals that they allowed to freeze, so the group would be well supplied even if they were delayed on the trail.

But something happened to postpone their departure further. It was late November, and as Ludwig predicted, the northern Inuit from Igloolik arrived at the seal-hunting site.

At first, the families were delighted to find Pinnaq alive. However, the woman who survived by eating her children and husband could not conceal her actions. When she told her friends and relatives the details of how she survived her ordeal, they grew silent, unsure whether they should shun the woman or forgive her, unsure if Pinnaq should be allowed to join them on their return to Igloolik.

That first day was tense for both camps. Pinnaq remained with the expedition group, in tears over the reaction from her community. She felt they were justified. Wasn't it a sin, after all, to eat one's beloved children and cherished husband? Shouldn't she be damned for eternity? Pinnaq became despondent and refused to eat, even though the party had an abundance of food. Kilabuk assured her that she could return with them to Black-lead, but his offer did nothing to change Pinnaq's mood. Kilabuk realized that the distraught woman would starve herself in the midst of plenty if he didn't take action.

He walked slowly over to the Igloolik camp, thinking about what to say. Kilabuk was a quiet, contemplative man who said little, never bragged about his exploits and always avoided conflict. But now he felt the need to mend this rift.

"I must ask my friends from Igloolik to please welcome back your sister." Kilabuk began solemnly when he'd gathered the people together. "Her husband instructed her to live. She did not harm the children or her husband. They died of starvation even though Pinnaq gave them the last of the small amount of food. If she had not eaten the flesh of her family, the fox and polar bears would have fed on them. Instead her husband offered up his body so she could survive and return to her family and friends."

The northern Inuit listened to Kilabuk. Several nodded in agreement. Others talked among themselves, weighing his words, remembering others in the past who had survived by eating human flesh. They believed it was evil to kill humans in order to eat their flesh, though it was not evil to survive when the souls of the dead had departed and when there was no other choice. The Igloolik people agreed to welcome Pinnaq back. They shared tea with Kilabuk and invited the expedition party to celebrate with them before parting.

With adequate snow to construct igloos, Kilabuk, Paloosie and the Igloolik men built a *qaggitt* large enough for both groups. They would celebrate Pinnaq's reunion with her family and take the opportunity to share stories and play games. Best of all would be the treats that the Igloolik group had in their stores—cigarettes, coffee, biscuits, sugar and flour for bannock. They were generous beyond the understanding of the outside world, even to sharing the last of their meager stores.

The celebration went on throughout the night. First, the wonderful seal stew and hot, tasty bannock. One of the Igloolik women even brought out a jar of precious jam. After the dinner, a drummer from Igloolik pounded out a rhythm while the group listened for a while and then, one by one, they got up to dance. Little Minnie was the hit of the group, copying her mother's dance steps, her tiny face beaming with joy.

Two teenage girls in the Igloolik camp had eyes for Paloosie. One of them danced next to the handsome young man and brushed her arm against him, smiling coyly at him. Paloosie ignored her advances because he only had eyes for Ashoona.

When the older dancers tired, it was time for the games. Eight young men lined up to compete in the ear pull. A length of soft leather was looped around an ear of each of two contestants, and the men then pulled their heads back until the pain became too severe and one of them gave up. Paloosie and a strong young man from Igloolik were the final contestants. Ashoona and Aula could not watch because of the pain Paloosie was enduring. Finally, when the two women could not bear it any longer, Ashoona pleaded for Paloosie to give up. She knew the hefty man from the north would last much longer, and Paloosie might end up with a bleeding ear or worse, no ear at all.

"Try the high kick," she suggested, knowing that Paloosie with his flexibility and agility would suit that game far better. Paloosie conceded to his opponent, and the two men shook hands.

The women set up the next game, hanging a bone from the end of a string and attaching the string to the high ceiling of the snow house. The contestants would kick the bone with one foot and try to land firmly on the foot they kicked with. If a contestant failed to hit the bone or declined to try the kick, he was eliminated. For each round, the bone was raised higher.

Paloosie and several of the Igloolik youngsters easily hit the target in the first round. However, the stocky winner of the ear pull could not do a high kick and soon yielded. In the fourth round, only Paloosie and an agile Igloolik youth remained. When the target was raised for the fifth round, the Igloolik competitor declined. Paloosie kicked the bone then asked that it be raised again. He caught his breath before making this final attempt. Paloosie took two long strides toward the dangling bone, leaped up, and kicked his target, amazing the spectators with his high leap and firm landing.

When the games finished, two teenage girls from Igloolik agreed to throat sing, after being coaxed by their parents. They stood facing each other, holding one another by the shoulders and began the rhythmic chant. The object was to continue until one of the singers started to laugh. The young women were full of fun and within a few minutes one of the girls broke out in giggles, and the performance ended in cheers from the listeners.

Chapter Fifteen

Return to Blacklead

It was long into the night when the Blacklead people departed, returning to their snow house. One of the Igloolik girls propositioned Paloosie, hoping to get him to sleep with her in the big igloo. He smiled pleasantly and turned back to the igloo that he shared with his family and the beautiful Ashoona. Pinnaq stayed with the Igloolik families.

The celebration over, it was time for the Blacklead group to begin the homeward journey. Pinnaq was now reunited with her community and would return to Igloolik with them, and Ludwig Reiner, only twenty-seven years old, was laid to rest on the barren coast where he had placed such high academic hopes. His name would endure forever at the site where he lay. Before departing, Kilabuk and his small band gathered around his grave near the river that they named after Ludwig. They prayed for the soul of the man who had seldom been at ease during the time they knew him.

As Kilabuk and his group passed through the valleys that connected the west coast of Baffin Island and Cumberland Sound, an abundance of caribou kept them well provisioned on their land journey. And soon they were speeding across the frozen water of Cumberland Sound, anxious to return to their friends and family before Christmas.

⌇

One of the villagers spotted the weary expedition members approaching Blacklead Island from the north. By the time Kilabuk and Ashoona drove their dog teams into the village, friends and families, including Reverend Worthington and Henry, had gathered near the mission.

"We have lost our dear friend," Kilabuk called out in anguish.

Ruby, with her newborn daughter on her back, along with Amo and their other three children, were there to welcome their erstwhile companions.

Kilabuk handed Ludwig's diaries and research papers to Reverend Worthington, once more expressing his regret that he was unable to save his employer.

"You are not to blame," the Reverend said. "I had a premonition that our good scientist would not survive such a brutal journey. We will hold a service tomorrow for Ludwig so the villagers can express their sorrow."

"Henry," Ashoona said, beaming at her benefactor, "I'm so happy to be back. I hope you will let me work with you again."

"You are more than welcome, my young assistant. I've lost staff, and we have much to do with so many Inuit afflicted by tuberculosis."

"What is that?" Ashoona asked, as they walked to the clinic. She wondered if Joanna was one of the staff members who had left, but she didn't feel comfortable asking Henry in case the subject was still painful for him.

"It is another disease brought by the whalers and traders and seems to spread like wildfire among the locals. It affects the lungs and causes coughing and chest pain. We can do little except recommend bed rest until patients can be transported to a sanatorium in the south."

———————

It was a strange homecoming of mixed feelings. Sadness for the death of someone the expedition members were charged with looking after, yet happiness because they had all returned safely. But anxiety also gripped the village because of the disease inflicting the Inuit community.

Ashoona settled in quickly to the routine of the clinic, but soon the staff members were overwhelmed with patients suffering from TB, a disease that far too often ended in death.

Ashoona was usually the one to explain the disease to the Inuit patients. A few days after her return, she met with a frantic woman from one of the outpost camps. Tina was set to be transferred to the sanatorium in Winnipeg.

"They won't let me take my baby; she is still on my breast. They snatched her from me and put me here like I am a criminal. Why can't I take little Paloosie with me? Please talk to them, Ashoona. You have their language; you can help me."

"I'm so sorry, but even Henry won't allow the children to go to the sanatorium with their mothers. I know how dreadful this is for you, and I'll do what I can to at least let you see him before you go. I may get in trouble for this, so please don't say anything."

Ashoona carried the six-month-old baby to the clinic. As she held little Paloosie, Ashoona felt a surge of motherly warmth for the small bundle in her arms.

I wonder when I will have a little one to warm my heart and a husband who will love us. What a wonderful feeling that will be.

At the clinic, Tina was waiting anxiously to see her baby. Ashoona passed the baby to his mother who immediately opened her breast to the infant; peace was restored, at least for the time being. Ashoona gave Tina directions on how to protect the baby from the disease, insisting that the baby's visit be as brief as possible and that Tina must be careful never to cough near the baby.

Ashoona waited with mixed feelings for the ship that would take the TB patients south. Treatment at a proper hospital was their only hope, but the disease was still so new that no one knew whether the Inuit sent south would actually be cured and return home. And the Inuit did not really trust the *Qallunaat* and did not believe the doctors would cure them. Many of the afflicted were hiding, because the thought of being shipped off for many years to some unknown destination was far worse than the discomfort of the disease.

"It will be better if you go on the ship," Ashoona tried to assure the Inuit patients. "They will take you to a hospital, and you will have the best of care. You must go to heal yourself so you can return to your family."

But the Inuit patients were unconvinced. "No one returns from the hospitals. Tell me of one person who has been healed and returned. You can't. I know you can't."

And so over the next month, Ashoona and Henry made every effort to find the TB patients who were hiding, take them to the ship for testing and then try to persuade them that getting treatment at a sanatorium was the only cure.

"Henry," Ashoona said, as the ship pulled out of Blacklead with twenty local Inuit, "I don't believe this is the best way for our people, and I hate having anything to do with this. Do you know that instead of being called by their names, they are given numbers. Numbers! What are we? Prisoners to be picked up and taken away? I thought that only happened long ago. Do you remember when the explorer took one of our people to England to show him off like a freak, and the poor man died there never to see his family again?"

"I agree Inuit patients should be cared for in their own communities. I have written letter after letter advising the government to expand the hospital in Panniqtuuq by adding a TB ward. All I received was an official response supporting the program that removes your people from their homeland. The department spends a measly four dollars a year on health care for each Inuit in the north, so it's no wonder they seek the cheapest solution.

"If we could treat the Inuit patients in their own communities, they would recover more quickly. Sick people need their loved ones around them. Sending the TB patients on the supply ship to distant places and then to big city hospitals in Winnipeg or Edmonton takes too long and results in even more deaths. Three months on the ship and being away for two to four years is too long for these people. Once I move to Panniqtuuq, I'll try to add a TB ward to the hospital, but I'll have to do it without government help."

"You're moving to Panniqtuuq?" Ashoona's voice was strained.

"Didn't you know that I've been appointed to that hospital? You must come with me, and together we can try to get beds in the community for TB patients."

"Panniqtuuq!" Ashoona exclaimed. "The village I grew up in, where my father abandoned me, where my mother died, where my aunt sold me to Qillaq. Oh, I can't go back there!"

"You'll be fine, Ashoona," Henry replied. "I won't let them mistreat you, and I'll see that you are protected from Qillaq. Panniqtuuq is bigger now, with a police force and churches.

The government is building a public school to replace the mission school. You will fit in much better now that you have a job, money, and thanks to Ludwig, your scientific training. It will be okay. I promise."

"I hope you're right, Henry, and I hope you will take our friends Kilabuk, Aula and her family. I need their support and love because once I'm back in Panniqtuuq, I'll be labeled as 'the little murderer' and be the brunt of racist remarks again."

"Your people were racist toward you?" Henry asked. "I thought only the *Qallunaat* were guilty of racism."

"You're so naive, Henry. Of course, racism exists on both sides. The Inuit make racist remarks about the *Qallunaat,* and the *Qallunaat* make derogatory remarks about the Inuit. Not everyone, of course. Many *Qallunaat* truly believe the two races are equal, and many Inuit accept *Qallunaat* without prejudice. However, those who believe in equality of Inuit and *Qallunaat* are in the minority."

Over the next few weeks, Henry and his staff prepared for the move to Panniqtuuq. This was a promotion for Henry even though he was not really career-oriented. He did not dream of rising to the top of the bureaucratic ladder in the Canadian government but was content in his small arctic enclave. He could live out his life in the north, making his rounds, dog mushing to the outpost camps and attending church on Sundays. He hoped someday to be fluent in Inuktitut, to treat his patients in their own language and be accepted as a member of the community. He accepted his new appointment because it would give him the opportunity to make changes to the system that would benefit the Inuit.

In early July, the supply ship arrived that would take Henry and his entourage to the hospital in Panniqtuuq. Ashoona felt a mixture of anticipation and fear. Did Aunt Amaruk still hold a grudge? Was Natsiq in the village, and had she married James? How would the villagers respond to her caring for them at the hospital? These questions warred within her and gave her little peace as the ship powered across Cumberland Sound toward Panniqtuuq fjord. She'd had her happiest and most miserable days in the little Inuit village. What was in store for her now that she was a young woman with a job and money and some level of prestige?

A pale moon shone in the half-light of the midnight sky when the ship dropped anchor in the fjord. The tide was high, so the passengers were able to go ashore immediately.

"Henry," Ashoona asked, "may I stay at the hospital tonight? I don't have a home here anymore. My dear, old friend Aula passed away while I was on the expedition. And even if she had lived, I couldn't stay in the same house with her grandsons because they are now men and certainly not marriage material for me."

"You are a staff member, and the hospital will be your home. Try to put aside the past and hold your head up high. Your aunt mistreated you, but you're on a new leg of your journey and should be proud of your accomplishments."

It was a difficult time for the hospital staff. Most of the Inuit in the village were afflicted with tuberculosis. Ashoona understood the anguish the people felt when they were told of their illness and informed that they would be sent for treatment far from their homes and their loved ones.

A few days later, Lucy, a friend of Ashoona's from her mission school days, arrived at the hospital asking to see her.

"You must help me," Lucy cried. She held the hand of her two-year-old, and on her back was her six-month-old baby. "The ship taking the TB patients away will be here soon. They'll force me onto the *Nascopie,* and they won't let me take my children. Please help me, Ashoona."

Hers was the familiar and heart-wrenching story that Ashoona had faced at Blacklead. She had to tell her friend she had little choice. But Lucy was the only one at the mission school who had not teased and bullied her. And when Ashoona's life was shattered by her father's departure and her mother's early death, Lucy had comforted her. When the community turned against Ashoona after Davidee's death, Lucy stood by her, believing in her innocence.

Ashoona had been certain that Lucy's life would always be perfect, and during Ashoona's tumultuous years living with Aunt Amaruk, Ashoona often wished she could trade places with Lucy. But now her friend's idyllic life was fractured. Lucy, a young dedicated mother, had studied at the Anglican mission, passing her grades with ease.

As was the custom for most Inuit girls, Lucy married while still in her teens. However, hers was not an arranged marriage; it was a love match and her husband was a loving and responsible man of her choosing.

Her husband, Joe, worked for the Hudson's Bay Company, hunting whales and rendering the oil. When the whaling industry failed, he continued to work, picking up odd jobs to supplement the seal and caribou he hunted.

But now Lucy's future was in jeopardy. If separated from her children for several years, they would see her as a stranger when she returned. She might also lose her husband because women who went south to the sanatorium often did not return. She was desperate.

"Let's hide you," Ashoona said quickly, trying to formulate a plan. "Don't get on the boat, but you can't stay with your children because you could infect them. Can you live outside the village while you recover? If you do, I promise to look after you."

"But what about my baby? How will she be fed? And my little Amo? Who will look after them?"

"Bring them to the hospital; the baby will have to take the bottle. I'll bring the children to see you regularly if you agree to be careful. Joe can look after them when he is not hunting or working. But you must rest. That is the only cure."

Lucy was one of the beauties of Panniqtuuq and regarded as a most desirable wife. She came from an important family; she could sew, speak both English and Inuktitut and write in both languages. But she was faced with a challenge that intelligence and status could not solve.

〜〜〜〜

Within a few days, Lucy left the community, crossing the fjord by boat along with Jonasie and Mary, an elderly man and his wife. Jonasie was infected with TB, but even though Mary was healthy, she refused to be parted from him.

The energetic woman with cheeks as round as a peach, and strong, stout legs insisted, "I will fetch whatever you need and care for you when the disease slows you down."

The trio set up camp across from the village in a spot called the Qulliq because the valley was shaped like the lamps that light the igloos.

From July to freeze up in late October, Ashoona crossed the fjord to check on the small group and deliver staples—flour, coffee, sugar from the clinic and meat supplied by Joe. Lucy's husband often operated the motorboat so that Ashoona could hold the baby and look after the toddler as they crossed the fjord. And Lucy was always waiting on shore as if she spent her days with her eyes glued to the ocean hoping to spot the boat launching out from the village.

"My little ones! You've grown so much!" The toddler ran to Lucy, but before she picked him up, Ashoona handed Lucy a mask.

"I scrubbed every part of me in freezing water," Lucy told her. Beside the camp, an icy stream tumbled down the valley. Ashoona shivered at the thought of immersing a foot, let alone bathing, in the water.

"Just one hug," Ashoona cautioned. "And please be careful not to cough."

"Are they happy? Have they been healthy? I miss them so much."

"Amo is content. He plays quietly with empty boxes, anything that can be made into a 'house.' He is old enough to adapt, but little Alukie cries and cries unless we walk her and sing to her. Aula helps me, and I'm getting very good at singing for hours at a time. She will be quiet as long as I sing, but the minute I put her down, she screams. Finally, I have to leave her because I have work to do. So guess what? Minutes later she is asleep and wakes with a smile. So don't worry; you must think about getting better."

Lucy was not known to be emotional, but she could not stem her tears when her babies had to be passed back. Before the visit ended, Ashoona gave her patients a box of supplies.

"Not too much sugar," Ashoona explained. "The government is rationing food—only so much sugar and butter for each person until the war is over."

"The war!" Lucy cried. "I hardly know what is happening in the world when I am home. Now that I live out on the land, the Germans could invade Canada, and I wouldn't know. What's happening with that horrible Nazi with the weird mustache?"

"The Germans are bombing England daily. We listen to the news every night and hear of cities blown apart by the Luftwaffe. The Brits are sending their children to Canada to keep them safe. But the Royal family has decided to stay in London and keep the Princesses Elizabeth and Margaret with them.

"The idea that we have to pledge allegiance to a king on the other side of the ocean used bother me," Ashoona continued. "But I admire the way King George and the Queen have acted while all around them the country is being bombed and there is real danger to their family."

At the end of the visit, Jonasie asked for just a little tobacco, but Ashoona had to refuse. It was Henry who had approved the supplies, and he was adamant that none of the patients be allowed to smoke. His involvement in hiding them would get him fired if word got out to officials in Frobisher Bay.

The first snow fell in September, blown in by one of the hurricane-force winds that assaulted the valley and prevented anyone from going out on the sea. After the storm, Ashoona crossed the fjord, but she did not have anyone to operate the boat, so she could not bring the children. Lucy met her on shore, disappointment clearly written on her face. However, Lucy looked much stronger.

"How are you doing? Are you still spitting up blood?"

"No sign of blood, and my cough is better. Before the fjord freezes up, I hope I'll be well enough to return and be with my babies. What about that man of mine? Has he found a new woman?"

"Don't worry about Joe. He's as faithful as the disciples of Christ."

"Didn't one of the disciples deny Christ?"

"Well, I should have said faithful as Mary Magdalene was to Christ."

"Yes. Women. They are faithful. Right."

In mid-October, Ashoona made one final trip across the fjord. The winds blew fiercely from the Penny Ice Cap, through Auyuittuq Pass and across the fjord. The waves kicked up against the motorboat, almost capsizing it. When she finally beached near Lucy's camp, the young mother and the two elders met her at the shore, their belongings packed.

Ashoona knew immediately that Mary had become infected. At least now the elderly couple would go together south to the sanatorium. As for Lucy, hopefully the tests would show that she was free of the disease. She looked healthy, and her cough was gone.

Chapter Sixteen

The Place Where We Take Our Clothes Off

The *Nascopie* floated offshore in deep water waiting for boatloads of Inuit from Panniqtuuq to come onto the deck of the ship the Inuit called, "the place where we take our clothes off." It was late October when Ashoona lined up with the other villagers to be tested for tuberculosis. She knew what awaited her. So did Henry. He held her hand as they walked to the small boats docked near shore. Before she stepped in, Henry took her face in his hands and kissed both cheeks.

"You will be back, Ashoona. Be strong, and get well." Henry's voice was unsteady. He felt responsible for Ashoona's illness. He had convinced her to accompany him to Panniqtuuq where they would be exposed to the disease every day, and he had reluctantly supported her when she asked to hide Lucy.

"I know what you're thinking, Henry," Ashoona said, kissing his cheeks in turn. "It was my decision to help care for patients, and I realize that my trips across the fjord in windstorms opened the door for me to get TB. I'll do whatever the

nurses and doctors down south tell me. Two years, maybe four...
if that is what it takes, but I *will* be back."

Apart from Ashoona contracting the disease, the past
year in Panniqtuuq had not been as dreadful as she had feared.
At fifteen, her life was taken up with work at the hospital and
community feasts and events. She tried to avoid Natsiq. The first
time they met was in the Hudson's Bay Store. Ashoona thought
it was Natsiq but had to look twice. She had a baby on her back,
a bright-eyed little boy. Ashoona's first thought was that he must
be James' son.

Natsiq was still as spiteful as ever. "So...you stole his gun
and dog team. You've disgraced my mother. And now you think
you are special, working in the hospital. Are you going to crow
over me now that James can be yours?"

"You didn't marry James? Then whose baby is this?"

"My baby. That's all you need to know."

"Natsiq, why can't you be civil and let the past go? I don't
harbor a grudge against you. Maybe your mother, but you were
only a child, and we do stupid things when we are young."

Natsiq did not answer. She turned and walked away. That
was last summer. But for now, winter was approaching, and the
Nascopie was anchored offshore waiting for passengers to board
for the trip to the sanatoriums down south.

From the dock, the people from the village were herded
onto cargo barges and then into a cargo net to be lifted onto the
ship. Treated more like commodities than human beings, once
on deck, they were lined up to be x-rayed, and officials gave each
Inuit a number on a metal disc that they wore on a chain around
their necks or wrists. As they waited their turn to be examined,
both Ashoona and Natsiq coughed. They knew.

The doctors spoke in English, directing a few fortunate
people back to the community—the Inuit whose lungs were clear
of the disease. The infected villagers were not allowed to return

to their homes, not allowed to pick up any cherished belongings, not allowed to say goodbye to their loved ones. The explanation for the harsh treatment was lost on them. Ashoona knew she would be sent south, and Natsiq understood enough to know she was infected. However, many of the elders, several who were seriously ill, did not understand.

"What are they saying?" the confused elders asked Ashoona.

"We are to go into the hold of the ship where they have sleeping and living quarters for the TB patients. We will be taken south to a hospital, maybe in Winnipeg or Montreal, perhaps in Edmonton."

"But they won't allow us to get our belongings. I cannot go without my Bible. Tell them, Ashoona, to bring my Bible." It was a woman in her sixties, crippled from years sitting crouched scraping sealskins, her face wrinkled from the fierce winds and sun of the north. "Why won't they let me go to my home to get my Bible, my sewing?"

"They are worried that people will not come back to the boat, that some will hide in the village and infect others." Ashoona did what she could, asking the people returning to shore to retrieve belongings for those that could not go ashore and to send messages to loved ones.

Natsiq was frantic when the doctors told her that her baby could not go with her.

"You bastards can't take my child!" she yelled.

Ashoona had to give Natsiq credit for her spunk. She admired how her cousin fought for what she wanted, sometimes to the detriment of others. But sometimes Natsiq's blunt approach got results.

Despite Natsiq's protest, the nurse reached into the young woman's *amauti*, lifted the baby boy out and handed him to the nearest woman.

"No, not her, stupid *Qallunaaq*, non-human!" Natsiq used the meanest expression the Inuit had for the *Qallunaat*. "Give to her," Natsiq ordered, pointing to Amaruk. "She is grandmother. She take him." Natsiq was furious. "And what milk he gets? That nasty stuff you give babies in the southern hospitals?" There was no end to Natsiq's fury. No tears. Just unrelenting anger pouring out in her broken English.

The Inuit were then loaded into the hull of the ship, separated from the crew and not allowed on deck. The *Nascopie* did not head south to Montreal immediately. It was on its supply run commissioned by the Government of Canada to drop off food and supplies and to take the medical team to every community in the Eastern Arctic to test the Inuit for TB. The journey from Panniqtuuq to Montreal would take three months.

The patients were not mistreated on the journey. They had the same food as the crew and the medical team, but the conditions in the hold were abhorrent. As more and more people came aboard the *Nascopie,* the patients' quarters became unbearably crowded. Children had to double up in the bunks, and by the time the ship loaded the last of the patients, several of the men were sleeping on the floor. The patients' quarters were noisy and hot. It was next to impossible to sleep because of the constant coughing, children crying and the older patients getting up several times a night to stumble to the toilet. Because of the length of the sea journey and the unbearably crowded conditions, the disease worsened in many patients, especially the fragile elders.

Except for the irritable Natsiq, most of the Inuit endured the inconvenience and suffering without complaint. They had spent their lives painstakingly scraping sealskins, mending every small tear in their clothing, stitching perfectly or sitting for hours at the seal holes and could patiently tolerate most any physical suffering. However, they were confused about where they were going and wanted to know how they could stay in touch with their loved ones. Most, if not all, had never been away from the arctic tundra. They also wanted to know more about the disease that afflicted them.

Ashoona became the link between the medical staff and the patients. She painstakingly translated Doctor Crowley's explanation of the disease, trying to find an Inuktitut word for everything he said. Unfortunately, she was so careful that the words fell like a cold wind on the Inuit.

"The doctor says the disease is sweeping across Canada's north, infecting eighty percent of the population, and that since the beginning of the twentieth century, tuberculosis has been the greatest cause of death in humans around the world. Except for the slums of Hong Kong and Africa, the Inuit of Canada are suffering the highest rate of infection."

"Ashoona," Natsiq interrupted, frustrated. "You speak like a *Qallunaaq*. We know the Inuit are getting sick, but we want to know why, and we want to know where we are going. You ask the doctor to tell us."

Ashoona put the question to the doctor. "He says that because we live in such small houses with so many people in one room, we pass the disease on to one another, then the entire family becomes ill. He says that out of ten people in the north, eight of them have the disease. It is what they call an epidemic."

"The *Qallunaat* gave us this disease. I know that. Now they don't even tell us where they take us." Natsiq was still fuming over being separated from her baby. She screamed at Ashoona in her native tongue, "Now all we are is a number; they take us from our family, our home. They take my baby away. It is not our fault. Why we don't stay in Panniqtuuq?"

Ashoona interpreted for Doctor Crowley. "He says they could not build a hospital big enough and soon enough to treat everyone, and it is less costly to send the TB patients south where they already have hospitals. He says we will get better faster there because we need fresh air, and we can be outside, not huddled in tiny houses with poor air quality and poor food."

Ashoona paused to speak to Doctor Crowley. "You are wrong about the food. The seal, caribou, berries in the fall, clams we dig and even the vegetation from the intestines…it is good food for us. The old people tell us that no one was sick until the whalers came and brought germs. I know something of this. Germs do not live when it is so cold. If we had been left alone, maybe we would have been hungry; some would even starve, but we would not have all your diseases and die before we get to live our lives."

"It's good that you talk back to him, not just be baby repeating words that are lies." Natsiq again offered her opinions with little self-restraint.

When Ashoona interpreted Natsiq's rant, Doctor Crowley looked sad, his face collapsing in on itself. He knew that hospitals should have been built in the northern communities, that for people who had family nearby, bed rest and fresh air would improve their health. He also knew that months cooped up in the ship would hasten the death of several of his older patients. He listened with interest to Ashoona.

"You are a bright one. You worked with Doctor Russell at the clinic in Panniqtuuq, isn't that right?" Crowley was a thin, short man with a graying beard and a stooped posture. Ashoona thought he was about fifty, which seemed quite old for an assignment in the Arctic. He appeared to be embarrassed by the situation, not wanting to mistreat people but aware that he had to follow the orders from Ottawa.

"If you worked in the hospital, you know a little about nursing. I need help with the patients because I have only one nurse, and she does not understand your language," he went on to say. "Would you interpret for us during the voyage? I can offer only little pay, but maybe the work will help you avoid the boredom of the long voyage."

"Yes, of course. I would like that," Ashoona answered.

"Oh, I should have introduced myself earlier. My name is Peter Crowley, and I work at the Edmonton hospital."

"Is that where we're going?" Ashoona asked.

"Yes, some of you. Others will go to Winnipeg, some to Montreal, wherever beds are available."

"The people need to know where they will go so maybe you can decide, and then I will tell them," Ashoona continued. "When do I start working for you?"

"You can't come to my office because patients are not permitted on the top decks. I'll come for you tomorrow, and we'll make the rounds of the sick quarters."

"Until tomorrow then, Doctor Crowley. Thank you."

"Peter…call me Peter."

Since Natsiq bunked next to Ashoona, she could not help but hear the conversation with the doctor. "So now the little murderer is to save people from death," she said bitterly. "I suppose you think you are important with that good English and that spoonful of medical training." She spoke Inuktitut so that the doctor could not understand, but other patients did.

Kiruk, an elder, came to Ashoona's defense. "Don't listen to your cousin's bitterness. She is angry because James would not have her, and to make James jealous, she flirted with Ron, also a young policeman, but a *Qallunaaq*. She had that baby with him, and she only drove James away.

"Ron also gave babies to a thirty-year-old mother and her two teenage daughters. That young Ron made so many babies in Panniqtuuq, enough to form…what do you call it…a hockey team? He had many things the young girls wanted, so he smiled, gave them gifts and then he gave them babies. The elders ran him out of Panniqtuuq before their young women were all ruined. So, Ashoona, don't mind her sharp tongue. She is a sad, angry girl, that Natsiq. Now the people talk about her in the community. They say she disgraced her mother."

Soon after, Kiruk and Ashoona became friends. Ashoona helped the elder cope with the hardships of the journey. The old woman was incontinent, often wetting her bed, so Ashoona found sanitary pads and showed Kiruk how to use them. Kiruk never uttered a word of complaint, although it was obvious that the disease was wracking her thin body. After years of kneeling over the sealskins to scrape them clean, her legs were bowed. When she got out of bed, she had to stand for several minutes to adjust to the pain of standing.

Ashoona watched, noticing how Kiruk shuddered with pain just to walk to the toilet. "I can see that it hurts you to walk. You weren't always crippled, were you? I'm sure it was you that the villagers in Panniqtuuq told me about. They said that in your second marriage to the man from Alaska you had finally found love after an unhappy marriage. What did they mean?"

"It is a strange story," Kiruk said, chuckling. "You know that in the old days, parents often arranged marriages for their daughters. If a family had too many girls, marriage to a good hunter assured the parents would be fed in their old age. If too few girl babies were born in a community, parents would go to other communities to look for wives for their sons. We were bartered off like possessions…like dogs.

"When I was barely a woman, not even having my first bleeding," Kiruk continued, "my parents forced me to accept Jacobie as my husband, a man three times my age. My parents made the arrangements when I was born. Jacobie had some sort of control over them, and they couldn't refuse when he came to claim me. He made my stomach sick just to look at his squat body, his short fat neck and his thin hair. Eeeee!" Kiruk shrieked.

"I tried to run away, but he found me, tied me to his dog sledge and took me away. The first night in the snow house, he forced himself on me. It was so painful and horrible for me that I wanted to take an *ulu* and slit my throat. I hated him every day until he died."

"What happened to him?" Ashoona was captivated by this story that closely paralleled her own experience.

"The following spring, he fell through a lead in the ice."

"Did you push him?" Ashoona asked with a chuckle.

"I would have, but it all happened by the grace of God."

Ashoona told Kiruk about her kidnapping and her escape from Qillaq.

"You were lucky to escape. You avoided having that awful man jump on you like a dog and treat you worse than a dog. I thought my life ended the day he came for me. But later, with my second husband, I was happy and found the best part of the day was getting under the caribou skins. I must rest now, but later tonight I will tell about the good man I married, the man from Alaska."

Once dinner was finished, Kiruk continued her story while they sat around the dining tables enjoying tea. At first, she spoke only to Ashoona, but soon others gathered to hear about Kiruk's days traveling with the explorers during the remarkable era when sailing ships tried to find a passage through the Arctic Ocean.

That first night when Kiruk began her story, Natsiq walked away, caught up in her own misery and unwilling to share in the storytelling. For most of the day and evening, Natsiq isolated herself. Her one solace were the forbidden cigarettes begged from sailors who could not resist the pleas of the dark-eyed beauty.

The next afternoon, Natsiq was smoking on the part of the deck cordoned off for the patients. She heard footsteps behind her.

"That's bad for you." It was Kiruk, also puffing on a cigarette.

"You're smoking too, so don't tell me what to do."

"I won't outlive this disease. You are young and beautiful; you should look after yourself so you can return to your baby."

"What do you know about me? You're not from my village."

"I lived many years in Qikiqtarjuaq, just across the mountains from your village, and I visited often. I know all about your baby, the boy's father who deserted you, and I know about the troubles between you and your cousin. Life treated you well until you went with a man to make James jealous. Now you smoke and do not rest. If you're not careful, the disease will create ugly lumps on your body. The lumps will grow and the doctors would have to cut your leg off."

"You're lying!"

"I don't lie, little Natsiq, but I do worry about you. Your father came from my village; he was a good friend to me. He asked me to watch over you."

"No one can help me. Just leave me alone!"

"I have a story I want you to hear. It is about a journey much like this one, a journey where people who were angry and selfish hurt one another, and others who cared and risked their lives to save one another. After supper, come and listen."

The old woman limped along the deck.

"It hurts you to walk. What's wrong?"

"Just my old body falling apart," she said, laughing. "Once I was a young woman, running along the ice behind the dog team. Now, all my joints ache. Each day I have a new pain, but all is bearable; it is just this aging sack I'm in that is falling apart. I'm still the same young woman who never tired, kept our igloo warm and my family clothed in warm caribou skins."

Kiruk's words gave Natsiq pause to think.

What the hell, Natsiq thought. *Maybe I'll go and listen to the old bag of bones. She can't make me any more miserable than I am already.*

Chapter Seventeen

Search for the Northwest Passage

Thulat night, after the evening meal was eaten and the dishes washed and put away, Kiruk continued her story.

"I was a young widowed woman when I married Karuluk, the man from Alaska. I met him when he traveled to Qikiqtarjuaq with the famous Captain Bartlett, the shipmaster who sailed our waters, led Admiral Peary to the North Pole and was respected and admired by the Inuit who worked for him. Bartlett chose Karuluk as his guide, because of his loyalty and his skills as a hunter.

"After our marriage, I left my home and traveled with my husband and Captain Bartlett far, far away to Point Barrow, a place where the explorers hired Inuit to hunt for their expeditions. Karuluk could find birds when no one else could see them. He could also shoot seals and keep them from sinking into their breathing holes.

"Captain Bartlett was hired by that lying, cheating Stefansson to sail north from Vancouver searching for the

Northwest Passage. But this time Stefansson planned to sail from west to east across the Arctic Ocean. Others had tried to find the passage beginning from the east. Bartlett hired my man Karuluk, my family and three other Inuit hunters. By then I had two babes, one three and the other five. Karuluk had traveled with Captain Bartlett before; he always served him well and was treated well in return. This was Bartlett's first trip with Stefansson. But what did the famous explorer do? Do any of you know?"

"I heard he received awards," someone replied.

"He should have been jailed for killing his own men and for putting my family at risk. As soon as the ship was caught in the ice near Herschel Island, he took his favorites and two Inuit hunters, abandoned the ship and walked to safety. If it hadn't been for Captain Bartlett and the Inuit hunters, we would all have perished. Many of the men on that ship died. Do you know why? Did you hear about it?"

"No. Tell us," Natsiq said, now transported out of her misery to the events in the land of no sun.

"Ah, that I will tell you tomorrow. Now, I go to my bed."

Kiruk painfully raised herself from the chair and shuffled over to her cot.

Time ground along slowly for Natsiq. For days she stayed on her cot, staring blankly, almost catatonic. She only moved to sneak out for a smoke and to listen to Kiruk's story. It was the old woman's tale that helped Natsiq endure the months at sea trapped in the *Nascopie*.

"So please tell us why they died. You said the ship was caught in the ice. Were they rescued?" Natsiq was impatient as Kiruk settled into her chair the next evening and waited for quiet.

"The ship drifted with the ice pack from Herschel Island across the Bering Strait. Then the ice cracked and the ship went down, but not before Captain Bartlett ordered the supplies loaded onto the ice. Four scientists asked for their share of supplies, loaded a sledge and walked away. Twenty-one were left, sixteen *Qallunaat*, one other Inuit hunter and our family of four.

"Few *Qallunaat* can survive in that land of ice. The four men who left were the most educated of the crew, doctors of this and doctors of that with years of university and knowledge of many, many books. But did they know anything about how to cross the arctic ice, hunt for food and find their way to Nome, Alaska? Of course not. I knew they wouldn't survive.

"Karuluk told them not to go, but they said he just wanted to keep their share of the supplies. What they said about Karuluk was not true. My husband wanted everyone to survive because he was certain they would all die out on the ice—fall through a lead, lose their way, run out of food and be helpless as babes. Of course, he was right. The four men never reached land, and no trace of them was ever found. They thought they were better than us Inuit, but they got lost in the bitter arctic winter.

"Not all the *Qallunaat* were so arrogant. Captain Bartlett respected the Inuit and treated us fairly. We all loved another young man, a mapmaker named Mamen. He was athletic, cheerful, always offering to take on the most difficult tasks. If all the *Qallunaat* were like Mamen, then the months we endured would have been more bearable.

"We built snow houses and settled in to live out that first winter camped on the ice close to where the ship sank. All we had were dry biscuits, canned pemmican, oil, tea and a little sugar, which was barely enough food to last until the seals returned.

"Miles to the west was Wrangell Island where the birds would nest in spring and where we could hunt for seal. We couldn't see the island from our camp, but the explorers, and of course Karuluk, knew it was there. Four brave *Qallunaat* struck out for the island. They had a gun, a sledge and enough pemmican to last them for two weeks. Once they found Wrangell Island, they would return, marking the trail, and then the camp would follow. We had to move before the returning sun melted the ice from under us. Days passed, and they did not return. I will tell you later how they died, but then it was left to the ones who remained to find our way across the Bering Strait to Wrangell Island.

"Captain Bartlett sent young Mamen, who was always willing to face danger. In his home country of Norway, he skied from town to town faster than a dog team. He didn't boast about it, but we found out later that he was a champion skier who went to other countries to race. Mamen set out across the rugged sea ice on his skis to mark a path to Wrangell. We knew it would take many hours for him to cross because he would have to struggle over the high ridges of ice pushed up by the sea.

"I worried that he wouldn't return, just like the other search party. We waited for days as the winds raged. I was sure he would die out there without a snow house to protect him from the cold.

"Just when we had lost hope of seeing him again, I saw a speck in the distance. I didn't know if it was Mamen or if my eyes were deceiving me. But the speck grew larger, and I saw it was the young Norwegian. My heart filled with joy knowing he had survived. He was frostbitten and exhausted, so we took him into the snow house and slowly warmed his frozen hands and feet. When he recovered, he told us he marked a trail to Wrangell Island, and that he would lead us there.

"Before the ice broke up, we packed our camp and followed Mamen's route to the island. He was a brave man. Because of him we survived and found our way to land. And if it wasn't for the Inuit hunters, we would have starved. All we had to eat during many weeks was foul-tasting pemmican. If the Inuit hunters did not hunt for seals, make clothes and snow houses, the *Qallunaat* would all have died.

"Once we got to Wrangell Island, the two Inuit hunters went out on the ice each day to wait beside the seal holes, but they came back with nothing. Again we were left with only the pemmican. Several *Qallunaat* became sick with swollen legs and their bodies bloated for no reason."

"What made their bodies swell?" Natsiq demanded. "Did anyone survive?"

"The Inuit survive even when we have only a skin to make soup. Mamen helped us through those dark days when the seals did not come to their breathing holes. He was such a good person, caring for the sick, wrapping their frozen feet, making tea. Another *Qallunaaq* was foolish and greedy. I sewed *kamiit* for him to keep his feet dry, and he would forget to stand them up to dry at night. He left the *kamiit* in a pile to freeze, and in the morning he couldn't put his feet in them. Then he walked on the ice in only his socks. When he stole food from my little family, I wanted to push him through the ice, but in the end, he died from frozen feet."

"You still haven't told us what caused the strange bloating," said Natsiq.

"Enough for now. I am weary. There is time. We still have to travel to Qikiqtarjuaq."

As they ate their meal the next evening, Natsiq again pressed Kiruk, "So what happened to the crew and your family?"

"Wait till later. That is the time of stories, not when there is food."

The patients gathered after supper, waiting quietly. Kiruk settled down in her chair, her tea nearby.

"The brave Captain Bartlett left with the other Inuit hunter. The captain planned to walk across the Bering Strait to

Siberia and then along the coast south until he could find his way to Nome. If he reached Nome, he would telegraph for a rescue ship. Before leaving, he told us not to fight, to share and to help one another. He took an Inuit with him because he knew that the hunter could find the seals and the polar bears and protect everyone from the bitter cold. Bartlett was a *Qallunaaq* with courage and intelligence.

"After Bartlett and the hunter left for Russia, trouble started because we no longer had the good captain to keep order." Kiruk cleared her throat and sipped her tea.

"What trouble? Just tell us a little more," Natsiq begged.

But the old woman broke into a violent coughing fit, and no one would think of asking her to continue. Ashoona helped her to bed and brought her a hot drink of honey and lemon.

"I want to live my life like Kiruk, helping people, even the ones who have been cruel to me," Natsiq told Ashoona, who was truly surprised at Natsiq's seeming change of heart.

"You find her story fascinating, don't you?" Ashoona asked Natsiq when they were getting ready for bed that evening.

"She makes me forget," Natsiq replied. "Goodnight, Ashoona. I…"

"Yes?" Ashoona asked.

"Nothing. I'm tired."

The next evening Kiruk continued her story.

"Where was I?"

"The captain went to get a rescue ship," Natsiq offered.

"Ah yes, when Bartlett left, we had no one to lead us. Everyone agreed to share food from the hunt, but two of the *Qallunaat* cheated. When they killed ten birds, they would eat five before returning to camp. Everyone knew they were not sharing their hunt and that they were stealing from the meager supplies in the camp. When Karuluk killed a seal, we split the meat evenly, with each person having a share. The *Qallunaat* argued over the food, yelling in foul language and scaring our two girls. Mamen knew who was stealing, and he didn't want to stay in our camp.

"He could not stand the fighting and decided to leave the camp. Mamen and three others set out to make camp on a smaller island, taking their share of the supplies with them, including guns, tents, ammunition and the pemmican. They left right away because the ice would soon melt, and they would be trapped on Wrangell.

"We were left with men who did not share, who argued and fought. I didn't want to stay in camp while Karuluk went out to hunt. I worried about the safety of my children, and so I asked Karuluk to take us with him and he did. The girls knew they had to be quiet while their father waited at the breathing hole. We watched them closely because sudden ice shifts caused cracks to open up.

"The sun grew brilliant, sweeping away the snow, melting the ice and bringing summer. The ice went out, and we could no longer hunt for seals. But then the birds came to Wrangell Island. We took the girls with us to help gather eggs near the tall cliffs.

"All through the summer, we waited for a rescue ship, hoping that Captain Bartlett and the hunter had reached Nome and would send help. As the seamstress for the *Qallunaat* and my family, I worked all summer till my lips bled, chewing skins to make boots for their feet and sewing *amautiit* and pants for the oncoming winter.

"The ice would soon form again, and already the birds had flown south. We were facing our second winter on Wrangell Island and preparing for death. The *Qallunaat* discussed how they would bury the ones who died first because the bears and fox would not feast on the bodies piled under rocks. We were sure that by next summer we would all be dead.

"My husband was very sad, but in his worse moments of despair, our youngest daughter, who was only three, would tell him not to worry, that we would live. Her good nature helped him when rescue seemed impossible. Karuluk loved our two daughters, and he worried that they would perish in that bitterly cold land because he had accepted this job. He could have taken us across the ice and traveled to safety, but my husband would not leave the others. The trip with the children would have been difficult, but he would have given his life for those girls; they were everything to him."

Kiruk paused in her story and sipped her tea. Ashoona thought of how her father had abandoned her. Again, she felt the pain in her chest, no longer anger, just an overwhelming sadness over something she could never understand. She fought back her tears and pushed aside thoughts of her father. She wanted to hear about the little girls trapped in the Arctic. Kiruk coughed, sipped her tea and continued.

"I thought someone was stealing food from our tent. I saw a *Qallunaaq* leaving with a piece of seal. We knew that two of the *Qallunaat* were taking our share of the hunts, and they stole from our tent, keeping food from our children.

"The weather grew bitterly cold, and all the animals left the island and the sea. We had no seal meat left, and all the supplies were gone, even the awful pemmican. We were ready to accept our fate as winter set in. Over the next month, a thin sheet of ice formed overnight and then melted during the day. We knew that in a few days or weeks, the temperature would drop and the ice would become too solid for a rescue ship to reach us. We huddled in our tents because there wasn't enough snow to build an igloo.

"We wondered about the four men camped on the other island. I was worried about Mamen and wished he had stayed in our camp. I wanted my family to be with a good *Qallunaaq* like the young Norwegian, not with these selfish thieves who cared only for their own survival. But Mamen was far across the strait, through a sea that was gathering ice flows day by day. Soon the chunks of ice would harden together, and we would be stuck on the island until spring when the people in the rescue ship would find only our bones.

"The ice had already formed solidly along the rocky coast when the captain of a passing ship spotted a tattered tent. The captain had heard that Stefansson's ship had sunk and that the survivors were in desperate need of rescue. Bartlett had made it to Nome, an unbelievable journey. He had telegraphed for help, and here was a ship. Although the captain saw no sign of life, he sounded the horn and set off flares. A man staggered out of the tent."

Kiruk paused, letting her story sink in. "What would you do if you were near starvation for nine months, if you had prepared yourself for death, and suddenly, you heard a ship's horn and saw the boat only a short distance offshore?"

"I would scream and wave my arms. I'd be the happiest person in the world." Natsiq seemed to have forgotten her own suffering in listening to Kiruk's tale.

"Two others crawled out of the tent, and the three men just stared out to sea at the boat. They didn't wave or yell. They were like stones; they couldn't believe they had been saved. One of the survivors aimed a gun at the rescuers. The rescuers landed their boat and approached slowly, raising their arms to show they meant no harm. One of the rescuers walked up to the man with the gun and gently pushed it aside. 'We've come to save you, not harm you,' he told them. Finally, the men realized they were being rescued, and soon the survivors were on board, and the crew bathed, fed and clothed the starving men.

"The best man among the Qallunaat, Mamen, was buried on that lonely island. He had spent the last month of his life caring for his three companions until he fell ill." She paused, thinking of the tragic death of one so young.

"Only three were rescued!" Natsiq could not mask the anxiety she felt for those camped on Wrangell Island. "Did all the others die, including your little children?"

"Be patient," the old woman cautioned. Storytellers did not appreciate being rushed and disliked being interrupted. "Listen carefully, Natsiq. Learn to help people; learn patience; learn that your life can be saved."

"I just want to hear the story," the young woman replied sullenly.

The old woman shook her head sadly.

"Natsiq is not the only one that faces severe difficulties on this journey to the land of the *Qallunaat*. Help one another or life in the south may trap and kill you like it killed many from that icebound ship."

The listeners nodded, then realized that Kiruk was going south but she would likely not survive, that she would die in a foreign land. They were silent and sad as the old woman continued.

"I am coming to the end now. Soon our ship will dock at Qikiqtarjuaq. I have family there. I need to go on shore one last time to see familiar land and feel the winds. When we dock, promise you will sneak me onshore. Maybe you need to tell a little lie to get me past the *Qallunaat* who don't want me to leave the ship." The listeners all nodded.

"Now we finish.

"The rescue ship sailed north, following directions from the three they had rescued. The captain spotted our encampment on Wrangell Island, two big tents. We immediately realized the ship was there to save us. We yelled and waved; my husband hugged our two girls, tears streaming down his face, and I knelt on the ground and cried. And so our suffering was over. The ship's crew cooked for us and gave us warm clothing.

"Out of the twenty-five sealed in the ice in the month of no sun, fourteen lived because of the people who shared and cared for one another. The three survivors from the other island told us how Mamen cared for them, that he gave them his share of the fresh meat and ate the putrid pemmican. They lived because of his sacrifices." Kiruk's voice faltered. She sipped her tea and her voice grew faint; she coughed, obviously in pain.

"You don't have to continue, Grandmother. Rest," Ashoona advised.

"I finish now," Kiruk said with difficulty, and in a tired voice, continued.

"So do you want to know why Mamen, strong and athletic and barely out of his childhood, died with his legs and stomach swollen?"

"Yes, please," they murmured. The listeners suggested lead poisoning, parasites in the bear meat, tuberculosis, diseases that brought death in the Arctic.

"Was it the pemmican?" Natsiq asked.

"Yes…the pemmican was the killer. The careless Stefansson did not test it, and the men who ate it met a horrible death. Stefansson would not accept responsibility for risking the lives of people who had placed their faith in his leadership. He had brought thin jackets, poor tents, a ship that could not withstand the ice and rotten pemmican. Several survivors supported one another. The Inuit and a few *Qallunaat*, especially the kind, young Mamen, always helped and always shared. Others fought and cheated.

"The four brave men who tried to find a route to Wrangell Island all died. When their skulls were found, they still had tins of pemmican, guns and ammunition. They died because of the foul pemmican.

"So now, you go south to the *Qallunaaq* hospitals. Care for each other and help others to endure this dangerous journey you are on. Assist the ones who fall ill and comfort those who lose hope. Be like Mamen; he sacrificed his life to help others.

"I have a rest now."

The old woman lay down, coughing and breathing fitfully. As the boat dropped anchor at Qikiqtarjuaq, Kiruk took her last breath. And so it was that Kiruk was buried in her own land by her own people.

Chapter Eighteen

The Sanitorium

The ship sailed south, and the days passed quickly for Ashoona, but for Natsiq each hour felt like a week. She missed her son, and although she was not as angry, she became more and more despondent. Kiruk's story had affected her. Natsiq wanted to be strong like Kiruk and help people, but she still felt she could not atone for wrongdoings during her youth. It seemed her baby son had been taken from her as punishment for her actions, and because she was unable to rest, her condition worsened.

"You should talk to her," Peter advised Ashoona. "She'll kill herself. I know she smuggles smokes into the sick bay. With Kiruk, I turned my head because I knew it wouldn't make a difference for the dear, old gal, but Natsiq is young and strong. If she continues smoking, she may be inviting death. Please could you talk to her."

"Natsiq and I have some bad history between us; I doubt she will listen to me." Ashoona tried to explain what happened during those painful years she spent with Natsiq's family.

"Come with me anyway, Ashoona, and interpret. I know she understands a fair amount of English, but discussing the details of the disease should be in her own language."

When they reached Natsiq's cot, she was staring blankly at the ceiling.

"Natsiq," Peter began softy, placing his hand on her shoulder. "I'm worried about you, and I want to ask you to do me a personal favor. Please, please, you must stop smoking and try to eat your meals. I know that most of your dinner comes back untouched. If you don't try to help yourself, the tubers will grow, and they will attack your legs and steal your beauty."

This got Natsiq's attention. Kiruk had said the same thing. Maybe the old woman wasn't lying. The thought of being physically repulsive hit a nerve.

Peter continued. "Walk with me early in the morning before the others in the ship are awake. We won't infect anyone if they are all snoring in their cabins. Would you do that?"

"Will that keep me from getting ugly lumps on my legs?"

"I can't promise anything. I can only say that if you continue smoking, not eating properly and not resting, you'll become very ill, and the disease will steal away your youth."

The next day, Natsiq became the doctor's walking companion, striding around the deck in the early morning as the ship powered along the rocky coast of Baffin Island. The sun shone overhead early in the day and cast its rays over the snowcapped mountains, creating a breathtaking pink landscape.

Peter remarked on the beauty of the land, and as their morning walks progressed, Natsiq began to appreciate the colors and shapes of the land and the beauty of the deep blue-green icebergs that floated near the ship.

By the time the ship reached the south end of Baffin Island, Natsiq's bitterness and restlessness had begun to dissipate. Peter tried to draw her out about the guilt she suffered, speaking slowly since her understanding of English was spotty. They also spoke about Kiruk and the message the old woman had given them before she passed away. Remembering the story-teller's words helped Natsiq understand that she could choose to be different, to help the elders and the sick and not just think about her own problems.

"I be like guys who fought and stole," she admitted in one of her morning walks with Peter. "I know I bad to Ashoona; and I tell her, but not yet."

"You will be with Ashoona at the hospital. You'll find the time and courage to talk to her. You and Ashoona will recover and return to your village, where you can help people and atone for the things that weigh on your conscience," Peter promised. "Your disease is not far advanced, and now you are eating and looking healthier. What about those cigarettes? Have you given that up?"

"That is hard. At night, I need one smoke. I know I should count sheep, like you *Qallunaat*. But I sneak on deck to beg for just one smoke."

"You're trying Natsiq. That's what's important. When you arrive at the hospital you won't find any cigarettes, so the sooner you cut down, the easier it will be when you are at the sanatorium."

"Where we go?"

"I'm not even sure, but I'll do my best to have you and Ashoona transferred to my hospital in Edmonton. Your English is improving, so maybe you can also help us as an interpreter. Someday, you must tell me about the bad blood between you and Ashoona."

"It her fault for coming into my family and spoiling everything. I still mad at her."

"Ah, Natsiq," Peter said, disheartened that she clung to the past, "that's life. If we hold on to anger, we lose the chance to move on. I have to see my patients now, so you go to your breakfast."

The ship sailed south, leaving behind the land of the Inuit. Many of the elders watched sadly as the *Nascopie* left Baffin Island and the familiar mountains they had known all their lives. They had no idea what awaited them in the land of the *Qallunaat*. Most of their experience with white people had been negative. Whalers invaded the north and treated the Inuit with disdain; the explorers, for the most part, did not appreciate the skills of the Inuit, and for this mistake, they traveled to the northern seas unprepared and perished. The traders were a mixed group. Some integrated into the Inuit community, like Ashoona's father, while others held strong racist views and treated the locals as if they were subhuman.

Government officials came to the North believing they could save the Inuit from disease and starvation. They were well meaning, but they did not understand the language and segregated themselves from the Inuit people. And now these Inuit were on a journey to a foreign land where they would be lost in a sea of white faces, in a strange culture. They wondered if they would ever return to their homeland and to their loved ones left behind. No one in the group of Inuit was convinced that life in the south would be bearable.

The ship docked in Montreal on a hot, September day. The older Inuit, still dressed in caribou jackets and sealskin boots, suffered from the oppressive heat.

"What's happening now?" they asked Ashoona, the person they turned to for information about their plight.

"We will go in buses. Some will go directly to the sanatorium here in Montreal. The rest will take a train or a plane to other cities."

People onshore stared as the strange entourage left the ship. Once the locals found out that the Native people were TB patients, they backed away. The disease was a source of fear for everyone.

"They act as if we are freaks," Natsiq muttered.

Peter noted that the patients were not only extremely hot but also disturbed at being the source of so much unwanted attention.

"We will go soon. Ashoona, help me get everyone on the buses. I'll call out the numbers; could you please translate and get them to board the bus. The first bus will go to the san in Montreal."

It was a slow process moving more than two hundred Inuit onto the buses. Peter told Ashoona to board the last bus, along with Natsiq.

"This bus is only the first part of our journey," Peter explained. "You interpret, Ashoona."

"We will go to a school where you will get a bunk for the night, and tomorrow, we will go to the airport and take a plane to Edmonton. It is a long trip, but you will get food on the plane and be able to wash up in the bathroom. Your long journey will be over when we arrive at the Charles Camsell Hospital."

The Inuit patients had heard of Montreal and Ottawa, but Edmonton? Where was that? What would life be like in this land that was as hot as a fire?

The next day, the plane was cooler and the food welcome, at least for the younger patients. They received a tray each with cooked meat and vegetables, then a sweet dessert and all the coffee or tea they could drink. Ashoona enjoyed the trip and was entranced by the scene from her window as they flew over cities and then west over the flat prairie. The trip was much more difficult for many of the elders, who had never eaten anything but wild game and felt nauseous when they ate salad or cooked vegetables.

The afternoon was sweltering hot when they landed in Edmonton. A tall, broad woman met them at the airport. She was dressed in a stiff white uniform, her brown hair neatly tucked into a nurse's cap.

"Ashoona, please interpret. This is Nurse Ann," Peter explained. "She will go with you to the sanatorium and get you settled in. I must go home because I have not seen my family for many months. I'll be at the hospital soon."

"*Ullaakkut*," Nurse Ann addressed them. "That is the only word I know in your language, so Ashoona will interpret for me. Please follow me across the tarmac to the airport bus. Later we will transfer to the local bus that will take us to the hospital. It's a long trip, but when we arrive at the hospital, I hope you will be comfortable."

The Inuit patients were encouraged to hear the nurse make an attempt to speak their language, but they were dismayed by her military-like approach. Nurse Ann was all business. They felt herded rather than accompanied, and when one of the patients paused to look around, Ann hurried him on.

"Please follow me closely, and don't dilly-dally." Ashoona had trouble interpreting that expression. Soon they reached the bus, and the twenty patients made their way to the seats. Boarding the bus was like walking into a hot oven.

"Take your seats quickly, please." Nurse Ann was not being unkind, but she was by nature assertive and accustomed to being obeyed. "Move to the back, and be quick like bunnies." Recalling the rabbits on Baffin Island, Nurse Ann's expression brought a chuckle from one of the older woman and a scowl from Natsiq.

"I not a rabbit."

Once underway, the bus took them from the airport across the city.

"Ashoona," one of the elders said in their Native language. "It is too hot for us. I feel sick."

"I don't know what I can do," Ashoona responded. "Peter might have helped, but I don't think this nurse will listen."

They all looked at the nurse sitting very tall and straight at the front of the bus. At nearly six feet, she towered over the diminutive Inuit people. Both Nurse Ann and the bus driver wore surgical masks, which just added to the elders' uneasiness.

"Please, Miss Nurse, could you help us?" Ashoona asked in a soft voice.

"Be quiet back there. We'll be at the hospital before you know it."

"I told you," Ashoona said to the elders. "She will not listen to a simple Inuit girl."

"Tell her they are ill in this heat. Go up there and tell her," Natsiq said emphatically.

"*You* go up to the front of the bus," Ashoona answered.

"She doesn't understand me. You go."

Ashoona moved slowly along the aisle to the front.

"Miss Nurse. We need some help for the old people."

"What's that?"

"The elders are not feeling well because of the heat. They still wear their caribou skins and their sealskin boots." Ashoona spoke softly, and Nurse Ann could barely hear her above the noise of the bus and the Edmonton traffic.

"Sit down, right now. I'm responsible for you, and I can't allow you to stand up in the bus." The nurse stood up to her full height and nailed Ashoona with a look that sent the young Inuit woman back to her seat.

As she passed Natsiq, her cousin lit into her, "You must tell her loud, not act like a baby fox that whimpers! I'll go see that...what do you call in English...that battleaxe."

Natsiq stomped up the aisle and placed herself firmly in front of the nurse. "The old people need clothes like them people. Not silly nurse clothes but clothes like them outside wear." Natsiq pointed to the lightly dressed people walking along the street in cotton dresses and short-sleeved shirts. "You gotta get water for the old and the children. And you do now. If old people die, it is because you let them die and you have big trouble."

Natsiq finally got the nurse's attention.

"We will transfer to another bus soon. It's getting cooler now, so the local bus won't be as hot. When we arrive at the hospital everyone will get cotton gowns."

"You do now," Natsiq insisted. "Stop bus now!" she yelled at the bus driver. "I see a store with clothes. They gotta have."

The bus driver looked at the nurse for direction. Ann shook her head.

"We will transfer to the other bus in one block. When we're there, I'll see what I can do for the elders."

The bus stopped on a busy downtown street.

"Now quick as a wink, everyone, off the bus. And you, young lady, get Ashoona. I'll need the two of you to help me. Ashoona, you go to the restaurant and ask for water. I will go to the store for clothes.

"I'll have to pay myself, and it's unlikely the hospital will repay me," Ann said as they walked across the parking lot.

"Thank the Good Lord that my husband makes big bucks and is generous. I certainly couldn't afford this extravagance on my wage. Look after the elders, Natsiq. Take them into the park. It's shady there, and they can use the public washroom. I'll be back in two shakes of a lamb's tail."

"Why is that woman talking about a lamb?" Natsiq shook her head, puzzled.

The nurse returned thirty minutes later, carrying several bags, and Ashoona followed with bottles filled with water. The girls passed the water around while the nurse approached the old people.

"Ashoona, tell them to take off their heavy clothes," Ann ordered.

Ashoona looked puzzled. "The women will not undress in front of everyone."

"Well, I never! Imagine modesty among the Eskimo! All right, you tell the women to change in the washroom. Hurry, hurry. Times a' wasting. Here are their clothes."

The women went into the washroom two at a time. Natsiq and Ashoona could hear the women giggling as they tried on the brightly colored cotton dresses, laughing at how funny their friends looked when they replaced the caribou *amautiit* with cotton dresses.

Ann's brusqueness disappeared abruptly; she could not resist chuckling along with her fun-loving charges.

The men also changed into cotton pants and shirts, which brought another round of laughter.

"*Qujannamiik*...Thank you," several elders said, smiling warmly at Natsiq.

She had helped them; they liked her.

"Enough now. Line up for our bus." Ann once more became the officious matron.

Soon the elders were seated comfortably, and the bus was underway again. The busy commercial center gave way to tree-lined streets and neat houses with green lawns and bright, flowered borders. As the bus continued, the houses were left behind, and eventually it slowed down and turned onto a rough dirt road and passed through a forested area.

Finally, the bus pulled up to a bleak-looking building. Here was the hospital, but rather than appearing like a place of rest and comfort, it looked like a prison. The imposing structure was three stories high, built of dark stone and surrounded by woodlands that included fruit trees. Before arriving in southern Canada, the Inuit had never seen even one tree let alone a fruit tree. Now they were surrounded by trees that closed in the views and made them feel uneasy. Everything was so different from their land of wide landscapes, cozy houses, tents and igloos.

"Are we really going to stay here?" Ashoona whispered to one of the elders. "Is this a prison?"

"We're here, folks," Nurse Ann announced. "Follow me as quick as a wink, and we'll get you registered and into beds."

"I not going to bed," Natsiq muttered in her broken English, intending that Nurse Ann hear her protest.

"Young woman, you are now under the supervision of the doctors of the Charles Camsell Hospital, and you will do whatever they say you are to do. Doctor Crowley has ordered bed rest for all patients, and bed rest you will do."

"You not my boss!" Natsiq yelled. "You Qallunaat think you better than us. You not. You could not stay alive for one day in our land, but here in your place you boss us around. I do what I want."

"We'll see about that, young woman. You'll learn to do as you're told or you may find life tough at the Camsell. Now, please line up."

The lobby of the hospital was oppressively hot, and the elders were weary as they lined up in front of a desk where a young nurse with fluffy blonde hair wrote numbers and names in a register.

"Your name, please." The elder looked at her blankly.

Ashoona stepped forward and interpreted. Even with her help, the nurse had difficulty spelling the unfamiliar names, so the line moved slowly. Ann noticed the older people were shifting uncomfortably, obviously finding the long wait tiring.

"Ashoona, please tell the older people to come with me and have tea. The younger patients can stay and get registered. Come to the cafeteria when you finish. We'll have a hot meal for everyone before you get assigned to your beds."

Well, I guess the old battleaxe can be human, Ashoona thought as she carried on with her job of spelling Inuktitut names.

The Inuit patients settled into a routine over the next two weeks. Dr. Crowley ordered complete bed rest for all the patients for the first week. Then after x-rays, patients with less serious symptoms were allowed to get up to use the bathrooms, while those more severely affected were not allowed out of bed, even to use the toilet. The elders turned to Ashoona to intercede with the doctors and nurses. They found it humiliating to be forced to use a bedpan. Natsiq was infuriated with the treatment.

"Tell the nurse they can walk to the bathroom."

"I told her that it's insulting for the elders to use a bedpan, but she insists on complete bed rest for Routine One patients. I'll ask her again, Natsiq," Ashoona responded, "but I heard the doctor tell Nurse Ann that the rules can't be changed.

I'm sorry, but maybe it will help them get better if they stay in bed and rest."

"You should talk to Peter. He is the big boss, right?" Natsiq added.

"Why don't you talk to him yourself, Natsiq? You became friends on the ship. Tell him that the elders are embarrassed."

Despite Natsiq's intercession, nothing changed.

"I'm sorry, Natsiq," Peter responded kindly. "I can't change the treatment. It's all we know for now. Soon there may be medicine to cure tuberculosis, but for now, bed rest is our battle approach."

"It feels like I in a battle here," Natsiq said. "The old people not like to have a bedpan."

"What I like about you, Natsiq, is that you're worried about your people and no longer dwelling on your own problems. When your symptoms improve, I want you and Ashoona to continue your education. Learn to speak English well, and you can help, along with Ashoona. It'll make the time go faster, and you'll be able to help the elders."

Natsiq and Ashoona shared a room with two of the seriously ill women, and both of the young women interpreted and helped the elders in every way they could. Natsiq even stopped hating Nurse Ann, who was diligently trying to learn their language. In fact, the strong-minded nurse had a soft side as they found out after a few weeks had passed, even getting a smile out one of the elders over the bedpan issue.

"Must be regular to be happy," Nurse Ann said in Inuktitut as she handed the hateful bedpan to the patient. The Inuit patients accepted the situation and gave Ann a warm smile for trying to learn their language.

The first year at the hospital was not as unpleasant as Ashoona had feared. Along with Natsiq, she attended high school classes at the hospital each weekday. Natsiq struggled with her studies, while Ashoona excelled, especially in science. Because of her training with the German explorer, Ashoona often knew more than the teacher. Ann approached Natsiq and Ashoona shortly before their second Christmas at the Camsell.

"You girls are now moving on to a different routine," she told them. "Since your very first week here, you were only allowed to get up to go to the bathroom, but now you can leave the hospital to go to church, and when the weather warms up, you can take walks in the park."

"We can walk in your winter," Ashoona told her. "In Panniqtuuq, our winter is windy and much, much colder. If we were home now, we would be going out with dog sleds to hunt caribou and would sleep in snow houses. It's not too cold for us. When can we go?"

"Sunday is a good day, girls. We have a beautiful valley where the Saskatchewan River flows. People walk there on their days off from work. But make sure you come back for dinner. I don't want to lose any of my patients."

"We would miss you, Nurse Battleaxe," Natsiq said with a chuckle.

Chapter Nineteen

Canadian Airmen

Ashoona and Natsiq were the only two patients from their village well enough to leave the hospital for outings. Though not best friends, they ended up spending a lot of time together. They never discussed the bad history between them. Ashoona felt that her cousin was sorry for what she had done, and Ashoona's life had improved beyond Natsiq's, so it was now possible for her to forgive, although she never forgot.

This was their second year at the sanatorium. A cool fall had replaced the oppressive heat of the prairie summer, and a blanket of snow covered the hospital grounds. After the confines of the stuffy hospital, Ashoona and Natsiq enjoyed the brisk cold of the Edmonton winter. The heat they could not bear, but wind and freezing temperatures were part of their lives. They strode out following Nurse Ann's directions to the valley trails in a landscape so different from the barren lands of the Arctic. The girls were unaccustomed to trees, and now as they walked the trail, the forest seemed to close in around them.

They wore their *amautiit*, made of heavy white cotton and decorated with brightly colored Inuit designs. Ashoona was taller than her cousin, taking after her Scottish father, with deep brown eyes like her mother. Natsiq was slim and petite, exotic looking with flashing eyes. Their dark complexions, beauty and unusual clothing turned heads wherever they walked. This day, they chose the river trails, where there was less likelihood of meeting inquisitive, and at times, bigoted locals. But today, others were walking the trails on this cold winter afternoon.

"Hey girls!" It was a tall, attractive Canadian airman, striding toward them on the snowy trail. His companion was a shorter, but equally handsome airman.

"Keep going, Natsiq," Ashoona whispered. "Soldiers are only after sex."

Ashoona averted her eyes as the men caught up; Natsiq glanced up and caught the shorter man looking at her. He gave Natsiq a warm smile, revealing even white teeth. His eyes were brown with dark eyelashes.

Natsiq's heart missed a beat. It was his beautiful brown eyes that captured her at first glance, and it was Natsiq's exotic beauty that stopped the airman in his tracks. When Natsiq paused, Ashoona grabbed her arm, steering her forward along the trail.

"I don't want anything to do with them. Come." Ashoona continued to pull her cousin away from the men until Natsiq resisted and shook herself free.

"I'm going back. You're making a judgment about them. You're just like the *Qallunaat* that say things about us. What fun is there in life if you are afraid?"

"No, Natsiq," Ashoona said. But it was too late; Natsiq turned back. The two men were waiting on the trail, watching the girls jostling and arguing.

"Hi, girls!" said the shorter man. "I'm Sandy, and this is my flying partner, Eddy." When Natsiq introduced herself and Ashoona, the soldiers had trouble pronouncing their names.

"Those are weird handles! No Mary or Susan, eh? So are you Indians?" Eddy flashed a smile that reminded Ashoona of James and his betrayal.

"No, of course not. We are Inuit from Baffin Island," Ashoona said in a cool voice. "I don't want any trouble with soldiers, and if you cause problems, I will yell."

"You have me wrong, Ashoona. I'm a farm boy," said Sandy, who was hurt by Ashoona's comment and struggled to find the right words to protest.

"Sandy is as safe a companion as your grandmother. He has spent his life pitching hay, cleaning shit...whoops, excuse me...mucking out the barn and milking cows. Sandy doesn't have any young women within sixty sections of your farm, do you, friend?"

"Eddy's nailed it. No women in my life, although my mother tried to marry me off to keep me from getting recruited. She found a fat farm girl and told me Mary Lynn was a good cook and can she ever sew quilts—Mom's idea of the perfect wife for me."

Sandy could not take his eyes off Natsiq. He could see that the lithe Inuit woman would never be fat. He fell in beside Natsiq, leaving Ashoona to walk beside Eddy.

"As you can see," Eddy told Ashoona, "Sandy is harmless. He doesn't know anything about women. What about you girls? What brings you to Edmonton?"

Ashoona told them about the TB hospital, explaining that both of them were free of the disease and that they were now studying for their high school certificates. She did not know what else to say to this polished man, and they walked in silence. Eddy felt her awkwardness and filled in.

"My parents ride me day and night to make something of myself. They came to this country with nothing and made a fortune through hard work. They expect me to be an achiever and make all their sacrifices worthwhile. Soon as this bum war is over, they want me to have my head in the books, so I really need a few days with a beautiful woman before I get into that Lancaster."

"Please don't expect me to keep you company. I'll be going to normal school and will need to concentrate on my studies." *Besides*, Ashoona thought, *I have to work hard for everything I want, while Eddy seems to just be floating through life with his parents' money providing a cushion.*

"We just want some company during our leave and to have someone back here thinking about us," Eddy responded.

Sandy and Natsiq found a bench overlooking the river and were enjoying the view. They moved over, making room for Eddy and Ashoona. A bright sun shone in a clear blue sky and the air was still with not even a whisper of a breeze.

Ashoona enjoyed the wide sweep of the valley. The land dropped down to where the ice-covered Saskatchewan River wound through the forested snowy valley. Ashoona missed her homeland, but the expansive view unspoiled by houses made her appreciate the beauty in the land of the *Qallunaat*. She enjoyed the scene while listening to Sandy talk enthusiastically to Natsiq.

"We expect to be fighting the Nazis when we get to England. Since the Yanks came in with us, the Krauts and Nips will get a taste of our airpower. For the first few years, it was one-sided with Goering and his boys bombing the hell out of the Brits. We're going to stop the air raids and give them back twice what they gave."

"You be careful. Too many young guys are coming home in boxes," Natsiq said as she took in the muscular farm boy with his closely cropped hair and pleasant face.

"We're both coming back, aren't we Eddy? You gotta get that college degree so your parents will feel their big bucks have been well spent. What was it that you were learning before you signed up?"

"Engineering. When the war's over, I want to build bridges and roads. Maybe I can build roads on Baffin Island. Well, I guess I'd have to build a bridge first."

Ashoona laughed at this idea. "There will never be any roads on Baffin Island, and they will never build a bridge to the mainland. We live near the Arctic Circle, and we travel by dog teams and lately, with those new snow machines. Build your roads down south. We don't like concrete and steel. We like our land as it is."

"Wow. You're very opinionated for an Indian." Ashoona was annoyed by Eddy's comment, thinking that here was an educated man who was cursed with money and family support that corrupted his behavior and attitudes.

"We told you we're not Indians, for Christ's sake!" Natsiq yelled. "We are Inuit, or I guess what you call Eskimo. You know, the people who build igloos and hunt seals. Indians are different from us as you are."

"Another lady with strong views," Eddy said. "Who would think that a quiet walk along the river would turn out this way?"

"Listen all of you," Sandy interceded. "Let's not waste time arguing. I have no opinions about anything except the price of wheat. But right now, I'd really enjoy a juicy hamburger. Can we take you girls out for supper?"

"I'd like that…" Natsiq replied before Ashoona interrupted her.

"Sorry. We are expected back at the hospital for dinner. If we don't return, Nurse Battleaxe will have the police after us."

"That's darn bad luck for us," Sandy said. "We start six months of training next week, then a short furlough before we fly to Britain. Can you give us a rain check for that meal until we complete our training?"

"Is that okay with you, Ashoona? You no longer think they're axe murderers?" Natsiq pleaded.

"For *Qallunaat*, they are acceptable." And to the airmen, Ashoona said, "But I'm still checking you both out. I will look forward to that restaurant meal."

Sandy was immediately likeable. About Eddy, Ashoona was unsure. Under his smiling, groomed exterior, slick uniform and shined buttons was a character Ashoona did not feel comfortable with. But it was just supper they had agreed to, and eating in a restaurant would be a wonderful break from the hospital food.

"I'm sure Nurse Battleaxe will let us stay away for dinner when you return," Natsiq said. "We don't have no hamburgers where we live."

***

Young men whistled at the Inuit girls and harassed them as Ashoona and Natsiq walked to the restaurant in downtown Edmonton. It seemed that many men immediately assumed that all young women with dark skin were prostitutes.

Natsiq and Ashoona arrived at the restaurant ahead of their dates and found a booth. Natsiq put a coin in the jukebox and "Chattanooga Choo Choo" came on. She bounced along the aisle, passing another diner on her way back to join Ashoona.

"Look what they're letting into this place. I ain't goin' ta eat with no squaws." The man was beefy-looking, with a gut that pressed against the buttons of his Macintosh jacket. He'd quaffed too many beers at the nearby saloon, and his words were slurred and loud. The patrons in the small restaurant stopped eating and stared, first at the drunk then at the two beautiful Inuit girls.

When Ashoona and Natsiq heard racial slurs, they usually walked away. But this evening they did not want to leave. They had been looking forward to the first restaurant meal of their lives.

"Ignore him," Ashoona advised. Natsiq's eyes flashed with anger and humiliation. She saw the restaurant owner approach.

"They gonna make us leave." Natsiq was almost in tears she was so angry. But instead the restaurant owner marched up to the drunk's table. He was Slavic in appearance, slightly balding, but sturdy and muscular. He wore a chef's apron over a white, pressed shirt and dark blue pants.

"Shut your gob. Dis here country has many different people, and in my place, dey is all welcome. When you finish, you scram, and don't come back." The unruly customer scowled, his face florid from too much booze. He bit on the toothpick he had stuck between his teeth and stumbled to his feet.

"Listen to him tell that jerk off," Natsiq said with a chuckle.

Ashoona walked over to the owner and put her hand on his shoulder. "Thank you so much for defending us."

"You are welcome, girls. Ready to order?"

"Our dates should be here any minute."

While this was happening, Eddy and Sandy were a block from the restaurant.

"I'm not sure if going out with the girls is such a great idea," Eddy said. "What if someone from our base sees us? We'll get ribbed all the way to London and every day during the war.

You know what the airmen call guys who go with the Indians? Squaw men."

"Hey, Eddy! They aren't Indians. Say that again, and Natsiq will dump me."

"Just tell me what you'll do if we get ribbed about our, what do you call them, Inuit gals."

"We'll tell them that our girlfriends are the most beautiful women we've ever met. If they continue to harass us, I'll give 'em a hiding." Sandy looked like he could tackle just about anyone. He was of average height but he looked powerful enough to throw a horse over a fence. His shoulder and arm muscles bulged beneath his heavy uniform.

"I guess you could handle them. Heaving hay bales must get you in fighting shape."

Shortly before Eddy and Sandy entered the restaurant, the burly drunk staggered past the girls.

"Bloody Indians ruining our town," he said under his breath.

"What an asshole," Natsiq muttered.

"Watch your language, Natsiq. Sandy and Eddy just came in. I get the impression Sandy is serious about you, and swearing won't go over well with his parents."

Sandy was all smiles as he approached Natsiq and squeezed in next to her. "You look even more beautiful than I remember. I bet you could eat hamburgers every day of the week and not spoil your figure."

"Stop flirting, Sandy, and let's order." Eddy waved at the waitress and gave their orders.

"Hamburgers!" Ashoona exclaimed after her first bite. "I've never had anything so delicious in my life."

"What do you eat up there in the Arctic?" Eddy asked.

"You will laugh at us." Natsiq had already suffered from the comments the hospital staff made. *You know they don't cook the meat. They just hack off raw pieces, even eating the intestines of the caribou.* These remarks were made in English in front of the girls before the staff realized that Ashoona and Natsiq understood English.

"I know what the Arctic people eat," Sandy said respectfully, "and it doesn't make me laugh. I'm impressed that in a land of ice and endless winter, people are able to survive. I can't imagine living in a land where I couldn't grow potatoes, corn, tomatoes and wheat for bread. In summer, we just go out the door and pick our food, and in the winter, we walk to the root cellar or freezer." Sandy ate steadily, but not fast, looking up at Natsiq between bites and smiling at her when their eyes met.

"I still want to know if you eat whale and seal, or was that just in the old days, before we came north and brought civilization."

Ashoona could think of nothing to say in response to Eddy's condescending remarks.

Another Qallunaaq *who believes that the English are the superior race, bringing civilization to the savages.*

At least supper was delicious, but she decided she wouldn't spend time with Eddy again.

The relationship between Natsiq and Sandy was taking a much more serious turn. The young airman was obviously besotted with Natsiq's beauty and feisty character. As they left the restaurant, Sandy invited Eddy and the two girls to his farm so Natsiq could meet his parents.

Ashoona felt caught. She knew Natsiq did not want to go alone, and she also knew that Eddy's attentions might become more and more objectionable.

Oh well, it's just one day. I can handle it, she thought.

Dinner with the Fredrickson family was another new experience for Natsiq and Ashoona. The large family ate around a big kitchen table loaded with vegetables, plates of beef, bowls of gravy, pickles and home-baked bread. The main course was topped off with cookies, custard and apple pie with homemade ice cream.

Sandy's mother was a short, sturdy woman with luxurious brown hair, a sparkle in her eyes and the energy of a teenager. She carried out the big meal with such competence and calm, getting up to fetch more food without missing a beat in the conversation.

"We already have one boy in France being pushed around by the Germans, now they're taking Sandy away from the farm. The only reason they get to take him is because we have two others here," she said, nodding at the teenagers. "And so we have to put a thirteen-year-old on a tractor and our fifteen-year-old on the combine, and two of them missing school in the fall to get the crops in! I don't want Sandy to go to England. Too bad we can't get you married off quickly so you can help your dad with the harvest.

"What do you think, dear?" she asked Sandy's father.

"What did you say? Oh yes, I'm all for Sandy proposing to the lovely Natsiq. Time you we had some grandchildren to keep you occupied."

Mr. Fredrickson was a quiet, broad-backed man. He didn't say much during dinner, deferring to his loquacious wife and occasionally giving an "umm hmm" to indicate his appreciation for the tenderness of the steaks or the perfect consistency of the mashed potatoes.

"Mother, did you know that Jimmy Weigan got himself hitched just the other day to a gal he doesn't care that much for and all because his family wants him to stay on the farm." Sandy's fifteen-year-old brother was protective of Sandy and not at all sure that a hasty marriage to the strange beauty was the best choice for his older brother. "Besides, we'll do just fine, and Sandy will have a great adventure. I wish I was eighteen, so I could sign up."

"Thank the good Lord you're not. It's worrying enough for us to have two sons risking their lives."

After dinner, Mr. Fredrickson, along with Sandy and the two younger Fredricksons, showed Eddy the farm buildings and the stock of cattle, sheep and pigs.

The girls helped clear the dishes, but when the men returned, Mrs. Fredrickson shooed the two Inuit girls outside.

"I'll finish up now. You go take a walk with your fellers down by the stream back of the place, and you might want to look at the Herefords we're raising. They're beauties."

"I think Sandy wants some time alone with Natsiq," Eddy said, as he reached for Ashoona's hand to begin their walk. "Come with me. I'll show you where they milk the cows with these new machines they have. Pretty modern place. "

Once they were in the dark cavernous barn, Eddy pulled Ashoona close, holding her so tight she had trouble pushing him away when he tried to kiss her. She reacted forcibly, remembering with bitterness how James had forced himself on her.

"No! I don't want you to kiss me. Let me go!"

"What's the matter with you? I've never had a girl refuse me before."

"Is that what these walks and our supper out were all about, just to get me into bed before you go to the front? Well, maybe other women have fallen all over you, but I won't spend another minute wasting my time with someone who is so self-centered. You think just because we are Native that we must be easy. Is that what's going on? I just hope Natsiq is not being treated with the same disrespect."

"Naw. Sandy is head over heels in love and wants to marry her. I just wanted one kiss, and yes, I had hoped you would be willing to go all the way."

"I wouldn't let you touch my hand again let alone have sex with you. Don't you see that?" *This man! If he wasn't in the process of attracting a woman and if he wasn't so self-centered, I would think he was ill.*

"You're just an Indian. Why are you so uppity? Every day I see girls like you selling themselves on the streets of Edmonton."

"You're disgusting. You look at someone's skin color and label them a prostitute." This remark finally registered with Eddy.

"I'm out of line; I apologize. I've been taught a lesson. I'm not really a bad guy. Look, why not have a drink with me, and we'll try to be friends. No more advances." Eddy pulled a mickey from inside his jacket.

"I don't drink, but you go ahead." Ashoona walked back to the kitchen, anxious to be away from Eddy and wanting to spend time with Sandy's pleasant mother.

The relationship between the other two young people became intimate. Natsiq and Sandy had found a quiet spot in the hay barn, and Natsiq did not feel any need to resist. Sandy was gentle with her, asking if she was ready to give herself to him. Natsiq yielded to his kisses and urged him on. Sandy and Natsiq were both overwhelmed by the feelings they shared. Neither had ever expected to fall so completely in love in such a short time.

"I would marry you today," Sandy told her, "and I mean it. But there's no time for a wedding, only for a promise that we will marry when I return from the war. It won't be long now. They say Hitler will be on his knees by Christmas."

When they dropped the girls off at the hospital, Sandy held Natsiq in his arms until Eddy pulled him away. Their leave was over, and they were going to be late.

After the airmen left, Natsiq was alternatively lifted by her love for Sandy and in tears knowing she might not see him for months. Ashoona hoped that Natsiq had not been foolish enough to get pregnant, but in three months, noticed Natsiq feeling ill at breakfast and guessed.

"Are you going to have Sandy's baby?"

"I'm happy about it. The war will end soon, and he'll be back before the baby is born. We'll get married, and I will find some way for Samuel to join us. Sandy will give me money for a plane ticket for Samuel and me. I miss my little boy as much as I miss Sandy, but soon we'll all be together. Can you imagine what a good life I will have living on that farm with all the food, never a worry and a guy who loves me!"

"You should have married him before he left."

"Why? Lots of people in Panniqtuuq never marry. They just move in together. In *Qallunaaq* land, I know you have to marry, but it's no big deal for me. I know he loves me and will be a good husband."

"He will. I am sure." But Ashoona knew what could happen if Sandy didn't come back, and she worried about Natsiq, especially since the two cousins would be separated, Ashoona going off to normal school to study to be a teacher while Natsiq would try to finish grade ten before being released from the sanatorium.

Chapter Twenty

Corbett Hall

O n a bright September weekend, Ashoona moved from the Charles Camsell Hospital to the Corbett Hall student dormitories located on the grounds of the University of Alberta. Ashoona looked around her residence. People in Panniqtuuq would think the dormitory was a house, but at college it was just a room for one person. No more crowded hospital room with old women coughing and getting up to pee during the night. She opened closets, checked the dresser and admired the sparkling clean bathroom with its aroma of disinfectant and window cleaner and the small desk where she would do her schoolwork. Once she had her few belongings stowed, she found her way to the cafeteria.

Other students were already seated, most in groups of four or six, giggling and talking loudly. Ashoona did not want to intrude. She saw a pale, slender young woman sitting by herself.

"Do you mind if I join you?"

"Please, sit down. I'm Brenda." She had fine features, startling blue eyes and hair the color of wheat. She did not smile, her voice almost a murmur. Brenda returned to her meal, not looking at Ashoona again before getting up and excusing herself. This first encounter with a fellow student upset Ashoona.

Will I be rejected because of my skin color?

The next day, the students lined up to collect their textbooks and attend an orientation. Ashoona gave her name to the staff person, who looked through the lists.

"Ashoona Campbell. Ah, so you are the girl from the Arctic with the scholarships. Your marks were so high that you won just about every grant and scholarship available. Someone must have been pointing you in the right direction."

"Nurse Battle…uhm, Nurse Ann. She encouraged me to go to college. She almost forced me to make this decision, saying that it will be the smartest move I've ever made."

"She's right. All your books and tuition plus your resident fees and food are paid for, and you'll get a small allowance, enough to buy personal items and go to the occasional movie."

The next time Ashoona ate at the cafeteria, Brenda was sitting by herself again, and she motioned to Ashoona to join her. This time Ashoona noticed what was different about Brenda. She wore a long-sleeved, cotton shirt, with buttons up to her neck and a skirt that reached her ankles, even though it was a sweltering fall day. Brenda's fair hair was pulled neatly into a bun. Although she appeared to be nineteen or twenty, she dressed like someone's great-grandmother.

Brenda smiled shyly. "Tell me about your classes. What are specializing in?"

Ashoona explained that she hoped to return to her Inuit village to teach grade school, and that her majors were social studies and science. "And what will you do when you graduate?"

"I'll go back to my children and husband and teach in the Celestial FLDS school."

Brenda had to explain the difference between the Fundamentalist Latter Day Saints and the Mormon Church. Ashoona had learned about the Mormons, a religious group that spread the prophecy of Joseph Smith and had strict rules about cigarettes, liquor and caffeine.

Brenda explained to Ashoona that the FLDS broke away from the main church, held all possessions communally and required its members to dress in old-fashioned modest clothing. Ashoona was most surprised to learn about the marriage arrangements that significantly separated the FLDS, not just from the Mormons but also from mainstream Canadians.

"You have children! How old are they?"

"Two boys and a girl, the oldest is six. That's Jeremiah. Adam is four, and Rachael is a year old. I miss her so much."

"You don't look old enough to have a six-year-old. When did you get married?"

"We marry young in the FLDS church. I was thirteen when I was chosen by the Prophet to marry my husband."

"That sounds too much like my arranged marriage. I hope your wedding was one that you enjoyed. I ran away before that horrible, old guy could rape me."

Brenda did not reply to this, but Ashoona could see a pained expression on her delicate, beautiful face as if sorrow was a permanent part of Brenda's life. But Ashoona sensed that Brenda was not yet ready to talk about her relationship with her husband. Lunch hour was over anyway, and they gathered up their books and headed back to class.

After that, they met each day for lunch and supper, and over the semester, they shared their stories. Most surprising for Ashoona was that polygamy was practiced in Brenda's church and community.

"Are you serious? Your husband has twenty-five wives, and one hundred children!"

"Actually, one hundred and one. The church prophets teach us that eternal life will only be achieved if a man has at least three wives. Women and children are the property of their husbands and fathers. I was chosen to enter a celestial marriage, not one condoned by the state but blessed by God. The first wife was able to get married under Canadian law; my other sister wives and I are celestial wives."

"Are you happy with this kind of marriage?" Ashoona wanted to ask how the sexual arrangements worked, but she knew the subject was far too private. She tried to imagine a household where the husband invited one of the wives to share his bed while the other wives listened at the door.

"We are two of a kind. I'm different because of my clothing and strict rules, and you look different to the rest of the students because of your dark skin."

"Some people in Edmonton accept me. My boss at the restaurant treats me like the rest of the staff. He's a great guy. His family suffered terribly when the Jewish people were targeted in the Ukraine. So now he defends minorities, and he helped me deal with some of the racial comments I've had to endure."

"You're working in addition to going to school?"

"I work on weekends waiting tables. I want to save money so I can buy all the nice things white people have, things that will make life easier when I go home."

"I'm surprised you want to go back to the Arctic. Won't Qillaq find you and hurt you or worse?"

"Natsiq heard from a new patient at the san that Qillaq was in Montreal searching for me. It's only a matter of time before he tracks me down. He'll never give up, but I will feel safer in my homeland."

"It's the same with me. If I dared to leave Elijah, the entire male priesthood would hunt me down and drag me back to Celestial. Of course, I would never consider leaving Elijah because he would take my children."

"What! Mothers always keep the children. At least that is what Ann told me."

"Not within the FLDS. The Prophet and apostles have incredible power over our lives. The children are used like pawns to maintain control over the women. We're never allowed to leave the house with all our children, even for a day. My cousin tried to escape, hiding the children in the back of the truck under cabbages she was taking to market. Her sister wife informed on her, and she was caught. They spoke about blood atonement, but in the end they did not kill her; they sent her from the house to live in a shack. Her children are being raised by a sister wife."

"You want to leave him, don't you?"

Brenda did not reply, her silence an answer, and the pain and helplessness in her face reflected the deepest sorrow Ashoona had ever seen. Ashoona changed the subject; she did not want to inflict that pain on her friend again.

On weekends, Ashoona took the bus to the Camsell Hospital to visit Ann and Natsiq and see how the other patients were faring. Often new patients arrived for treatment, and along with them came news of relatives and friends in the north. Someone always seemed to have an update on Qillaq's whereabouts, as if a telegraph mysteriously carried news between the sanatoriums in Canada.

"He left Montreal, and he is making his way to Winnipeg," Natsiq told her. "He speaks about you as if you're a witch that must be burned, your limbs torn from you, your...well, I won't repeat what else he is saying."

"How can his family in Igloolik survive when he is not there to hunt?" Ashoona asked. "He has three wives and a dozen children. God help them trying to manage through the winter with only his young sons to hunt for the family."

"In his madness, he believes you are responsible for the suffering of his children. He tells everyone that his youngest died of starvation because of the spell you cast."

During lunch the next day, Ashoona confided in Brenda, telling her the story of her abduction.

"What is it about some men that they must own and control women?" Ashoona asked in exasperation.

"But you've resisted marriage and saved yourself. I agreed to marry Elijah because my parents, the priesthood and everyone else expected it of me. During the ceremony, they asked if I would take Elijah for life everlasting. My mouth was dry as if stuffed with cotton. I paused, wanting to say no in my loudest voice. But my mother pinched my arm and ordered me to agree. And that was it. I was in his bed that night and had a baby to care for when I was only fourteen."

Ashoona and Brenda were from very different cultural backgrounds than the rest of their classmates. Many of the young women came from farm families or remote communities—not Inuit or Mormon but Scottish, English and Irish. They were not unkind to Ashoona and Brenda, but they made no effort to make friends with the dark-eyed Inuit or the strangely attired Fundamentalist Mormon.

When Christmas break approached, Ashoona wondered what she would do rambling around in the school residence while Brenda and the other students returned home for the holidays.

"Go back to the Camsell," Brenda suggested. "You'll at least have Natsiq and Nurse Ann for company. And doesn't Natsiq need your help to translate those mushy letters that arrive regularly from overseas?"

"Oh, yes, Sandy's letters. He is a sweetheart of a man. I didn't find myself attracted to him, but he is the salt of the earth. We should be so lucky to find husbands like him."

"Well, I won't be looking for a husband. I have one, and even though he is forty years older than me, I'm stuck with him. As it is written in the Book of Mormon, "for time everlasting," and that includes being his obedient wife in the afterlife."

"Well, if you ever consider making a break for it, just let me know. If I could escape from Qillaq across the frozen Arctic with him chasing me by dog team, I'm sure I could find a way to rescue you from an unwanted, abusive marriage, which is not even a real marriage. You are more like a sex slave."

"That could never happen." Brenda's words had the deafening finality of someone dealt a prison sentence.

Ashoona packed a bag, left the dormitory and walked through the snowy streets to catch the bus to the Camsell, where she joined Nurse Ann and Natsiq for Christmas.

"More news for you," Natsiq announced when Ashoona arrived. "So hold onto your hat. Qillaq was asking about you at the sanatorium in Winnipeg. He started off in Quebec because that is where most of the Inuit patients are taken, but he is narrowing down his search. You best keep your eyes in the back of your head." As Natsiq's command of English improved, she had picked up many of Nurse Ann's cliché expressions.

"Good gracious! What do I have to do to rid myself of that beast? Kill him?"

"There's a plan," Nurse Ann's commented bluntly. The buxom nurse was a law-abiding and upstanding member of Edmonton society, so it was doubtful that she was serious about counseling murder. "It gives me the heebie-jeebies just thinking about that monster. But since we can't cut his throat with a scalpel, we'll just have to make sure he never finds you. Only a few of us know that you're attending college, and we'll keep it that way."

"He'll find out I was here. What will you tell him?"

"Leave it to me, girl, and don't you worry. I want you to enjoy your Christmas holiday. Just put your feet up, eat chocolates and go to a few movies."

"Actually, I have a job during the holidays. Natsiq, do you remember the Cocky Bull Restaurant where that bozo badmouthed us? Well, when I went there one day for a coffee, the manager asked me to work a few shifts."

"You sure don't let the grass grow under your feet, girl!" Ann said warmly. "That's the way I hope my daughter grows up, ready to work hard and get ahead. The war will be over soon, and opportunities will come a-knocking. And what about the restaurant? With a name like that, are you sure it's a safe place?"

"We get a few drunks and misfits, but the owner is as good as gold. He defended Natsiq and me when one of the customers wanted us thrown out. By the way, Natsiq, if you're feeling well enough, you could put in a few hours there, too. You'll make good money on tips during the holidays."

"I gotta study through the break if I want my certificate. It doesn't look like I'll have too many chances to make money, even after I graduate," Natsiq said, pointing at her growing belly. The smock provided by the hospital was now tight against her middle.

"I just hope that man of yours is willing to put a ring on your finger when he returns from the war," Ann remarked. "How is he doing over there? He's a fighter pilot, isn't he?"

Ashoona had just finished reading Sandy's most recent letter, and Natsiq was buoyed by his assurances of love and his exciting plans for their life together.

"He wrote that the pilots are treated like royalty, living in a mansion with the best of food and everyone bringing them gifts. He even has a batman, another service man who waits on him, polishing his shoes and keeping his uniform pressed. Doesn't that just knock your socks off?" Natsiq exclaimed.

"Getting him back safe is what counts," Nurse Ann offered.

Natsiq gasped almost too quietly to be heard. She left them to return to her studies, but Ashoona thought she might be in her room crying for the man who fathered her child, a good man, whom they all knew was in serious danger.

The next letter to arrive increased Natsiq's anxiety. This time, Nurse Ann read it.

My dearest wife:

May I call you my wife even though we have not seen the minister to exchange our vows? Life here continues to be amazing. I have never eaten so well, even on the farm, but don't tell my mother. I guess the air force wants us to enjoy every meal because for some of us, it might be the last. We have steak, lobster, shrimp and desserts you've never heard of, all served up on dazzling table linen with fresh flowers in the center.

The guys don't care that much for the table set-tings, but I like it. They're all after the women here, and a couple of the guys got married. They sure go after those English gals, who want to get hitched right away so they can go to Canada. "War Brides" they're called. But don't you worry about me, sweetheart. My heart only belongs to you and the little baby we will raise together. When I'm flying, your picture is on my instru-ment panel. That helps me keep away from the German spitfires.

"He's a good man, Natsiq. You are lucky," Ann contin-ued. "Are the two of you going to live on the farm with his par-ents and his brothers?"

"Well, first I have to go home to get Samuel."

"How old is your son now?"

"Let's see. He was a year old when they yanked him away from me, so he will be turning five this year. I can't believe I've been here almost four years!"

Ashoona had also been away from her homeland for a long time. She hoped Henry and a few friends from the expedi-tion had not forgotten about her. At least Natsiq had a child to return to in Panniqtuuq.

Why am I going back there, to the village that shunned me? She wondered at her decision to teach school in the village where she had experienced so much pain.

She could go to Frobisher Bay where they were desperate for Inuit teachers. She could even teach in Alberta because her marks were well above average. She was being pulled back home by the faint hope that her father would seek her out. It had been eleven years since he left, and Ashoona still could not under-stand how a father that loved her so dearly could abandon her.

When she agonized over his betrayal, Nurse Ann always tried to find a reason for his actions. "When was that? You were seven, and the country was in a deep depression. Have you ever considered that he could not buy passage up north, that he was sick or conscripted into the war? How do you know he's not over there fighting on the ground while Sandy flies overhead protecting him? It's not as if there is mail delivery to your doorstep in Panniqtuuq. Even if a letter arrived for you, would your aunt give it to you or throw it in the fire?"

"He just left, Ann. I have to accept that and not harbor false hope that he will miraculously reappear. All my encounters with men have been unlucky, and I feel I will never find a man I can love and admire."

"Not that doctor...what's his name? The man who encouraged you in your studies."

"Henry? Yes, he is goodness itself. It will be a lucky woman who snags him. He would never be interested in me; his heart is still scarred from his experience with the man-eating Joanna."

"See, my girl. Women can be vicious and hurtful, too, and people can change. Look at Natsiq. Didn't she falsely accuse you of killing her brother and then arrange to trap you in the marriage with Qillaq? She may never be your best friend, but the two of you get along, and I know she regrets the past."

"If she regrets her false accusation so much, then why doesn't she apologize? Why won't she admit that she pulled the trigger and not me?"

The old hurts made Ashoona's stomach churn and her face flush with the memory of being shunned and persecuted. "It was so unfair, and yet no one, except old Aula and my friend Lucy, believed me."

"My point exactly. Some people will always help you. Look at how we started out. You thought I was the devil himself.

What did you girls call me? The Old Battleaxe? And now you have quite a different opinion of me. Right?"

"I'm so sorry for that, Ann. And yes, it took me a few months to realize you only wanted what was best for us. Gotta go now. The Cocky Bull calls."

"Just be careful there, my girl. Don't let any of those drunks pinch your behind!"

Ashoona laughed as she put on her heavy winter coat, wool hat, boots and mitts before heading out into the frosty December air.

Chapter Twenty-one

An Unwelcome Visitor

The Christmas holiday had ended when a heavy-set Inuit man entered the hospital asking for Ashoona. He was a tree-trunk of a man, short with powerful arms. When he spoke a few hesitant phrases in broken English, his halting words sounded as if he had practiced the phrases over and over but had not really grasped what each word meant.

"What is her last name or her number?" It was the receptionist with the fluffy popcorn hair and a cheerful face.

"Don't know number. Last name? What that is?" he asked gruffly. "We go by one name. Her Ashoona."

"I'll try." The receptionist pulled out a ledger, searching through all the first names. "It will take a few minutes. Please sit down and wait. We have the names organized by numbers or by last names, if they have a last name. There are two hundred patients here."

"Our language. Speak it." A sharp ache began snaking its way up the back of his head, sending throbbing pain across his temples. He was not accustomed to having a woman make him wait or order him around. His eyelids grew heavy, and his eyes glittered with evil petulance.

"I'm sorry, but I can't speak Inuktitut. I'll call my supervisor. She understands a bit of your language and may be able to help you."

He clutched his temples. He could not bear to wait. He had traveled for three months from the Arctic in a ship, searched for Ashoona in Montreal, then jumped a train west and searched for her at the Winnipeg sanatorium. It took him several months to figure out where Ashoona might be and two more months to find a way to get to Edmonton. Now this snippet of a woman was asking him to sit patiently and wait.

He paced the floor. Several minutes passed before Nurse Ann appeared.

"And who did you say you are looking for?"

"Ashoona. You speak Inuktitut? "

"A little," she said in his language.

A torrent of angry words poured out of his ugly mouth. "She owes me. She is a relative," he lied. "I need to see her now, not wait like this ignorant *Qallunaaq* tells me. I not get ordered around by silly women."

"Oh, is that right? Well, Sally, did you find someone named Ashoona on the list of patients?" she asked, knowing that Ashoona was no longer on the active register.

"I haven't found her name yet. I asked the gentlemen to take a seat, but that just made him angrier."

"Keep looking, Sally." Then she faced the angry Inuit and asked in Inuktitut, "What is your name?"

"I'm..." He paused, and then said, "Adamie, uncle from Panniqtuuq."

"Ann, there's no one with the first name Ashoona, said Sally. "But wasn't there an Ashoona here last year? A really bright girl who completed her senior matriculation, passing with high marks?"

"I don't recall, Sally. So many came out of the north. Ashoona...uhm...no. I don't think so."

"You lie. You know where she is!" he shouted in Inuktitut. "I can tell. Tell me, you *Qallunaaq* bitch." He glowered at Ann, clenching his fists, threatening her. "I strangle you, you useless piece of *Qallunaaq* flesh. Who do you think you are dealing with here? A helpless savage that you can boss around like you *Qallunaat* always do. No, you cannot fool me. Tell me where the little witch is!"

Ann could not understand what he was saying, but from his tone, she could well imagine. She remained steady as an ocean liner.

"Sally, call the police." She seemed unafraid despite the anger she faced.

But before Sally could reach for the phone, the enraged stranger grabbed Ann around her throat, choking her till she could barely breathe. Sally was so terrified by the violence she had trouble dialing the numbers.

"Be steady," Sally told herself.

The stranger had Ann in a death hold. But the matron, who was a hefty woman and did not put up with any nonsense, brought her knee up, catching her attacker in the groin. He roared in pain and released his grip on her throat.

"We don't know where Ashoona is, so you get out of here and leave us alone!" Sally shouted. It was the first time the novice had ever raised her voice in her life.

"Shush, not a word more," Ann said to Sally, barely able to get more than a croak out of her injured throat.

He stared at the receptionist. "So I right? You know something. Where she is?" He reached across the desk, bearing down on Sally like an evil storm.

"I don't know. She left. They all went back to the place they came from. She's not here. That's all I know."

Sally backed up behind her desk, believing she would be the next one to have the breath squeezed out of her. The huge man pushed aside the desk, his jaws clenched and his face livid. He towered over Sally and grabbed a fistful of her fluffy hair.

Ann moved with surprising speed for her size, picked up a chair and brought it down on his head. He let out a holler that reverberated through the hospital, then he staggered and fell to the floor.

Sirens screamed outside, and two policemen rushed in to find the big man groaning in pain on the floor.

"I know who you are, you despicable bastard!" Ann yelled as they handcuffed him and dragged him to the police car. "I hope they lock you up and throw away the key." When Ann reported the incident to Ashoona, it was like a cold finger pressed against her spine. "He's found me, and now I'll never be free."

"He will be locked up, and when and if they let him out, he won't know where you are, and no one here will say a word. Just go back to school. You have four months left at normal school, and then you can get a job anywhere in the English-speaking world."

Ashoona did not feel reassured. She learned from Ann, an inveterate newspaper reader, that Qillaq received a sentence of six months for his attack on the two women.

Six months, and he will be free again! Ashoona's thoughts swirled like a hurricane in her head. *What then? He's not dumb. He is obsessed, and I know he won't give up until he finds me and both of us are dead!*

Ashoona's nightmares were filled with Qillaq. She would wake up in a sweat, Qillaq strangling her, raping her, and she felt exhausted afterwards. Her studies began to suffer. She had always prided herself on being the top student in her class, but her grades were slipping. Her emotions were in a jumble; she felt depressed one day, and tense and nervous the next.

Brenda tried to help. "Look, my friend, the law is on your side. I think you can get a restraining order if you can show that your safety is threatened. You are lucky compared to me. Most of the policemen in my town are members of our church. If I tried to run, they would help Elijah hunt me down and even take me into custody."

"I don't feel lucky. How can I make it through to graduation with the threat of Qillaq hanging over my head?"

"He won't be out until after graduation, after you've left for Panniqtuuq. Concentrate. Study. Don't let that beast take away the most important thing in your life. It is your passage to a better life, where you will have the respect of your community. That bastard needs to be put in jail and kept there till he is an old man and too weak to chase you."

"Oh, so you can swear!"

"I know you won't believe me, but I have problems that can't be solved. I can't move to another community. I can't refuse sex with Elijah. I am bound to him, forced to obey him. He can beat me, and I can't go to anyone for help. And worse, his first wife mistreats my firstborn and has taken my baby from me. She wouldn't even let me hold my little one while I was home during the Christmas holidays." Brenda's voice cracked, and a tear tricked down each cheek.

"I'm sorry, Brenda. I've been so obsessed with my own problems I haven't asked you about your visit home. You're living a nightmare."

"Esther, the first wife, hates my oldest son, Jeremiah, and no matter what he does, she yells at him and beats him. I complain to Elijah, and he tells me to pray. Jeremiah has become withdrawn, and Esther wouldn't even let me touch my own baby girl. Of course Esther, who hasn't been able to get pregnant, is delighted to have a baby to cuddle."

"That's unreal. How can she do that? Rachael's your child, for goodness sake."

"Yes, she can do it. Esther controls the household, the kitchen and all the children. Elijah lets her get away with it. It's often like that in FLDS households. The husband has sex with the young wives and then an older wife wields the power in the household."

"What about your middle child? He's four, right?"

"Adam is always happy to see me. Such a cheerful little soul. He doesn't get upset no matter how much conflict swirls around him. But I can't sleep thinking about the other two—Jeremiah getting a beating for not holding his fork the right way and my baby taken from me. My children are my only happiness in a marriage I despise."

"Maybe you need to run, just like I did."

"I've been thinking about escape. Have you any idea how difficult that would be? I've heard of women escaping, but no one has left with all her children. And the women who are caught and brought back live a hellish life. If only I could have gone home and had the arms of my little Rachael around my neck and been able to sing to her." Tears filled her eyes, and violent sobs shook her thin body.

"I'm so sorry," Ashoona said, putting her arms around Brenda. "I didn't realize how bad things had become. "You had to listen to my complaints when your life is far more painful. At least I'm not forced to have sex with someone I despise. Thank God, I was able to escape."

"I am trapped, Ashoona. You have a life ahead of you, while I'm forced to spend the rest of my life with a man I hate. If I leave, I lose my children. They are the center of my life; so precious to me that I will never risk having them taken from me."

"I think you should come with me and talk to Ann about this. I disliked her at first, but she has become a great friend. She can't stand men who control and abuse women. She is part of a group pushing for women's rights. She might be able to help you because she has a respected position in the community, she knows the laws and is not afraid of standing up for what is right."

"That's the matron in the hospital, the woman you called Nurse Battleaxe. Are you sure about this?"

"We can all make mistakes in our initial judgments about people. I was dead wrong about Ann. I believe she would do almost anything to protect me from Qillaq. If we tell her about your situation, I'm sure she will try to help you. Come, let's go and see her."

They arrived at the Camsell shortly before Ann's shift ended. The two young women knocked on Ann's office door.

Chapter Twenty-two

The Rescue

Ann drove her 1940 Chevrolet west across the mountains heading to Celestial, a compound that housed a few hundred followers of the Fundamentalist Mormon sect. Ashoona was in the passenger's seat checking the map and giving directions. Classes had ended, and Ashoona and Brenda were on a two-week reading break preparing for exams. It was an amazing spring day. The sky was an expanse of blue, and in the distance they could see the blue outline of the Canadian Rockies.

"We have plenty of time to get to our rendezvous with Brenda, so we're staying in a special hotel tonight," Ann told Ashoona as they drove up to an impressive stone building reminiscent of a Scottish castle.

"I've always wanted to stay in the CPR hotel and soak in the Banff Hot Springs. When we go on vacation, I'm always with a brood of children and a husband who thinks sleeping in a tent and freezing my tootsies is a holiday. This is a pricey place, and when I told hubby that I was driving across the Rockies to Celestial, he peeled off a wad of cash. This is my birthday treat."

"It's your birthday? How old are you if you don't mind me asking?"

"Twenty-nine and holding," Ann laughed.

"Thank you so much for giving up your birthday to rescue Brenda."

"I bought you a bathing suit because I've heard that nobody swims in Baffin Island."

"You're absolutely correct. The Arctic Ocean is freezing cold, and we don't have swimming pools. I doubt whether more than a couple of Inuit know how to swim."

"We'll be soaking in the hot pool, not swimming. It'll do us a world of good and set us up for the long drive over the Rockies."

After unpacking in their room at the Banff Springs Hotel, the two women walked along the trail leading to the upper hot springs. The setting sun caught the mountaintops, turning the snowy peaks pink. Ashoona could not take her eyes off the towering mountains. Since leaving her arctic village, this was the first time she'd seen ice-covered mountains.

"I could never live in Edmonton where the land flattens out like a sea of brown dirt. I could live here, though, nestled in the Rockies. Take away the trees, and this is what my land is like, except we don't have hot springs."

They spent a pleasant evening at the hot springs and enjoyed a good night's rest at their hotel. The next morning, they drove through the mountain pass over a rough road and then headed south to Big Fork, a small town nestled at the foot of the Rockies in southern British Columbia.

"Let's drive past Celestial and see what the place looks like. We have an hour before we are to meet Brenda," said Ann.

They could see the farm buildings and the sprawling houses. "Wow! There must be twenty rooms in that house!" Ann remarked.

"I guess you need lots of bedrooms when you have twenty-five wives and over a hundred children," Ashoona explained.

"Good grief! Why doesn't our government do something about this? We are in Canada. Polygamy is against the law. At least last time I heard."

"Brenda told me it's the politicians. The FLDS were able to elect a member to sit in Parliament. He has argued against enforcing the legislation. The cult also has a hold on the provincial politicians. They're afraid they'll get thrown out of office if people claim they are trampling on religious rights."

"What about Brenda's rights? Even her children can be taken away."

———— ～ ————

While Ann and Ashoona drove by the compound, Brenda was preparing for what was planned as a trip to the doctor for Adam, her four-year-old. Doctor appointments were the only times she was allowed to travel into town without a sister wife or Elijah. Taking all three children with her would be the problem.

The baby was down for her nap in the large sleeping and living quarters. It was Brenda's chance to take her without Esther noticing; that is, if Rachael didn't wake up and alert one of the sister wives charged with watching over the sleeping infants.

Brenda, her two boys and Esther were in a separate building where the kitchen and dining room were located.

"Why are you so quiet, Brenda?" asked Esther. "You're as pale as a ghost." Like all women in the compound, she wore a long dress of simple cotton, with her hair neatly pulled back. She had lost the bloom of youth. Once a pleasant-looking woman with a Roman nose and big blue eyes, Esther's nose had become too sharp and she had gray bags under her eyes and wrinkles around her mouth from the ever-present scowl.

"I'm fine, just worried about Adam. He still has a temperature and a sore throat. Hopefully the doctor will give me something for him. Oh, I'm also taking Jeremiah with me. I noticed he was coughing yesterday. I'll have the doctor look at him as well."

"I haven't heard him cough. Are you coughing, young man?"

Jeremiah looked at Esther but did not answer.

"Answer when you are spoken to," Esther demanded.

"I want to go with Mommy."

"That's an answer? I don't think so."

Brenda stepped in. "Jeremiah, remember you coughed when you were bringing in the wood last night."

"I remember, Mommy."

"Now finish up your lunch, children. You have to brush your teeth and get ready to go into town."

Brenda's hands shook as she cleared away the dishes. Her stomach felt like a rock was planted there.

She took a few deep breaths, trying to compose herself, so that Esther would not see through her and discover that Brenda was planning to escape rather than make a routine trip to the doctor.

If Esther suspected anything, she would call Elijah and have all the priest heads after her before she could rendezvous with Ann and Ashoona.

Brenda finished her work in the kitchen then changed Adam's clothes while Jeremiah dressed.

"Take your jacket and wool hat, and put on an extra sweater. I heard it might get cold before we get home."

Brenda put several layers of sweaters and an extra jacket on Adam. "It's hot, Mommy. Take off."

She kissed and hugged him. "Please just keep them on until we drive to the far fence."

She took Jeremiah and Adam to the car, placing Adam in the front seat and Jeremiah in the back. "I have to go back in the house for something, and I want both of you boys to be very quiet. If anyone asks where I am, tell them I forgot my purse. We are playing a game now, and I need you to follow the rules. If you're very good and quiet, I'll buy you an ice cream cone."

Brenda's heart pounded as she walked toward the nursery. "Please let her be sound asleep."

Rachael was curled up on her side with her Teddy bear tucked under one arm, her soft fawn hair moist from sleep. "She could sleep through a hurricane," Brenda whispered to herself. "Now please just stay asleep."

Brenda had not held Rachael since the beginning of the college term. Slowly and carefully she put her hands under the sleeping child and gently lifted her. Rachael nuzzled against her mother. The feel of her daughter against her breast brought tears to her eyes.

The house was quiet as Brenda tiptoed down the long hallway to the front door. Rachael did not stir. Now down the stairs, six steps, carefully. No one was outside. Several of the sister wives were in the field preparing the gardens, and the other children were either in school or napping.

Brenda thought about the school. *Thank God, I don't have to send you to the Celestial school where some lecherous old man will have you assigned to him when you are still a child.*

You're going to be my little girl again. Brenda was again close to tears as she placed the child next to Jeremiah.

"Shush. Don't wake her."

She closed the car door as quietly as she could. Rachael stirred and opened her eyes.

Brenda drove slowly out of the compound. Just as she reached the gate, Rachael let out a cry that Brenda was certain could be heard as far away as the fields. In order to leave the compound, she had to stop the vehicle, open the gate, drive through and then get out again to close it. Her hands shook as she tried to close the gate latch. Rachael's cries could be heard over the sound of the engine. Jeremiah rocked his little sister, trying to quiet her. One of the priest heads, a thin man with a sinewy face, was outside chopping wood. He paused in his work and stood for a moment listening. He put the axe down and walked toward the kitchen where Esther was working.

"Oh, my God," Brenda whispered.

"What's the matter, Mommy?" Jeremiah asked over the cries of his little sister.

"Nothing. Give Rachael her soother. Try to get her to stop crying. We're going to be okay." But there was little conviction in her voice. She knew the man would tell Esther, and within minutes, they would be after her.

Brenda drove down the gravel road into town, keeping her eyes on the rearview mirror. *I know they'll follow me. No mother has successfully left Celestial with all her children. Esther won't let me take Rachael. I know it.*

It was only ten miles to the parking lot where she was to meet Ann and Ashoona. As she drove, Brenda whispered a prayer, "Please, dear God. I know you don't condone what they're doing. I know you're a good God who protects mothers and children. Please, please help me."

Jeremiah had managed to sooth Rachael back to sleep. It was a blessing that the children were quiet. Adam sat calmly beside his mother looking out the window, unperturbed. *Was there ever a day in his life that he caused her grief? And responsible Jeremiah, always willing to discuss anything with me and stay by my side when there were conflicts among the sister wives. I am blessed to have such wonderful children.*

Brenda started to cry again, so filled with terror and with the wonder of escape. She fought the temptation to press the accelerator to the floor and race the Ford to the meeting place.

Only a mile to go. Just a few more minutes. Would Ann and Ashoona be there as planned, and can I get there before Esther catches up with me? Brenda's stomach was in knots, and her breath came in short gasps.

Suddenly, she spotted Elijah driving toward her in his old gray pickup. Her heart pounded, and she felt sick with fear.

Stay calm; he knows you're going to the doctor's appointment.

But she was anything but calm. The truck slowed down once he recognized the car. He pulled up on the side of the road and began to get out of the truck, lifting up his thick arm, signaling her to stop. Instead she drove slowly past, pointing to her watch to indicate she was late. She smiled nervously, waved and continued on to town.

When she looked in the rearview mirror to make sure he carried on to Celestial, what she saw almost stopped her heart. The farm truck from the commune was barreling down the road, clouds of dust erupting behind the vehicle. The truck slammed to a stop next to Elijah, and soon both trucks were in pursuit.

Brenda floored the gas pedal, and the 1939 Ford kicked up gravel and swerved across the road so close to the ditch that Brenda feared she would roll the car. She steered into the skid and brought the vehicle back to the center of the road. Her hands felt numb as she held the steering wheel in a death grip. She could not take her eyes off the road to check the rearview mirror. She knew her pursuers were closing in on her.

I just have to find Ann and Ashoona. They're my only hope.

When she took the last corner heading into town, Elijah's truck was tailing close to her bumper. He laid his fist on the horn. She could feel his anger in the sound of the horn, but she didn't stop. Now she was in the town and slowed down.

Rachael was awake and screaming. Jeremiah crooned to Rachael but could not stem her crying. Little Adam, never one to be rattled, just looked out the window, curious about the stores and oblivious to his sister's protests or his mother's erratic driving.

Elijah gunned his truck and moved up beside her vehicle, motioning to Brenda to pull over. She did not even look at him. Her face was grim and determined. Just one block to go.

What if they aren't there?

But they were waiting when Brenda drove into the parking lot. "Jeremiah, lock the doors in the backseat. Boys, just stay in the car." Brenda locked the door beside Adam and jumped out of the car. Elijah reached Brenda at the same time as Ann and Ashoona.

"I'm leaving with the children, so don't try to stop me." Brenda forced her voice to be steady, knots of fear caught in her throat. Her stomach tightened, and she felt ill. Her already-pale face was drained of all color.

The bulk of him and the roar of his voice terrified her. "Apostate! Whore! You won't leave me. No one leaves Celestial. You will go to hell, and so will the children. My children!" he yelled, bringing a liver-spotted fist close to her face and threatening to punch her.

Elijah was sixty-two, a barrel-chested man and still robust, although showing years of too many steaks and potatoes packed around his middle. He looked clean and tidy in his pressed cotton work shirt, cowboy boots and black pants. The smile that he usually flashed at the townspeople was replaced with an angry scowl, and his eyes glittered with fury.

Elijah was always self-assured and confident that he was doing God's work. But Brenda had learned the hard way that behind the glad-handing, backslapping and hearty laugh was a scheming man who would do almost anything to retain the kingdom he ruled.

Ann stepped between them, seemingly unafraid of the powerfully built man. "Leave her be. It's against the law to prac-tice polygamy. She has every right to leave, and I'll make certain she is safe from your abuse."

"Get out of my way, you meddling bitch. Brenda, just come quietly. No one will hurt you, I promise. Just get in the truck and give me the keys to the Ford. Esther will drive the chil-dren home."

"I'm leaving with the children, and I'm never coming back." Her voice was shaky and faint. "You can't stop me because I'm not your legal wife, and even if I was, you have no right to stop me. That's right, isn't it, Ann?"

At this point, the other truck pulled up, and Esther and the woodchopper piled out and tried to grab Brenda. Ashoona and Ann stepped next to Brenda, flanking her.

"Lay a hand on her, and I will see you all in jail." Ann's look of determination was enough to give Esther pause.

"I won't allow someone like you to come between me and my wife. She belongs to me as much as my horse, my dog or my shovel belongs to me. Who are you to take her from me?" Elijah yelled. "The daughter of some whore and a whoremaster, an unbeliever trying to break up my family? And this abomination! This Lamanite! What is she doing here?" pointing at Ashoona.

"You call this a family?" Ann countered. "Twenty-five wives and how many children? One hundred. What are you running, a breeding farm and using women like prize cows? You're disgusting!"

"Get out of my way, you bitch!" Elijah shouted, fury erupting over the knowledge of his wife's repudiation, the humiliation he would suffer when the Prophet learned that he could not control his women. The shame would be too much!

He had tried to follow the scripture, and he did not condone violence, but even the Book of Mormon spoke of blood atonement for the worst crimes against God. Wasn't this the worse crime, to refuse to obey your husband? None of his wives had ever contemplated escape, and no one was going to leave him, especially not with his children, children that belonged to *him*.

His eyes glittered in their fat sockets. He went for the shovel he kept in the pickup. "You won't leave me, you whore. You will be dammed forever and spend your days in hell."

Ashoona stepped in front of Brenda protecting her from her jailors, while Ann ran toward the crazed man, pushing her way past Esther and the other man. The sturdy nurse stood unyieldingly in front of Elijah. He raised the shovel, ready to bring it down on Ann. But she stood her ground.

He paused. If he assaulted a woman in broad daylight, the law would come down on him because he was in the town and away from Celestial. He lowered the shovel.

"Do you want a knuckle sandwich?" Esther yelled, as Ashoona blocked the older woman from trying to get at Brenda. Esther pushed Ashoona, but Ann stepped between them. Esther was no match for the sturdy nurse.

"Get away from her. Brenda's coming with us!" Ann had a voice like a foghorn.

Their cries reverberated down the street, and in minutes, several townspeople arrived, some curious, others there to help. Fortunately, they were not members of the FLDS. Elijah saw them, dropped the shovel and rushed at Brenda, grabbing her with his meaty hands. His fingers closed around Brenda's slender arm as he pulled her toward his truck.

"No! No! Leave me alone. I won't go with you. Help me!"

"Elijah, you have to let her go." It was one of the businessmen who had heard the ruckus and had come out of his store. "You know the law. You can't restrain a woman if she wants to go. The courts can get involved regarding the children, but this woman, who is not your legal wife, is free to go."

"She will pay!" Elijah had let go of Brenda's arm, but his fists were clenched, nails digging into his palms. He could do little now. Too many non-believers around; he needed to get Brenda back to Celestial where he had support.

Elijah could not give up. Rage ruled his actions. But he knew that showing his rage here would just cause trouble. He wanted to reach out and strangle Brenda, but no. He had to control himself. His pulse thundered in his ears and temples, his mouth was as dry as sand, and his closed throat would not allow a word to pass.

"We have to leave, Elijah." Onias, the woodcutter, placed his hand on Elijah's arm and said quietly, "We'll track her down later, and she will be punished for this crime." He was a short, wiry man, his face lined with wrinkles, not from age but from anger and conflict. His stringy hair and piercing, ebony eyes were frightening; he was a man you'd not want to cross.

Elijah listened to Onias but did not really hear the words. He knew that the skirmish was lost, but he could not let the matter go. Brenda was *his* property, as were the children. That is what the Prophet taught him.

"Listen to Onias, Elijah." The gas station owner walked over to Elijah. "You have to let Brenda go. We don't want an incident here. If you use force against this girl, there will be nothing but trouble for the town. Give it up, at least for now."

Many of the townspeople depended on Celestial through the purchases made by the prosperous commune. No one wanted to lose Elijah's business, but no one wanted to look the other way when a young woman was being forcibly restrained. More important, the town's leaders did not want the government to come down on the practices at Celestial, despite the illegal marriages. They remembered how the Sons of Freedom had their children taken away and the parents jailed; the town emptied of paying customers because of conflicts such as this. They remembered the bombings, fires and nude demonstrations, and they did not want their community to become a ghost town.

Elijah knew he was losing. The veins in his temple throbbed as he stomped across the parking lot to his truck.

"You will regret this," he said, pointing a sausage-like finger at the gas station owner. "You'll never have my business again. And you evil women who have led my wife astray, I'll see you in hell. I will hunt you down. You, Brenda, and you, dark daughter of the lost tribe, the evil people who killed the Nephites, you are condemned to everlasting hell."

His tirade ringing across the parking lot, Elijah stormed back to his truck. With each step, he shook his fists, cursing Brenda, her rescuers and the town's people.

He turned back for a final word. "Brenda, your only salvation is to come with me now. I'll forgive you and take you back. Ours is a celestial marriage. It can't be broken by you or any of your meddling friends from college."

"Elijah, you know it's unlawful to restrain anyone, even if she is your wife. As far as we know, your only lawful wife is Esther." The shopkeeper spoke in a calm voice. "There will only be trouble for our community if word gets around that your women don't have their freedom."

"She is taking my children. I won't allow it. They belong to me."

"Well, you might just be wrong there, Elijah," said the shopkeeper." I think Brenda can leave. We don't want the newspapers to get hold of this. Before you know it, they will shut you down, and I'll lose my best customer. After all, everyone knows that what you do out there is against the law."

"I've built your businesses, and yet you won't help me keep what is mine. You are going to support these evil women. You are going to help her take my own children from me. It is written in the Book of Mormon that women must obey their husbands and that children belong only to the priesthood. You apostates will be dammed for life everlasting as will this evil woman and my children. And if she leaves, I will not achieve everlasting life. I'll be dammed as well."

"Elijah," the shopkeeper tried to be patient, "the Mormon Church has given up polygamy, and the government has laws against it, so you are living contrary to the laws of your own church."

"I live by the Book of Mormon. Joseph Smith received direct word from God that men must take at least three wives in order to gain everlasting life. The Mormon Church was wrong to reject the principle."

"Well maybe so, Elijah, but the law is the law. And ya know, women have a lot of rights these days. Gittin' those wartime jobs has changed things, maybe for the better, but for us men, well, we just have to change with the time. You can't win this one right now."

"Now, why don't you all come to the Blue Moon" he continued, "and sit down with us for a coffee. You too, Esther and Onias."

"We don't drink coffee," Esther snarled back, "and we don't associate with townspeople that do not support us. You'll pay for this."

The shopkeeper did not respond to the threat, although he knew how much power Esther wielded and did not take her words lightly.

He turned to Ann, "Take the young woman and the little ones and git out of town. We don't want no ruckus here."

Esther and Onias had given up. They could see they were outnumbered and were already thinking of better ways to get the children back. Esther would be happy if she never laid eyes on Brenda again, but she would turn heaven and earth to get Rachael back into the cult, and if possible, the two boys.

Brenda stood shell-shocked once her would-be captors had gone.

"Thank you," Brenda said to the business owners. She was close to tears, her voice breaking as she spoke.

"Don't thank us. We will rue this day. Elijah will never do business with us again. So just leave, lady."

Brenda opened the car door and lifted Rachael out. She was screaming at the top of her lungs.

"A future opera star," Ann said with a chuckle.

Adam was his usual unperturbed self, and Jeremiah, looking worried, hugged his mother tightly and burst into tears.

"It's over, my lovelies. Jeremiah and Adam, this is Ashoona and Ann. They are going to take us to our new home. We are going to live in the city."

Ann did not hesitate for a second. "Brenda, put the children in my Chevy. Ashoona, give her a hand, and let's get out of here quickly."

Brenda was so frightened at the confrontation and their narrow escape that she felt like her legs were going to give way, but she had all the children in the car in minutes.

"Ice cream," Adam ordered. "You said ice cream."

"If you were promised ice cream," Ann said, "then that is what we must get. And more important, we'd better get a bottle of milk for Rachael before she breaks my eardrums. Brenda, there are some baby cookies in that lunch box. That will quiet our little screamer until we get her a bottle.

"Adam, I give you my word we will have ice cream once we reach the store out on the main highway. It's just a few minutes away," Ann promised. "Why don't you count cars, Jeremiah? That will help pass the time; or better still, teach Adam to count. Right now, we have to drive because I am darn sure we haven't seen the last of dreadnaught Esther or her skinny, evil-looking sidekick and certainly not the last of the man who thinks it's all right to have a harem in Canada. Who does he think he is? The Sheik of Arabia? And remember, Brenda, the law is on your side. When you stay at our house, the police are only a phone call away."

After a restaurant meal and the promised ice cream cone, the children fell asleep. On the car radio, Frank Sinatra crooned "Sentimental Journey," and Bing Crosby sang "Accentuate the Positive" as Ann drove the Chevy through the mountains. The three women sang along, feeling release from the tension of the day. They stopped in Nelson late that night and carried the drowsy children into the motel.

"Brenda, I'm puzzled by something that Elijah said about Ashoona," Ann said. "In fact, I was puzzled by everything he said, but he called Ashoona a Lama...something."

"A Lamanite," Brenda replied. "He was referring to the passage in the Book of Mormon about the dark-skinned people. I don't pay any attention to the section because it doesn't match actual history. A Lamanite is supposedly a descendant of two rebellious Israeli brothers who crossed the ocean to North America hundreds of years ago. One of the brothers was cursed with dark skin color in punishment for his actions against the good brother, Nephite, and his followers. Eventually, the Lamanites exterminated all the Nephites. North American Indians, and that would include Ashoona, are said to be descendants of the Lamanites. Mainstream Mormons don't accept that section of the scripture, but the belief remains strong among the fundamentalist sects."

"What a bunch of hogwash!" Ann declared. "Just another way for whites to discriminate and despise people of color."

"It's not just the Mormon religion that looks at dark-skinned people as subhuman. When the churches first sent missionaries to northern Canada, they were told to convert the 'savages,'" Ashoona added. "We're used to being mistreated and called names, but this is the first time I've heard of a religion characterizing all dark-skinned people as evil, or descendants of an evil tribe. What next?"

Chapter Twenty-three

Graduation

The prairie sun baked the city of Edmonton in an unusually warm spring. Ashoona yearned to return to her arctic homeland, to the cool breezes coming off the ocean. She longed for the magic evenings of perpetual light when the midnight sun sends streams of pink across the mountaintops for a few minutes and then bursts over the snowy peaks to begin a new day of brilliant sunshine. Ashoona also loved the winter of perpetual night, when the stars guided her path, their illumination bouncing off the icy white landscape. It was never really dark in the Arctic, not like the winter nights in Edmonton where the sun fell below the horizon bringing on a night as black as pitch. Arctic light is magical, the midnight sun in summer and the mystery of the northern lights during the months of no sun.

Only a few weeks and Ashoona would return to the north. But first she and Brenda had to sit their exams and attend graduation.

The war was drawing to a close. The Allies were bombing Germany, and everyone knew it was just a matter of time before

Hitler capitulated. Natsiq had progressed enough in her studies to read Sandy's letters, but she still shared the news with Ann and Ashoona and had added Brenda to her circle of confidants.

"Listen to this," Natsiq told them during a Sunday visit.

I'm a pilot on a Lancaster bomber and making raids over Germany every night, giving the Jerries back a little of their own. They bombed London every night without any thought to how many children and innocent people they killed. Of course, we are told our targets are strategic bridges and munitions factories, but after we dropped our load and flew back over Dresden, I saw houses and churches in flames and even a scorched playground.

We were bombing the people of Dresden, not military targets. Old man Churchill cooked that one up to bring Hitler to his knees. Other guys told me the raid on the German cities was to display Britain's air power to Russia. Everyone knows Britain rules the sea, but now King George has the strongest air force in the world. That raid on Dresden made me sick. I just want it to end and come back to you.

"Oh, there's one more thing," Natsiq added, laughing. "He wrote that all the young air men wear these handsome bomber jackets and that the girls in the town are always after them. But my Sandy never pays them any attention. Listen to this. 'Some of the girls call out at us, "You're just cannon fodder for the Jerries!" And the old men in the town call us the "Crib Kids" because most of us pilots are barely out of our teens. I guess the old guys can't believe we can handle ourselves against the German Luftwaffe, but we can.'

"Oh, I have another letter from Sandy about the war. But half of the letter is blacked out by the censors, so I had to read it several times before I figured it out.

"Listen to this:

I'm going on my last mission tomorrow night. We're flying out with a thousand bombers in formation, one squadron after another. We each carry one bomb, drop it and turn for home. Then the Messerschmitt come after us. The Jerries' fighter planes are just waiting for one of us to break out of the formation and start down to our target. It only takes twenty minutes to unload that one bomb and get out of there. The rear gunner has to keep his eyes on our back. He'll yell out, "On our left, roll starboard! Drop, he's coming at us from above!" I tell him to shut his gob because there's not much more I can do. The plane is dropping, rolling, shifting starboard and aft like a boat in a wild sea. The men are all yellin', thinking that we're going to get it just days before the end of the war. I tell you, sweetie, I need a strong shot or two when I land this girl. The crew in the plane, they don't wait till we land. I have to stay sober, but they break out the gin and cordial, and by the time we land this baby, the boys can barely stagger out of the plane. I'll miss the Lancaster. She's a beaut of a plane. If I didn't love you so much, my first love would be the Lanc.

"He's funny, isn't he," Natsiq said, more bubbly than Ashoona had ever seen her in all their years of their often-strained relationship.

"He'll be back soon," Natsiq added, almost jumping up and down despite her heavy belly. "I want to have the baby first and then the wedding. His parents don't mind. His mom told me a lot of farm folk start families before walking down the aisle. Elisapi, the old woman at the san, tells me it will be a boy because of the shape of my belly. Sandy's mother hopes it's a girl, but Sandy wants a boy, and I just want a healthy baby and my man home safe."

———————

"The war's over! Peace at last!" It was Ann who phoned Ashoona to give her the news. "Hitler, that Jew-hating monster, surrendered, took cyanide, put a gun to his head and then blew himself up in his Berlin bunker taking Eva Braun with him. Too bad the Russians will occupy that part of Berlin. I wanted to see a picture of Hitler's body so I could be sure the world was rid of him and that he hadn't escaped with his girlfriend."

On the day that news of the surrender reached Canada, there were parades and dancing in the streets. Ashoona and Natsiq joined the crowds in the happy craziness. Soldiers kissed girls on the street, girls they had never met before. Someone even kissed Natsiq, telling her he hoped her man would come home safely. People cried and partied into the night. Even the school children joined the celebration—V-E Day they were told. They were unsure what it meant.

Ashoona and Brenda had to ask Ann for the news about the surrender. The two students were too preoccupied with their studies to read newspapers or listen to the radio. Ann was always up on the latest news and filled them in one Sunday when Ashoona and Brenda broke away from their books for a short visit with Ann and Natsiq.

"The Allies landed on the beaches of Normandy a year ago, June 6, I think," Ann told them. "The Allies freed occupied Holland where those poor Dutch people had been persecuted and starved throughout the war. Then we marched into France, freeing the French from the Vichy traitors and collaborators. Finally, Berlin fell, and the evil Nazi era crumbled. Hopefully, it won't be long before Japan surrenders, and we'll have peace."

"I don't give a hoot about what happened in the war," Natsiq told them. "Sandy promised to phone me as soon as the war ended. I'm on pins and needles waiting for his call and wondering if he'll be back in time for our baby's birth."

"And when is your due date?" Ashoona asked, as they shared coffee and cookies around the table in the stark, sanitized hospital cafeteria.

"Just three weeks to go." Natsiq did not look like she was in her third trimester. Throughout the pregnancy, she had gained little weight.

"Our grad is next week; maybe you can attend if you're well enough. At least Brenda can go to her own graduation now that she has escaped from Elijah and Celestial," Ashoona added.

"Are you saying that Elijah would not have allowed you to go to your own graduation? Why?" Ann asked.

"I was only allowed to go to normal school so that I could return and teach in the FLDS school. My graduation was a triumph for Celestial, not for me. No one is allowed to go to college or university until they have children because children are the security for the priesthood. They know we won't bolt if our children are back in Celestial. As soon as I finished classes and exams, I had to return. Esther came to the school one day to make sure I wasn't seeing other men and to check that my marks were high enough."

"She has got to be the nastiest women I've ever had to deal with," Ann offered, "and in my line of work, I meet some pretty snarly types. Why does Elijah favor her? She has a face like a washboard and a body like a sumo wrestler."

"Elijah is afraid to cross her because of her violent temper. But when it comes to sex, he seldom sleeps with her. As you might expect, he prefers the young wives. Once he even asked for me and another sister wife to come to bed with him together. When we refused, he beat us. Wives have a duty to obey their husbands, no matter how offensive."

"So," Ann continued, "they wouldn't let you attend graduation because completing the program was their accomplishment, not yours. Well, enjoy your grad, my girl. It's a wonderful accomplishment for you and a ceremony you'll remember all your life. I'll look after the children while you get your certificate, and I'll bring my youngsters along. They're older, going into high school now, and I want them to follow your path, well…not the path of getting stuck with a polygamist…you know what I mean."

"And you, Ashoona, I have to tell you how proud I am of you." The once hardheaded nurse choked on her words, and Ashoona could see tears in her eyes. The young Inuit girl put her arms around Ann, hugging her until Ann patted her and pushed her out at arm's length, "Enough. Enough. I love you, girl. You did well. I adopt you as my daughter. I have three sons, and finally on the fourth try, we had our little girl, but I would like to have an older daughter."

The ceremony was everything Ann said it would be. The students wore blue gowns and caps. Ann and Natsiq sat together in the audience, with Ann's two youngest and Brenda's children.

Ashoona won three awards—one for science, mostly because of Ludwig's teaching; one for social studies; and one for physical education. When the president of the school handed out the certificates, he made special mention of Ashoona.

"'This is our first graduate from the Northwest Territories. Ashoona Campbell has been a brilliant student. And instead of remaining in southern Canada, Ashoona is returning to her home village on Baffin Island in the Arctic. She will be the first Inuit teacher, or for that matter, the first Native teacher, in all of the Canadian territories. Ladies and gentlemen, let's all applaud the achievements of this bright, inspiring young woman."

After the ceremony, the four women and the children gathered in the auditorium to enjoy tea and cake. Natsiq could barely contain herself, she was so happy.

"Sandy called me from London. Guess what? He gets to fly the Lancaster right to Edmonton. He'll be here tomorrow and will phone me as soon as he lands. Can you believe it?"

"Wonderful, Natsiq," Ann replied. "We all know how worried you've been. I'm looking forward to seeing you walk down the aisle with your man. And remember, if you ever want to continue with your studies, just give me a dingaling on the phone. The Camsell is continuing with its classes and will always be there for former patients."

Natsiq had passed grade ten, not with high marks but sufficient to allow her to continue her high school. However, the young Inuit woman thought only of the return of her beloved Sandy and the impending birth of their child.

"We'll tie the knot this summer. Too darn bad you'll be in Baffin and can't be my bridesmaid," Natsiq said, smiling at Ashoona. "I'll miss you both, but I understand you have to find jobs, especially you, Brenda. I can't imagine having to support three children all on your own."

Although Brenda did not receive top honors, she managed a respectable A-minus average and was delighted to receive her diploma.

"I can teach anywhere. I can earn money and look after my family," she said excitedly.

"Why not come to Baffin Island? They are desperate for teachers, and the pay is good. The new patients who arrived at

Camsell last week told us the government is moving the people off the land and into communities. Frobisher Bay would be a great place to work because quite a few English-speaking people live there, and many of the Inuit speak both languages."

"Oh, I will consider that seriously," replied Brenda.

Ashoona warmed to the topic and could not say enough about her beloved homeland. "And you'd love it there, Jeremiah. I remember going out to hunt whales with my father and hunters from the community. I was about your age when my dad let me paddle the boat along with the other women while the men speared the whales. It was so exciting."

"Whales!" Jeremiah exclaimed. "You kill whales! Why?" The little boy was obviously dismayed by the picture of the beautiful animals being hunted down and killed.

"Oh, Oh! I..." Ashoona stammered trying to find the words to calm the boy's anxiety, when Brenda interrupted.

"Jeremiah, you know that we raised cattle, pigs, chickens and sheep, which we kill to feed our family. The Inuit people don't have farm animals, so they hunt seals and whales in the ocean and caribou out on the land. The ocean and the land is their farm; that is how they feed themselves."

Jeremiah's brow furrowed as he listened to his mother's explanation, and then sat quietly turning the new information over in his mind.

With the celebrations over, Brenda and Ashoona took Ann out for lunch to say goodbye and thank her for Brenda's rescue. Ashoona had money from her waitress job, and since the end of the war, tips had been pouring into her pocket.

By this time, the world had learned of the horror of the Nazi regime. Newsreels of the concentration camps had reached Canada, and everyone was talking about the atrocities inflicted on the Jewish people.

"Germans are not bad people," Ann declared, "so how could they let this happen and not stand up and protest? They must have known what was going on when they saw their Jewish neighbors taken away at gunpoint and marched through the streets as if they were criminals. Millions of Jewish people exterminated. It's unbelievable!"

"I don't believe in war," Ashoona added, "but in this case, I'm glad we fought the Nazis. The pictures of those tortured Jewish people found at Auschwitz will never leave my mind. When the army freed them, the people who had lived through the horror looked like the walking dead. Can you imagine how they felt when the U.S. Army arrived and freed the inmates and imprisoned the guards?"

"Apparently, the released prisoners did not smile, did not cheer," Ann continued. "They were like zombies. They had lost children, wives, husbands. They had nothing to celebrate. Their lives will be marked forever by the horror of what they endured."

"Ann, let's not talk about it any longer. By the way, where's Natsiq?" Ashoona asked. They had expected her to join them for lunch at the Cocky Bull.

"Sitting by the phone waiting for Sandy to land his Lancaster at Edmonton airport and call her on the phone. She's a nervous wreck because he was scheduled to arrive two days ago."

"Well maybe no news might be good news. He survived the war; he must be safe." Brenda was thinking of how dreadful it would be to find love, be expecting a baby and then lose it all.

"The authorities wouldn't inform Natsiq if anything happened," Ann said. "They'd telegraph the parents and then send one of those 'I am so very sorry' letters that the squadron leader has to write. He's probably written hundreds of those. Oh, my God! I just remembered. I heard a news story this morning about two planes colliding in mid-air near the Canary Islands. Both pilots died."

The grim possibility hit them all, and the mood changed. The three women had a premonition that something was wrong.

"Ashoona, best you come back to the hospital," Ann suggested. "I'll phone Sandy's parents to make sure he's safe. Natsiq is going to go out of her mind if she doesn't hear from him soon."

But there was no need to call. When they returned to the Camsell Hospital, Natsiq met them at the door, sobbing so violently her entire body shook. She was so overcome she couldn't get a word out.

"We know, Natsiq," Ann said, taking the distraught young woman in her arms. "I am so sorry, my darling. So sorry."

There was no consoling Natsiq. She went to her room and stayed there for days, lying on her cot sobbing. Nothing could bring her out of her depression, even though everyone in the hospital tried to find a way to give her hope for the future. Brenda came over with her children, hoping that if Natsiq held Rachael and saw the boys, she would come around and look forward to having Sandy's baby.

Ashoona and Brenda were completing their plans to move to the Arctic. Brenda had landed a job on her first application and would fly to Frobisher Bay, her flight arranged and paid for by the Department of Indian Affairs. Ashoona and Natsiq, like all former TB patients, had passage on one of the government supply ships going to Baffin Island.

Brenda and her three children were staying with Ann in her roomy house in the Glenora district. Ann's husband, George, was a senior administrator for Edmonton's Department of Finance. He never spoke about his work and he never raised his voice; he was a solid provider who enjoyed working in his garden and mowing and watering the lawn. In the evenings, he liked to read the newspapers, and along with Ann, listen to the news.

George was happy to open their home to Brenda and her family and was interested to learn about her life in the infamous FLDS cult. His first thought was how enraged he would be if his sweet daughter was forced to marry an old man the day she turned thirteen.

Ann and her husband wanted the best for their family. Their children were in middle school and high school and busy with after-school activities. Ann and George didn't indulge their children. The children walked or took a bus to soccer, baseball or ballet lessons. A roster of duties was taped to the fridge, chores that were religiously carried out by Ann's daughter and eleven-year-old son. The two younger children folded their clothes at bedtime and made their beds in the morning. The two older boys, now fourteen and fifteen always had excuses: "I couldn't set the table because my soccer practice went late. I forgot about the garbage this week because I was studying."

Ann and her husband dealt with the older boys by trimming their allowance and adding extra duties, but no loud retributions, just a simple approach of responsibilities and accountability.

The calm, loving environment helped Brenda's children adjust to the significant changes in their lives. Ann's four children, even the older boys who never had time to wash dishes, played with Jeremiah and Adam and entertained Rachael. Brenda appreciated their support. She knew that life as a single mother would be difficult at times, so for now, she enjoyed the company of Ann's family and the comforts of their modern, well-appointed home.

Brenda's flight north was only three days away. She had trouble sleeping as the magnitude of her move to the Arctic, to a new home and her first job overwhelmed her. Would Jeremiah fit into the school system where most of the children were Inuit? Would Rachael and Adam adapt to daycare? At least Elijah was not likely to track her down on Baffin Island. She slept fitfully, waking in the night with disturbing dreams about an unknown future. Rachael woke and smiled at Brenda through the bars of the crib. Brenda's worries evaporated as she held her child.

She joined the family for Sunday breakfast and was amazed to see George standing over the stove flipping pancakes. Never in her life had she ever seen or heard of an FLDS man cooking or cleaning in the kitchen. George was neatly shaven and dressed in pressed suit pants and a crisp white shirt covered with a large apron. With his round face and easy smile, he was a man she could easily hug.

After breakfast, Ann's family left for church, and Brenda read to her children. When it was Rachael's naptime, she let the boys play outside. Ann and her family would soon be home for lunch, and in the afternoon, Ann had promised to take Brenda and all the children to see the legislature buildings.

Brenda was standing at the kitchen window, watching Jeremiah and Adam play ball in the backyard when she heard a vehicle in the driveway. She was puzzled because it seemed early for Ann's family to be returning from church. She waited for the front door to open, but when no one came in, she felt a sense of panic a second before screams erupted from the backyard. From her vantage point, Brenda saw Esther and Elijah chasing Jeremiah and Adam.

Ann told me to phone! The number was taped to the refrigerator. Brenda grabbed the phone, and with shaking hands, dialed the number for the police department.

"My children are being kidnapped!" she yelled into the phone. "Please come immediately!" Her heart thumped in her chest as she gave the address.

Brenda burst through the front door in time to see her two boys being pushed, pulled and dragged toward Elijah's truck. Jeremiah kicked at his captors and screamed for his mother. Adam, usually unperturbed, burst into tears.

Brenda's usually calm nature took a complete about face. She was like a grizzly sow whose cubs were being threatened. She rushed at Esther, pushing the big woman to the ground, then she beat at Elijah with her fists.

"Let them go! I'll never let you take my children!"

But Brenda was no match for the hefty FLDS leader. He raised his fist and brought it down on Brenda's nose. She staggered and grabbed the side of the truck to steady herself. Her head spun and she tasted blood.

By this time Esther had recovered, grabbed Adam, threw him in the truck and locked the door. Elijah had a firm grip on Jeremiah's collar. The young boy was crying, and in between sobs, kicking at his captor. Brenda regained her strength and once more rushed at Elijah. But it was too late. Elijah lifted the boy into the truck, got in himself and locked the doors. Meanwhile Esther turned and dashed into the house. Brenda saw her just as Esther was opening the door and ran after her, aware that Esther was going to get Rachael.

"Come back here, you whore!" Elijah yelled out the truck window. "No woman will ever leave me! You're mine. Come peacefully, and you can have your children back."

I need to save Rachael. Please let the police stop Elijah.

Esther was no longer young enough to move quickly up the stairs, and by the time she reached the top landing, Brenda was at her heels.

The frantic mother tackled Esther, grabbed her feet, and the would-be kidnapper toppled over at the top of the stairs. Brenda knelt on top of Esther, holding her on the floor while the older woman kicked and screamed.

"You're never touching my baby again!" Brenda screamed. "You have no power over me and my family. You can't have your way anymore. You and Elijah have flaunted the law, taken children from their mothers, forced girls into marriages with old men and evicted women from their homes. The law will make you pay for your crimes."

Brenda could not believe that she could triumph over the woman who had dominated her life for the past seven years.

"Bah! The law," Esther sneered. "Elijah ignores the law. He has the government in his pocket. No one can touch us. Our religion protects us. You will see."

Just then, they heard sirens and the screech of tires in front of the house.

"The police are here, and this time you don't have the local FLDS policemen to come to your defense."

Two officers burst through the door.

"Which of you is Brenda?"

"I called you." Brenda tried to catch her breath. "She stole my boys and is trying to steal my baby. Her husband has my boys in his truck. Please, catch Elijah before he gets away with them!" Even as she said this, her inner voice told her that Elijah had already escaped and had her two sons with him.

"He's not in the driveway, but we saw a truck speeding down the road just as we approached the house. We had no time to chase a speeder when children were being abducted."

"Please, go after him. It's a gray Ford truck with BC license plates," Brenda yelled, her stomach in knots at the thought of losing her boys.

One of the policemen ran to his vehicle and took up the chase, calling in to the station for backup.

By this time, Ann's family had arrived to the turmoil at their home. A policeman was taking Brenda's statement, and Esther sat scowling in handcuffs.

Ann was furious at having her home invaded. "Get her out of here, and lock her up. I can't bear having her in my home another second."

Ann knew what Elijah's truck looked like, and she insisted that her husband join in the chase. Their children stayed at the house with Brenda. They were concerned for the safety of their young charges but also a little excited about the drama that had come into their normally staid lives. What would become of Jeremiah and Adam if the police couldn't rescue them? The older boys had listened to Brenda talking about the FLDS, how some children were taken across the border and given to new parents, beyond the reach of the law and their natural parents.

Ann thought she had a rough idea of the route Elijah would take. "Keep the pedal to the metal, George!" Ann urged her husband. "He'll take the road south toward Calgary and head for the U.S. border. If he gets into the states, he'll take the boys to Utah, and Brenda will never see her sons again."

When George and Ann reached the intersection with the main highway, they looked around anxiously, trying to spot Elijah's truck.

"He's coming up behind us, George! Can you block his truck?" Ann grabbed George's arm, no longer the calm, collected hospital matron.

George swerved his vehicle across the road and brought it to a stop, blocking all vehicles heading in both directions. Elijah's gray truck pulled in behind them. Angry drivers honked and yelled until George got out and explained the situation to the drivers nearby. The man in the car immediately behind Elijah understood the problem and offered to help by blocking the truck from turning back.

George walked up to Elijah's truck and tried the passenger-side door where the children were being held. It was locked.

"Let them go. The police are on their way."

"I will kill them before I let you take what is mine!" Elijah screamed, red-faced and out of control. He smashed his fists on the truck dashboard and leaned on the horn.

Not one vehicle moved. Jeremiah was holding his little brother, and both were sobbing. The boy wanted to be strong in front of his younger brother, but he couldn't hold back his tears. Little Adam had always been stoic, but he was terrified of Elijah and sobbed along with his older brother.

Elijah turned his anger on the boys. "You brats, stay in the truck. If I see you open the door, I'll kill you!"

Elijah jumped out of the truck, picked up the shovel from the truck bed and approached the driver whose car blocked Elijah from turning around. Elijah swung at the driver, who dodged the shovel and got back in his vehicle. The enraged man smashed the car with his shovel, denting the hood and cracking the windshield.

"Apostates! I will kill all of you! Don't you realize you will burn in eternal hell? These are my children. My possessions! You have no right to interfere with a man's family." He continued his ranting until he heard the sirens. He realized it was over, and the hateful government would put him in jail. He was finished.

To Adam's delight, the two boys were taken home in the police car. Even Jeremiah found the trip exciting, especially when the officer let them turn on the siren. Ann and George followed the police car home, but not before they thanked the other drivers and offered to pay for the repairs to the man's car.

Brenda wept with joy when she saw her boys getting out of the front seat of the police car.

Chapter Twenty-four

The Return

To Brenda's dismay, Elijah was let off with only a fine for trying to kidnap her children. The wealthy cult leader appealed to the judge on the basis of his family's finances, and he worked the community to get references swearing to his excellent character. He was soon back in Celestial searching for another child bride to replace Brenda. Esther was sentenced to a few months in jail, and she never regained her dominance within Elijah's household.

After Brenda's escape, Elijah increased vigilance on the Celestial wives and children and commanded complete obedience. Members of the community who objected to Elijah's orders or complained in any way were told to "be sweet." A husband who could not control his wife's behavior could be excommunicated and never see his family again. His wife could be reassigned to a new husband. Despite the polygamist practices, government funds flowed to the community for the school and family allowances. Elijah laughed at the gullibility of government officials as he continued to "milk the beast" for welfare benefits and grants.

———————

Natsiq's baby was born at the Camsell Hospital, weighing a little over five pounds. The grieving young mother not only had an infant to care for but also one who wouldn't sleep for more than an hour at a time. Natsiq had decided to return to Panniqtuuq, believing that her mother would help her with the frail infant and that her older son Samuel would bond with her despite her four-year absence.

"I've named my baby after his father, Sandy," she told Ashoona. Natsiq was still unable to talk about her loss without choking up. "I know I should be happy to have Sandy's baby because it will be something of him to keep with me always, but I just can't feel any happiness. I deserve this punishment, don't I, Ashoona?"

"Why on earth would you say that?"

"You know why. You know I have harmed you and now I'm being punished for my bad behavior."

"Good Lord, Natsiq, don't feel that way. Let's put the past behind us. We've moved on. I'm pleased you're returning to Panniqtuuq. You need to bond with Samuel again, and you need some help in caring for your new baby."

Ashoona's friends had written that it was Adamie who took care of Samuel, not Amaruk. Ashoona wondered if Aunt Amaruk would actually be capable of helping Natsiq look after a colicky infant given the mean-minded treatment Ashoona had suffered.

"In any case, Natsiq, you will get help from the government. There's family allowance now for parents, and as a single mother, you'll get government relief. You can be with your children; you won't have to work until they go to school, and even then you'll get relief if you can't find work. When we leave for Panniqtuuq next week, I'll give you a hand with the baby during the trip home."

⁓⁓⁓

The ship dropped anchor near Panniqtuuq on the last day of June, and the passengers waited on deck for high tide. The returning TB survivors waved enthusiastically, but they were too far from shore to see their families and friends. Ashoona joined the others on deck, scanning the dock to try to spot familiar faces in the crowd. So many emotions ran through Ashoona's mind. This village had shunned her, much like women in Celestial who disobeyed and were shunned. But she was returning as a fully qualified teacher, the very first Inuit teacher. Life held much promise.

Natsiq's future, however, was far from sunny. Little Sandy had trouble nursing and never seemed to get enough milk to keep him satisfied. It was as if he was fighting her when she tried to nurse him. He would latch onto the nipple, try to nurse but keep losing his grip, and then he would scream.

During the flight across Canada and then the month-long journey by sea from Montreal to Baffin Island, Natsiq was often in tears from exhaustion and grief. Ashoona tried to help Natsiq by walking the baby on the deck and singing to him so that the distraught mother could catch an hour or two of sleep, but by the time the ship reached Panniqtuuq, Natsiq was fatigued and haggard looking.

"No one will want to marry me; I look like an old woman," she complained, checking her reflection in the mirror. Natsiq applied lipstick and put on her new clothes that had been provided by the hospital. When it was her turn, she held Sandy close as she stepped into the cargo boat that carried them to shore. Her parents were waiting on the dock, her father holding a little boy's hand. Natsiq barely recognized Samuel. Natsiq stepped on the dock and hugged her parents, but when she bent to hug her son, Samuel hid behind his grandfather and turned his head away.

"This is your mother," Adamie told Samuel. But to Samuel, Natsiq was a stranger. He did not want to be near the strange woman who was supposed to be his mother. He left his grandfather and ran up the dock to watch the boats coming in and the town's supplies being unloaded.

"He's a good boy," Adamie said, smiling as he watched his grandson. "Give him time."

Even more strained was the meeting between Amaruk and Ashoona. All Ashoona could manage was a cold, "*Unnasakoot*...good afternoon."

Other villagers welcomed her with open arms. They knew Ashoona had come back to be a teacher, and the animosity among the elders was replaced by admiration for her accomplishments. For some of her peers, especially a few of the young men, Ashoona sensed resentment. Times were changing among the Inuit. Men were no longer central to the well-being of a family now that other jobs were replacing hunting. And the jobs were taken not by the men, but by their women.

One young man, however, was obviously glad to see her. A tall, lean man, just slightly younger than Ashoona, rushed up to her and threw his arms around her.

"Paloosie? Is that you? Have you ever changed!" She had a warm smile for the teenager from the German expedition whose first love in life was the beautiful Ashoona. Obviously his attraction to her had not diminished during the years of their separation.

"But where is Henry? Did he finally chase Joanna down and get a ring on her finger?"

"You mean Doctor Russell?" Paloosie asked. "He's the chief of the Frobisher Bay hospital, a big wig now. You'll see him when you go to the city for meetings. All the teachers go to Frobisher at least once a year."

Ashoona watched as Amaruk and Natsiq with Sandy in her *amauti* walked up the hill, followed by Adamie and a young boy. The old man held the boy's hand, the two looking like a bonded pair.

"Is that Natsiq's little boy walking with Adamie?" Ashoona asked Paloosie.

"Yes. Samuel is a good boy, and he and his grandfather are inseparable. I remember you told us that Natsiq's little brother had been killed, and you were blamed."

"Natsiq has never apologized for lying about Davidee's death. Maybe it doesn't matter anymore. I'm happy that Adamie has someone who loves him and someone he can care for. I can't imagine what Adamie's life has been like living with the mean-spirited Amaruk for the past thirty years."

"Oh, and there's your new school principal coming toward us, Ashoona. He's my boss, too. I'm the caretaker and general fix-it man at *Atagoyak Ilisiviak*."

Ernest Macpherson was a Newfoundlander, appointed by the government to run the new school in Panniqtuuq. He had a round face, balding head and a portly build. With his fair skin, it was obvious that he suffered during the twenty-four hours of sun. Already, his smooth, chubby cheeks were a rosy pink from the effects of the brilliant summer sun. He wore glasses that failed to make him look scholarly; instead he had the appearance of a friendly grocer.

"I'm Ernest Macpherson, the principal at the school here in Panniqtuuq. We've been expecting you, Miss Campbell, and I'm pleased to welcome you to *Atagoyak Ilisiviak*."

Ashoona took an immediate liking to Ernest. He treated her as an equal, not looking down on her as many of the *Qallunaat* did. Her only problem with him was his heavy accent. During their brief meeting at the dock, she had to ask him to repeat himself several times. And then to make matters worse, when she couldn't understand him, Ernest exaggerated his accent.

"'Er ya deaf, girl?" he said lightheartedly. "'Er might it be me brog dat gits ya?"

Ernest had a jolly voice and a big laugh.

———————

School was out for the year by the time Ashoona had arrived, but the graduation ceremony was planned for that weekend. Ernest asked Ashoona to come to the school and help prepare for the celebration as soon as she moved into her government row house. He also offered to help her get settled. The government row houses were furnished, but teachers had to bring their own dishes, linens, stock of food and other miscellaneous items. Ashoona had only the clothes given to her by the Camsell hospital and a few belongings she had bought with her earnings from the Cocky Bull, so it didn't really take her long to get settled.

Ernest was married to an equally jovial wife. Judy was about as round as she was tall, with a wonderful warm smile like her husband. They were both middle-aged and had many years of teaching experience on "The Rock." Teachers from Newfoundland were often recruited for the North because the climate there is similar to that of Baffin Island, long winters and cold bitter winds.

The day after Ashoona moved into her row house, Judy arrived at her door, her ever-helpful husband in tow carrying boxes filled with household items.

"I hope you can use these things," Judy said after introducing herself. "My place is filled to the rafters with all the stuff we brought from St. John's. I just want to do a clean sweep so I can get into my storage area and closets."

Judy had brought a set of dishes, pots, cutlery, towels and bed sheets.

"You'll be going to the store for your food, girl, and you'll find the prices there will floor you. So if you need to borrow some food until you can put in an order to come on the next supply ship, let me know. I have tons of flour, sugar, rice, whatever you might need."

"Judy runs her own store. The only difference is that we don't charge. Even after she gives flour and sugar to the locals, we are never without, as you can see by our expanding waistlines."

"The Lord loves the little children," Judy kibitzed. "I'm trying to cut back on the chocolate bars, but I guess you haven't noticed that I lost three pounds."

"Are you sure you didn't find them again?" Ernest shot back.

"Lord 'a mercy, Ernest, watch what you say." His wife gave him a fake cuff and laughed. "May your big jib be full of wind, and I see that it is."

———

Ashoona walked along the dusty path to the school, happy to join Ernest and Judy in the preparations for the graduation ceremony. Ernest needed Ashoona's help as the other English-speaking teachers had already flown south for the summer break, and the Inuit staff had left for the fishing site at Clearwater Bay.

"Only three graduated out of eleven grade eight students? Isn't that low?" Ashoona asked as she helped Judy string paper streamers above the gym stage.

"And they are all girls. They're anxious to move to Frobisher Bay and stay in the residence while they complete their junior matriculation. Just four more years. If they can make that, these girls will do something with their lives other than have babies."

"I worry about the others who aren't graduating, especially the boys. They can no longer survive as hunters, and going on social assistance isn't the answer."

"Every family in the village will be getting the government check each month. That was the deal when the hunters were forced to move into the villages—a house, a check and a school for the children." Judy paused in her work, dangling a colored streamer from a chubby arm. "School is so difficult, especially for the younger ones. They come to class speaking only Inuktitut and then have to learn English almost overnight, and from the likes of Ernest with an accent as thick as molasses on a cold winter day!"

Now that Judy was revved up, she had no difficulty going on about the problems the Inuit faced. "And the girls. I worry about them getting pregnant as young as thirteen. I'm pleased that at least three of them will escape the pressures from their boyfriends. I had to intercede between my best student and her boyfriend. He was forcing her to have sex. I faced him down and told him to leave her alone, or I would get the police to have a talk with him. That went over well as you can imagine. I hear the young guys making nasty remarks about me whenever I go to the store. But I don't give a cotton pickin' hoot what they think. I saved little Alukie from having a baby when she was not more than a baby herself."

"There you go, pontificating again instead of working on the decorations," Ernest said with a broad smile on his round, pink face and a twinkle in his eyes.

"Are we doing all this for just three graduates?" Ashoona asked softly, not meaning to criticize but curious about the extent of the celebration being planned.

"Ah. No. All eleven will be included in the ceremony, along with their families. The students who didn't pass will receive a certificate of attendance. It's the party that is important," Ernest explained. "If the students who failed can be part of the celebration, they may come back next year and pass their exams. I can only hope."

"I wish life on Baffin Island had stayed the same as when I was a child. Families hunted and fished. They did all right." Ashoona thought back on her life as the child of the Hudson's Bay factor. "My life was perfect up until the day my father left."

"You're still angry about that, aren't you? Now that you're back, maybe you could talk to your uncle and try to find out what happened to your dad. Don't let it corrode your insides. Deal with it straight on."

Judy and Ernest could hardly wait for the grad ceremony to be completed so they could return to St. John's, a trip northerners refer to as "going outside." The couple had been in Panniqtuuq for a year, and they were anxious to see their children and grandchildren and visit friends. The summer holiday would be a respite from the isolation of the Arctic.

Ashoona had no desire to travel south, at least not so soon after returning to the north. However, she would be going to Frobisher Bay for the Labor Day weekend. The Department of Education arranged for the teachers from remote communities to attend the orientation meeting just before the beginning of the school year.

The trip to Frobisher would also be a chance for Ashoona to go to a movie and eat in a restaurant. She looked forward to seeing Brenda and wondered how her friend was settling into her new life. She would also visit Henry. It had been four years since he had hugged her goodbye on the dock at Panniqtuuq.

For the summer, however, Ashoona took up the routine of the village, attending Sunday services at St. Luke's Anglican Church and the many community gatherings to celebrate a christening or mourn the death of an elder. Increasingly, deaths occurred among teenagers and especially among the young men. The changes affecting life in the north disrupted the centuries-old hunter-gatherer culture, often leaving the young men without hope for the future.

Aunt Amaruk and Adamie attended community events along with little Samuel, but Ashoona never saw Natsiq. Ashoona found it difficult to speak to her aunt without her stomach turning into knots. It was different with Adamie. She saw him and his grandson walking to the Hudson's Bay Post one day and caught up with them.

Adamie initially looked embarrassed and hesitant to talk to her. He glanced down at his feet when Ashoona greeted him, mumbling a response.

"Adamie, you do remember who I am, don't you?"

"Oh yes, I do. I have to go now."

Ashoona found his behavior quite uncharacteristic of her uncle. Adamie had always liked her, even loved her when she first came to stay with them.

"What's the matter?" she pursued.

"Your aunt has decided the family will have nothing to do with you. She says you have taken on *Qallunaaq* ways, that you think you're better than us with your college education."

"That is so untrue and so unfair, Adamie. I still want you to be my uncle, and I want to see Natsiq because we became friends when we were at the Camsell. I worry about her."

"I worry, too. She stays in bed all day, getting up only to change and nurse the baby."

"May I visit her?"

He paused before replying. "Come to the house when Amaruk goes to the craft circle on Friday afternoon." His eyes never left the ground, and he shuffled his feet as if wanting to get away from her. Adamie took young Samuel's hand, gently leading the little boy away from Ashoona.

As Ashoona approached her aunt and uncle's house a few days later, she saw Samuel playing with his friends, laughing as they ran through the streamlets that trickled over the rocks. Summer was a liberating time for children. Released from the confines of school and overheated houses, they spent their days outside amusing themselves until their parents called them in for the evening meal. Samuel seemed to be a happy, healthy child. Ashoona hoped that Natsiq had been able to reestablish her bond with her firstborn.

She knocked on the door of the wood-framed shack. When no one answered, she opened the door, poked her head in and called out. In Panniqtuuq, everyone just walked into other people's houses, but Ashoona did not feel comfortable entering her aunt's home without some warning.

The room was stuffy and overcrowded with a table and chairs where Adamie sat, an old, worn couch, and a crib where Sandy was sleeping. If that wasn't enough furniture pushing out the walls of the small house, she also spied a double bed where Ashoona assumed Amaruk, Adamie and Samuel slept, and a single bed where Natsiq was sleeping. Ashoona wondered how they coped in such a cramped space when she had two bedrooms, a living room, a kitchen, plus a storage area.

Adamie was polishing a stone carving. He looked up at Ashoona with wary, watery eyes. Ashoona's uncle had aged greatly over the past four years. He was a small, slightly built man, and although just in his fifties, he was now stooped and frail. Adamie always had a kindly face, but after years of domination by a shrewish wife, he had become withdrawn and sad. His only solace was his grandson Samuel, whom he cherished.

"Uncle, how are you?" she whispered, not wanting to wake the baby or Natsiq. "And how is Natsiq managing with little Sandy?"

"Natsiq is tired all the time, and the baby, well…he is sweet but such as skinny little one. Not like Samuel at all. I worry about Natsiq, sleeping all the time, not wanting to talk, not able to say a word to Samuel or play with him."

"She needs time. Is Amaruk helping with the baby?"

"Not Amaruk. She says she doesn't want to be grandmother to a *Qallunaaq* baby, and I'm too old to care for the poor little thing. With Samuel, I'm fine. I am teaching him to build a *qamutik* and to carve. I am able to guide him, not indulge him the way I did with Natsiq. The pain Natsiq suffers is because I wasn't a good father, and Amaruk not a good mother. And I tell you now, I wasn't a good uncle to you, my sister's child."

"It's in the past, Adamie. Don't blame yourself for Natsiq's problems. She is young and will find a husband and get her life together. I want to help her, if I can."

With some trepidation, Ashoona launched into the topic that had disturbed her since she was eight years old. "Uncle, I can't help but wonder why my father never wrote me and never came back even after mother died. Is there anything that I should know?"

He shuffled his feet and avoided eye contact with Ashoona. Then to signal the end of the conversation, Adamie got up stiffly, placing his hands on the table top to help push himself to his feet.

"I must check on Samuel." His eyes were again glued to the floor as he excused himself and left the house.

Adamie's behavior puzzled Ashoona, but she pushed it to the back of her mind. After he left, Ashoona went over to Natsiq, who was stirring.

"Cousin, it's me, Ashoona."

Natsiq opened her eyes, looked at Ashoona and turned her head to the wall. "I have no energy. I have to sleep."

"Come for a walk, Natsiq. The sun is shining. The supply boat brought lots of new things to the store. You could put Sandy in your *amauti* and show him off to the people in the village, and we can buy a new outfit for him."

"I look terrible. I don't want anyone to see me this way."

"You just need to braid your hair and put on your best clothes and that *amauti* your mother made for you when you were just a teen. You've lost so much weight, it will fit you again, and now you have a wee babe to tuck under your *amauti*. Sit up, and I'll do your hair. Please do this for me."

Natsiq complied. Her hair had grown long enough to be styled in the traditional Inuit fashion of two braids twisted in attractive circles on both sides of her head. The style flattered

Natsiq's flashing dark brown eyes and oval face. Her petite figure was accentuated by her loss of weight, whereas Ashoona was several inches taller with a full figure and a small waist.

Ashoona found a mirror and held it up. "There. See. You're beautiful."

The sun was dazzling and the weather warm. They wore the traditional summer *amauti*, made of white cotton and decorated around the edges with colorful blue and red stripes. It was never really hot in Panniqtuuq, so no one went out in short sleeves. They always wore at least a light jacket because the chilly winds could come up in minutes. That day the air was calm, and most of the village people were out walking.

"So why does your mother object to us to seeing each other?" Ashoona asked.

"I don't know," Natsiq said unconvincingly.

As they strolled to the store, women stopped to talk and inspect the baby, commenting on the boy's similarity to the mother, grandmother or grandfather and making no mention of the father. Natsiq wanted to tell them that Sandy's father was a war hero, and that if he had lived, she would be a married woman with a house and everything she could ever want. Instead, Natsiq barely acknowledged their comments and greetings. She mumbled, *"Qujannamiik"* and hastily broke off the encounters.

"We must get going, Ashoona."

At the store, Ashoona picked out an outfit for Sandy, offering to buy it.

"I don't want your charity," Natsiq retorted. Ashoona understood and tried to move on to safer topics. They walked through the store, admiring the new items that the post-war period had brought. Ashoona mentioned that it was great that they no longer needed coupons to buy sugar and butter. Rationing had been lifted at the end of the war. Ashoona felt so much hope for herself, and she wanted her cousin to regain her feisty attitude.

They could not spend too much time at the store as Natsiq insisted they return home before Amaruk returned. Leaving the store, both women were surprised to see someone from their past. James was wearing his police uniform and flashing the dazzling smile that had captivated Natsiq and Ashoona when they were younger. While his smile had not changed, James was no longer the fit, slim young man of the past. He had put on weight, not to the point of obesity, but enough to detract from his movie-star good looks.

"Look who's back in Panniqtuuq, and little Natsiq with another babe. You are a busy girl, aren't you? And Ashoona, still in love with me, I hope?"

Ashoona just stared at him, wondering what she had seen in this self-centered man. Even Natsiq, who in the past would always quip back, could not come up with a retort. Her face flushed. Ashoona noticed Natsiq's embarrassment.

"Natsiq's man was killed defending this country from the Germans and is a Victoria Cross recipient. The little one is his son."

Ashoona took Natsiq's elbow and gently steered her away. "Goodbye, James."

"My mother still believes I should marry James," Natsiq told Ashoona as they walked up the gravel path between the rows of small shacks and hastily built government houses. "Remember, I was promised to him, a deal made between the two mothers. But I don't want anything to do with any man. All I want is to have Sandy back alive, and that can't be." Natsiq's voice broke, and she choked back the tears as they walked slowly up the path to Natsiq's shack.

Neither Ashoona nor Natsiq could avoid seeing James. It was a small village, and most people bumped into each other unless they never left their house. Natsiq did not want to see James if he was going to humiliate her, but Ashoona knew that it would be worse for the young mother if she stayed home all day in isolation. So, over the summer Ashoona often called on Natsiq. Aunt Amaruk was aware of their walks. If Amaruk was home when Ashoona knocked, she ignored her niece, but no longer outwardly objected to the visits.

On a dazzling August afternoon, when Ashoona and Natsiq walked down the hill to the beach, they saw several families loading their motorboats to head out to the fishing spot at Clearwater Bay. A few had camped out on the land since breakup. One of these was Kilabuk's family, who was back in Panniqtuuq for a day of shopping.

Ashoona spotted Aula loading up their motorboat and hurried over to her friend. Aula now had a glass eye, replacing the one she had lost when she stepped in to protect Ashoona from Padluk. Aula and Kilabuk had been at the fishing grounds when Ashoona returned from Edmonton so this was their first chance to see each other since the day Ashoona was diagnosed with tuberculosis and sent away on the ship.

"Ashoona! You're even more beautiful than ever!" Aula cried. "And I hear you are a teacher. Congratulations!"

"And congratulations to you. Two more children. And is this Minnie? She's a little girl now...no longer the screamer or the dust-mop baby." They both laughed remembering the baby's first year when Minnie was the beloved child on the expedition, the only one unaware of how close to death they had all been.

"And Aula. You look so healthy and happy."

"You mean I'm fat," Aula laughed. A chubby baby boy squirmed in her hood and a toddler was trying to keep up with Minnie as the sturdy six-year-old toted bags of groceries over to the motorboat.

"Minnie, you're such a big girl now, even helping your mama. And are you fishing and hunting too?" Ashoona remembered how her father had taught her how to shoot at that age.

"I fish and caught a big 'un," She stretched her chubby arms out wide. "But Paloosie, he caught a bigger fish. He caught a walrus. See. There's my big brother."

Ashoona turned to watch Paloosie walk down to the beach hefting a boat motor.

"Hello, Paloosie. I see you're going out with your family to Clearwater. Is your work at the school finished?"

"I'll be back when the school opens this fall. Besides looking after your school, I'm also contracted to work at the Frobisher school for a few months each year. I'll be doing school maintenance and taking the students out on a cultural awareness program."

Paloosie lifted the motor onto the transom of the boat and tightened the lugs. "By the way," he continued, "I met a friend of yours from Edmonton."

"Brenda?"

"I helped her move into her apartment and built shelves for her."

"Brenda and I were at normal school together. I'll see her next week when I am in the city. "

"I know. She says you're her savior."

"And you are my savior! I'll never forget how you saved me from Qillaq. I owe you my life, Paloosie. But how is that leg of yours?" Ashoona asked.

"It healed and remains a good memory because every time I look at the scar, I think about you." He smiled warmly.

Strange how much he reminded her of Kilabuk, always calm no matter how difficult the circumstances, always with a smile as if to say *"ayunqnaq…*it can't be helped and so let's laugh instead of complain."

Ashoona decided not to press Paloosie for more news about Brenda. She'd heard something in his voice that reminded her about the expedition when Paloosie had a crush on her.

Ashoona rejoined Aula to wish her good fishing. "Your skinny teenager has become a giant, Aula. He's taller than Kilabuk. What have you been feeding him, lots of Arctic char, caribou and *muktuk*?"

"He's grown into a wonderful young man and has even become the conversationalist and joker in the family," Aula said. "I'm pleased that he is no longer tongue-tied as he was on the expedition."

The two women laughed and hugged again, happy to be reunited. Ashoona was so happy to see her friend that she had forgotten about Natsiq.

"Oh! Sorry. You know Natsiq, don't you?"

"Yes, hello, Natsiq," Aula answered coolly.

Aula took Ashoona aside and asked her why she was out walking with Natsiq, the cousin who had caused her so much grief.

Natsiq, realizing that Aula was talking about her, became annoyed. "Ashoona, I'm going. You coming or not?" Ashoona said goodbye to Aula and rejoined Natsiq.

"You told her bad things about me, didn't you?"

"It was a long time ago. We were together for months on the trail, and of course, the women on the expedition asked me who had arranged my marriage with Qillaq and why Aunt Amaruk disliked me so much. Does your mother still believe I was the one who shot your little brother?"

"Why would she think anything differently? Why would she believe you over her own daughter?"

"Maybe it's time you told the truth so that old wounds can heal. You're not the same person you were as a young girl. I thought we were friends, Natsiq. I'm sorry I told Aula about your treatment of me, but I was angry and hurt. I no longer feel that way."

"I just wish you wouldn't talk about me."

"I only speak well of you, now."

"Sure. I bet."

Ashoona dropped the conversation. Natsiq's bad mood was affecting her, and Ashoona wished she was sailing out to Clearwater Bay with Aula and her brood. The tide had rushed in, rising ten feet in the last few hours. The sun glistened on the bay and bounced off Kilabuk's silver boat. The two young women were silent as they walked up the hill to Natsiq's parents' shack.

"I'm going to Frobisher tomorrow for the teachers' orientation meetings," Ashoona announced as she was leaving Natsiq. "Take care of yourself."

"Yeah, right."

The next day, Ashoona boarded the Beaver single-engine plane for the hour-long flight to the city. She was to meet with officials from the Department of Education and teachers from Frobisher and the outlying communities.

Ashoona looked forward to reuniting with Brenda and wondered how she and her children were making out in a city where most of the residents were Inuit. She thought about a reunion with Henry and wondered where life had taken him.

Was he married now? Will he even remember me?

As soon as the plane landed in Frobisher, Ashoona phoned Brenda and was invited for dinner. Brenda lived in a two-story apartment block built to house the teaching staff. As Ashoona walked up the hallway she was met with a mix of cooking aromas.

A lot of you must be frying fish, she thought as she caught the familiar smell of Arctic char.

Chapter Twenty-five

Inuit Romeo

Brenda opened the door and spread her arms to hug her dear friend. Ashoona noticed immediately that Brenda had abandoned the long, old-fashioned dress and austere hairstyle. She wore a modest blouse with a high collar and a wool skirt that fit firmly around her small waist and fell below her knees. The outfit accentuated her slender build.

Brenda led Ashoona into the living room where the children were playing. Jeremiah remembered Ashoona.

"We're learning about seals, and we even eat seal meat. When the ocean freezes, Paloosie is going to take my students in a *qamutik* to hunt seal and sleep in an igloo."

"It sounds like you've forgiven me for eating whale meat."

"We don't hunt whales, only seals and caribou. I still like whales. Paloosie said we killed too many whales, and we shouldn't kill them anymore. They are dangerous."

"Maybe you mean *endangered*?" Brenda corrected.

"Endangered," Jeremiah repeated. At seven, he could carry on a serious conversation about the success of the seal hunters and the problems with too many people drinking alcohol in Frobisher Bay. The weight of the world's problems rested on his little shoulders now that he no longer had to worry about his mother and his cruel treatment from Esther.

Adam and little Rachael were quite the opposite, just happy, carefree children busy playing with a small wooden toy *qamutik*. Rachael had turned two, and having learned to speak much earlier than her older siblings, now commanded them to give her toys she wanted or fetch things for her.

"So, you know my friend Paloosie from Panniqtuuq," Ashoona said to Jeremiah.

"He will be our outdoor leader at school. This summer he took us out on the ocean in his fishing boat, and we went caribou hunting, too. He's Mom's friend."

They enjoyed a wonderful dinner of fried chicken and spaghetti. Rachael dug into her bowl with both hands, covering her cheeks and the tray of her high chair with tomato sauce. Jeremiah ate slowly, poking at his food, more interested in the adult conversation than his meal while Adam ate quietly and quickly, giving his full attention to the food. Brenda and Ashoona had so much news to share that the time passed quickly.

"Children. Sorry, but it's time for bed."

Brenda read to the boys while Ashoona sang nursery songs to Rachael. Ashoona loved the warm sensation of holding the healthy, chubby baby and thought about having a family of her own one day to love and care for.

"So tell me, what are you and Paloosie up to?" Ashoona asked Brenda. Once the children were all tucked in, the two friends settled in the living room with their tea.

"Paloosie was with you on the expedition, right? Were you involved with him? I never even thought to ask you."

"No. He's just a friend. But how on earth did you meet?"

"Actually, he was the first person I got to know here. Since he does maintenance work at the school, he came over to fix the locks, and then he helped me move in on my first day in Frobisher. The department hired Paloosie to take the students out on the land, you know, a sort of cultural awareness program. He'll be here for several months each term. Goodness, that man can fix everything!"

"He's good with his hands, I'll give you that!" Both women laughed at the double meaning. "When Paloosie was on the expedition, his father taught him how to build kayaks, *qamutiit* and igloos."

"I know this is sudden but, I loved him the moment I saw him, and I know he feels the same about me. He wants to become a Mormon. We have a small group in Frobisher, just ten or so members, but we support each other. Next summer, Paloosie and I will be married by the local prophet from the Church of Latter Day Saints." Her face lit up with happiness as she spoke of Paloosie.

"Are you serious about continuing in that faith?"

"Of course," Brenda replied. "Mainstream Mormons do not support polygamy and have modern ideas. What Paloosie and I like about the faith is the dedication to hard work and the rules against smoking and liquor. He's wonderful with the children, and he's so funny he makes me laugh more than I've ever laughed in my life. After spending seven years with a man I hated, one who abused me, I could never have imagined how wonderful it could be to fall in love and have someone truly love me.

"Don't tell me you are going to settle down here?"

"Why not? The children are happy here. I've hired an Inuit woman to help with the children, and she is teaching them Inuktitut. Jeremiah will start school next week, and he can already speak a few sentences in your language? Adam and Rachael are happy, always full of smiles and giggles. In the summer, Paloosie took us out in his fishing boat, and we camped on one of the islands. The children were the happiest I've ever seen them."

"He is a few years younger than you, but that can be a good thing when you are long in the tooth and need a younger man to help you up the stairs."

They broke out in giggles. "We'll never really be old, Ashoona. Well, maybe we will, so don't you think it's time you got married? You should find yourself a fellow and have a few babies. It's the best life."

"I've been disillusioned in love, mostly because of my father, I think. I believed in him with all my heart, yet he abandoned me. Then I fell in love with James, who turned out to be a lout."

"If your father was such a good man, then disappeared, there must be an explanation. What did your aunt say?"

"At the time, both my aunt and Natsiq used that against me, calling me a bastard. Since returning to Panniqtuuq, I haven't been able to get a straight answer from anyone in that family. It made me angry, but I just want to get on with my life."

The next day Ashoona attended the teachers' orientation meeting. It dragged on until late into the afternoon when the superintendent of schools took over the microphone and droned on for almost an hour.

Ashoona slipped out of the meeting to look for a phone. She had been thinking about Henry and hoped to see him later that day. However, when she called, the secretary explained that

Henry was at a meeting and asked Ashoona to call back the next day. When Ashoona returned to the conference, the superintendent had finally wrapped up his presentation, and the teachers were gathering to socialize.

Ashoona was the only Inuit teacher in the group. Most of her colleagues admired her; others spoke to her condescendingly.

An overweight woman in her late twenties tapped Ashoona on the shoulder. "I guess you're one of the teaching assistants." The buxom teacher was wearing a roomy top, a short skirt that fitted snuggly about her ample hips and high heels that were out of place in this northern city of gravel roads and dusty walking trails. She had a pretty face framed by shoulder-length, frizzy hair bleached to an unattractive shade of yellow.

"No. In fact, I'll be teaching grade six and will be the science teacher for grades seven and eight in Panniqtuuq."

The news was met with a blank stare as if the hefty young woman thought Ashoona was making it up.

"Well then, since you're educated, maybe you can convince the women to stop serving raw meat to their families."

"Why would I do that? There are more nutrients in raw meat. We have always eaten raw caribou, seal and even *muktuk*, but we also cook the meat and make good soups and stews. What concerns me is that too many Inuit families are getting most of their food from the trading post and eating too much sugar, bread and cookies, and they're putting on weight."

Ashoona did not have to say that the plump teacher should also cut down on the mashed potatoes and sugared treats. That ended their conversation.

The last day of the conference ended early, giving Ashoona time to walk to the hospital. When she asked after Henry, she was once more met with condescension.

"Doctor Russell is the administrator and is very busy."

"Please tell him Ashoona is here."

"I'm sorry, but I can't do that."

Ashoona realized that the bureaucracy of the *Qallunaat* had already taken over Frobisher. Outsiders now seemed to be running the city, and their attitude was that anyone with a dark complexion was beneath their notice. She stood at the desk fuming, angry at once more being treated like a second-class citizen.

Ashoona wished she had Natsiq's spunk. Her cousin would tell the secretary, "You will go and get Doctor Russell right now, or I will walk through that door and find him myself." But Ashoona was raised to be polite, so instead of making demands, she said nothing and sat down to wait.

The receptionist ignored her, and Ashoona sat patiently for an hour until the door to the administrator's office opened and Henry walked out. When he saw Ashoona, he opened his arms and embraced her warmly.

"Ashoona! You're back. Come in. We must talk."

He led her into his office. "I hear you're a teacher. I couldn't be happier for you. But tell me how it's going in Panniqtuuq." Henry seemed younger than when they last met. When Ashoona first worked with him in Blacklead, she was just turning thirteen, and Henry seemed too old for her. Now that Ashoona was nineteen and Henry thirty-two, the age difference seemed inconsequential. Time had been kind to Henry. He was fit and healthy. She had never taken much notice of his appearance during their years at Blacklead and Panniqtuuq. Now she took it all in—his gray eyes, even white teeth and disarming smile.

"So I hope Qillaq has been locked away in jail and won't be coming after you again."

"Qillaq tried to find me at the san; he made a lot of trouble and ended up in jail. Thankfully, my friends protected me.

He's probably out by now. He doesn't know that I am back in the north."

"Just keep an eye out for him, my dear friend. Every year we have too many battered women admitted to hospital. Their abusers will stop at nothing to get the women back, only to beat them again. These men are obsessed. When we release the women, they eventually return and need help again."

"Don't worry about me. Everything is going well. I start teaching the day after I return to Panniqtuuq. I have a comfortable home, and I'm making good money. But look at you. The big boss with a cadre of women protecting you from dangerous woman like me," Ashoona laughed.

"I apologize for the receptionist. I must emphasize to the staff that the locals must be treated the same way as the *Qallunaat*. Let me know if it happens again. I can change some behaviors, but deep-rooted prejudices still persist. So, my dear Ashoona, I have a meeting shortly, but are you free for dinner tonight? We can have steaks in a real restaurant and a long talk about your experience outside Baffin."

Having dinner with Henry was the first time Ashoona had spent an evening with a man whose company she enjoyed. They had shared so much in their lives. Both had suffered heartbreak, and their shared pain was a bond, along with their work in caring for the sick in Panniqtuuq and Blacklead. They understood one another and could say anything to each other.

The evening ended too quickly for Ashoona. The pleasant experience made her wish that she had taken a position in Frobisher so she and Henry could become closer. But she had to be on the plane early the next day.

Henry arrived at Ashoona's hotel to drive her to the airport. When her flight was called, Henry took her hands in his and bent to kiss her. It was sweet, just a light touch on her lips, but Ashoona felt a rush of warmth that stayed with her during the hour-long flight. As the plane flew over the mountains and across Cumberland Sound, Ashoona daydreamed of Henry, hoping she would soon see him again.

───────

It was a beautiful September morning when Ashoona walked to Judy's house, rapped on the door once and walked in. Judy was nursing a coffee and poring over a recipe book.

"I thought we could walk to school together. I want you to tell me everything about your trip back to Newfoundland," Ashoona said, greeting Judy with a big smile.

"It's still early even for the first day of school, so sit down and have a coffee. I just need a minute to find a recipe."

"Another low-fat dessert for tonight?" Ashoona joked, knowing that nothing Judy put on the table was low fat. The last time Ashoona came for dinner, Judy served Devil's Food cake, topped with thick chocolate icing.

"Why cut back on tasty food? I don't want to be skinny. Ernest likes me the way I am. Good love handles, he says. Someone who needs to eat my cooking is Natsiq. She's all skin and bone. Have you seen her since you came back from Frobisher?"

"I'll be seeing her after school today."

Judy and Ashoona enjoyed the walk to school. It was a typical fall day, cool and calm with brilliant sunshine that glistened on the water of the bay. Winter might arrive any day, but this morning was dazzling.

After classes ended, Ashoona walked to Natsiq's shack in the older part of town. She passed a row of government houses, some still under construction, before reaching the rundown area of matchstick houses. Adamie met her at the door, looking weary and sad. Aunt Amaruk was cooking at the stove and did not acknowledge Ashoona.

"Not a good time for us. Little Sandy is asleep, and Natsiq needs to rest," Adamie said. Then he whispered, "I need to talk to you."

"Anytime will do. Maybe come to the school. I'm there every morning by eight."

A few days later, Adamie showed up at her classroom door with little Samuel holding his hand. They were so close, those two. Ashoona gave Samuel crayons and paper, and he played quietly while Ashoona took Adamie into the staff lunchroom.

They spoke in Inuktitut. "It's Natsiq. She won't get up: she just lies there, not even caring for little Sandy. Amaruk won't look after the baby, not a *Qallunaaq's* baby, and I'm too old to change diapers. I worry about Natsiq. We need help for her and the baby."

"I'll try to get her out for a walk again. We're having a feast at the school to celebrate the safe return of the fishermen and hunters. I'll get her up even if I have to dress her myself."

As Adamie got up to leave, Ashoona called him back in the room. "Adamie, is there something you know about my father that you should tell me?"

"No. Nothing." Adamie left the room quickly before Ashoona could ask anything more.

His reply left Ashoona exasperated. She realized she would not get information out of him, but she was certain he was hiding something.

Natsiq was not easy to budge, but Ashoona used a bribe that she was sure would work. "I'll buy you a pack of cigarettes if you just come to the store with me."

At Ashoona's suggestion, Adamie had refused to buy Natsiq cigarettes, and Ashoona knew her cousin would be desperate for a puff.

Despite her weight loss, once Natsiq's hair was braided and she was dressed in her beautiful amauti, she looked stunning. Her lean face had a haunting appearance that drew men's stares. There were so few unattached women in the village that a beauty such as Natsiq, even one with two children, was sought after, maybe not as a wife, but as a sexual partner.

After leaving the store, the two young women made their way to the school where the festivities were about to begin. The hunters brought in the seals, caribou and *muktuk* they had caught and they placed the raw gutted meat on tarps in the middle of the gymnasium floor for everyone to share. Two village musicians were setting up on the stage, and the school staff was busy arranging chairs along the edge of the gymnasium. Ashoona was in charge of looking after the tea, coffee and cookies.

"You okay?" Ashoona asked her cousin.

"Yah, good," Natsiq lied, unable to hide the depression that engulfed her.

Natsiq had little Sandy tucked warmly under her *amauti*. Babies were always the center of attention, and the elderly women greeted Natsiq warmly, asking if they could hold Sandy. Most of the villagers did not discriminate against the babies of *Qallunaaq* fathers; it was the mother who was the subject of gossip. The little one was brought into the circle of the community. He was one of them now.

James came over to say hello, flashing his brilliant smile and working his beguiling charm on the vulnerable young woman.

"It's good to see you come out of that little shack, Natsiq. Come to my place, and we'll share a beer. Bring your baby, as long as he naps while we visit. I have a house now that I've been promoted to sergeant. More money and bigger digs."

The thought of getting out of the cramped quarters was a draw for Natsiq. The next evening, she dressed carefully in her best clothes, tucked Sandy under her *amauti* and walked to the center of town where the newer houses had been built as residences for teachers, police and other officials who were mostly *Qallunaat*. James and Ashoona, who were part Inuit, were exceptions.

Natsiq knew before she arrived at James' home that she would be expected to have sex with him. She was not apprehensive about the physical contact; she was going because the alternative was far worse. She was hoping that the visit would at least jolt her out of her malaise. But Natsiq's inner voice told her she was sinking into a world that would lead to disaster. Natsiq's ability to love with all her heart died in the Lancaster bomber that blew up over the Canary Islands.

James met her at the door and sized her up for a moment before inviting her in. "A beer for the village beauty?"

"Just a cigarette, please. I don't do very well with booze."

"Don't be a spoil sport. I hate to drink alone. One of my few rules." He opened a beer for her and lit her cigarette. She inhaled deeply, trying to relieve the tension that had been sapping her energy ever since Sandy's death. Soon she was gulping the beer, feeling relief as the alcohol reached her blood stream.

"This goes down well," Natsiq said, feeling more relaxed than she had been for months. "I shouldn't drink, but when the pain in my stomach turns to a warm feeling, why not?"

The baby was sleeping peacefully for a change, giving the young mother a break. "Do you got another one of these?" said Natsiq, slurring her words and pointing to the two empty beer bottles.

Soon she was laughing and telling James stories of the san, her misery forgotten for a brief interval. James led her to the bed. Natsiq felt some physical satisfaction in having a man touch and desire her again. But James was a rough lover. He didn't spend time on foreplay; he quickly removed her panties and pushed her legs apart. He pushed his fingers into her and then thrust into her, coming quickly and without any words of endearment. It was over so fast that Natsiq was left unsatisfied, and feeling even emptier than before. The physical act was for James alone and had nothing to do with Natsiq or any affection he might have for her.

"You're a good lay." James rolled off Natsiq and offered her a cigarette. She lay beside James until the baby awoke, by which time James was snoring.

Natsiq cleaned herself up in the bathroom, dressed and walked home. Her head ached and the knot in her stomach returned.

If only I had some booze at home, she thought. *At least it would relieve the constant ache in my gut and let me relax.*

But her parents kept no alcohol in their home. Her mother was adamantly opposed to drinking and was working with a group of prohibitionist women who were pressing the church and government authorities to turn Panniqtuuq into a dry community. Natsiq's mother was a force to be reckoned with in the village.

Amaruk had been a leader in the formation of the craft circle, encouraging the women to create the beautiful wall hangings to sell to the *Qallunaat*. She also nagged the men into carving items the *Qallunaat* wanted—bears and seals, instead of the more obscure and interesting art pieces that reflect Inuit culture.

Adamie uncharacteristically defied his wife when deciding what to carve. His sculptures depicted the shift spirits instead of the all-too-common bears and seals. He carved large pieces that took him months to finish and were difficult to sell. It was his one escape from his wife's tyranny. Adamie spent most of his day hiding out in the shed, working on the green soapstone carvings, often with his grandson Samuel watching and, at times, helping.

One evening in early winter, Ashoona walked by the shed and spotted Adamie and his grandson.

"Hello, Adamie. That's such a beautiful piece. That's Sedna, the ocean spirit, isn't it? When I save enough money, I want to buy one of your carvings. I want art that reflects our culture.

"You know Adamie," she continued, changing the subject, "I still wonder how my father could have abandoned me. He loved me so much; it just doesn't make any sense to me."

Adamie quickly averted his eyes and changed the subject.

"You must see Natsiq. She's taken up with that young police guy that you used to have a thing for. He's a fair policeman, but he's bad news for Natsiq. Talk to her."

"It's not really my business, but for your sake, Adamie, I'll talk to her." Ashoona saw grief and regret in Adamie's eyes, not just because of his daughter's troubles, but something else that was gnawing away at him.

Ashoona found Natsiq getting ready to go out.

"Do you want some company?"

"No. I'm going to meet a friend," Natsiq answered sullenly.

"It's James, isn't it?"

"You're still jealous, aren't you?"

"Are you joking? I don't care about James. I care for you. You should stay away from him. He is…"

"I'll do whatever I want," Natsiq shot back. "You just want him for yourself."

"Have it your way, Natsiq. I'm just warning you. James isn't one-tenth the man Sandy was. You're selling yourself short just for a few bottles of beer."

"Get out of here, Ashoona. We are no longer friends. I wish you had not escaped from Qillaq. In fact, maybe you haven't. I'm told he's coming back to get you."

"What have your heard? Tell me!"

"The government is moving families into the communities, so he and his brood of wives and children will be relocated here. Guess what he will do when he finds you?"

Ashoona felt her heart sink at the thought of having to deal once more with her abductor.

"I can't believe that you still hate me after what we went through together. I thought we had become friends, but I guess I was wrong." With that, Ashoona turned abruptly and left, feeling betrayed and hurt by Natsiq.

The news that Qillaq might come to live in Panniqtuuq was something Ashoona had never thought possible when she made her decision to return to her village. If Qillaq moved to Panniqtuuq, she would never feel safe until someone put a bullet through his brain.

Despite the conflict between the cousins, Ashoona still worried about Natsiq. She knew her cousin was overcome by despair. James would hurt Natsiq just as he had betrayed Ashoona years ago. Ashoona could not understand how Natsiq could sleep with James after being with someone as wonderful as Sandy.

And Qillaq...was he really coming here to live?

Ashoona's stomach tightened at the very thought of the vicious man. She had no defense against a man who was obsessed with hatred, lust and revenge. She knew that he would never stop chasing her because, in his twisted mind, she belonged to him. Ashoona understood that if Qillaq arrived in Panniqtuuq, the expert hunter would not fail to catch his prey. She had no place to hide and no way to avoid him. He would come for her; she was certain of that. Rather than the safe haven she imagined, Panniqtuuq had become a trap.

What was I thinking when I decided to return to Panniqtuuq? Who did I think would protect me?

Ashoona was nervous as she walked to her row house. It was such a beautiful evening. The stars reflected against the brilliant ice and snow, and a half moon cast a fairyland light on her path. Despite the beauty all around her, she could not dispel her fears. She picked up her pace, wondering when he would arrive, wondering if he was already stalking her.

She reached her house, turned the key in the lock and let herself in, relieved to be safe in her own home. Five rooms and a locked door.

Tomorrow, I will go to work. No one can harm me at the school. And I am safe in my house, she told herself, but she was unconvinced.

She slept fitfully, awakened by nightmares. Qillaq was in her room. She gasped and woke up, then lay in her bed, tense and unable to get back to sleep.

Tomorrow I must get up, go to the school and teach my class. I won't have my life controlled by this monster.

———

Her teaching responsibilities took up most of Ashoona's life. She walked to school each morning with Judy and was buoyed up by her friend's lively conversation. Ashoona worked hard throughout the day, and after classes, she walked home like a zombie, wondering when Qillaq would appear.

He's coming. She knew it in her heart. *He's not dumb. He will find where I live and where I work.*

Her row house overlooked the bay. The long days of summer had been replaced by equal days and nights. In two months, the sun would disappear completely, and winter was already upon them. Dusk fell as Ashoona returned home from work. She opened the curtains on the window that overlooked the ocean. She loved to watch the glimmer of lights from the village houses dancing on the waves and the shimmer of moonlight bathing the mountains that framed the inlet.

She wrote to Ann, her mentor from the Camsell Hospital, and jokingly described her home to the head nurse as "waterfront property." Ann had admired the lakeshore cabins they had passed on their trip through southern British Columbia. Well, maybe the twenty-four hours of darkness in winter in her village and the driving winds wouldn't be great selling points. But Ashoona appreciated the panoramic view, the ocean on the living room side and the vista of Mount Duval from her kitchen window.

During the night, visions of Qillaq returned. Awakened by another nightmare, Ashoona struggled out of bed to splash cold water on her hot forehead. She shook her head and staggered back to bed. The dream seemed more than real, and from that day on, Ashoona remained on alert like a bird aware of a prowling cat. He would come for her; he could not bear losing a woman that he believed was his. Her nightmares haunted her every night, and every morning Ashoona felt disoriented and suffered from pounding headaches.

Ashoona felt tense as she walked to Judy's later that week. Her buxom friend was her usual ebullient self, and she did not hold back on offering advice.

"Why do you let him control your thoughts? You have a teachers' degree and everything you ever wanted—status in the community, a good job. He's not even here yet, so don't let that monster dominate your life."

"I know I should get him out of my head. But I can't. He is evil. I hate him. Yet I can't stop the thoughts churning in my head. As soon as I am home for the night, I feel trapped."

"And why do you worry so much about Natsiq," Judy went on. "She has made her bed and must sleep in it. Help her if you can, but don't let your cousin's problems drag you down."

"James is the most heartless man I've ever known," Ashoona continued. "Natsiq will regret getting into his bed. All he wants is sex. He won't marry her; he'll use her and dump her."

But Natsiq continued to find escape in her relationship with James. She wanted the booze and cigarettes, and clung to the false sense of comfort she felt when they had sex. She went to his apartment every evening about the time James got off work. As soon as Natsiq entered the apartment, she pulled a beer from the refrigerator.

"Help yourself," James said sarcastically.

"The least you can do is give me a drink. You never talk about the future; you fuck me and give me beer and cigarettes. It's not enough; I need more." Natsiq's attitude toward James was shifting. He was far from the kind and loving partner Sandy had been, but he could rescue her from the poverty and cramped conditions of her parents' house.

"Do you really think this is going anywhere?" James asked.

"Why not? You enjoy sex with me. Besides, our mothers arranged our marriage. Everyone in the village knows I'm sleeping with you. If we don't get married, everyone will gossip."

"You're already a target for the old biddies. You're unmarried with two children, both *Qallunaaq* babies. And are you stupid enough to cling to that agreement our mothers made when we were babies?"

"There's no one else in the village you could marry. Ashoona thinks she's better than the Inuit, and all the other girls are hooked up or too ugly to interest you."

"My parents have other plans for me. Even my mother agrees that I should marry a white girl, maybe one of the officers' daughters from Regina. I'm not staying in this dump for the rest of my life."

Natsiq looked at him blankly. She finally got it. She understood that she had been used. The painful ache in her stomach returned with vengeance.

How could I have been so gullible? Why didn't I figure it out before?

Natsiq tucked her baby into her amauti and walked out into the cold night. The winds were so strong she had to lean forward in order to keep moving, the icy wind blasting into her face. As she plodded home, the tears fell.

How could I be so stupid?"

When she reached home, her father was in the house and saw the anguish his daughter was suffering.

"He isn't the right man for you," Adamie said, an unusual comment for a man who so rarely expressed an opinion about anything.

"Oh Papa! I'm so unhappy."

Ashoona awoke one morning, and as she sipped her coffee, the nightmares dispersed. Nights were the worst, of course. Once she'd had breakfast and prepared for the school day, her mood brightened. She even told herself that if Qillaq tried to hurt her, the people in her village would protect her.

They like me now; they treat me like I'm one of them, no longer "the little murderer" to be traded off to a beast. They won't let Qillaq near me. Even James would help me. He must uphold the law; he has the responsibility to defend me. Imagine that!

Ashoona stopped at the post office the next day, hoping there would be letters from friends. Nurse Ann and Brenda wrote to her regularly; Ann with updates on TB patients and her teenage children, and Brenda with news about her new job and her life in Frobisher Bay.

The postmistress had been on the job since Ashoona was a child. At that time she was the only Inuit hired into a government position. Although she was near retirement, she had a face that would never grow old. Despite the passing of the years, she seemed as young to Ashoona as she did years ago.

"What ever happened to your father, Ashoona? I remember he wrote to you after your mother passed away, and then suddenly, the letters stopped."

"He wrote? Are you sure?"

"Of course, I'm sure. I passed the letters on to your aunt. I guess she didn't give them to you. You were just a child then."

Ashoona was stunned. She walked out of the post office, burning with anger.

She ran to her aunt's house in a rage.

"The letters!" Ashoona yelled. "Tell me about them." Natsiq and Adamie were home with the children; Amaruk was out.

"What letters?" Natsiq said, unconvincingly. Adamie stared at the floor.

"Adamie, for God's sake! I can tell that you know about them. Is my father still alive? Why didn't he come back to look after me?"

Adamie got up slowly, his shoulders bowed.

"Come." He led Ashoona to his carving shack behind the house. It was a small plywood shed with a roof and three sides. On one wall was a worktable, and along the back wall, a shelf for tools and rough-cut soap stones. He shuffled over to the shelf and took out a bundle wrapped in caribou skin. Without a word, he passed the package to Ashoona.

"Did Natsiq know about this, too?" Ashoona demanded.

"Natsiq knew, but Amaruk made us swear we would never tell you. She told me to burn the letters, but I couldn't. Natsiq was just a little girl when this started and should not be blamed. The guilt wears on her."

"I'm supposed to feel sorry for Natsiq?" Ashoona said, angrily.

"Yes," Adamie answered, his voice shaking. "She needs your forgiveness."

Ashoona went back in the house and carefully unwrapped the parcel. Inside were dozens of letters neatly arranged by date. She read aloud while Natsiq and Adamie listened in shamed silence.

"He wrote me just after mama died. He said he would come to Panniqtuuq on the supply ship and that he would take me to Montreal to live with him. In the next letter, he enclosed money to pay for mama's headstone."

She opened the next letter, this one addressed to Adamie and Amaruk. A letter filled with anguish over the news of Ashoona's death.

"You lied to him? Told him I died? That's why he never came for me. He never abandoned me, and you didn't tell me." Ashoona was so angry her words came out in a torrent of sobs.

"I wanted to tell you about your father's letters when we were at the san." Natsiq was close to tears. "I don't know why I didn't. Maybe I thought you had so much, and until I found Sandy, I had so little. I'm so messed up."

"But there's more for you to say, isn't there, Natsiq? What about Davidee? Isn't it time for you to admit what really happened? Isn't it time for you to ask me to forgive you, not just for the letters, but for lying about your brother and for conniving to sell me to Qillaq?" Ashoona's voice rose to an angry pitch as the knowledge of Natsiq's deception flooded back like a dam releasing powerful uncontrollable waters.

"I have no more to say." Natsiq, who was lying on her cot, turned her head to the wall and ignored Ashoona.

"Go home, Ashoona. Read the rest of the letters, and write your father. He may still be at the same address. Then come back to see me." Adamie was a sad figure, slumped with age and guilt.

Ashoona returned the next day, furious thoughts broiling in her mind. Adamie opened the door, a dejected look on his haggard face.

"He sent money for a tombstone for our graves, mine and my mother's. There are no tombstones!" Ashoona yelled. "Where did the money go? You stole it, didn't you?"

"Talk to your aunt," Adamie said despondently. "She had her reasons, and we didn't have the courage to oppose her."

Just then, Amaruk walked in the door and saw Ashoona holding the bundle of letters. She looked like she had sunk her teeth into a lemon.

"You, you...!" Amaruk yelled at Adamie, her anger rippling across her face. "What have you done? You will destroy our family? How could you side with Ashoona? I should have thrown the letters in the stove myself. I should never have trusted you to keep the secret."

"Amaruk," Adamie said softly. "You must beg Ashoona's forgiveness." He was confronting his formidable wife for what may have been the first time in their marriage. "You took away her only remaining parent, and we will all have to atone for our wickedness. How can you go to church every Sunday and pretend to be a Christian, when you have treated our own niece so miserably—my sister's child, the little girl we promised to love and care for?"

Ashoona did not want to spend another minute with this tortured family. The last letter still had an address. She would write her father immediately and try to find him.

———

Ashoona was pleased to learn that a charter plane had landed, bringing mail and supplies to the village. She had written her father two weeks earlier and didn't expect an answer for some time, but with this flight, there was a chance of an early response. When the postmistress handed her a letter, Ashoona's heart missed a beat.

"It's from your father, isn't it?" the postmistress asked. "I recognized his handwriting."

"Thank you! Thank you!" Ashoona hugged the postmistress and looked at the familiar writing. She tore open the envelope, her heart almost bursting.

"He's in Montreal! He's coming to Panniqtuuq this weekend! He's remarried, and his wife will come too. He loves me. He never stopped loving me and can't believe I'm alive, that I didn't die. You have no idea what this means to me!"

"I think I do, Ashoona, and I wish I had questioned Amaruk about the letters all those years ago. I thought something was wrong when the letters stopped so abruptly."

Ashoona was in tears, but they were tears of joy. She ran to see Judy and cried on her shoulder. She wanted to tell everyone that her father had not abandoned her, that he loved her and would be coming to see her that very next weekend. Ashoona did not tell anyone about Amaruk's treachery. Their household was in enough misery without having the entire village condemn them.

After visiting Judy, Ashoona ran to Aula's house to tell her friend the good news. She was planning a big dinner to celebrate her father's visit and hoped that Aula could help her. Kilabuk was on a fishing trip, but Aula and her little ones were home.

"So everything is working out for you, Ashoona," Aula said, hugging her friend. "All you need now is a husband and a few babies, and life will be perfect. I think you've waited too long because Paloosie tells me he has found a new love. The only problem is that Brenda lives in Frobisher, and if they get married, I will only see my grandchildren during holidays."

"You don't have to wait for the grandchildren to be born. She has a ready-made family."

"I've met Brenda and the three little ones. They are so well behaved, and that Jeremiah, he spoke to me in our language. Can you believe that?"

The door opened, and Paloosie walked in. He smiled and opened his arms to hug Ashoona.

"You've heard that Brenda and I will be married? I know the two of you share almost everything." Paloosie chuckled at the thought of the two women chatting, one who was the subject of his teenage infatuation and the other who had his deep love and a lifetime commitment.

Ashoona was relieved to notice that his teenage smile had not been replaced by a man's aloofness or arrogance. Ashoona felt assured that a loving man like Paloosie would be wonderful for Brenda after the years she spent subjected to Elijah's sexual and emotional domination.

Paloosie could not say enough about Brenda—how beautiful she was, what a good mother and teacher. He was deeply devoted to Brenda, his love so much more intense than the puppy love he once felt for Ashoona.

Ashoona was relieved that Paloosie had found his true love. Ashoona could be his friend and not worry about leading him on just because she enjoyed his company.

"I heard that you took the students and staff out on the land to fish and hunt."

"Teaching the *Qallunaat* to live out on the land is an endless source of entertainment. The skinny, bald gym teacher from Frobisher Bay came on the trip with three female teachers, and they all slept in the same tent. I told them to tie down their tent with rocks and use good-sized boulders, or the wind would blow away both them and their tent. But they used only small stones.

"In the middle of the night the winds bore down on our camp. When I looked out of my tent, I saw four pale *Qallunaaq* bodies running around in the freezing wind, trying to find boulders big enough to weigh down their tent. The women had on only their panties and T-shirts, and the gym teacher wore skivvies, displaying a pair of skinny, white legs and looking just like a ghost. I was afraid if the children woke up they would think the dead had risen from the tundra."

Ashoona and Aula had a good laugh over Paloosie's story, enjoying the gossip and his colorful storytelling.

"I came here to ask for your help to put on a dinner for my father and his wife, and I've stayed too long. There is so much for me to do."

Ashoona's next visit was to Lucy, the only classmate from her school days who did not bully her during that most painful time in Ashoona's youth.

"Well, maybe it's time Natsiq also admitted to shooting her little brother. I feel sorry for Natsiq, and I know that only admitting her treachery will let her move forward with her life," Lucy said. "She often comes to the Welfare Office, distraught and pleading for us to help her. She wants us to find her a government house of her own or give her a plane ticket to Frobisher. She is desperate to escape; she feels trapped."

"I'm no longer angry with Natsiq and Adamie. I can't forgive Amaruk, but I can forgive my cousin and uncle. Amaruk was forcing their silence. But let's not talk about that miserable family; let's plan the feast for my father. You cook the best caribou steaks in the village, and Joe always kills caribou with the tenderest meat. Do you have time to help me with the dinner now that you have a big government job?"

"Of course, I'll bring the steaks. Work is going well at the Welfare Office. I can't believe that I'm actually the manager for a few months. Me, a simple Inuit woman with a big government paycheck."

"Why is the appointment temporary?"

"The usual. Indian and Northern Affairs won't permanently hire a local Inuit for a manager's job. More important, I don't have a college degree, just the six-month-course I took in Frobisher, one in office administration and one in social work. The federal official in Frobisher is recruiting a manager and another social worker, both from Ottawa. It's okay. Once the new staff arrives, I won't have to work late anymore, and I'll have more time with my family."

"I'll be checking on developments once your new supervisor is here. I met many wonderful people in Edmonton. Hopefully you'll be lucky enough to have a boss like Ann, my friend from Camsell Hospital who was the staff supervisor. But...no more talk about work. We're going to cook up a storm and have a wonderful party when my dad and his wife visit." Ashoona clapped her hands together excitedly.

Ashoona couldn't wait till the plane landed. She had dressed carefully that morning before walking to the airstrip. She wondered what her father would look like. She had childhood memories, but thirteen years later, he would be older. He would look different.

But Ashoona recognized her father immediately. Of course that was not difficult because only two *Qallunaat* disembarked. Her father walked across the gravel airstrip, an attractive middle aged-woman at his side.

Her father swept Ashoona up in his arms. With tears in his eyes, his voice choked, "My little girl! I can't believe it. I'm so happy, so happy!"

He hugged Ashoona closely, and as they embraced, Ashoona could not keep from sobbing. For years, she had been so angry with him for leaving. Now, she knew it was not his fault. Aunt Amaruk had betrayed them both, and Ashoona had a father again and a family.

Dugan Campbell stepped back, holding Ashoona at arm's length.

"Oh, please excuse me, Ashoona. Let me introduce you to my wife, Lynne."

Ashoona held out her hand to the tall, well-groomed woman sensibly dressed in a fur coat and sturdy winter boots. Instead of taking Ashoona's hand, Lynne opened her arms, smiling at her stepdaughter and trying to hold back her tears.

"Oh, Dugan, she is lovely!" Lynne enthused.

Ashoona returned the hug, pleased that the new member of her family was so warm and welcoming and obviously prepared to love Ashoona. Lynne could never be a replacement for the mother Ashoona had lost, but maybe a woman she could share her problems and thoughts with.

"Come to my place. I have a spare room, and tomorrow we will have a feast. Well, in Panniqtuuq we call it a feast. It will be a dinner with many friends and a spread of fried caribou steaks, seal stew, bannock and a cake made by my friend, Judy, who is an amazing cook. My friends are helping me with the meal, and some of your old friends will be there."

"What about Amaruk and Adamie? I suppose it would be awkward if they were to come."

"I haven't come to grips with my feelings about that family's deception. All of them, Amaruk, Adamie and Natsiq were part of the lies, and they even stole the money you sent for the gravestones. I still can't understand how Aunt Amaruk could do what she did. And for Adamie to go along with such wicked behavior is beyond my understanding. He betrayed his sister's family, for God's sake. I tried to help Natsiq after her baby's father was killed in the war, and all the time I defended her, she knew about the letters and never said anything."

"Put it behind you, my girl. You have a new life now. I'm so proud of you. I always knew you would be a success. You were such a bright child. Now you have your teaching certificate."

The next day was the big dinner. It was an exceptionally pleasant day for October. A scattering of snow dusted the tundra, but for once, no wind. Ashoona decided to hold the dinner in the afternoon near the ocean where there was a fire pit and rocks surrounding a dip in the tundra. Aula had made the seal stew and bannock, Lucy's caribou steaks were grilling on the campfire, and Judy brought one of her extraordinarily delicious cakes. It was a cream cheese and pudding Bundt cake, so moist and light and topped with thick chocolate icing.

Neighbors who heard the celebration joined the gathering, adding baked Arctic char and turbot to the feast. The sun dipped below the horizon in the afternoon, painting the mountain peaks pink and sending shafts of rose light across the quiet ocean. When they finished their tea, Jimmy Atagoyak picked up his fiddle and played for them. It was a melancholy tune that brought tears to their eyes because the music told of the years of sadness for both Ashoona and her father. His next tune was a jig that got couples up dancing and old people stamping to the rhythm. For Ashoona and her father, the song told them of the joy that had returned to their lives.

Once their friends had drifted away, Ashoona, her father and Lynne gathered up the dishes.

"Look out to sea!" Ashoona remarked. Not far off shore, they saw two young Belugas breaching in the calm water. Soon the whales would migrate to a stretch of ice-free ocean west of Greenland. They watched the beautiful animals leap and play until they disappeared from view.

"So tell me this story about you being sold to Qillaq?" Lynne asked. "Another unbelievable treachery perpetrated by your aunt. How could something like that happen in this day and age, a young girl being traded off to an old man," Lynne said, a look of distaste furrowing her smooth brow. "It's so disgusting. Isn't that against the law? Won't Amaruk be jailed for her actions? And what about Qillaq? Why isn't he in jail?"

"I only wish," Ashoona said, her happiness momentarily torn away.

"Now that you're safe, better just let the past go," Ashoona's father added. "I would imagine that Amaruk and Adamie are burdened by guilt over their actions. Even Natsiq will suffer knowing how wrong it was to keep the secret of my letters."

"I'm not really safe, Papa." Ashoona told him that Qillaq's three wives and his brood of children had been relocated to Panniqtuuq, and that Qillaq was expected to arrive sometime after Christmas. "I even have one of his sons in my class. The poor child is struggling with English and finds books and lessons so foreign that he may not pass his grade. It will be hard for him to be left back because he'll be so much older and bigger than his classmates. He may be able to kill a seal with a single shot, but school is a struggle for a child brought up in hunting and fishing camps."

"You actually feel sorry for his son?" Lynne was becoming more and more impressed with Ashoona as she got to know her. "You're a kind teacher; they are lucky to have you. About this Qillaq, do you have someone looking out for you? Dugan, aren't you worried that this obsessed man will come after your daughter again? Shouldn't we make sure she has a protector, someone who walks her home and watches out for her?"

"You're right. I won't sleep well when we go back to Montreal unless I'm assured of Ashoona's safety. She was taken from me once. I could not bear to lose her again. Is there someone that I could ask to keep an eye on you?"

"There's Paloosie—Aula and Kilabuk's son. He's going to Frobisher Bay to work for a couple of months but will be back after Christmas. He's grown to be a strong man and a good hunter. He saved my life when Qillaq confronted us during the expedition. I know he will make my safety his utmost priority."

So before Dugan Campbell left for Montreal, he made arrangements with Paloosie to be Ashoona's protector. Nothing could have pleased Paloosie more. He wanted to watch over her; he promised to never be intrusive and to be always polite and respectful. Ashoona didn't mind; she enjoyed the young man's company and laughed at all his jokes and funny stories.

Ashoona's friends and several other villagers came to see Dugan and Lynne off. The Inuit villagers conversed amicably in Inuktitut with Dugan, while Ashoona and Lynne chatted with

Judy and Lucy. Judy brought up the treachery perpetrated by Ashoona's relatives.

"At least now you're no longer bitter about your father, but I'll bet my bottom dollar you'll hold a grudge toward your aunt and uncle for some time."

"They are sad people who have to live with what they've done. I feel sorry for Adamie. He wants to do what is right, but he is so browbeaten, and except for his decision to hide the letters, he never stood up to that dragon lady. I'll always be thankful that he kept the letters that brought Papa back to me and gave me a stepmother and a new friend.

"I worry about Natsiq," Ashoona continued. "Her behavior is self-destructive. She can barely look after her beautiful baby, and Amaruk has the mothering instincts of a rat."

"Right. A mother rat eats her young," Judy added with a chuckle.

"We need to consider the well-being of the baby," Lucy added, giving the discussion a more serious note. "Adamie is a good and loving grandfather to Samuel, but he can't help Natsiq with the little one. I'll talk to Natsiq and ask her to come see us again.

"The new supervisor from Ottawa has a raft of degrees in psychology," Lucy continued. "She's been describing, or to be more accurate, bragging about her past accomplishments working with mentally ill clients. Maybe she can help Natsiq."

Ashoona was about to question Lucy about her new boss when the pilot gathered up the passengers and led them across the gravel runway to the plane.

Before Dugan and Lynne boarded the plane, Ashoona agreed to fly out to Montreal at Christmas and join them for the holidays. Father and daughter could not believe their good fortune. With the reunion of Ashoona and her father, the only dark part of Ashoona's life was Qillaq's expected arrival in Panniqtuuq.

———〰———

Someone was always spreading news in the village, and by the time Ashoona returned from her Christmas break in Montreal, the gossip mill had been at work, and the entire community knew of the letters and Amaruk's deception. Adamie had spent his married life intimidated by Amaruk. He was a good man and a loving father and grandfather, but he was also submissive and avoided conflict at any cost. He knew that Amaruk had written to Ashoona's father that his only daughter was dead, buried in the little gravesite near the ocean. He agonized over the lies, often telling himself that he should confront his wife, that he should insist she right the wrongs she had inflicted on Ashoona. He also knew about the money Dugan sent to erect two headstones.

Ashoona had not visited Natsiq since the episode with the letters. She had seen Adamie during her trips to the store or the post office but only nodded. She did not want anything to do with her relatives. When she ran into Amaruk, Ashoona did not even acknowledge her.

Amaruk had become a sad figure. For years, she had been a community leader, the center of the craft circle and the local person government officials consulted prior to making major decisions that affected the village. Now she was shunned by the church congregation and unwelcome at the craft center. Ashoona wondered how the churchwomen could not forgive her. *Wasn't that what Christians do? Forgive the sinner?*

The grip of winter had broken, and sunlight beamed down on Panniqtuuq the day Adamie approached Ashoona at the Hudson's Bay Post.

"I'm worried about Natsiq. She talks about guns now, asking me where my rifle is. When she sleeps, she cries about her brother, Davidee. It's the voice of someone who suffers every minute of her life."

"What about James? I thought they were together."

"She broke it off. Natsiq didn't love him; she just wanted booze and cigarettes. These days, she goes over to Kakik's house. One of his gang members is making some awful hooch, and Natsiq is drinking every day. One night, she came home with a black eye and bruises all over her arms. Little Sandy no longer has a mother."

Ashoona remembered Aula's dissolute grandson, Kakik. Ashoona felt a tug of sorrow thinking about how much she missed Aula, the old woman who had defended her so many years ago. Kakik was now in his late twenties, and instead of hunting, he had joined a group of young men who spent their nights boozing. James might have moral shortcomings, but Kakik was violent. Ashoona learned from the villagers that James had arrested Kakik for assault twice in the past month.

"I'll come to see Natsiq tomorrow, but I don't want to be there when Amaruk is around. I cannot forgive my aunt."

***

"Natsiq," Ashoona said approaching her cousin's bed the next day. "It's me. I know what is troubling you. I've known for years that you wanted to tell everyone about Davidee. Please tell your parents that you pulled the trigger and that it wasn't me. It will help you."

Natsiq bowed her head and was silent. Ashoona waited. Would she finally admit what really happened years ago? Natsiq broke into gulping sobs so violent it was difficult to understand what she was saying.

"Yes, Ashoona, I killed my little brother." Natsiq's weeping shook her thin frame, and Ashoona bent down and put her arms about her cousin.

"What did she say?" asked Adamie, who was close by. "Did she say something about Davidee?" The elders believed it was wrong to utter the name of a deceased loved one, but Adamie's concerns for Natsiq overrode the cultural taboo.

"Papa, I'm so sorry! I killed him, not Ashoona. I'm so wicked, and everyone in the village hates me. I can't stay here. I want to leave and take Sandy with me. I must get out of here before this village kills me." She sobbed uncontrollably. "Papa, Samuel loves you, and I want him to stay here with you."

Adamie was speechless. Yet another evil deed that the family had to live with. It was almost too much for him. "What can I say? It's more than I can take, knowing how we've treated you, Ashoona."

"I forgave you, Adamie, the day you gave me the letters, and I forgive you, Natsiq. When we were at the san together, you tried to tell me, and I know you're sorry, but you have to forgive yourself, Natsiq. You have to pull out of this and be a mother to your beautiful baby. He is the son of the man who truly loved you."

"I miss him so much," Natsiq cried convulsively. "Why did he have to die and leave me alone? Our lives should have been perfect."

"I think you should go to Frobisher. Remember Brenda? I'm sure she'll take you in, and Henry could help you find a program so you can kick your addiction."

"Okay, I'll try, but don't say anything about this. If Kakik hears I'm planning to leave, he'll beat the shit out of me."

Ashoona left them alone in the house filled with pain and grief—no place for a little baby. Samuel was managing because he had the love of his grandfather and the companionship of his friends, but the baby should not stay there.

Chapter Twenty-six

Kakik

Natsiq was spending far too much time with the unpredictable Kakik, at times taking both children with her and putting not only herself but also her two boys at risk. Natsiq's addiction to alcohol and cigarettes was controlling her life, and both were available at Kakik's shack. One afternoon, she tucked Sandy into her *amauti*. Adamie was not home, so she took Samuel along. Although Samuel was afraid of Kakik and did not want to go with his mother, he obeyed. The young boy was so much like his grandfather, sweet natured and quiet, a follower who demanded little from his caregivers.

The tiny family painted a sad picture as Natsiq walked with her two children through the village. Natsiq's shoulders slumped, and she walked with difficulty, exhausted from the stress and constant gut-wrenching pain that crippled her except when she was drinking. She grieved for the past and was terrified of the future. Her beauty was fading; she was too thin and her hair was stringy and unkempt.

A beer. That would take away the pain.

Kakik was already drunk and in a temper when she arrived.

"We're out of beer, so get your butt over to Jimmy's and bring back a dozen. And don't sell your sorry ass to get the booze either! I know you'll do anything for a drink. I'll pay him when I get my welfare dough."

Natsiq forced her voice to be steady. Acidic knots of fear hit her stomach making her nauseous. "Jimmy's place isn't safe for the children. You get the beer."

Kakik saw red. Fury erupted in him, uncontrolled and fueled by the alcohol.

"If I tell you to go, you go! You're my woman, and you do what I say. Leave the children here and get the beer."

"You're drunk and not making any sense. I gotta go home."

It was difficult for Natsiq to leave without a drink, but at least she had enough motherly instinct to know that her children were in danger. When he was drunk, Kakik had assaulted Natsiq with such rage that she feared for her life. Thankfully, that time she did not have the children with her. She couldn't expose them to his rage.

"You never loved me, you little bitch. I heard you've been asking around about getting passage on the supply boat to Frobisher. You're planning on leaving and taking your bastard children with you, aren't you?" He grabbed her chin and pushed his face to within an inch of hers. "Just like you to hang around me drinking my beer and then sneaking onto the next boat out of here and fuck that son of a bitch waiting for you in Frobisher."

"Don't be crazy, Kakik. I don't have a guy in Frobisher, just Brenda, the woman I met in Edmonton. She offered to give me a place to stay while I dry out. I have to get out of here before this place kills me."

"You're not leaving me, you bitch! Don't even think about it. I took you in after James dumped you, and you're mine now. Women don't run out on me. Ever!"

"Kakik, calm down. I'm not leaving town until the supply boat comes in this spring. That's three months away at least. But right now, I have to take my children home. You're drunk, and you know what happens when you get tanked."

"I'm not drunk!" he yelled. In his inebriated state he saw himself as a reasonable man. Hadn't he given Natsiq beer and cigarettes, put up with two children not even his own flesh and blood, and worse, fathered by a *Qallunaaq*? How could she consider leaving him even if she was telling the truth?

Natsiq moved toward the door, holding the terrified Samuel by the hand.

"Get back here! You're not going anywhere."

The doorknob wouldn't turn. Natsiq's throat tensed with fear. In two long strides, Kakik grabbed her, pulling her back by the hair.

"Please! Not in front of the children. Please, let me go!"

The thought of Natsiq leaving him made Kakik lose it. He was no longer thinking clearly. Losing his temper made him feel sick and afraid for what he might do. Last time he hit her, she was knocked unconscious, and for a few minutes, he thought he might have killed her. When she came to, he was sitting on the floor holding her hand and asking for her forgiveness. She forgave him that time, but now she had plans to leave the village. He knew she wouldn't come back to him. He couldn't let that happen. He couldn't let her go.

"You bitch! You whoring little cunt! I'll teach you to cheat on me. Tell me who you're meeting in Frobisher. Don't lie to me. I know it's not your Mormon girlfriend. Don't try to fool me! You need to be taught a lesson so you'll stop fucking me around."

A lesson. That's what Kakik always called his attacks on Natsiq. In his liquor-crazed mind, he thought beating her would make her stay and give up her plan to leave the village.

He yanked on her hair, and she landed hard on the floor, the baby still clutched in her arms.

"Oh God, please don't!"

Samuel stood stiff against the door, his face white as a ghost.

"Run, Samuel! Run!"

But Samuel couldn't move or leave while his mother screamed in pain and while his baby brother cried.

Natsiq curled up on the floor, tucking the baby under her as Kakik's blows rained down on her back. He brought his foot back and kicked the side of Natsiq's head.

Kakik finally stopped when he realized Natsiq wasn't moving. He didn't mean to seriously hurt Natsiq…just teach her a lesson…bring her into line. His mind was racing. He could change; he could try to make life with Natsiq work. She'd brought this on herself. If she could be faithful, he would stop drinking, become a hunter and go out on the land where all the poison would be cleansed from his body.

Suddenly, he was remorseful. As Natsiq regained consciousness, he begged her forgiveness, promising he would never beat her again.

She let her breath out in a whisper of fear. Every muscle and bone ached. But she gave no thought to herself, only to her children. Sandy was still screaming, a good sign, but Samuel was quiet, a statue-like figure nailed to the door.

Natsiq picked herself and her baby off the floor. She had to be careful. One wrong word, and he would lay into her even more viciously.

I must remain calm, not provoke him. I have to get the children out of here before they become victims as well.

"Kakik, I have to go home now. The children need their lunch. I'll come back tomorrow, and we'll talk."

"You'd better not be lying to me. If you do, I'll kill you next time. Do you understand me?"

Natsiq just wanted to get out. She never wanted to see him again. She gathered herself together and rocked Sandy to calm his crying. Then she knelt down near Samuel and gently took his hand.

"I want to go home to Grandpa. I don't want to come here again."

"We're going home, Samuel." She spoke to Kakik, trying to steady her voice, so that he would not guess at her plans to escape. "See ya tomorrow. Okay?"

She was out the door, walking as fast as she could into the cold afternoon. Summer was months away, and a spring storm raged down on the village. Her head throbbed from the pain of the attack and her mind was reeling as she weighed her options. She had to get out of the village; it was her only chance.

Instead of going home, she made her way to the Welfare Office. They had to help her. It was their job, wasn't it? To protect women and children from abuse. She hoped Lucy would be there, someone who could speak to her in her own language, someone who understood how violent some young men could become over their girlfriends.

Lucy no longer occupied the manager's office. Instead, she shared an office with Donna, the newly hired *Qallunaaq* social worker. Natsiq couldn't unload her problems in front of a white woman. What would this neat modern-looking girl think of Natsiq's life? Two children out of wedlock, a violent boyfriend and a family whose reputation was ruined.

Lucy would understand, but not Donna, a *Qallunaaq* just out of college who had grown up in the safety of her family—a young woman, who at twenty-two, was likely still a virgin.

Donna was tall and husky; she looked like she had eaten too many helpings of potatoes and bread and quaffed too many sodas.

Natsiq let herself into the Welfare Office and noticed that Lucy was not alone. Donna was there, and the battered young mother felt uncomfortable in Donna's presence.

Lucy often thought how difficult family life would be when Donna married and had children. She had a vision of the overweight, domineering woman grabbing her daughter by the arm and dragging the child to the supper table, rather than simply asking her daughter. Inuit parents believed spanking was not the proper way to teach children right and wrong. They learned by suffering the consequences of their actions. Inuit mothers would never drag a child to the supper table. Lucy was certain Donna was the kind of person who would use physical force to make her co-workers or her children comply.

One day at work, Lucy was filling out her timesheet when Donna actually cuffed Lucy on the arm, demanding that Lucy fill it out later. Lucy, always one to avoid conflict, simply complied, although she felt so humiliated at the physical abuse that it made her nauseous.

"I need to talk to you alone," Natsiq told Lucy in their language.

"What is she saying?"

"She would like you to leave if you don't mind. She's embarrassed to talk about her problems in front of you."

"Of course, I mind. I'm the senior worker here and responsible for recording the interview and making the recommendations to our supervisor."

When Natsiq asked again if she could talk to Lucy alone, Donna told Lucy to get on with the interview, ignoring Natsiq's request.

Natsiq described the attack and Kakik's threats, begging Lucy to arrange for a plane ticket to Frobisher for herself and Sandy.

"I promised to go back to him tomorrow. If I don't go, he'll come after me. You have to help! There's a flight tomorrow to Frobisher. Please get me and my baby on that plane. If you don't, I'll be dead by tomorrow night."

"Tell me what she's saying, and speak English so I can take notes," Donna demanded.

"I was hired so that the locals could speak in their language. When so much emotion is involved, it's difficult for them to speak in a foreign language."

"What are you talking about? We're in Canada. English is not a foreign language."

But Lucy knew she was right. Natsiq's well-being depended on her being able to communicate her problem clearly in her own language. Lucy told Natsiq to continue in Inuktitut.

But when Natsiq spoke in her own language, Donna grabbed the young mother and pushed her so hard that little Sandy woke up screaming, and Samuel curled up in the corner weeping. "Mommy, I want to go home to Grandpa."

It was impossible to continue the interview with two children crying and Natsiq on the verge of tears. Natsiq spoke in English trying to emphasize the urgency of her situation.

"Lucy, you got to get me on the plane to Frobisher. Please! I gotta go now. The children are hungry. Miss Donna, you understand, don't you? I gotta go tomorrow."

Donna did not reply, but Lucy promised to take Natsiq's concerns to the manager and to try to get a plane ticket issued for the next day's flight to Frobisher.

With the baby crying and Samuel once more in shock, Natsiq left for home. She had a sinking feeling about the interview. If Lucy had remained as the manager, she would be certain of an escape, With Donna in charge, she had little hope.

Lucy knew all too well that Natsiq's situation was urgent. She knew of several young men who committed suicide and young women who had been beaten by their partners, one was even killed in a violent attack. Lucy understood the violence that erupted between partners in such an isolated community. When relationships fell apart, the men became aggressive, even to the point of murder, or alternatively one of the partners would commit suicide. Lucy felt strongly that it was her role as a welfare worker to take action quickly and decisively to protect Natsiq from Kakik's violence and to prevent Kakik from taking his own life.

"Let me write the report, Donna. We must urge Karyn to issue a plane ticket for Natsiq. We have to get her out of the village."

"No. I'll write the report."

Instead of asking Lucy for her notes, Donna grabbed Lucy's hand, prying Lucy's fingers from her notebook. When Donna realized the notes were in Inuktitut, she handed the notes back to Lucy and asked for a translation.

"I'll translate the notes, Donna, then I'll make my report and give it to Karyn as quickly as possible. This matter is urgent."

"Everything is urgent for you. This can wait until tomorrow morning. Give me your report, and I'll make a recommendation to Karyn in the morning. She told me I am in control here, although you're a valuable first line of contact for the Inuit. So do as I say."

Lucy was exasperated by Donna's heavy-handed judgment. She quickly translated her notes, punching out the words on the typewriter and adding a strong recommendation to immediately relocate Natsiq and her child to Frobisher Bay for treatment and for their safety. It included a recommendation for police protection for the young mother until she was safely on the plane.

"We should see Karyn together," Lucy proposed, concerned that Donna would not communicate the urgency of the situation.

"You go home to your family. I'll give this to Karyn."

"You promise you'll give this to Karyn as soon as she comes back to the office?"

"Yes, although I don't share your view of Natsiq's situation. If we gave an airplane ticket to everyone who walked into the Welfare Office, our budget would be in deficit. Go home. I'll deal with it."

Donna put her strong hands on Lucy's shoulders and propelled her out of the office. Lucy wanted to shake loose from Donna's grip, but she was too unaccustomed to this kind of bullying to stand up for herself. As Lucy walked home, she felt confused and then angry about her co-worker's aggressive approach and frustrated by her own submissiveness.

I'm her equal and even more experienced. Why am I being treated like a child, someone to be pushed around? I should have gone directly to Karyn.

Chapter Twenty-seven

Deception

When she arrived at the office in the morning, Lucy's worst fears were realized. Karyn was not in, and Lucy had a sick feeling about Natsiq's situation.

"Donna, did you give my report to Karyn?" Lucy was tense and sensed that something terrible had happened.

"I put it on her desk. That is exactly what I told you I would do. Our manager will deal with it."

"Karyn has to make a decision immediately if Natsiq is to leave on today's plane. Natsiq has to get her baby ready and has to pack. There is barely enough time now. Natsiq will be here any minute."

Just then Natsiq walked into the office, looking drawn and nervous.

"I need to know if I'm on the plane. I have to get ready." She appeared frantic and looked disheveled as if she hadn't slept the previous night.

"Karyn's in a meeting," Donna replied, "and I don't know if she'll give in to your demands."

Lucy and Natsiq both had a sinking feeling. Obviously Donna had not pressed Natsiq's case with any urgency. Natsiq wouldn't get her ticket. She was trapped.

"I promised Kakik I'd see him today; if I don't, he'll find me and beat me. I can't take another beating." Natsiq made one last plea for help. "That was the last time I will let anyone lay a hand on me. Please help me, Miss."

"Everyone asks for trips to Frobisher. We can't give in to every request. That would be unprofessional."

Natsiq's thoughts swirled in her head. She could say nothing more to the unsympathetic *Qallunaaq*.

What can I do? She won't help me, and Lucy is powerless.

Natsiq left the office. She was doomed. Her feet were leaden as she plodded home. Her mind was made up; she knew what she had to do.

Lucy understood Natsiq's depth of despair. "You didn't give Karyn my report. You lied to me. Now tell me where Karyn is or I'll…" Lucy caught her words, telling herself to stay calm. It would not help Natsiq if she created a conflict with her co-worker.

"If you must know, she's in a meeting at the school."

Lucy threw on her coat. As she ran out the door, she noticed Kakik across the street, walking toward the Hudson's Bay Store.

God, I hope he didn't see Natsiq here.

Lucy ran as fast as she could to the school, arriving out of breath. She barged in on the meeting without knocking.

"Karyn, we have an emergency. I need your help with an urgent matter."

Karyn was not pleased to see her employee barging in without warning.

"Go back to your post, Lucy. I'll deal with it when I get back to the office."

Karyn was dressed in a gray suit with a pencil-slim skirt, her hair in neat curls from a perm she'd had before leaving Ottawa. The officious manager contrasted with the school staff members around the table, who were mostly dressed in denim or casual pants.

"But Miss Singer…"

"I will finish this meeting and speak to you later. Go back to the office." Karyn's anger was palpable.

Lucy could not break through Karyn's indifference. The tough-minded supervisor refused to listen when Lucy explained that Natsiq's life was in danger.

Karyn's intransigence barred her from taking interest in what Lucy had to say. But Lucy was perplexed. Had Donna even given Karyn the report? Nothing made sense, and Karyn refused to listen. Frustrated, Lucy turned to her friend Ashoona, who was one of the people meeting with Karyn.

"It's Natsiq. Ashoona, can you help me? Her life is in danger."

Ashoona excused herself from the meeting. As they walked to the school's exit, Lucy explained the case and asked Ashoona to go to the police with her. Ashoona knew about Kakik's violence and feared for the safety of anyone who was around when Kakik became enraged.

Ashoona ran to the police station, convinced that Natsiq's situation was indeed urgent. Lucy, who was slower than her friend, arrived in time to hear what Ashoona's was saying to James.

"I'm worried about Natsiq. If I told you that she is suicidal, would you be able to confiscate Adamie's guns, and if you knew that Kakik has threatened her, could you protect her?"

Ashoona described the circumstances, even adding the old history of little Davidee's death. Although James was a consummate womanizer, Ashoona had heard in the community that he was a fair policeman—one of their own, they said, someone who could speak their language.

"I appreciate that you've come to me for help," James said. "Yes, I can ask Adamie to turn over his guns, and then I'll hang around to protect Natsiq in case Kakik shows up. We broke up under bad circumstances, which may be adding to her depression. I know a little about the psychology of the human mind from my studies in Regina."

On the way to Natsiq's house, they met Adamie, who was headed to the Welfare Office for the family's monthly check. He was carrying Sandy and holding Samuel's hand. James talked to Adamie about confiscating the three guns he kept in the house.

"But why do you have Sandy with you?"

Ashoona did not wait for an answer. She broke into a run, James and Lucy following but unable to keep up.

No one was home in the little house. Ashoona felt momentary relief.

Maybe she went to Kakik's as she promised? Yes, that made sense.

If Natsiq showed up at his place, he would not be suspicious unless she was unable to conceal her plans to get to Frobisher, not in a few months, but today. Whatever was unfolding with Ashoona's cousin, Natsiq was not safe.

James and Lucy arrived as Ashoona came out of the house.

"James, could you go to Kakik's?" Lucy asked. "I saw him outside the Welfare Office just after Natsiq left. He'll know why she was there. He'll figure out that Natsiq was trying to get out of the village, and he'll go after her. He beat her yesterday. If Natsiq breaks up with Kakik, he may kill her or become suicidal himself."

Something out of place caught Ashoona's attention.

"Wait a minute." Ashoona walked toward the shed, apprehension growing as it became clear what she had spotted. "Oh, my God! No!"

James and Lucy ran to the shed and saw Ashoona bending over Natsiq's body, blood pooling and soaking into the snow.

Natsiq had fired the gun into her chest, missing her heart the first time and then firing a second deadly shot. Her suffering and anguish ended with the same gun that had taken the life of her little brother all those years ago.

"Oh Natsiq! Why didn't you ask me for help?" Ashoona sobbed uncontrollably beside her dead cousin. Ashoona was unable to move; her regrets and sorrow overwhelmed her. Lucy reached down to help Ashoona up.

"I am so sorry, Ashoona."

"It's my fault she is dead, Lucy. I abandoned her because I was angry with her family. I could have helped her. I could have bought a ticket for her." Lucy held her friend while Ashoona sobbed.

James took a blanket from the house and covered Natsiq's body.

"I'm sorry for your loss, Ashoona. Lucy, look after her. I'll try to find Natsiq's parents and give them the sad news. I also have to contact the Frobisher officials about the death."

"Adamie was on his way to the Welfare Office," Ashoona whispered between sobs.

The two women held each other until Lucy, shivering from the cold, gently led Ashoona away from the heartrending scene. As they walked back to Ashoona's house, the distraught woman continued to cry, while Lucy's feelings hardened.

This is their fault, Donna's and Karyn's. They didn't care. They let Natsiq die even though I told them over and over again that she was in danger.

Lucy flew into Karyn's office, anger rising in her like a storm.

"You should have issued the ticket for Natsiq. Now she's dead. Just like I said in my report."

"Your report said nothing of the kind. You recommended Natsiq remain in the village and attend counseling at our office. I agreed, based on your report."

"No. That was Donna's recommendation, not mine. Ask her. She will tell you. She took my report and promised to give it to you last night. This is crazy. Talk to Donna; she'll tell you that I was adamant that Natsiq leave town before something dreadful happened to her and the children."

"James came here to inform Adamie of his daughter's death. I knew Natsiq had been at the office yesterday, so I spoke to Donna immediately. She told me that *you* recommended Natsiq remain in Panniqtuuq."

Lucy could hardly speak she was so upset. *This is a nightmare! How could this happen?* Not only did she fail to protect Natsiq, but Lucy was now also being blamed for Natsiq's death.

"Karyn, that wasn't my report. You've got to believe me."

"Then give me a copy of your report, and do it quickly. The village will be up in arms over this unnecessary death, and they will want the person responsible to be dealt with severely."

"Donna took the only copy of my report, but I have my notes. They're in Inuktitut, but you could have James translate if you don't trust me."

"Well, get it."

Lucy ran to her desk, her heart racing. The notebook was gone. She rummaged through her desk drawers thinking that she may not have left it in its usual place beside her typewriter. No notebook, no proof that Lucy had tried to save Natsiq.

"It's not here." Lucy felt sick to her stomach.

"You're out of this office as of today. We can't have an employee who makes such a disastrous decision and then lies about it. Your poor judgment cost the life of that young woman. Clear out your desk, and leave immediately."

Lucy could not believe what she was hearing. She was stunned. Never before had she been told her work was less than perfect. In school she had been a top student. When she took courses in Frobisher, she was touted a role model for other Inuit students. Now this obstinate woman was dismissing her and blaming her for a report Donna had written. It was so unfair, so unjust.

Lucy cleared out her desk, but before leaving, she knocked on Karyn's office door.

"Karyn, it was Donna who didn't want to send Natsiq to Frobisher. Please talk to both of us at the same time, and you'll learn the truth. You have to believe me."

"I don't have to do anything. I've made up my mind, and I'm not changing it. If you want, call our senior manager in Frobisher."

Karyn's suggestion was the lifeline Lucy needed. Bruno liked her. She'd worked for him for the past three years with no problems. He often congratulated her on her careful work and organized management of the office. He had appointed her into the temporary position of manager.

Lucy's voice quavered as she spoke to Bruno. She explained the mix-up with the reports, emphasizing that Natsiq would not have committed suicide if she had been sent out to Frobisher.

"It was Donna who made the error in judgment, not me. I've worked for you for years, and you know I would never have risked the life of a young woman and her children."

He has to believe me. Someone has to be fair.

Instead of saving Lucy from being fired, he supported Karyn's decision.

"Karyn filled me in on this earlier. She told me that you have a history of errors since she took over management of the office. I have to back her up on this for the well-being of the office in Panniqtuuq. We have to let you go."

Lucy was beside herself with grief. How could this happen to her? She was doing her job. How could Donna get away with such a bold-faced lie? Lucy had no more fight in her. She left the office in tears and cried all the way home. Her children were home with Joe, her husband. Lucy could not even hug them.

She closed her bedroom door and wept uncontrollably, saying over and over, "It's so unfair! She lied! How can they do this to me when I was such a loyal employee, such a reliable and conscientious worker?" Lucy cried herself to sleep.

In the morning, Joe brought her coffee in bed and took her in his arms, trying to coax his wife out of her despondence.

Meanwhile, the villagers had learned of Natsiq's death and believed that it was Lucy who refused to protect the young mother. When Amaruk met Joe in the village later that morning, she screamed at him.

"Natsiq went to see Lucy and that wife of yours refused to help her! My daughter's death is on her head. I'm glad Lucy was fired! At least some justice is being handed out at the Welfare Office."

Joe explained that Lucy had tried to protect Natsiq, that it was the new staff member who opposed sending her to Frobisher. Amaruk wouldn't listen. She yelled back that Lucy might as well have pulled the trigger.

Ashoona heard the gossip at school and immediately realized what had happened. She had only met Donna and Karyn a few times, but she was uncomfortable around both women. Donna was far too controlling to be a welfare worker. And Karyn, though well educated, had little empathy for the Inuit. Ashoona remembered when they were children, how Lucy had defended her when everyone else bullied her. Now, it was time for Ashoona to help Lucy. She wanted to grieve for Natsiq, but instead she rushed to Lucy's defense.

Lucy staggered out of bed, her head pounding and her eyes bleary from weeping. Despite her grief over Natsiq's death and the unfair treatment she had received, she had to look after her children.

As soon as she saw Ashoona at the door, Lucy began crying again.

"They lied about me. I asked to have Natsiq sent to Frobisher for her safety, and Donna objected. Donna said she would give my report to Karyn, but she didn't. Karyn believes Donna because they are friends from Ottawa. It doesn't matter what I say. Karyn decided I was to blame without even talking to Donna and me together. It's so horrible, I can barely stand it."

"I know it's not your fault, and we will prove it. Guess who's the administrator for the Department of Health and Welfare? It's Henry. Our Henry knows you and would not believe the word of a newcomer who won't last in the community past her first monthlies. Donna doesn't belong here. She's a bully and a coward, blaming you for her mistake. As soon as she heard of Natsiq's death, she lied to Karyn about the report and destroyed your notes. She's willing to ruin your life to save her own skin. "

"Do you really think you can clear my name? I feel so awful. I never imagined someone would lie to get me fired. My life has always been blessed. Even when I had TB and thought I would lose everything, you helped me."

"I will help you again. We'll get to the truth."

"But this incident is more than I can bear. I can't even properly grieve over Natsiq. All that I can think of is how I've been mistreated. The community will shun me because they believe I was responsible for Natsiq's death. How can I go on? I can't put it behind me because the villagers will never forget. They'll ostracize me just like they did you when they thought you killed Davidee. The village can turn against a person so quickly. Do you really think Henry can help? Can you talk to him?"

"That will be easy because he's arriving on tonight's plane in order to carry out the autopsy. I'm off to meet him, and I'll invite him to stay at my place. We'll get to the bottom of this mess."

───── ∿ ─────

Ashoona met Henry at the airstrip. He kissed her on both cheeks and held her close to him. She leaned into his warm embrace, and the tension she'd felt over the last twenty-four hours was swept away. But she had to talk to him about Natsiq's death.

"I should have done more to save Natsiq. I knew she was desperate. Can you imagine Natsiq making the decision to take her own life?"

"I'm sorry about Natsiq, but it's not your fault, Ashoona. You're not responsible in any way."

As they walked to the police station, she told Henry about Lucy's predicament and how the entire community had condemned her.

Henry was dismayed over Lucy's treatment. But he could not be biased without investigating the incident. However, knowing Lucy's reputation in the community, he found it difficult to believe that she would lie. He arranged to meet the three employees involved in the incident. Lucy's dismissal could not be reversed immediately, but Henry would report his findings to their senior manager in Frobisher. There was a process, but Henry was certain he could get to the truth.

Before investigating Lucy's grievance, however, Henry had the sad task of determining the cause of death of the beautiful young mother, the cousin who had been Ashoona's friend, and at times, her tormentor. Now the entire community only felt love for Natsiq and grief over her untimely, tragic death.

———

The meeting at the Welfare Office was strained. Lucy asked Ashoona to attend because the aggrieved employee was so upset that she had trouble speaking without bursting into tears. Ashoona was Lucy's steady voice during the proceedings.

Henry led off the discussion. "I will give everyone a chance to be heard. The purpose of this meeting is not to assign blame, but to find the truth and learn from the incident so that future suicides can be prevented.

"Let's start at the beginning with Natsiq's visit to the Welfare Office. Donna, please begin, and I want you to tell the truth. You will not be disciplined, no matter how this comes out. I promise. Mistakes are often the cause of tragedies like this. We are human, and we work in difficult jobs, often dealing with people in distress."

Donna was no longer the arrogant colleague that Lucy had come to know. Instead she spoke in a subdued voice, unable to look directly at Henry, her eyes glued to the floor. In a leaden voice, she repeated her version of the interview with Natsiq and stated that it was Lucy's report that led to Natsiq's death.

"I left Lucy's report on Karyn's desk," Donna said, unconvincingly. "Lucy left the office early and did not sign the report.

The next day Karyn asked me who wrote the report, and I told her it was Lucy."

"Karyn, please tell me what time Donna told you that Lucy wrote the report. Was it after you heard the news of Natsiq's suicide or before?"

"Why does that matter?"

"Please answer the question."

"We both knew about Natsiq's suicide."

"Is it possible, Karyn, that Lucy's report never got to your desk?" Henry asked.

"Donna wouldn't lie about the report, would you, Donna?" Karyn asked.

Donna looked increasingly uncomfortable, fidgeting with a paper clip and twisting it compulsively.

"It was Lucy's report; she didn't want to give Natsiq a plane ticket." But Henry could see from Donna's posture that her words did not ring true.

Henry asked Lucy to tell her side of the story. Ashoona reached over and touched Lucy's hand. "Just be calm, and tell Henry what happened. Speak slowly, and try not to cry."

"Natsiq came to the Welfare Office yesterday; she had her two children with her." Lucy's voice was soft, and she seemed close to tears as she continued. "Natsiq was badly bruised from an attack by her boyfriend and begged us to give her a ticket to Frobisher so she could leave the next day. The interview ended abruptly when Donna pushed Natsiq and made it clear that she opposed sending Natsiq to Frobisher." Lucy paused for a moment to gather her thoughts.

"After Natsiq left, I transcribed my notes of the meeting from Inuktitut to English, wrote up a report and gave it to Donna. In my report, I recommended that we put Natsiq and her baby on the next plane to Frobisher. I wrote that they were at risk if they stayed in the village another day."

"Do you have your original notes, Lucy?"

"I looked for them, but my notebook and my typed report are both missing. I typed my name on the bottom of my report and signed it. I assume that Donna wrote her own report, and that is what Karyn received."

After everyone had finished speaking, Henry sat back in his chair, contemplating what he had just heard.

"Karyn, I believe that Lucy is telling the truth. I will speak to Bruno and ask that he reverse her dismissal. Donna, now is the time to tell the truth about what happened. This will not go on your record. Lucy has been terribly distressed, and the people she has lived with all her life are angry with her because they believe she betrayed one of their own. This is her village. They believe that Lucy failed to protect Natsiq. So for Lucy's sake, I ask you to search your soul and tell me the truth. We will only admire you if you can admit that it was you and not Lucy that opposed issuing a plane ticket to Natsiq."

He spoke to Donna in such a kind manner that she burst into tears. "Yes. I'm sorry. I tore up Lucy's report as soon as I heard of Natsiq's death, and I took her notebook. I was afraid."

"That makes it easier for your senior manager in Frobisher. We have Donna's admission, and as far as I'm concerned, Lucy is to be re-instated immediately and the issue closed. My only follow-up will be to ensure a more frequent evaluation of your performance, Karyn, and careful scrutiny of Donna's involvement in difficult issues. Have faith in Lucy. She knows the community; she worked here several years before you came on staff. She deserves to be treated with respect and fairness."

Lucy and Ashoona left the office, relieved at Henry's decision. Lucy could not believe that the anguish she faced only an hour ago was lifted. She could now grieve for Natsiq and share in the community's sorrow. The two friends held hands as they walked to Judy's to share the news.

"I knew you would have looked after Natsiq," Judy told Lucy. "I never believed the story that it was your fault that she took her own life. And really, it isn't anyone's fault. It's the clash of the old and new life in the Arctic. Young fellas just can't adapt, and young women become pawns in these isolated villages."

"Hey, Judy, you're sounding off like a politician. You know that you can't get elected in this community," Ashoona laughed.

"I'm serious," Judy went on. "If I am not electable, women like you two better get into politics. You both come from Inuit aristocracy, and you, Ashoona, have already made your mark by becoming the first Inuit teacher. The North may appear to be run like a colony, but the federal government will not rule the Arctic forever. Eventually, Ottawa will have to loosen its hold on the Arctic and replace colonialism with democracy. When that happens, young women like you could get elected and do something about the problems here."

"What can we do to prevent youth suicide?" Ashoona asked. "Natsiq showed troubling symptoms ever since Sandy's death. I've come to realize that she had been walking toward her own death for many months. Her despondency, lack of attention to her appearance, her inability to re-establish a bond with Samuel and then her loss of interest in the baby...we knew she was spiraling downward but could do nothing to save her."

"But we have to recognize that her motherly instincts surfaced," Lucy added. "She made sure that Kakik did not harm the children, and she talked Adamie into taking the children on a walk so they would not witness her suicide. I wish I had been more assertive and insisted on putting the report on Karyn's desk myself. I had a premonition that Donna would make a mess of things."

"At least the villagers will know it was Donna, not you, that failed Natsiq. As quickly as they condemned you, they'll now turn on Donna and Karyn. And Amaruk, who easily becomes enraged over real and imagined injustices, will demand their heads."

"I hope I'll be able to work with them again and that they won't resent me," Lucy said. "Karyn is smart, even though her personality irritates me, and Donna has learned her lesson. If the department lets them stay, I may be able to tap into their resources to help Natsiq's baby."

"What do you mean?" Judy asked as she poured coffee and placed a plate of pastries on her kitchen table.

"Adamie is too old to care for the baby, and I wouldn't leave Amaruk with a puppy let alone a precious little child. No one else in Panniqtuuq could adopt little Sandy, but maybe Sandy's parents will want to take him."

"I've met them," Ashoona said. "The baby looks just like his war-hero father, and now that Sandy has finally put on some weight, I can see the resemblance between him and his Alberta grandmother. When we had dinner with the family, Mrs. Fredrickson impressed me with her energy and love for family. Adopting Sandy might help her deal with her son's death. Sandy will grow up to be a muscular, handsome young man with a bounce similar to his grandmother."

"How can Karyn be of any help?" Judy asked.

"Before she took the job in Panniqtuuq, she was head of adoptions for the Province of Ontario. She knows how to work the system."

"What about Adamie?" Ashoona asked. "He might object to the baby leaving the community and being raised among the *Qallunaat*."

"I don't think so," Lucy answered. "He doesn't share Amaruk's prejudices, and as you told us, Ashoona, he admits he's too old to be changing diapers."

Chapter Twenty-eight

Henry

Even though Ashoona was exhausted after the meeting that resolved Lucy's position, she met up with Henry and suggested that they take a walk. They took the path toward the entrance to the fjord. The trail was rough, with hard snowdrifts to negotiate and wind-blown bedrock. The trail skirted the cliffs that defined the edge of the frozen sea. Ashoona felt an increasing sense of relief as they continued along the trail.

"It's been a crazy month, Henry. It's as if all the constellations suddenly clashed and created a different world. I have my father back, the village knows that I didn't kill Davidee, and I have a job I love. But I feel so sad about Natsiq's tragic death. Surely I could have done something. I had enough money to buy her a ticket to Frobisher. I should have looked after her."

Henry knew he could do little to soften the guilt Ashoona felt over Natsiq's death, so he took her hand and drew her into his arms. His warm embrace restored Ashoona and washed away the heartache she'd felt since she found her cousin's body.

They walked until they reached a place on the trail that had been obliterated by a rockslide. Although they both enjoyed the walk, they did not feel like clambering over boulders so late in the day when they were both emotionally and physically exhausted.

"How about we go back to your place for something to eat? I've had only a sandwich and a snack on the airplane. Far from filling or appetizing. What are we having for supper? I suppose you have a raw seal dish for me because I suspect you've become a more traditional Inuit in the past year."

"We're having caribou steaks. Lucy's husband provides me with the best meat in the village. I don't have time to hunt, but as a member of the communal Inuit, I get to share in the hunters' harvests. In return I bake cakes. This is the best place in the world to live."

"It's too bad for me that you like it here so much. I suppose I'm out of the running as a potential husband unless I move to Panniqtuuq."

Ashoona felt her face flush, but then told herself that such an intimate comment was just Henry's way of teasing her. She interpreted his comment as something a close and caring friend would say. She didn't want to jump to the conclusion that he would ever be serious about their relationship.

"Maybe you'll move to Panniqtuuq once you've tasted my cooking. Or perhaps I'll reassess Frobisher as a future home. It's still the North. They hunt, fish and make traditional clothing there. Maybe we need more people like me who speak the local language to balance the tide of *Qallunaat*. I could teach the children to appreciate where they come from, explain that Frobisher Bay's name is really Iqaluit, meaning "the place of many fish," and teach the boys that they have a place in this changing world."

"Sounds like you're on a soapbox. Has Judy's political bent been influencing you?"

"I should keep my views to myself." Ashoona shook her head. "Strange that I can't defend myself in a personal conflict, but when it comes to speaking out about injustice, I never shut up. Let's go home and enjoy a dinner without any serious discussion of the future of the Inuit."

Ashoona gave Henry the spare bedroom down the hall from where she slept. She felt calm and peaceful knowing he was close by. When she was alone, Ashoona listened to every creak in the building, every whisper of the wind. Tonight she fell asleep feeling safe and comfortable, as if her body drifted on a pillow of clouds.

Ashoona woke early and tiptoed downstairs to make coffee. But she didn't need to be quiet because Henry was up and had opened the curtains to look out at the jumble of tidal ice in the sound. As the morning sun caught the tip of the mountains across the fjord, Ashoona suddenly felt full of hope and promise. Soon there would be long days of sunshine; darkness and the bitter winter were months and months away.

"Come over here," Henry said, holding out his arms. "I need a morning hug to start my day off right." Ashoona wanted to hold him and once more feel the comfort of his arms.

It was not just a brotherly hug. Henry held her tightly and looked into her eyes. She tilted her head and his soft lips came down on hers. He kissed her passionately, holding her head with both hands.

They pulled apart, and Henry held her at arm's length, looking at her with a questioning look in his eyes. She smiled up at him, and he took her lips again, this time pulling her close and wrapping his arms around her completely. It was a long, loving kiss that left Ashoona breathless.

Ashoona waited, hoping he would say something of his feelings for her. Instead he smiled playfully.

"Am I too old for you?"

"Definitely," Ashoona laughed. "I should find a younger man," she continued lightheartedly. "Women always outlive men, and I don't want to be a widow for decades. Then again, you're a healthy specimen and may beat the odds and outlive me." Ashoona paused, looking thoughtfully at Henry. She was hesitant to bring up a topic that had been so painful for Henry. "I wonder, Henry, are you still in love with Joanna?"

Henry bowed his head as if ashamed. "I assure you I am over that infatuation. Watching her jump from a relationship with me to an affair with the captain was hurtful, but now that I look back on it, I see that she was the wrong person for me."

"Both of us have changed. Remember when I was young and all I wanted was a husband, children and everything the *Qallunaat* had? Now I have hopes and dreams beyond being a wife and mother, and material things don't mean as much to me. I want to be a successful teacher, but I also hope I can do something worthwhile for the Inuit community."

"In what way?"

"Natsiq's tragic death has affected me deeply, made me aware of the problems people in the Arctic are facing. I don't have a clue about the answers, but one thing I do know, these problems won't be solved by a bunch of *Qallunaat* sitting in Ottawa."

"I understand your worries about your people, and you know I share your concerns. Your interest in improving the lives of the Inuit doesn't mean that you cannot have a happy marriage."

"Not many men want a wife who wants to make changes to the system; they want someone to have babies, enjoy sex and cook for them."

"Sex is good…. But we're getting too serious for so early in the morning, and I haven't even had my coffee. Why not be a submissive woman and pour me a cup?" Henry said with a grin.

"Yes, Master. How do you take your coffee?"

"Black as hell and sweet as love." He smiled at her.

Ashoona felt a warm shiver and wished they could spend the day together, wrapped in each other's arms. She believed that Henry felt the same way. She was sure of it.

But Ashoona was due at school, and Henry had an appointment with James regarding the autopsy. They walked together as far as they could.

When Ashoona arrived at school, Judy looked at her mischievously, having noticed that Ashoona had an overnight guest. Judy was quick to tease but did so in private so other members of the staff wouldn't hear. In any case, Ashoona was aware of the gossip mill in the little village and that the news of Henry's overnight stay would be known around the town in no time. But Ashoona didn't mind. There could be a lot worse rumors than talking about her friendship with a respected man like Henry, someone who had been her friend since she was a young teenager.

Ashoona listened for the plane when it took off that morning, wishing she could have skipped out of her class to see Henry off. Once he was gone, the day seemed to drag. As soon as school was out, she made her way to the Welfare Office. It was imperative they get in touch with little Sandy's Alberta grandparents regarding the adoption.

Ashoona remembered the name of the farming community where Sandy's grandparents lived and located their phone number for Karyn. Ashoona made the first call in order to sound out the family regarding an adoption, which would be a big decision for the family.

Mrs. Fredrickson was in her mid-forties. The family was well off because grain prices were skyrocketing, so their finances were in good shape to be able to take on another child. However, the loss of their second-oldest son had left a pall over the household. Although this would normally be a time in their lives for the elder Fredricksons to use their extra money to travel, Mrs. Fredrickson had no interest. She spent days looking at photos of her dead son, her usual happy chatter gone. Mr. Fredrickson seemed to have lost interest in the farm, leaving the job to his oldest son and the two teenagers.

"It's been the worst time of our lives," Mrs. Fredrickson told Ashoona. "We can't seem to get over losing our boy."

Ashoona related the tragic story of Natsiq's death and then told Mrs. Fredrickson about Sandy and his need for a safe, loving home. When Ashoona asked if they would consider adopting the baby, Mrs. Fredrickson's initial reaction was to say no. But she said she would talk to her family and have a decision the next day when Karyn was to call her.

The family sat around the big kitchen table—now only three sons—John, the eldest, safely back from the war, and two teenagers, George and Robert. What surprised Mrs. Fredrickson was the strong argument the two teenagers made in favor of adoption.

"We'll help you with little Sandy," George promised, and Robert nodded in agreement. "We'll even change diapers," George continued, "just not the poopie ones."

"When he gets older, I'll teach him how to drive the tractor," Robert added.

No one seemed to object, and the more Mrs. Fredrickson thought about holding her dead son's little boy, the more she warmed to the idea. In fact, she realized that she hadn't felt as good since before her son left for Europe. Even Mr. Fredrickson was excited about having Sandy's son under his roof.

This baby will bring a lot of work, Mrs. Fredrickson thought, *but maybe my grandson will help to heal some of the*

grief I have felt every day since the arrival of that dreadful tele-
gram with the news of my son's death.

"Instead of traveling to Europe, which many of our friends are doing," she suggested, "let's take a trip to the Arctic. We should meet Sandy's other grandparents, check on Ashoona and bring our little Sandy home."

"You could probably fly to Italy and back for the price of the plane ticket to Baffin Island," her husband informed her. "Are you sure you want to give up on your dream of traveling to La Scala to hear a real Italian opera?"

"We'll see one of the most beautiful regions of Canada. I've read about the North and the Inuit people. The men hunt seal and caribou, the women make the most beautiful clothing and people from all over the world seek their art. It'll be an adventure we will cherish, just as we'll cherish our little grandson."

Instead of waiting for Karyn's phone call, Mrs. Fredrickson called Ashoona at the school to inform her of the family's decision to take Sandy. When she said that her husband and their two teenagers were planning a trip to Panniqtuuq, Ashoona invited them to stay with her.

Karyn was an efficient manager and worked swiftly to get the adoption papers in order. She explained on the phone to the Fredricksons that it would take a few weeks to get signatures and paperwork through the courts, but that Henry had agreed to bend the rules and let them take the baby home to Alberta as soon as possible. And Ashoona and Lucy promised to help out with the child as often as they could until he was safely in his grandmother's arms.

Natsiq's funeral was held on a cool, windy Sunday. Amaruk and Adamie sat in the front pew with Samuel. Sandy's new parents and stepbrothers had arrived the day before the funeral and had taken over the baby's care. Although he was now a little over a year old, Sandy did not make strange. He seemed to take to Mrs. Fredrickson and the two boys almost immediately; they had little Sandy smiling in minutes.

As soon as Lucy learned that the grandparents had agreed to adopt Sandy, she asked Ashoona for advice as to Mrs. Fredrickson's size and had an *amauti* ready the day the family arrived in Panniqtuuq. Mrs. Fredrickson tucked little Sandy under the *amauti*, and he snoozed peacefully throughout the service.

The community rallied around to support Adamie and Amaruk, putting aside old grudges to join in the couple's sorrow over the loss of the daughter that belonged to the entire community. As the Anglican minister led them in prayer, the villagers keened in sorrow.

Even Kakik came to the funeral and was not shunned but greeted with expressions of regret for his loss. They knew Kakik had treated Natsiq cruelly, but they felt he could not help himself. Like Qillaq and Padluk, he was seen as an aberration in Inuit culture. He did not possess the happy, gentle nature of his people. Unlike the Inuit, he created chaos and lived in violence.

In the old days, Kakik might have become a shaman, but Christianity was replacing the old beliefs, and men like Kakik who did not fit into the pattern of Inuit culture turned to antisocial behavior. People would say that he was the type who was crazy during a full moon, not in hatred of him, but with understanding that his behavior was not his fault. They said, "*Ayunqnaq*...it can't be helped."

Donna and Karyn did not attend the funeral. Ashoona knew this was a mistake on their part. The villagers may have forgiven the welfare workers their mistakes had they come to mourn along with the community. But Judy and Ernest were there. Judy wept along with the Inuit women and hugged Amaruk after the service. It was a day of healing for everyone who attended.

After the funeral, the congregation moved to the school gym where everyone participated in the usual feast of caribou, seal and *mukluk*, with warm bannock and pots of tea. What was different from past Inuit social gatherings was the table of desserts that Judy and Lucy prepared, including Judy's amazing, rich chocolate cake slathered with thick chocolate icing.

Then came the speeches, praising Natsiq for completing her studies and returning to her community. Akulukjuq, the Anglican lay minister, spoke first of the need to address the problem of youth suicide. Then his speech turned to happier memories of how the young woman's beauty turned heads and how well she could play cat's cradle. As usual, the speeches were overly long especially for Judy and Ernest who understood only a few words of Inuktitut. At the end of the service, Judy heard her own name and asked Lucy to translate.

"He thanked you for making the delicious cake and said that you and Ernest were the type of *Qallunaat* who add to the well-being of the community. That means you are one of us."

"Well, Ernest, I think it's time we learned the language. Right? Lessons start next week. If locals are going to say nice things about us, I want to understand what they're saying."

A month had passed since the Fredricksons had attended Natsiq's funeral and picked up their grandson. Now the spring storms were affecting air flights.

Lucky the Fredricksons left soon after the funeral, Ashoona thought. *If they had waited to return to Edmonton this week, they would have been out of luck.* The airstrip had been shut down for a week. No one was able to fly in or out while the winds raged and villagers huddled inside their homes.

As Ashoona prepared for school, she listened to a wind warning being broadcast over the radio. She would only have a half-day of school because the students would be sent home before the winds became too fierce. In spring, gales regularly blew through the village, but winter hurricanes like this one were unusual. April was typically the month Arctic dwellers looked forward to for relief from winter's grip. On her way to school, Ashoona was barely able to move forward in the icy blast. And as she bent into the gale, she saw a figure off to the side in the shadows, a big man who seemed to be watching her. Ashoona tried to walk faster, but the wind was too strong. Her heart jumped into her throat.

It's him!

She did her best to hurry and reach the safety of the school. She felt like a trapped animal. Just then she heard footsteps approaching quickly from behind. Her heart pounded; she imagined the worst.

He's right behind me, so close I can hear his breath!

"I decided to check on you this nasty morning." To Ashoona's great relief, it was Paloosie. "It looks like someone is tailing you. He'll never touch you if I'm near. I'll get you to the school and back each day; that is, if you don't mind my company. I can even tell you a few jokes," he said with a grin.

When they reached the school, Ashoona invited him into the staff lunchroom for coffee. The teachers were discussing the latest school and village news and helping themselves to cookies, coffee and tea. The female teachers were charmed by the handsome Inuit man who spoke better English than the average young Inuit.

When Paloosie left, they teased Ashoona. "So will you be walking down the aisle soon with that good-looking man?"

"He's a sweetheart. But we are more like brother and sister. His true love is my friend Brenda. He is so in love with her that he can't speak without mentioning her name. Remember studying Romeo and Juliet? Well, he's an Inuit Romeo. Loves to be in love. Even if he once had a crush on me, his heart now belongs to Brenda."

"You shouldn't give your friends such precious belongings. You should have kept this one for yourself," Judy advised with a smile.

"Well, he's my bodyguard. My father arranged it before he left, because of Qillaq. Actually, I like having Paloosie walk me to school and home. I feel safer. Besides, he can be quite entertaining. When he was a young teenager he was tongue-tied when I was around, but these days he is quite the chatterbox, telling me stories that would make you roll with laughter."

"A man with a sense of humor is worth a thousand good hunters these days. Maybe you should try to get him back from Brenda. At least you'll have a good laugh along with whatever else he wants to give you each day," Judy chuckled.

Just as classes were about to begin for the day, the teachers in the staffroom heard the wind rattling the windows of the school and decided the winds were too strong and they would close the school for the day. They contacted as many parents as they could and asked them to pass the word around. A few children had already arrived at the school and were pleased to be sent home for an unexpected day off.

By the time the staff left the school, the weather had worsened. The wind rocketed down from the Penny Ice Cap high in Auyuittuq Pass and swept down the steep walls of Mount Asgard before roaring into the narrow gully where the little village of Panniqtuuq lay exposed to its fierce power. The hurricane-force wind rocked the fragile houses, tore the roof off the Hudson's Bay Post and pushed over snowmobiles and machinery. Mothers kept their children indoors because if they were outside, the little ones could be tossed in the air. Even adults took shelter during these hurricane-force gales.

Paloosie came back to the school to retrieve Ashoona. The winds were fierce, and icy snow battered their backs as they struggled to get to Ashoona's home. As they passed the church and got close to Ashoona's place, they spotted Qillaq watching them from the corner of the church.

"Hurry! Let's get you inside and lock the door."

The wind was so strong that is was difficult to close the door against the force of the storm. Paloosie managed to close the door and lock it behind him.

"Do you want me to stay the night? I promise I will be a gentleman, sleep on the couch, get up and make you coffee in the morning. I'd feel better if I could be here. I don't want to leave you alone."

"People will talk if you stay here. Gossip is the village entertainment, especially when the weather keeps them indoors and they don't have anything else to do. I would be finished as a teacher if word got around that you stayed overnight. I suppose you know that Henry stayed here, and that is enough gossip to hand over to the busybodies. Don't worry. I'll be fine once I lock the doors behind you."

Paloosie left reluctantly. He checked around the house and up the street, trying to spot Qillaq. Just thinking about the vicious man made his old gunshot wound ache. Recalling the fight to save Ashoona during the expedition reminded him of just how obsessed Qillaq was. He wondered if even a government-built row house would keep him out. Paloosie was the only person out that night. The other villagers had all taken shelter from the gale.

Ashoona spent the afternoon planning the next day's lessons. She prepared her supper of turbot and rice but found she could not get a single fork of food down her throat. She made a cup of hot chocolate and listened to the radio, then put on her pajamas and sat up in bed trying to read until she felt sleepy.

The winds pounded at the building, rattling the house so much that Ashoona worried it would sweep the roof off and leave her exposed to the storm. The noise was incessant. Ashoona couldn't tell if it was the wind battering the house or someone knocking down her door. She couldn't sleep even though she was exhausted from her early-morning start.

She was reading F. Scott Fitzgerald's *The Great Gatsby*, an intriguing story but so removed from life in Panniqtuuq that Ashoona had trouble concentrating. What would Fitzgerald think about life in her community? No cars, fancy clothing or mansions, just a land of ice and snow, hunters, fishermen and women who could sew and run alongside a *qamutik* for hours.

Remarkably, Fitzgerald understood that racism existed everywhere. His unsympathetic character ranted about the superiority of the whites and his concerns that the colored races might submerge the white race "if the whites don't watch out."

Strange that a writer from the land of the *Qallunaat* who understood the tension between races in the United States could also likely understand the reality of the Arctic.

The noise of the wind would not let her rest.

It's him; I know it!

She heard the door smash in, but then the wind rocked the house and caught part of the metal roof, making such a noise that Ashoona told herself it was just the damn wind.

She put the book down and closed her eyes. She tried to ignore the loud flapping as the wind caught a corner of the metal roof. Finally, she dropped off into a fitful sleep.

Chapter Twenty-nine

The Predator Returns

Ashoona woke in the middle of the night, certain that she'd heard heavy footsteps on the stairs leading up to her room. It was difficult to discern the difference between banging caused by the wind and footsteps. She steeled herself, so terrified that she couldn't move.

I should get out of bed, run down stairs to get my gun or grab something...anything. But it's just the wind. I'm being paranoid.

She lay in bed, tense and frightened, listening intently. She heard it again. A step on the stairs, then only the wind and then another footstep.

She jumped from bed and shrieked.

Suddenly, he was there, a huge form in the doorway.

"You fucking bitch! You think you can run away from me. I will fuck you all night then cut your pretty face into ribbons and slice off your breasts, all while you are alive. I have suffered because of you. I have harmed my children because of you. Now, you will pay."

420

Ashoona dodged as he lunged for her. She slid under the bed, hoping that Qillaq was too big to squeeze under.

No one could help her. She was alone. If only she had let Paloosie stay the night. She screamed again, hoping against hope that someone would hear her voice above the howling wind.

"No use yelling, you bitch! No one will hear you. Shut up, and come quietly. If you come without a struggle, I promise I will kill you quickly." He bent down, sweeping a muscled arm under the bed, trying to grab her. "Come out from under there, and I won't torture you. Just come and make it easy on yourself. That little fuck will be back, and I need you to myself for the night—a long night of revenge I've been wanting you for too many years."

"You'll have to drag me out, you beast. I won't go with you. You're crazy! Even your wives know you're crazy! They talked to me at school. Do you know what they told me? That you ate human flesh, that you ate your own child when there were no seals. You even killed and ate your daughter when your wife killed and brought a seal home. You told her you preferred human flesh. Your own little girl! What kind of monster are you?"

"Who told you that? I will find out, and she will be the next to die."

"Your wives and the village people. Everyone knows you're crazy."

Ashoona's accusations momentarily halted Qillaq's attack.

Didn't he realize how he was despised in the community? Ashoona wondered. *Can I use words to turn back his violence?*

"You don't have to control women and bring the hatred of the community down on you. You can change."

"You shut up! You don't talk!"

He jumped up quickly, flipped the bed over and grabbed Ashoona by her arm, dragging her down the stairs. She was barefoot and dressed only in pajamas. She shrieked and kicked as he pulled her out the door and into the storm. Her feet burned when they touched the icy ground, like tiny knives nicking at her soles.

As they turned the corner toward the trading post, Ashoona felt trapped. She was not strong enough to defend herself against a two-hundred-and-fifty-pound man who was consumed with rage. He smelled of booze and sweat, his hands as rough as wrinkled steel. She knew her only chance was for someone to see or hear her. But it was the middle of the night, and the streets were empty, the houses dark and the raging wind drowned out her cries. She yelled louder and bit his hand as he dragged her toward the old shed behind the Hudson's Bay Post. She knew she'd die there unless she fought to free herself.

He shoved her into the shed and pounced on her, dragging her pajama pants down.

"Help me! Someone, please help me!"

"Shut up, you slut." Qillaq slapped her face. She felt warm blood trickle from her nose, but she yelled even louder. "Help me! Please, help me!"

Ashoona kicked and fought. She rolled out from under Qillaq and dodged away from him. She looked around for a weapon or a place to hide, but she could see nothing to help her. Although he was stronger, Ashoona had the advantage of speed. She made it to the door when Qillaq pulled a knife.

"Don't move, bitch, or I will slit your pretty throat."

I need a weapon! Ashoona thought. But it was dark, and her eyes had not adjusted to the dim interior of the shed. She grabbed the door handle, but before she could turn it, Qillaq threw his weight against the heavy wooden door, cutting off Ashoona's escape. She tried to get away, but Qillaq pressed the knifepoint lightly against her chest. Ashoona couldn't move. Her breath came in gasps. She could feel the point of the knife digging in through her pajama top.

This can't be the end; this can't be happening to me.

"Move away from the door, or I will kill you right now."

Ashoona took a cautious step forward; she trembled with fear, knowing her abductor could end her life in one quick movement if she opposed him. Qillaq moved back a step into the dark storage shed, keeping the knife on Ashoona's breast. He raised his hand and backhanded her face, sending Ashoona sprawling onto the floor. He held the knife blade to her heart as he pinned her down with his heavy body.

"Help me! Someone!"

Just then, the door crashed open. Paloosie had heard Ashoona's cry as he walked by the shed on his way back to check on her.

"Oh my God. No!" He yelled, "Get away from her!"

Ashoona screamed, blood running from her nose as Qillaq held the knife to her breast, ready to slice her open.

"Paloosie! He has a knife!"

Paloosie took two long strides into the shed and using his great skill at the high kick, landed a sharp blow on the side of Qillaq's head. The big man was stunned by the surprise attack and rolled away from Ashoona.

"You bastard!" Paloosie yelled, kicking at Qillaq again, planting his booted foot in Qillaq's exposed flank. The heavy-set hunter reeled for a moment and then staggered to his feet. He whipped his knife through the air, slicing into Paloosie's leg.

"Take that, you little shit. Come for me, you skinny little fuck! You no match for me. I kill you both. This is my woman, and no one is going to stop me this time. She made a fool of me, took my dog team, my gun, and tonight she will die by my hand!"

Paloosie winced and backed off, blood seeping from his leg. Qillaq stabbed again at Paloosie, but even though he was injured, the young man was quick on his feet, easily dodging the knife. He ducked away and danced around the lumbering madman.

"So you think you can fight me, you little runt. I could wring your neck with two fingers."

Paloosie watched Qillaq's every move, ready to dodge, waiting for his chance. Qillaq moved toward Paloosie again, and Ashoona scrambled to her feet, feeling her way around the shed for anything she could use as a weapon. Piles of junk were strewn around the old shed—barrels used for rendering whale oil, paddles for the whaling boats and old ropes coiled up on the floor.

Suddenly, her hand landed on an *ulu*. It felt rusty with age, but it was made of good strong steel. She grabbed the handle, and when Qillaq lunged again at Paloosie, the agile young man sideslipped the crazed Inuit, giving Ashoona a chance to pass Paloosie the weapon. The battle was even—Qillaq with a sharp long knife and Paloosie wielding the large *ulu* with its semi-circular blade that could open the throat of a caribou in one swift move.

Qillaq raised the knife, thrusting it at Paloosie's chest. Paloosie deflected Qillaq's outstretched arm and slashed downward with the *ulu*, slicing through the big man's parka and opening a long, shallow cut down the crazed man's chest. Qillaq staggered for a moment. Paloosie stepped back.

"Give up, Qillaq. I don't want to kill you."

Blood poured down Qillaq's parka; the bulky hunter appeared to have given up the fight.

Ashoona watched her attacker, hoping that the battle was over, that she and Paloosie could tie the evil man to the shed post and turn him over to James.

But his thirst for revenge would never be over for Qillaq. He glared at Ashoona.

"You die!" Qillaq moved unbelievably fast for a bulky, injured man. He swung the knife at Ashoona.

But Paloosie was there in a second. He caught Qillaq's arm and sliced upward with the *ulu*, opening Qillaq's throat. Blood spurted from the hideous man's neck, and with a throaty gasp, Qillaq fell at Paloosie's feet.

Paloosie and Ashoona stood still, stunned for several moments.

Ashoona cried, "Oh my God, Paloosie. You saved me!" She wrapped her arms around her guardian and sobbed with relief. "Is it really over? Is he really dead?"

Paloosie held her for a few minutes while both of them trembled, Paloosie from the fight and Ashoona from her brush with torture and horrible death.

Paloosie took Ashoona by the elbow, gently guiding her to the door. "I'm taking you home with me so my mom can look after you. Tonight you need a shot of rum."

He picked Ashoona up in his arms and carried her out into the fierce wind. Paloosie's foot hit an icy patch and he staggered momentarily under Ashoona's weight, but he regained his balance and struggled through the wild winds that screamed around them.

Aula opened the door for them. "What happened? My God, the blood!"

Paloosie's jacket and pant leg were splattered with blood, and Ashoona's nose bled down her lips and onto her pajama top. "Who hurt you? It was him, wasn't it? That monster, Qillaq! "

"He's gone, Aula. Paloosie killed him. Once again, I owe him my life." Ashoona broke down weeping, and Aula held her and rocked her until the shaking stopped and Ashoona's tears dried up.

Paloosie brought her a dram of rum. "Drink it down. It'll relax you. And believe me, I would take a drink as well if I hadn't promised Brenda I would never touch the stuff. Until you found the *ulu*, I thought I was a goner."

"This is the second time you've saved me. I guess I'll have to call you my knight in shining armor."

"Like in the days of kings and knights in old England. Now I have a second wound to remind me of you." By this time, Aula had bandaged Paloosie's leg and wrapped Ashoona in a cozy robe.

"The lady will be your dearest friend forever." Ashoona kissed his cheek and hugged Aula, relief flooding through her entire body.

———

Ashoona felt like she was walking on air. The shadow that had stalked her since she was twelve was gone. The investigation into Qillaq's death determined that Paloosie and Ashoona were in fear for their lives from the attack, and it was ruled self-defense.

Ashoona felt lighthearted as she boarded the plane for Frobisher. She had arranged to meet her father and Lynne for a weekend trip to Frobisher, and more importantly, she would see Henry. Ashoona had two days of teachers' meetings in the city, and her parents had arranged to rent a small suite at one of the hotels. As the plane took off and flew down the fjord and over Cumberland Sound, she left behind years of pain and anxiety. So much of her life had been fraught with stress that it was difficult for her to relax and enjoy the flight. She felt jumpy and tense.

The village people know I didn't kill Davidee; my father didn't abandon me; and the monster that stalked me for almost a decade is gone. I don't have to worry about him ever again.

Dugan met Ashoona at the airport. He had a taxi waiting, and they drove along the bumpy streets to the hotel. Lynne
had a stew bubbling on the stove.

"Do you remember me writing you about Doctor Russell?" Ashoona asked her father.

"Was he the doctor who hired you to work at the clinic in
Blacklead, the one who encouraged you to study? When you
thought I had abandoned you, Doctor Russell stepped in and
took my role, didn't he? I owe him."

"No one could replace you," Ashoona replied with
a smile. "But I do want you to meet him. May I invite him to join
us for dinner? He told me the hospital food is horrible, and he
never cooks for himself because he works too much."

"He's the hospital administrator, isn't he? That must keep
him busy in this town," said Lynne. "Of course, invite him. I've
made more stew than we three can eat."

Lynne expected to meet an older man, so was surprised
when she greeted Henry at the door, a kind-looking man in his
early thirties.

Ashoona had looked forward to this reunion even more
than she cared to admit. As they ate dinner, she caught Henry
looking at her. His eyes were a light gray and the warmth in his
smile made Ashoona's heart race.

"Tell us about the hospital in Edmonton, Ashoona? Were
there only Inuit people there?" Lynne asked.

"No. Not at all. The Inuit were the minority; the hospital
was huge and most of the patients were from the Yukon and
northern British Columbia. The elders initially hated it there.
But in our second year, that changed. They settled in and referred
to Camsell as 'their hospital.' Sadly, I don't recall one single elder
surviving to return home."

A pall settled over the dinner table until Ashoona continued. "Henry wanted to treat the people in the communities,

427

but the government refused." She looked at Henry. "If you had the chance you would have done what was right for our people. That is what I admire about you."

Dugan and Lynne looked at each other and smiled. They sensed that the relationship between Henry and Ashoona was much deeper than a casual friendship.

———————

The next day, Henry arrived with a bouquet of flowers. When Lynne opened the door, she joked, "Ah, flowers for me?"

Ashoona's father invited him in. "Lynne, I think our daughter has a suitor."

"That's pretty old-fashioned," Lynne replied with a smile. "Come in. Ashoona is getting ready."

"So what are your intentions?" Dugan asked with a chuckle.

Just then, Ashoona came out of the bedroom. "Shame on you, Papa. Don't torment the poor man, or he will never take me on a date again. We're going to the movies to see *Meet Me in St. Louis* with Judy Garland."

Henry held her hand during the movie, and when the film ended and before the lights went on, he lifted her hand and kissed the palm, sending warm shivers through her body.

Henry held her hand as they left the theater. "The street is like a skating rink," he said, making his way gingerly down the sidewalk and steadying her with his arm.

An early thaw had melted the snow, and when the temperature dropped at night, the streets became coated with ice. She moved closer to be nearer to him.

Northern lights streaked across the sky in ribbons of green and red. In the quiet evening, they could hear the crackle as the brilliant display swirled and changed colors. When they reached her hotel, he took her face in his hands and brought her lips to his. She melted into his kiss, excited by the touch of his body against her. Henry released her and stepped back.

"I remember thinking how beautiful you were when we walked the hills above Blacklead, but your beauty today is beyond description."

Ashoona trembled from his kiss. She wanted to tell Henry that she loved him. Something held her back, a worrying thought of wanting him too much and then losing him.

Ashoona could barely sleep that night. Each time she imagined the touch of his lips on her palm, a shiver of anticipation rippled through her. She hoped he was sincere when he told her that his obsession with Joanna was over. But she worried that his infatuation with his previous love was so intense that he could not love another, or that he would not want a young, inexperienced woman. She put aside these worrisome thoughts and imagined lying beside Henry, his arms about her, both of them naked. She removed her pajamas and felt her full breasts, touching her nipples and anticipating Henry's touch on her naked body. Finally, sleep came, a delicious sleep with dreams of lovemaking.

Ashoona had an early plane the next day, and Henry was unable to see her off. He had a budget meeting with the federal government officials. Lynne and Dugan flew back to Panniqtuuq with Ashoona. During the short flight, Ashoona had a seat by herself. She wanted to be alone and quiet, to replay Henry's kiss in her mind. She wondered if the kisses meant as much to him as they did to her. It would be three months before she would see Henry again, a lifetime for someone in love.

There was a purpose in Lynne and Dugan's visit to the little community where Ashoona was born and where her mother died. Dugan had arranged with one of the local artists to carve a gravestone, and on a windy spring day, they gathered at the cemetery overlooking the bay.

The beautiful gravestone was carved with an angel and the inscription in both languages read:

Minnie Aglulak Campbell

Born 1908 ~ Died 1934

*Beloved wife of Dugan Campbell and loving
mother to Ashoona*

The turmoil in Ashoona's life at the time of her mother's death left the little eight-year-old saddened but unable to grieve. She had been angry at her father's abandonment. Now tears flooded down Ashoona's cheeks. Her father held her as she wept. The gravestone for her mother was now in place, and the young woman knelt beside the grave remembering a soft voice, a loving touch and the warmth that had surrounded her as a child.

She recalled the long winters when her mother sewed their sealskin pants and decorated the caribou skin *amautiit*. While her mother sewed, she taught Ashoona how to crochet the warm woolen hats, adding a design along the edge. If she missed a stitch, her mother would gently tell Ashoona to start over. At six years old, starting over was hard for the little girl, so at times, her mother would begin the first few rounds, smile at her daughter and hand the work back.

"You will be a wonderful seamstress. You've learned that everything must be done slowly and perfectly. That is the way of our people. That is how we survive in this land."

Ashoona could not stem her tears at the gravesite. She had cried little when her mother died so many years ago because all her emotions were focused on anger at her father. But he had not abandoned her. He had been faithful to her and had never stopped caring. Now she could grieve for her mother and think of her childhood with warm thoughts, not bitter regret. Her world seemed whole again.

Several villagers joined them at the gravesite. Akulukjuq spoke at the gravesite, chanting the Anglican burial service in Inuktitut. Gathered at the edge of the group was Adamie with little Samuel at his side. Ashoona's uncle looked thinner. His clothes hung loose on a bony frame. He stood at his sister's grave, shoulders slumped and weeping as if weighed down by guilt, guilt for the mistreatment his niece endured at the hands of his wife. Worse for Adamie was Amaruk's wicked lie in a letter to Dugan telling the already distraught man that his daughter had followed his wife to the grave.

After the service, Dugan walked over to Adamie, offering his hand.

"Ashoona told me that it was you who gave her my letters. I forgive you for any part you had in her despicable treatment. You are suffering from the loss of your daughter, while I have my daughter back with me. Go in peace, Adamie. Don't torture yourself over what is past."

Adamie was speechless. Dugan had offered forgiveness.

"How can you forgive what we have done? It is too much for me to bear when I think of the evil we waged. Our family is damned. But you don't know all; there is more for me to confess."

Ashoona was listening as well. "What is it Adamie?"

"You must have wondered why we agreed to give you to that evil man, Qillaq."

"I thought it was revenge for Davidee's death."

"There's more." He paused, afraid to continue because he still felt Amaruk's control. Could he possibly reveal the bargain Amaruk had made with the vicious hunter?

"Get on with it, man," Dugan said, his anger rising.

"We made a bargain with Qillaq that Ashoona's first-born son would be given to us to replace Davidee. That was Amaruk's revenge, even though both of us suspected that Natsiq had pulled the trigger, not Ashoona. That is all. There is no more."

Ashoona shuddered at the thought of bearing Qillaq's child.

Thank God he never raped me. Thank God I did not have a child who would have been ripped away from me. It's over at last.

Ashoona's parents spent a night with Ashoona, making plans for a summer vacation together in southern Quebec and Ontario. Both Dugan and Lynne had jobs to return to, but they had one last obligation to meet. Dugan and Lynne paid a visit to Kilabuk to ask his help in keeping a promise Ashoona had made to the people at the shaman's camp.

"Next summer, when you take your family to Clearwater Bay, could you deliver a box of gifts to the people who survived the tragedy at Padluk's camp? I left the box with Ashoona."

"The survivors moved to Blacklead, but I'd be happy to deliver these gifts because we have friends and family there," Kilabuk promised.

Chapter Thirty

Above the Falls

Ashoona did not hear from Henry for the next two months, not even a letter. The ecstasy of blooming love was replaced with worry. Did his kisses mean nothing? It was unlike Henry to be insincere.

Time dragged. The weather was unusually warm in June; the students were restless, anxious to be released from the hot schoolroom and wanting to be out on the land. The children, teachers, hunters and parents watched the ice, hoping for an early break-up so the families could take to their boats to fish, hunt and camp at Clearwater Bay.

At last, school was out, and Ashoona was winging her way to Frobisher Bay to be Brenda's bridesmaid. The happy event was overshadowed by Henry's desertion, or so it seemed. She should have written him to let him know how much she cared, but she had expected to hear from him first. So, they would meet at Brenda's wedding, and she could judge for herself. If she saw him, she would know immediately.

A member of the Mormon Church performed the ceremony for Brenda and Paloosie. Brenda wore a white satin dress with a high collar and elegant, sweeping train. She had ordered the dress from Eaton's catalog months before the wedding. She looked like a princess, with her slim figure and elegant gown. Her light blonde hair was styled in soft curls, and she looked radiantly happy. Rachael wore a flouncy white dress and walked down the aisle followed by Adam and Jeremiah, who each carried one of the rings. Although Brenda had invited her parents, none of her family attended. They were well off and certainly could afford the flight, but they could not accept Brenda's rejection of her polygamist marriage and FLDS membership.

Kilabuk took Brenda's arm, delighted that his son had found such a beautiful, sweet-natured wife. Aula sat in the front row with her children. She wore the traditional Inuit dress of soft caribou skin, decorated with rows of beads.

Paloosie turned to watch Brenda approach. He was dressed formally in a black suit and tie with an artificial buttonhole carnation in his lapel.

Ashoona wore a sky-blue gown that hugged her slender waist. As she walked in the procession to the altar, she saw Henry. She was about to smile at him when she spotted Joanna, sitting at his side. Ashoona felt an agonizing pain in her heart and turned away quickly.

So that explains Henry's silence over these past months. How could he have misled me?

Her faced burned, and she felt ill as she listened to Brenda and Paloosie repeat their vows. She had so looked forward to this day as a joyous occasion not only for Brenda but also for herself. She was devastated.

Brenda and Paloosie were pronounced man and wife, and the groom bent to kiss his bride. Seeing their expression of true love brought tears to Ashoona's eyes. Her love was gone, stolen by a viper of a woman who could never be faithful. It was all Ashoona could do to keep from crying as she followed the happy couple out of the church and into the dazzling Arctic sunshine. She avoided looking at Henry as she passed. All she wanted to do was escape, never to see him again.

Outside the church, Ashoona hugged Brenda, trying her best to smile despite her broken heart.

"You look like your best friend just died, rather than married happily. I thought only mothers cried at weddings."

"I...it's nothing, Brenda," Ashoona lied. "I was just thinking of my own mother and how I will miss her on my wedding day." The words caught in her throat.

Ashoona walked away from the gathering. She had rented a car. All she wanted to do was escape.

"Ashoona, wait! Where are you going? You must come to the reception."

"Brenda, please forgive me. I seem to have suddenly come down with something. I must go back to the hotel and sleep because my head is pounding."

"I'm so sorry. And here I thought you and Henry would be dancing the night away and that you might even catch my bouquet."

At the mention of Henry's name, Ashoona had to turn her head so Brenda wouldn't see her tears.

Ashoona drove along the rough roads of the burgeoning northern city, parked her car on the outskirts and got out to walk. The sea ice had broken up, and the rafts of heaving ice glistened in the bright sun.

"I knew this would happen. Nothing good ever comes to me without punishment. I have my father back; my name has been cleared of Davidee's death; I'm a teacher. I should have known I could never find a faithful man to love me."

Just like the devastating experience with James, the loss of Henry's affection sent her reeling. At twenty, she was older now and a little wiser, so she shed fewer tears, but she felt that Henry's betrayal was hardening her heart.

"Damn men. Are they all the same?"

Ashoona returned to her hotel room and slept until her plane was due to leave the next day. She was flying to Montreal to spend time with her parents. It was a long flight and a miserable one. Ashoona could not get her mind off Henry. Watching a couple cuddling in the seats across from her just intensified her sense of loss.

Dugan and Lynne were shocked at her appearance when they met her at the airport. Ashoona's eyes were red from crying, and her face looked drawn.

"My darling girl, what on earth is the matter?"

"Oh Papa, I thought he loved me. Instead he's taken up with Joanna again. I should have known."

Lynne and Dugan could not find anything to take Ashoona's mind off her heartache. They had wonderful plans for her visit, and Ashoona accompanied them politely but found little joy in the walk up Mount Royal or even the visit to Niagara Falls. As she stood above the falls, Ashoona imagined leaping over the guardrail hundreds of feet down into the deadly foaming water. Although she spent the rest of the summer break with her parents, the holiday passed with little change to Ashoona's emotional state.

If only I didn't have to go back to Frobisher Bay. I am sure to meet Henry and Joanna, and seeing them together will be more than I can bear.

But Ashoona had to attend a staff conference and a tutorial on teaching indigenous children. The instructor was known around the world for his work with Aboriginal children. Ashoona plunged into her studies, thankful for the workload and to have a challenge that took her mind off Henry.

The staff conference, however, had the opposite effect. School superintendent Steve Frame was a large, self-important man, with a loud, commanding voice. When he took the microphone, several teachers glanced at one another and groaned, knowing his speech would be endless, boring and filled with self-congratulatory remarks. He droned on, oblivious to his audience.

"They say when Mr. Frame enters his office and plugs himself into the circuit that the lights go out in the government building." Judy had joined Ashoona and was trying to bring her young friend out of her doldrums. Ashoona smiled but soon returned to a picture of sadness.

"Hey girl, remember I told you that your father may have had a reason for not writing to you or returning to find you. I was right. Maybe Henry has his reasons. Have you asked him why he didn't write?"

"He is with Joanna. I saw them together. His infatuation with that woman shows no bounds. She broke his heart, but all the misery she caused him seems to be healed. She may even stay with him, get her children back and get married. After all, she is getting a bit old to be constantly on the hunt for a new man, and Henry, with his big government salary, is a good catch. No, Judy, it's no use. I have to try to forget him."

"You're such a little pudding, Ashoona. You wear your heart on your sleeve, and you love with abandon. It's a dangerous approach to finding a life mate."

Ernest approached, a warm smile lighting his round cheeks. "Judy, what have you said to bring tears to my sweet, young teacher's eyes? You need cheering up, Ashoona. Come with us for dinner. After that boring speech, I need a beer, a thick steak and my baked potato slathered with sour cream, chopped onions and bacon bits."

"Lord, help the little children, Ernest. Can't you see our darling Ashoona needs comfort not a description of the Frobisher Hotel menu?"

"Food *is* comfort. A tasty meal and a glass of good red wine will cheer you up. Well, maybe not good wine. Such a rarity does not exist on all of Baffin Island, but a sip with your meal will help you forget your cares and bring back that sparkle we love about you."

They left for the restaurant, walking up the steep hill to the largest hotel and the only reasonably good dining establishment in the city. They sat near the large bay window with its panoramic view of the city, its government offices, staff residences and small wooden houses and shacks at the edge of the swollen sea.

"It is beautiful," Ashoona remarked. "Thank you for inviting me."

Ashoona tried her best to put aside her dark mood. They discussed the new school year, and Ernest outlined the responsibilities of the newly recruited teachers and Inuit helpers. Ernest and Judy were staying at the hotel, but Ashoona had a room in the teachers' residence down the hill.

When Ashoona walked down the footpath that led to the residence, she heard footsteps behind her on the gravel trail, someone with a long stride and a pace that had quickened. She knew about the problems with alcohol in the frontier community; often, men who were no longer able to hunt lived on welfare and were just waiting for their next check. The drive to drink was the root of petty crime, and at times, violence. Ashoona quickened her pace, knowing it would be unwise to let a stranger catch up to her. She glanced over her shoulder but could only make out the shadowy figure in the fading August light.

"Wait, Ashoona."

She recognized Henry's voice.

"Just leave me alone, you, you..." The word "bastard" was on the tip of her tongue, but despite her anguish over Henry's desertion, she couldn't utter the word.

"Just listen to me, please."

"Get out of my life. I never want to see you again."

Ashoona broke into a run.

Henry shook his head and turned back to the hotel.

———

Ashoona had one more day in Frobisher. She had to shop at the Hudson's Bay Store for school supplies. She had planned her projects for her new classes, purchasing paints, colored construction paper, gold stars and a newly released book. She chose a Dr. Seuss book, knowing that her students, only recently exposed to English, would enjoy a book with colorful illustrations. Along with *And To Think I Saw it on Mulberry Street*, she bought E.B. White's *Stuart Little*.

"So, it's my little helper from Blacklead." Joanna fluttered up the aisle toward the checkout counter.

"Joanna." Ashoona didn't know what to say.

"I guess you know I'm working at the hospital with Henry. Well...not working with him every day because he's a big shot now running the whole show."

"I thought you and Captain Littleheart were together—Osgood, the wealthy fellow from England. What happened?"

"It didn't work out. Children weren't in the picture for him, and I still hope to get my two young ones back. Besides, his family hated me. They were just a bunch of stuck-up phonies. It's great to be back in the north and with Henry again." Joanna's voice was filled with the thrill of the hunt.

"I imagine it is. Well, excuse me, Joanna, I have a lot to do before leaving tomorrow."

"Why not have a coffee with me. I want to find out what Henry was up to while I was away."

"I have nothing to say. You'll have to ask Henry."

Ashoona thought of Henry's kiss and the promise it held and how Joanna had so quickly and completely stepped back into Henry's life.

"You and Henry are you back together?' Ashoona asked timidly, forcing the words out despite the tightness in her chest.

"Why, yes. Why do you ask? You remember how close we were in Blacklead?"

Maybe it was wishful thinking, but Ashoona thought that Joanna's voice revealed a subtle note of uncertainly, her once perfectly formed smile was now tight. Ashoona studied Joanna, seeing the minute lines that had appeared about her eyes. Unlike the arrogant self-absorbed captain, Henry would not care if the woman he loved aged.

Why would Henry return to Joanna, knowing how unfeeling she was, dismissing his love to run off with the captain, seemingly uncaring of the misery she put him through? But of course, men can be easily seduced, and Joanna had a kind of lustful power over Henry. The memory of his passionate affair with Joanna would be rekindled and the heartache he had suffered in Blacklead completely erased…until the next time. But Ashoona would not be there to witness it.

"Are you coming for coffee with me," Joanna repeated, "or are you just going to continue glaring at me? Is there something between you and Henry that I should know about? Were you lovers during my absence? Is that the shadow crossing your pretty little face?"

"No, Joanna. You have his heart once more. And no, I cannot join you for coffee."

Ashoona paid for her purchases and left the store. She couldn't bear to spend another minute with Joanna. The conversation with the flirtatious nurse made the blood rush to Ashoona's head. If Henry could dismiss Joanna's betrayal in the past, then maybe they deserved each other. Angry and hurt, Ashoona walked back to her room and slept until her flight to Panniqtuuq.

———————

Life at the school became routine. Ashoona knocked on Judy's door one fall morning. Her friend was sipping her coffee while she flipped through recipe books.

"Time for a coffee?"

"Thanks, Judy, I need a minute with you to ask you what you think about Henry. I have been devastated because I believed he loved me, and yet, it seems he is once more under Joanna's spell."

"I never met the black widow spider nurse, but knowing Henry, it's difficult to believe he would be caught in her web yet again. Are you sure Henry is with her?"

"Yes. Joanna told me."

"And you believe anything that comes out of that woman's mouth?" Judy asked, incredulous.

"Why is it so hard for me to find someone who will truly love me?"

"Ernest still loves me after thirty years, three children and five grandchildren. Occasionally, I have to tell him to move over to his side of the bed because his sex drive has not diminished despite my expanding waistline. But otherwise we are quite content."

"If only I could find a man as loyal and loving. Maybe I'm just unlucky with men."

It was an uncharacteristically warm fall. As usual, the days grew shorter and the dark nights returned, but there was enough light at the end of the school day for Ashoona's walks in the hills behind the village. Judy was not much of a walker, but Lucy joined Ashoona on weekends, happy to be freed of the constant demands of her young family.

They took the path along the river, first a gentle slope between giant boulders, then steeper as it wound up a rocky path toward the waterfall. The two rested on the cliff above the waterfall and watched the play of light on the pool below and listened to the roar of the water as it cascaded and boiled through the narrow gorge. Both were silent—Lucy felt at peace watching the beauty of the river; Ashoona, still stinging with the pain of her loss. The sound of the waterfall was too loud to allow for a conversation.

"My friend, your sadness encloses you," Lucy remarked as they descended the trail to the village. "I thought all your problems were solved, but I can see you are no longer my lighthearted, happy friend. Do you want to tell me?"

"Oh, Lucy. Thank you again for always being there for me. This time, no one can help."

"Life cannot be that dismal for a beautiful woman like you, young and educated. Is it Henry?"

"Yes," Ashoona whispered, "but this time I know it's hopeless." Ashoona told Lucy how she thought Henry was in love with her, yet quickly went back to Joanna.

"That's strange because Henry was in Panniqtuuq shortly before you returned from visiting your parents. He spoke of you in every other sentence. If he's not in love with you, I would be most surprised."

"Henry may have loved me, but he is mesmerized by Joanna. She has a powerful hold on him, one that he cannot shake loose no matter how much damage she causes. And of course, he would ask about me. He was my mentor when I was younger. He will always want the best for me."

"If he cares about you and wants you to be happy, why did he lead you on, then abandon you? If he did abandon you, that is. Are you sure? Did you ever speak to him?"

"He followed me from the hotel in Frobisher. He wanted to talk to me. I told him I never wanted to speak to him again. I wish I had at least asked him why he went back to Joanna. I want to understand men, to figure out how I can be deeply in love while the men I love are disloyal."

"Joe is a good and loving husband, and I know Henry would be as well. I simply cannot believe he would marry someone like Joanna, a mother who abandoned her children, the woman who seduced him and then so quickly left him for the flamboyant Captain Littleheart. Henry is someone I trust. Remember how he came to my rescue when Donna lied and Karyn wouldn't believe me. He saved me from the worst situation in my life."

"That's why I'm so confused. Nothing fits anymore. I feel my future is being stolen from me; not my career, but my hopes for a loving husband and a kitchen full of children."

"You'll get over him, and you will find someone to love and who will love you the way you deserve."

"I don't think so, Lucy. When it comes to love, I am no longer hopeful."

The two friends reached the village as the sun settled over the mountain ridge to the west. Streams of pink, rose and purple splashed across the sky. Ashoona's heart lifted momentarily, buoyed by the spectacular beauty of the arctic sky.

The warm fall days continued. Early snowstorms failed to arrive, and when a dusting of snow fell, the autumn sun soon melted the light covering. Ashoona continued her evening walks along the river. She felt angry with herself each time she reached the towering boulder where she first fell in love with James, who hurt and betrayed her in the end. So she had a new wound weighing on her heart. She reached the waterfall, and as she watched the icy streams pour over the steep drop, churning and boiling against the cliffs of the gorge, she lost herself in the wonder of the scene.

The roar of the water masked the sound of footsteps on the rocks. Ashoona sensed a presence nearby but dismissed the thought and continued to gaze at the water, mesmerized by its beauty. She remained still until the setting sun caught the outline of a man, and a shadow fell across the rocky ground.

"Henry! What on earth are you doing here?"

"Ashoona, what is going on with you? Why wouldn't you talk to me in Frobisher Bay? Why did you run away?"

"You're asking me to explain *myself*? Have you lost your mind? You're back with Joanna, and you question my behavior? I don't understand why you led me to believe you had feelings for me and then, as soon as Joanna shows her face, you fall under her spell and abandon me."

"Abandon you? You think Joanna and I are lovers again? No, my sweet girl. You are so wrong. I have thought about you every day since we last met."

"But you didn't write to me...no word for months! I trusted you, and then you disappeared! Can't you see how you've hurt me?"

"I'm so sorry! I wrote to you, but you were in Montreal, and my letter was returned. I guess the regular postmistress was on vacation, and her replacement from Ottawa didn't know who you were."

"You aren't with Joanna? But..." Ashoona felt the tears spring up, and she couldn't speak. She tried to choke back a sob.

"Did Joanna tell you we were together?"

"Yes!" Ashoona cried, the tears flowing freely with raw grief.

Henry reached for Ashoona, but she backed up, stepping close to the edge of the sharp drop-off down to the water.

"Be careful! It's dangerous."

"I need to know why you ignored me after you kissed me and when I believed we were becoming close. It was months! I trusted you. Then it seemed clear you were not serious, that our kisses meant nothing. That you were just like that philanderer, James."

"Oh my dear. You didn't know...?"

"Know what?"

"My mother. She was dying, and I went to Ottawa and stayed at her bedside for two months, helping her, watching over her during the pain-filled months before her death. When I returned to Frobisher Bay, I expected to be with you at Brenda's wedding, but you disappeared after the ceremony. Then after the teachers' conference, you ran away from me. I had no idea that you thought I had taken up with Joanna again."

Henry reached for Ashoona's hand, pulling her away from the steep drop. Her heart skipped a beat as he took her in his arms for a long, warm embrace, lips tentatively touching and Ashoona melting into his caress.

"I love you, my darling Ashoona, and I will be yours forever."

"Henry. I love you, too."

Henry took Ashoona's hand and led her to the path that wound steeply down to the village. His gentle touch and warm smile made her heart sing. She felt she must be dreaming.

"Come, my Inuit beauty. The light is fading, and I don't want you to slip over the edge. I almost lost you through a foolish misunderstanding, and I don't want you to fall into the rapids and leave me forever." He smiled, took her hand and softly kissed her fingers.

As they reached the village and her front door, Henry said softly, "I think I'll stay at the clinic tonight. Don't ask me to sleep in your guest room because I'll be unable to keep myself from your bed.

"No school tomorrow, right?" Ashoona nodded. "I will call for you at sunrise." Henry kissed her lips, and held her tightly.

The next morning, Ashoona was up early, almost dancing across the floor and feeling lightheaded with love and hope. She was sitting on the steps enjoying the earliest rays of the sun streaming across the eastern mountaintops and warming her body and her heart. She saw him cross the bridge and remembered how much she loved his graceful walk.

"Come, my gorgeous woman, I want to take you to a magical spot overlooking the bay. I've heard it's the place where a man takes his beloved to watch the whales dance out in the sea."

When they reached the sandy bay, Henry sat down on a large, flat rock and drew Ashoona down beside him.

"I think hidden treasure is buried in the sand beside us. Should I look and see what it is?

"You're teasing me."

He dug his hand into the sand and brought up a small, white leather box. He stood up, got down on one knee before her and opened the box.

"This is my mother's ring. She asked me to give it to you. While I was with her, I told her how much I loved you and wanted you for my wife. Please, Ashoona, will you marry me? I promise to love you with all my heart and never give you cause to cry."

"Before I accept, I need you to understand me. I won't be just a housewife. I have to do more in my life. I will cook for you because I love cooking, but I want the freedom to do more with my life and my career. Can you live with that?"

"You can change the world, and I will be at your side, loving you always."

"We are good for each other. My dearest Henry, both of us learned a lesson about love. I will never again doubt the ones who truly love me. I believe in your love and I promise to love you forever with all my heart."

They looked out to the bay. A pod of belugas danced through the waves as the morning sun glistened on the water and rosy streams of light touched the snow-capped mountains.

Yvonne Harris

Yvonne Harris lived in Pangnirtung, Nunavut, on Baffin Island for two years. During that time, she was a substitute teacher at the elementary school and an instructor at Nunavut Arctic College. While there she also hiked, skied and kayaked. She is a marathon canoeist who has competed seven times in the longest canoe race in the world, an event in which she and her partner held the women's record. This avid outdoorswoman has guided whitewater raft trips and has spent many summers on family canoe trips.

Yvonne has a degree in Regional and Urban Planning from the University of British Columbia and has worked for many years as a regional planner in the Canadian north. She is the author of several children's books as well as a hiking guide to Hawaii and a white water canoeing book.